ROSALVIVA

Also Available from Valancourt Books

GASTON DE BLONDEVILLE
Ann Radcliffe
Edited by Frances A. Chiu

CLERMONT
Regina Maria Roche
Edited by Natalie Schroeder

THE MYSTERIOUS WARNING
Eliza Parsons
Edited by Karen Morton

THE VEILED PICTURE
Ann Radcliffe
Edited by Jack G. Voller

MAD MAN OF THE MOUNTAIN
Henry Summersett
Edited by James D. Jenkins

THE WITCH OF RAVENSWORTH
George Brewer
Edited by Allen W. Grove

THE IMPENETRABLE SECRET, FIND IT OUT!
Francis Lathom
Edited by James Cruise

THE DEMON OF SICILY
Edward Montague
Preface by Jo Beverley

Gothic Classics

ROSALVIVA,

OR,

THE DEMON DWARF!

A Romance.

BY

GRENVILLE FLETCHER, Esq.

Que de grandes qualités,
Sans vertu! Que d'amour sans honneur!

ROUSSEAU.

THREE VOLUMES IN ONE.

Kansas City:
VALANCOURT BOOKS
2012

Rosalviva, or, The Demon Dwarf! by Grenville Fletcher
Originally published in 3 vols. by Matthew Iley, London, 1824
First Valancourt Books edition, 2012

Cover illustration by Odilon Redon

ISBN 978-0-9792332-6-5

Published by Valancourt Books
Kansas City, Missouri

Composition by James D. Jenkins
Set in Dante MT

10 9 8 7 6 5 4 3 2 1

A NOTE ON THE AUTHOR AND THE TEXT

Peter Garside's website *British Fiction, 1800-1829* indicates that of the 2,272 works of fiction published between 1800 and 1829, 379 of them are still considered anonymous; this works out to nearly 17 percent, and of course this does not include many works published pseudonymously or works originally anonymous whose author has later been identified. If one factors in those novels, the number of novels published anonymously in the early 19th century is probably closer to one in four. When we stumble upon these old novels, some of which, like *The Animated Skeleton* (1798) and *Love and Horror* (1812), have been republished by Valancourt Books, we are struck by a sense of mystery and frustration. "Who is the author?" we wonder, as, in the case of some titles, readers and scholars have wondered fruitlessly for two centuries or more. We feel instinctively that there is some important riddle to be solved, that if we knew the author's identity we might have a better understanding of the work itself, or of the context in which it appeared. Was the author a man or a woman? Wealthy or poor? Perhaps he or she was famous in some other regard and did not care to be known as the author of a "trashy" Gothic novel?

In the case of *Rosalviva, or, The Demon Dwarf!* (1824), however, we know the name of the author from the book's title page: he is one Grenville Fletcher, Esq. It seems at first, then, that in this case there is no mystery to solve. Surely one can type in the name of Grenville Fletcher on Google or Wikipedia and read the details of his life, when he was born, when he died, and what he did when he was not writing Gothic novels like *Rosalviva*. And yet that is not the case. In Jess Nevins's excellent *The Encyclopedia of Fantastic Victoriana* (2005), he notes simply that "Little is known about Fletcher," and, there, it seems, history and scholarship have been content to let the matter lie.

However, thanks to modern search technology and the wealth of information on the World Wide Web, we may be able to glean a few details of Fletcher's life. The Mormon church's Familysearch.org website discovers a Samuel Grenville Fletcher, born in 1801 and died in 1881, who lists his occupation in the census as "retired author and journalist." In the preface to *Rosalviva*, Fletcher notes that his first work, presumably referring to his *Rhodomaldi, or, The Castle of Roveggiano!*, published April 1, 1822, was "the first production of an author (scarcely twenty)." If *Rhodomaldi* were completed in 1821, some months before its April 1822 publication, and if Fletcher were twenty at the time, as he states, this would correspond to the 1801 birthdate given for Samuel Grenville Fletcher, strongly suggesting that they are the same person (how many authors named "Grenville Fletcher" could have been born at the same time?)

One wonders whether the author of *Rosalviva* may also be the same Grenville Fletcher who published a series of works entitled *"Parliamentary Portraits," Past and Present* beginning in 1847. That Grenville Fletcher is described on the title page of the 1881 edition of that work as "Late Editor of the 'Kentish Champion,' 'The Parthenon,' 'Mirror of the World,' 'Hants Standard,' 'Court Chronicle,' &c." This Fletcher, then, was a journalist, and given that the 1881 edition appeared the same year that Samuel Grenville Fletcher, self-described as a journalist, died, one suspects that it would be too coincidental for them not to be the same person.

If Fletcher was born in 1801, then, he was born seven years after Ann Radcliffe published her *Mysteries of Udolpho* in 1794 and five years after the appearance of M. G. Lewis's *The Monk* (1796). The Gothic novel's popularity had long been on the wane, and some modern critics have declared it dead with the publication of Charles Robert Maturin's *Melmoth the Wanderer* in 1820. Thus, by the time *Rosalviva* was published in 1824, it was already remarkably anachronistic, and somewhat of a strange choice of subject matter for a budding young writer, who apparently moved in literary circles, and seems from internal evidence in *Rosalviva* to have been acquainted with some of the popular novelists of his day, including Leigh Cliffe and Mary Gogo Lewis, who published as "Miss M. G. Lewis," but was no relation to "Monk" Lewis. By 1824, critics had moved on from ridiculing Gothic novels to ignoring them entirely. *Rosalviva* apparently only garnered one notice—a decided snub, since in the 1820s, only a few dozen novels were published each year, only a handful a month for the reviewers—a dismissive paragraph in *The London Literary Gazette*, which stated, in its entirety:

"*Rosalviva, or, The Demon Dwarf!*—About as utter rubbish as could be connected together by means of friars, banditti, love and murder. Rosalviva is written in the worst style of a now exploded style of romance." For the reviewer, then, the Gothic novel was not only quaintly old-fashioned, but actually "exploded," that is, entirely rejected and discredited as a viable literary form. So, then, the publication of a novel by a young writer some twenty-three years old, written in a style that had started its decline from popularity before he was even born, is something of an oddity, much in the same way it would be in 2012 for a musician or film director to release an album or movie in the style of those popular in 1985.

And yet, for today's reader there is much to like about *Rosalviva*. The novel's titular character is decidedly wicked and depraved, the book contains wonderfully gloomy and atmospheric scenes set in subterranean vaults and dungeons, and Valfroni, the Demon Dwarf, is a worthy addition to the Gothic bestiary, joining his contemporaries such as George Brewer's hideous Hag in *The Witch of Ravensworth* (1808) and Mary Shelley's monster in *Frankenstein* (1818). Although today's literary critics would likely share the 19th century reviewer's sentiment that the novel is "utter rubbish," modern readers and fans of Gothic novels of the period will be prepared to excuse its faults and absurdities and enjoy it as a fun novel of yesteryear, with its fair share of twists, turns, and surprises, including an unexpected and delightfully improbable ending.

A few words remain to be said about the editing of the present volume. *Rosalviva* was originally published in 1824 in three volumes by publisher Matthew Iley of London. Iley was not a prolific publisher of fiction, issuing a total of only nine novels between 1815 and 1824. An extant letter included on Garside's website indicates that Fletcher shopped his novel around before settling on Iley as his publisher; on December 22, 1823, Fletcher wrote to Cosmo Orme of the well-reputed publishing house of Longman and Co. as follows: "Mr Fletcher's compts to Mr Orme & will he have the goodness to signify whether he has had an opportunity of perusing the MSS of 'Rosalviva or the Demon Dwarf'. Mr. F. would not have been thus pressing save that he has some literary occupations upon the carpet, & remains as yet undetermined which to complete in the first instance." Apparently the Longmans publishing house declined, as *Rosalviva* appeared some six months later, issued by Iley. A reproduction of the title page of volume I is reprinted in this volume.

My editorial philosophy has always been one of restraint: in editing these lost Gothic novels for publication by Valancourt Books, I have tried to present them to modern readers in a form as close as possible to what original readers would have enjoyed, including preservation of old-fashioned or odd spelling and punctuation. However, the present volume has sorely tested this policy of editorial restraint. The 1824 edition is riddled with errors of spelling, punctuation, and grammar. Most of these pose no problem of understanding for the modern reader and have thus been retained for this edition. Thus, the reader will find inconsistent spellings, such as ardor/ardour, honor/honour, cemetry/cemetery, tranquility/tranquillity, suspense/suspence, and many others. A few spelling mistakes that were obviously the work of the original typesetter and not of Fletcher have been silently corrected, so two instances of "thurst" have been altered to "thrust," one instance of "least" has been changed to "lest," and "mein" has been emended to "mien." Fletcher's use of semi-colons, commas, and quotation marks has been retained as in the original, even where modern usage might punctuate differently, although a couple of extraneous or omitted quotation marks have been silently fixed. Fletcher's Italian and French are not any better than his English, and no attempt has been made to correct errors in foreign grammar, spelling, or accent marks.

The most significant problem that confronts the editor (or reader) is that there are numerous instances in the text where the word used by Grenville (or his publisher) simply does not seem to make sense in the context in which it appears. Thus, we find "momentary" where "momentarily" would be expected, "impervious" for "imperious," "impelled" for "impeded," "nominated" for "denominated," "emotion" for "motion," "expatiated" for "expiated," "lighting" for "blighting," and many others. Unfortunately, when an editor begins changing the words written in a book, he starts down a slippery slope. To correct all the errors of grammar and usage in this novel would essentially be to rewrite the book and to present to readers something quite different from what the book originally said. Rather than try to draw arbitrary lines and distinctions and present an amalgam of Fletcher's work and my "editing" (or rewriting), I have chosen to present the text as it originally appeared, faults and all, aside from the few minor corrections noted previously. This gives a much fairer representation of what popular novels of the early nineteenth century actually looked like: they were quickly and often shoddily produced, and errors (even significant ones) were not infrequent. To be certain, I have consulted two different copies of the first edition, and the errors alluded to appear in both copies. The reader, then, is advised that errors appearing in this text are errors that appeared in the original edition.

James D. Jenkins
Kansas City, Missouri

August 12, 2012

ROSALVIVA,

OR

THE DEMON DWARF!

A Romance.

BY GRENVILLE FLETCHER, ESQ.

AUTHOR OF "RHODOMALDI," &c.

> Que de grandes qualites,
> Sans vertu! Que d'amour sans honneur!
>
> ROUSSEAU.

IN THREE VOLUMES.

VOL. I.

LONDON:

MATTHEW ILEY, SOMERSET STREET,
PORTMAN SQUARE.

1824.

TO

LADY CAROLINE LAMB,

THIS ROMANCE

IS INSCRIBED,

BY THE AUTHOR.

PREFATORY ADDRESS.

The tolerable success attendant upon the first production of an author (scarcely twenty) may be some privilege for his reappearance: It is hoped that these volumes will be equal to a second endeavour. For the flattering encouragement he has received at the hands of his Reviewers, he begs to submit his best acknowledgments, to the Literary Chronicle, *and* La Belle Assemblée *more especially.*

London, May, 1824

ROSALVIVA.

CHAPTER I.

———————"Know'st thou not,
That when the searching eye of Heaven is hid
Behind the globe, and lights the lower world,
Then thieves and robbers range abroad unseen
In murders—and in outrage, bloody here.—"

SHAKSPEARE.

THE vespers on the eve of St. Rosalia had nearly closed, when from a half revealed gleam of moonlight, which threw its faint reflection beneath the porch of the chapel of St. Mark, the figures of two men, habited in long cloaks and black masks, were seen in earnest conversation under one of the columns. An attendant, not so conspicuously attired, and of less noble appearance, stood at a respectful distance along the piazza.

"Twice," rejoined one of the masks, "had I nearly given the Conte his errand to the other world, during our last night's festivity, but for the meddling interference of that poltroon the Signor Napoli."

"'Tis not too late to obtain thy purpose," softly spoke the attendant, who was named Gioeni, and who had approached during the conversation, "for hither comes the old Conte, and with no less a personage than his friend Napoli." The principal speaker, after a short deliberation, signified to the other, that provided he and Gioeni could intimidate the person of Napoli, he himself would undertake the punishment which the Conte merited, and which nothing but his sword could bestow.

Retiring down the Arcade, where the spot was dark and less frequented, they awaited the step of the Conte Reo Cardoni and his friend.

The principal masked stranger rushed upon the surprised

Cardoni, who instantly drew his sword and spiritedly resisted the attack.

"Either thy weapon, Conte, or mine," angrily exclaimed the aggressor, "will decide a quarrel which the house of Romagno thinks to offer with impunity—now, Signor, to its termination;" and half frantic he thrust his sword full at the breast of Cardoni.

The intended stroke was successfully parried by the Conte, who, grasping the arm of his antagonist, cried—"speak, villain, by whom am I thus threatened?—thou must be a coward indeed, thus to resort to the means of resenting whatever injury thy imagination may shape, and with an assassin's mask attempt to avenge it!—speak, ruffian! for I have still an arm strong enough to defeat thy malicious efforts."—

"This is no malice," replied the stranger, disengaging himself from Cardoni; "question thyself as to the few events which have transpired within thy knowledge during the last few days, and further explanation on my part is unnecessary. But this is no time for parley—I feel myself wronged by you, Signor Conte, and from you only, at this moment, do I seek atonement." The stranger became violent—a serious rencontre ensued, and the Conte Cardoni at length fell, dangerously wounded.

Napoli had easily been put to flight; for on perceiving his friend so powerfully attacked, and dreading the result, he, without further hazard, made the most precipitate retreat—nor paused to take breath, until he attained the Castelli di Romagno, the residence of Cardoni.

One of the strangers, on finding the Conte apparently lifeless, hurried his friend from the scene; and sheathing their weapons, hastily withdrew to the extremity of the villa.

Napoli summoned the utmost strength of the domestics, each bearing a torch, and well armed, they followed him to the Piazzi, where Cardoni was still bleeding from his wound.

It was with much difficulty the Conte could be moved to the Castelli; all animation had seemingly forsaken him, and the attendants conveyed their nearly-expiring master, amidst feelings of regret and dismay.

The daughter of Cardoni was upon a visit at a neighbouring district, it was thought expedient to announce to her the dreadful catastrophe, as the father, skilled in pharmacy, who attended the Castelli, had declared the wounds to be fatal, and that in a few hours, in defiance of every hope, the Conte would be no more!

Rosalviva, the only offspring of Cardoni, felt the shock with the feelings of filial affection; and throughout the lingering period of her father's struggles she quitted not his presence.

"Rosalviva, my child," faintly articulated the Conte, at a lucid interval prior to his decease, and taking her hand within his, "the hour is arrived when my spirit will be resigned to its Creator;"—turning to his confessor, he motioned that the attendants and each person should withdraw. Vivaldi closed the portal that excluded the household, and kneeling beside the couch, offered his orisons to Heaven for the dying Cardoni. A brother, likewise, of the same order, was bent before a crucifix, in earnest prayer to the throne of mercy.

"Rosalviva," repeated the Conte, "observe, and in the presence of these pious members of our holy religion, promise me that when my remains are deposited in the silent tomb, you will not discard from your memory the unhappy calamity that ushered in his untimely end."

Rosalviva was silent; but her tears were falling in fast succession. The solemn serenity that pervaded the apartment, and the cessation of the Conte's harrangue impressively awakened her sensibility; and looking sorrowfully on the contorted features of her parent, she cried, "Speak, my dear father, I will be devoted to all thy wishes."

The priests drew closely to the pillow of Cardoni, in compliance with his request, and fixing him in partly an erect and easy position, he addressed his daughter.

"Rosalviva, I am not insensible to all your tokens of obedience and affection, and will impose with confidence my departing commands. It is obvious, my child, that the shaft, aimed at this feeble existence, was not guided by an indifferent or common hand, or impelled by the dictate of the felon who would seek my property—no, the weapon was guided by an enemy to my family and felicity; and the spirit of interest and injustice must have been the motive of the wilful act."

One of the father's devoutly crossed himself, and mildly bade the Conte to proceed. A pause succeeded, Vivaldi applied a balsam to the lips of Cardoni—it seemed to give him temporary relief, and he again resumed.—"I have but little to remark—by my decease, Rosalviva, you inherit the ——, but I lose breath in giving the detail of that which my will and final decree fully and clearly authorises, and which, to the care of Vivaldi, are the documents consigned until the necessary obsequies of my burial shall have been performed. Vivaldi, the communication received by you this morning, I would have my daughter peruse."

The Confessor handed to Rosalviva a document couched as follows:—

"The Conte Reo Cardoni has not fallen by disinterested hands—the title of one known to the house of Cardoni bears the stain, and the day must arrive when its name will be revealed."

A cold tremor crept through the frame of Rosalviva as she glanced over the anonymous epistle.

"It is upon this suite, Rosalviva," pronounced her father, "that I now adjure your obedience—from the confirmation which you perceive, you can, in conjunction with myself, declare that my doom has long been prefixed, and that a secret and dreadful agency has at length succeeded in bringing forth my hour of dissolution."

"I can indeed, see, my father, that a horrible and demoniac arm has been raised for thy destruction."

"It has, it has," agitatedly spoke Cardoni, "and you, Rosalviva, only can avenge it—the last descendant of the race of Cardoni must not sink into his grave covered with abhorrence; they who directed this event have doubtless an efficient tale to varnish its apparent opprobrium.—I must not close a career my child with sullied laurels."

"Never, never," eagerly exclaimed Rosalviva, "I will live to blight such evil and desperate malevolence."

"You will, Rosalviva," repeated the Conte, momentary elated by her earnestness.

"Yes, my murdered parent—as the God who decrees our existence may herewith record."

The fathers crossed themselves, and in silent devotion directed their looks to Heaven.

"Thanks, my child," spake Cardoni, "I die blest in the assurance that you can forget not thy father's latest wish; and that you will never suffer to fade from your memory the horror of his assassination—pledge thyself my girl here, in the presence of these holy fathers, that to no human being shalt thy hand be given, until thy parent's murderer be discovered."

The eyes and countenance of the Conte attained a wild and delirious aspect.—Rosalviva was about to obey, when he interrupted the reply, adding, "Record too, that on whom this blood may rest, you will with hatred and revenge pursue, and when the mask be removed, that you will lead him to the scaffold."

"All this I swear," firmly pronounced Rosalviva, "and in the moment wherein I forget my oath—in the moment wherein I forget thy slaughtered remains—may thy injured spirit haunt me, and amid the most horrid of human torture, hurl my perjured soul to endless destruction."

"Enough, enough, my child—bless thee, bless thee—fathers ye witness the allegiance—remember it."

The Conte fixed his last gaze upon his daughter—his sufferings appeared dreadful, and in hard and pityable struggles his soul sunk to the charge of his Redeemer.

At the age of nineteen, Rosalviva found herself in the enjoyment of every gift that the summit of pride, or the arrogance of riches could demand—to her person, formed by nature into a shape of beautiful symmetry, was gifted a strong and peculiar mind, equalled by a sensibility and force of passions which the value of her charms heightened, and threw into her commanding features, a power and a fascination that appeared to possess every sweetness that could engage and attract—every hope and brilliancy that could allure. The property of the Conte falling to her entire disposal, the magnificence of the Castelli de Romagno, which was situated upon the borders of the populous town of Palermo, and surrounded by the picturesque and romantic Val di Mazzari, brought to her notice a numerous train of admirers, whose adulation was unceasingly offered—homaged too by her inferiors, and flattered nearly to infatuation by her equals; her young heart throbbed exultingly, and for some months she reigned supreme in the vortex through which she moved.

Leontini, a young nobleman of distinction, who had acquired

an enviable fame in the ranks of his countrymen, against the oppressors that had invaded the rights of Sicily, was, at the close of a meritorious campaign, honoured with the favours of Rosalviva, and became eventually the most fortunate of her admirers; his attentions were unceasing—they were sincere—and a period of some length witnessed their mutual regard.

Rosalviva was invited to pass the autumnal season at Messina, some leagues distant from her Castelli; with the approbation of Leontini, her compliance was immediately dictated, and the following day was signified for her departure.

The occupations of Leontini relative to matters of public importance, withheld his most strict attention, so much, that his mind and time was almost wholly engrossed by its arrangements.

The distinction of cold indifference, and the authoritative obedience to the duties of Leontini's station, was not duly observed by Rosalviva—her inclinations were strong and uncontrouled, and she treated but lightly those who felt not an equal perception with her own.—The late few and limited intervals that had permitted Leontini to appear at the Castelli di Romagno, were imagined by Rosalviva as the result of carelessness and danger; and she imputed to him, in the full tone of her belief, the neglect and coldness with which he treated her.

In frequent appeals did the lover of Rosalviva attempt to convince her of the error of her suppositions, and in language that spoke the pure sentiments of his heart, he avowed the sincerity and ardour of his affection—and which, to ought but Rosalviva, could not have failed in reducing the mistaken perceptibility.

The evening previous to her departure, the engagements of Leontini had detained him to an unusually late hour, he was thereby prevented from obeying his customary visit to Rosalviva; but in his heart her image was immoveably fixed—and though divided from her presence, its warmth and finer feelings were alive only to her admiration, and the study of completing her future felicity. He was apprehensive that his seeming inattention would call forth her reproach, and he dispatched a hurried epistle containing the fondest expressions of his attachment, and breathed a tributary vow to her happiness.

Rosalviva had retired for the evening earlier than her usual hour, mortified and vexed at the neglect she had met with—and in the confusion of her ideas, she resolved to think less of one she considered undeserving her esteem; and in the smile of a suitor more capable of appreciating her worth, she felt satisfied in discharging from her memory that of Leontini.

Had the pure and hallowed flame of love ever lighted the bosom of Rosalviva, it would never have formed sentiments so decisive as the present. It was not that she mourned his absence, or that his total separation would have caused one sigh, or one tear; it was that she considered her pride and magnified value but indifferently prized by him, on whom she had conferred her greatest esteem, and for whom she had forfeited the assiduous overtures of others, who would have doubtless repaid her with more than common fervency.

"Fool," she exclaimed, "that I was, thus to have secluded myself for one whose platonic soul is so unmindful of the charms which numbers have aspired to in vain. But I will hazard its coldness no longer; and as a proof of my freedom, this night terminates the conference. It will at least teach him that the merits and attainments of a being like Rosalviva are not to be purchased with indifference."

The latest moment expired in which he had sometimes visited the Castelli, and in the heat of her resentment she directed the subjoined communication:—

"I cannot but be sensible of the trifling situation I hold in your esteem. The very frequent instances of your neglect, and my subjection to the most painful disappointments, have together broken that confidence I had reposed; and to prevent a recurrence of the forfeiture of promises made by you, or my own unhappiness, you will consider this as the conclusion of a correspondence, yourself only can be blamed for."

The astonishment of Leontini by the introduction of a messenger with Rosalviva's letter, at an early hour, demanded an instant perusal—the effect of its contents is easily imagined.

He prepared to defend the conduct under which he had been circumstanced; but the susceptibility of his feelings to the unmerited charge, was too painful to suffer him to proceed, and he determined personally to endeavour to acquit himself, and soften the asperity of her decision.

He traversed one of the anti-rooms of the Castelli with much disorder, before Rosalviva acknowledged his presence. He had no cause to dissimulate; he still retained every feeling of his earliest ardour.

"Rosalviva," he tenderly pronounced, on her entrance—"can it be possible that the language dictated in this letter is the sentiment you would really acknowledge; surely you have formed too rash an opinion of my character, or am I the victim of some malignant reptile, whose invidious purposes are endeavoured to be effected at the price of the misery of him who sincerely loves you. Such let me consider, Rosalviva, to be the incitement, rather than the genuine feeling of one so amiable, so lovely as yourself."

"Leontini," answered the heiress of di Romagno, "the ideal suggestion of a rival approaching, under the mask of a slanderer, you will suffer me to remove; in whatever respect my opinion has been conveyed to you, it is exclusively my own. You cannot be ignorant of the truth of its assertion, and in its confession, you may in some measure restore, if not the affection, the credit due to a nobleman, and a man of honour."

Leontini replied at considerable length upon the sincerity of his professions, adding, that circumstances alone, of which she was perfectly acquainted, ought sufficiently to plead in mitigation; and that in any shape wherein he could offer atonement, it should be completed.

He attempted to engage the hand of Rosalviva; but her hauteur resisted the effort and at his seeming embarrassment a triumphant smile lighted up her bold features.

"Well, Signor Leontini, for delicacy sake further interrogation shall be avoided. Your future merits will speak for themselves during my absence. This evening I proceed on my journey, I may doubtless expect your company until then?"

"Dearest Rosalviva," pronounced her lover, in tones of real pathos, and clasping her extended hand within his, "how much have you wronged me—hence let me pledge myself in trust for your goodness: when I forget it—when I cease to remember that there is one being on earth who lives for Leontini, may that moment number the last of my existence. Promise me, too, Rosalviva, that you will not give me cause to forget you; promise me that when you feel incapable of returning Leontini's passion, that you will in candour and honour declare it; and whatever may be the affliction this doating heart experiences in the separation, it shall bear with it in silence, since it would be for the happiness and prosperity of a Rosalviva."

Rosalviva's heart felt a pleasing throb at the humiliating and warm expressions of his regard; and in an exclamation of sensitive ardour, she cried, "I am satisfied, Leontini, thou art mine; and in exchange of thy pledge, believe that Rosalviva will never inflict the smallest wound, or sacrifice a heart that has vowed to love her." Leontini felt assured of her forgiveness. His bosom throbbed in successive emotions of rapture, and taking her in his embrace, their fervent kisses testified a mutual sensibility.

Evening at length arrived, which pronounced the departure of Rosalviva. It was the first time that she had ever moved beyond the province that gave her birth. She anticipated delight in change of scene, the expectation of being ushered into society, the most splendid and inviting, and the enthusiasm she felt in the forthcoming enjoyment of the numerous entertainments which she had been proffered the introduction to, were each too powerfully impressed on her thoughts to admit of discomposure at a short separation from the man she esteemed. Her heart and mind were alert on the realization of gaiety. She received the assurances of Leontini's ardour, and bidding a fervent adieu, the carriage was speedily lost that conveyed her from the Val di Mazzari.

CHAPTER II.

"To love, the softest hearts are prone,
But such can ne'er be all his own;
Too timid in his woes to share,
Too meek to meet, or brave despair;
And sterner hearts alone may feel
The would that time can never heal."

LORD BYRON.

AN entertainment, given in honour of the nuptials of a Sicilian nobleman, afforded the first interview with Leontini and the heiress of di Romagno. Its impression was strong and powerful; the amusements of the evening ceased to delight him; he was thoughtful, and the more he gazed on the fine figure of Rosalviva, his attention and admiration became the more lasting.

Some friends of Leontini observed the charm under which he was bound; but to the lightness of their remarks, he returned a coldness that ill accorded with his usual manner and friendship.

The stature of Leontini was below the middle height, but accurately formed. A kind of stern decision marked his features; but gloomy as they would occasionally appear, there was still many a sunny tint of warm and pleasing generosity that beamed in its lighter shade.

His attachment for Rosalviva gradually increased. Her lightness of disposition would at intervals afflict him; but he had at length arrived at the satisfaction that he lived secure in her affection, and he supported the temporary separation during her stay at Messina, with sensations of mingled gratification and felicity.

He had twice perused a letter from Rosalviva, some few weeks after her arrival at her friends, written in the pure language of affection and expressions of sincerity, when the entrance of a domestic broke upon his pleasing meditations, and presenting a billet, carefully folded, withdrew.

Leontini was not acquainted with the characters of the envelope, and tearing it open, he read, "a friend to the Signor Leontini, in respect for his character and worth, embraces the present moment of signifying that the Signora Rosalviva has this instant quitted Messina; an assignation made in the cloisters of the Castel á Marri, within the hearing of the writer, summoned his closer observance, and as a warning to the Signor Leontini, in the case of confidence, this communication is submitted."

The astonishment of Leontini was painfully excited. He glanced upon the communication of Rosalviva, bearing the previous day's date; and after some few moments of reflection, he uttered, amidst the contest of his feelings, "Rosalviva is innocent; she could not so betray, so deceive her Leontini—obscure and villifying wretch, that would pollute her name, I treat thy attempt with the scorn it deserves." And at the same instant he destroyed the letter of his unknown correspondent, with implicit satisfaction.

"Rosalviva will never inflict the smallest wound, or sacrifice the heart that has vowed to love her," recurred to his remembrance with increasing assurances in behalf of her fidelity, and his reply to her epistle was fraught with all the ardour of a heart doting on the object of its enthusiasm.

An elapse of several days moved on with increased anxiety on the mind of Leontini. No communication had he received from Rosalviva. The instance of his unknown correspondent, and which he had treated with contempt, appealed somewhat earnestly to his credulity as to the truth of its intelligence. He perused the several letters in his possession from Rosalviva during their intimacy, in each was breathed a language progressively ardent and affectionate; he meditated on her behaviour towards him; he reviewed the various instances of her peculiar inquiry and sympathy which she had manifested for him. Her manner had always been disinterested and genuine. Why she could have held forth that show of regard which she had, why she could have concealed her affections for another, and yet have exchanged with his, was alike mysterious. The proud and lofty soul of Rosalviva he considered as too superior to admit of, or hazard reproach. She had frequently given him proof of her contempt, at advancements and conduct that were coloured with the slightest dishonour. Independently he knew that her will was decisive; she lived under no control; her own authority, to her own inclination was only liable—few ventured to oppose it. Why then she should have stooped to so pityable an act of duplicity was the utter surprise of Leontini. He still treated the idea of her capability of falsehood with indignance. It could not be possible, nor would he entertain a thought that appertained to her dishonour. He composed his mental agitation with the belief, that the hurry of engagements had precluded her from embracing the length of communication, which he had ever been in the habit of receiving from her. He had himself at times thrown aside correspondence, merely because opportunity was wanting to give it an immediate and real value; still his neglect was not questionable—and in the like manner did he construe the circumstance of the present moment with regard to Rosalviva.

Somewhat dejected at the unpleasant ruminations before him, Leontini hurried for a temporary change of scene. He was returning to his Palazzi, after a few hours absence, when from the dim light of a lamp, a man of mean appearance was seen loitering near the portico through which Leontini was entering.

The attentive survey of the stranger caught the eye of Leontini, and in a voice of stern enquiry, demanded the nature of his curiosity:—

"I was in waiting for the Signor Leontini," replied the man, with more brevity than caution.

"And your business with the Signor?"

The stranger drew from his cloak a small dark lantern, and turning its reflector full upon the features of Leontini, cried, after some few moments' elapse in a rude inspection, "Your pardon, Signor; you are the object of my mission."

Leontini was for the moment confused at the singularity of the affair; and desirous of a closer interview with his communicant, he retired some few paces, where the light of the portico lamps was more vivid. The man followed; but his countenance offered no trace of information to Leontini, as to his character, and he directly questioned the purport of his errand.

"The narrow street, Signor, which leads from the St. Esprit College, is terminated by an arcade of small but splendid buildings. The last house, at the right hand entrance, is kept by Signora Millezzani, by whom I am commissioned to request your attendance, at the hour that may be most convenient to yourself, Signor, after the tolling of to-morrow's evening bell for prayers."

"The Signora Millezzani?" repeated Leontini, and his imagination encountered a series of opposite constructions. "You have mistaken your adventurer; to my certain knowledge I never before heard mention of the name of Millezzani; and how I can be known to the Signora, or my presence required, is too apparent, not to show the error which you have committed."

"I am not aware, Signor, of the nature of the acquaintance; I was simply directed to remain at your residence here, until your appearance—so much that the Signora is acquainted with your habits, and certain of the character, that she promptly told me the hour which you in common was to be met with, to a minute within the hour I was in waiting. My information was not erroneously given; for but a few moments passed, when, Signor, I had the honour of addressing you: moreover, I have the superscription here of your abode."

He presented a small scroll to Leontini, on which was written his name and residence. He thought it strange, but deeming it the effect of a curious or idle moment, he resolved to humour it, and noting down the spot of assignation, he promised to be with the fair supplicant at an appointed hour.

"And is the Signora young and handsome?" jocosely questioned Leontini, as the messenger was about to depart.

"Both, Signor, though the cares of the world, perhaps, to a certain degree, may have impaired the one, and not altogether burdened the other."

Leontini was at liberty to draw his own conclusion upon the answer of the messenger; but wishing to extract, if possible, some intelligence of the family of Millezzani, he contrived to put a few florins into the hand of the stranger, and at the same time, in an indifferent manner, enquired if she was married.

"Ho, Signor—for that matter I am in complete ignorance, so long as my employers please to reward my endeavours, I never touch upon family secrets. You will be to your time, good Signor;" and with the most perfect ease and familiarity, he wished Leontini good night, and hastily withdrew.

Reaching his apartments, Leontini freely indulged in the humour of the incident. He knew the arcade to be respectably inhabited, and under whatever influence his presence was necessary, he could have no hesitation in affording it.

He waited the close of the following day with some degree of anxiety, and to the moment the evening bell announced the hour of prayer, he repaired to the dwelling of the Signora.

Leontini was ushered into a room of considerable neatness, where a packet directed "for the Signor Leontini" was handed to him—upon unfolding it, a few lines in the wrapper addressed him as follows.—"The Signora Millezzani has much to hope in pardon for this visit of Leontini—feelings overpowered by the acuteness of sensibility, has even now defied her resolution of coming to the appointed interview—she is sensible of his goodness, and doubts not his forgiveness at this strange behaviour; when he may have perused the enclosed epistle, and which the Signora Millezzani further trusts will be deferred until his return to his Palazzi."

Leontini was uncertain how to act consistent with his rank, but putting some questions to an attendant, whose replies were satisfactory, he quitted the house and proceeded to his own apartment. Breaking the seal of the Signora's letter, he discovered the signature of "Viola di Morini." A sensation of quick and thrilling astonishment seized his faculties, and in almost breathless emotion, he read its contents.

In earlier days, and amidst tranquil scenes, Viola di Morini had been the devoted object of Leontini's attachment, the assurance of each other's passion had united in them but one instinctive and affectionate tie: they saw each other with the eyes of fondness and delight—they cherished feelings known only to the heart which breathes its first love. The friends of Viola were averse to an alliance at so early a period, (neither of the lovers having attained their twentieth year) and before the nuptial rites had been considered as appropriate, the father of Viola was no more—her situation was distressing, her nearer relatives, whose views promoted their arbitrary conduct, assumed an authoritative right and severity towards her protection—to their establishment only had she refuge; her obedience to all their commands was imperative—her fortune was at their disposal, and so long as she was prohibited from accepting the hand of her lover, so were they more fully enabled to enjoy the advantages which its power maintained. Further intercourse with the only being on earth on whom she had fixed her heart, was ultimately proscribed, and a short elapse moved her to a remote part of the capital.

Separated from the man she loved, and excluded from every hope of society; it was not possible that her mind retained its energy, her heart its ardent hope. A few months saw her entire expectations blighted; her fine brilliant eye no longer possessed its lustre, the cheek faded, and the smile of joy and happiness had left no other trace but that of grief and despair. Her friends could not be indifferent spectators to the change which their cruelty had wrought—the engagements of a suitor to their choice was proposed, their marriage followed. She made no pause to question the dictates of her heart, it was silent, cold and withered—she was led to the altar a willing sacrifice, and the extent of her relief was in the embrace of almost a total stranger.

Leontini subsequently learned her fate, his happiness was equally broken, and the dull course of his future existence seemed as one irretrievable blank—he wandered about, the victim of despondency and insanity; he quitted the spot that had marked all his felicity—that had linked him with all his misery, every amusement appeared hateful to him, he cared not with whom he associated, and of whatever description might be the society that chance threw him upon, his apathy was so rooted, that not the ordinary means of life could awaken it to a sense of its interests.

Paoli Golfieri was a visitor in one of the many haunts frequented by Leontini, it was the receptacle for beings whose broken fortunes and ruined prospects brought them to a familiarity with desperation; it was here the experienced enthusiast watched with an "eagle eye," for the opportunity of plundering his unsuspecting victim; it was here that the passions of ferocity and dissipation had their free scope; it was here that man hunted his fellow, nor left him till fortune, family, and feeling were alike condemned.

Golfieri appeared at such a moment. Leontini snatched him from the precipice which yawned before his heedless tread. To a figure the most perfect, was blended a mind and disposition of peculiar energy; and his friendship with Leontini became warm, disinterested, and binding. He had alike associated with the horde of Catalines, in an unguarded moment; but with the aid of the

Signor Leontini he had summoned sufficient prudence to retract from their pursuits—there was an opportunity to escape the snares—it was seized with avidity, and the interests and welfare of the two signors became willingly united.

Time, and a repetition of entertainment in the most splendid society, had worked a beneficial change in the mind and enjoyments of Leontini, and the recollection of his unhappiness at the loss of Viola was materially softened; she was, indeed, almost wholly forgotten. It was at no great distance, subsequently, that he beheld the Signora Rosalviva.

There was a difference, notwithstanding, in his amour with the Comptessa, that almost applied itself to coldness; but his behaviour and very precise attention at all times towards her, needed no distant doubt to pronounce its character. It was not the heat and enthusiasm of boyhood that taught him to bow to the throne of her beauty; it was a progressive and earnest attachment brought on by incessant opportunity—by the strict sense of honour and sincerity that seemed to guide her mind and principles; and by all her pleasing endearments and assiduous endeavours to obtain his smile, and sense of happiness.

Four years had elapsed since he had taken his last farewell of Viola de Morini, when he received the communication from her under the fictitious title of Millezzani.

Viola had perceived the brink which the hurry of her irksome existence had thrown her upon. It was reviewed in all its disgust and sadness; and every succeeding day brought with it her further disquietude.

Viola had been introduced, at the early part of her alliance, to a portion of splendour and entertainment, and which for a time diverted—at least it helped to frustrate those recollections which hours of solitude are too apt to sketch. Up to a certain time, those enjoyments that Viola participated in were anxiously promoted by her husband;—they were at length tedious to him—her comforts became the least of his thoughts, and at last were wholly disregarded. At this stage of her alliance she had but attained her twenty second year.

At a public festival, where Viola with reluctance had consented to be present, and that only at the earnest entreaty of a valued friend, was announced, some time after its commencement, the Signor Leontini and the Comptessa Rosalviva.

Viola heard the name of her former lover. She saw the attention with which he escorted the Signora Rosalviva. Her feelings with poignance acknowledged the sentiment her heart still retained for him; and unable to endure their conflict, she pleaded indisposition, and hurried to her abode.

The anguish of past events, the idea that preyed on her mind of her present misery, and the happiness of Leontini, alternately pressed within her bosom. She felt a desire once more to see him—to converse with him—to question his felicity—to mark if he still respected her memory. Various thoughts collectively rushed upon her mind, and she felt determined to discover their reality.

She frequented numerous resorts, in the hope of his presence; but a period of some months witnessed her ill success. Her perseverance was not to be defeated; and its success at length brought her to the height of her wishes.

The name of Millezzani she knew was not familiar to him, and with its aid she effected her endeavours.

Leontini again perused the epistle—his heart abounded with too much of sympathy to withhold the tribute due to her remembrance, and to the sufferings of Viola its influence gave a tear.

He returned a few lines to Viola, in token of his sense of her confidence. The same evening he undertook to be with her, and conformable to his promise he met once again the woman of his "first love."

It needs no art to sketch the effect of such a meeting—it requires not language to tell the rapture of such a moment, to those who have known the feeling of love—to those who have borne a separation, and which time has rendered its reality only the more susceptible—it is with facility imagined the present sensations of Leontini and Viola di Morini.

Through hours of painful silence *she* had wept the loss of a Leontini—she had wept over the correspondence of happier days; and even when her husband was unmindful of her happiness, she had welcomed no other solace but the indulgence of solitude, and to bring back the remembrance of the past, for with it was impressed the caresses and affection of her Leontini. So much had she cherished the pang which was rapidly undermining her existence, that at the period of her communication with Leontini, sorrow and oppression had so altered her "fair form," that it seemed but a desolate wreck of that which it once had been.

Leontini had equally suffered during the intercourse; it had nearly cost him a life that was already drooping into lethargy and debility. The banner of his country waved with conquest—he flew to it with ardour; and in the path leading to glory he hoped to forget all his wretchedness. Fame had seemingly marked his efforts for her own, and in the thickest of danger his valour was successful. From a stranger in the ranks of military enthusiasm, he acquired "a leaders name."

The shores of Sicily echoed with the praises of its heroes, and the name of Leontini was not pronounced but with acclamations of applause.

Palermo hailed her repellers of the Moorish invasion with ardour, and in the esteem of its inhabitants, Leontini held a prominent feature, and for some time his mind and spirits enjoyed a seasonable tranquility.

Rosalviva, too, the envied heiress of Di Romagno smiled upon him, and when sensible of the weakness that attended the regret at Viola's loss—sensible that she was irrevocably in the possession of another, and probably happy, he endeavoured to prize the opportunity that might render *him* equally so; and in the favours of Rosalviva di Cardoni, he had partly realized his wishes—this then was his situation, and thus was formed the outline of his heart, when the presence of Viola di Morini claimed his remembrance. He embraced her respectfully—he could not look upon her with indifference, though the image of Rosalviva filled her place in his bosom.

Several moments expired before either ventured to break the silence.

"Leontini," she sobbingly exclaimed, "this is a painful meeting, prudence ought to have spared *me* its anguish; but, however great may be its reprehension; it ought to merit forgiveness."—Tears followed the confession of Viola, and she indulged in their relief, supported in the arms of Leontini. Her sobs were loud and impetuous—it was that convulsive sob that breaks from a heart, lit up with joy and yet depressed by sadness. There was a solemn serenity in the scene, that would have wrought a mind of the most repulsive cast, into compassion and pity; it was a scene to Leontini too affecting to admit of severity. He was convinced how far the sway of her disorder had extended, he marked the artificial gleam of brightness that darted from her eye, he marked the feverish tint that coloured her cheek, and he knew its full effect; he knew that it was the uncertain hectic flush that preceded consumption, there were no false shades in it, the reality was but too apparent, and he gazed upon her during a contention of agonizing feeling—he pronounced her name, and kissing with respectful tenderness her lips that quivered immoderately, remarked, "and you are still the wife of ——"

"Yes, yes," she eagerly replied, wishing to impede the observation, "but do not throw me from this glad embrace, do not disdain to hear me—I have not much to ask, my stay in this world cannot be long, I am satisfied with what grief and misery have done here;" and placing her hand upon her heart, she lifted her eye, still streaming with its tear, to those of Leontini, its expression denoted all her suffering; that look, that conscious look of sorrow with which she gazed upon him, penetrated into his very soul. Leontini would have retired—but she eagerly caught his hand.

"Leontini, this is a moment I have prayed for, long have studied to obtain; do not, if you ever loved me, do not leave me yet. I have something to say, it is the first solicitation the unhappy Viola has made to any being since your smile was lost upon her, it is the last—the trifling gleam of happiness which hope afforded me will soon fade."

"Viola you must desist from this unpleasant discourse, tell me the state of your unhappiness, I may possibly have the power of its alleviation."

"You did love me once, Leontini?" uttered the unhappy Viola, in tones so imploring and so benignant, that its accent seemed to be breathed by more than mortal form. "You did love me," she again repeated in anxious intercession.—"I did, Viola, nor is its power wholly extinguished—it were impossible to renounce the recollection of events gone by, it were equally impossible to view with indifference their fatality—had I ere this ceased to cherish them, what pain might I not have escaped."

"Circumstance, Leontini," she articulated, still detaining his hand—"decreed by Providence, foiled the union of two hearts bound as ours were—there requires no narrative of the collective miseries that followed my separation from Leontini—the only aid that extended itself to relieve them, was that of my present husband's; we were united, I am still his wife—nay, do not look reproachfully, Leontini, do not wholly break the remnant of a heart that is still your own—do not scorn me."

"I do not, Viola, I must be exempt from feeling and humanity, indeed, were I unable to recognize the agony and confession of this moment. Heaven is witness how much I loved you, and when I knew the truth of your alliance, when I had heard of all your suffering, my heart shed burning tears; whatever might have been your endurance of woe, mine was not less parallel—it brought me Viola to the shadow of earlier days. The pale and colourless features, the sunken eye, the habitual gloom and coldness towards society, all of which I bore the stamp of, was a sufficient portrait to a mind capable of susceptibility, to tell of its unfortunate cause, and for nearly three years, Viola, I prostrated myself to whatever destiny which might befall me."

"The rest is not unknown to me, Leontini, I have learnt it all, and am well persuaded of the value of your felicity, it shall not be disturbed by the presence of a wretched woman. This interview was the extent of my hopes, I can part now, Leontini, with tranquillity, and the latest moment of life shall witness my exhortation to God for your happiness."

Leontini wished to change the nature of the discourse, and enquired as to her circumstances. She entreated to be excused from reply, she intimated that her stay at Palermo was limited, she forbade interrogation, and concluded with stating her intention of quitting her abode the subsequent day—but by whom accompanied, or for a reference to her route, her information was silent.

The night was getting far advanced, Leontini requested a further meeting prior to her departure, it was assented to.

He held her to his heart some few moments, he pressed her lips in ardent warmth to his own. What sympathy, what intelligence did those few moments not impart. He broke from her embrace, and in the assurance of another meeting they separated.

CHAPTER III.

"Friendship is constant in all other things,
Save in the office and affairs of love;
Therefore all hearts in love use their own tongues,
Let every eye negociate for itself,
And trust no agent; for beauty is a witch,
Against whose charms faith melteth its bond."

Much Ado about Nothing.

ENTRANCED with the profusion of magnificence and gaiety that seemed to throng with the amusements of Messina, the Signora Rosalviva knew no thought or retained any delight beyond that which was centred in her present pursuits. She entered with the most buoyant spirit into all society that admitted a probability of splendid attraction, and warmed by the blaze of fashion and gallantry that spread itself around her, her mind would often repeat, "these are pleasures which solitude and retirement can never produce, their value will find a difficult compromise." An invitation to a Sicilian masque, of the highest rank, was an honour too great to the hopeful and innate vanity of Rosalviva to be declined; she sought its revelry, and whilst her elegant mien commanded the admiration of most beholders, her soul was filled with every degree of triumph and rapture.

There was one amongst the crowd whose eye had marked her, and by no inducement was its gaze drawn from her during the entire fete.

The character of the mask, and his close observance, could not fail in meeting with the perception of Rosalviva, there was an unusual trait of pleasantry in his manner, and his politeness and attention were not less distinguished.

Rosalviva enjoyed a thrill of triumphant pride and satisfaction, at the thought which gave rise to her being the peculiar object of the stranger's preference, and with agreeable confidence she encouraged his assurances.

As the great part of the company appeared to be separating, at the same moment the young Comptessa simultaneously followed, much trouble attended the procuring of conveyances immediately to the wishes of the masqueraders, and Rosalviva was of the number whose patience was excited by the delay; the Mask, whose pretensions she had not reviled, was by her side, and in a tone of well-behaved familiarity intimated the use of his carriage; it was not unacceptable, and the vehicle was soon clear of the prevailing confusion.

A trifling space of time occurred when the stranger, who was seated opposite to Rosalviva, implied, "Signora, the honour I receive in your assent to my proffered assistance, is one I can never forget; it will bear the date, lovely lady, of the happiest hour of my existence."

The Comptessa felt a momentary blush suffusing her cheek, at the complacency of the remark, and endeavored to offer in conceding terms her sense of his kindness; hoping, at the same moment, that she might not be kept in total ignorance to whom she was so infinitely indebted.

"To one, Signora, who has been no idle spectator to your goodness; to one who has, with more than common assiduity, studied its merits—the Signor Leontini, lady—but pardon me."

A resistless hesitation marked the reply of the stranger, he threw a glance of quick penetration into the countenance of Rosalviva—the cold rays of the moon which reflected through the window of the carriage, pourtrayed its almost colourless expression as he mentioned the name of her lover; he saw the momentary surprise which it excited, he knew that it maintained a kind of governance upon her mind and feeling, and he wished to ascertain the extent of its vibration; in an articulation then of passive compliance, he added—"since your silence, lady, seems to crave the conclusion of my interference, I would observe, the Signor Leontini, who is your established lover, cannot prize those merits more richly than he who now speaks of them."

Rosalviva recovered the trifling embarrassment which the introduction of Leontini's name had certainly created; and desirous of rallying the discourse with seeming levity, she asked the stranger if she had the devout felicity of being the debtor to the Signor Leontini's confessor.

"Not morally so," he answered, "but I have the distinction of his confidence, Signora, I have also that of his friend, the Signor Conte Golfieri; upon that matter I could narrate circumstances which might not be immaterial or unconnected with yourself Signora—you being the object he professes to love."

"Professes," echoed the voice of Rosalviva, astonished at the earnestness with which that word was pronounced.

"Yes, Signora, my own decided knowledge of his sentiments and principles will not allow me to change its affinition. It is not unfrequent that we profess to admire—aye, and ardently, that which we have but a mere distant, casual respect for, the adage, Signora, of 'all is not gold that glitters,' may serve figuratively in the instance of my friend, the Signor Leontini; but the carriage I perceive has stopped some moments at the Palazzi, where you requested to alight—I claim pardon for the detention."

The present separation with the stranger was a period which the Çomptessa would willingly have prolonged; but the opposition to such a wish was implicit. She had reached the residence of her friend, and prudence withheld further communication. He assisted her from the vehicle; it was a moment that was to divide her from an intelligence she might profit by—it would not admit of an entire forfeiture, and without further apology, she intimated that on the succeeding evening she should pass the Strado di Voli, towards the residence of one of her friends.

The stranger comprehended the tenor of the information, and pressing her hand to his lips, whispered that his family were noble, his fortune princely, and that the endowments of his ancestry were added to the most illustrious of record.

Rosalviva numbered with anxiety the moments that noted the time of her passing the Strado di Voli, and she hurried to the spot; disguise was no longer requisite, for in the stranger's mask of the previous evening stood the Conte Golfieri.

Their meetings were frequent, and to every scene of public assembly the Conte Golfieri was her devoted ciceroni.

The return of Rosalviva to the Palazzi di Romagno was gladly hailed by her admirers; and several days were occupied in receiving the congratulations and visits of Palermo's nobility.

A week had terminated since her announcement at Di Romagno was publicly acknowledged—no wish, no invitation, no notice was intimated by Rosalviva with regard to any conference or meeting with Leontini; and he supported the conflict which his feelings sustained with pain little short of distraction. His pride was hurt at the singular treatment he had received at her hands, and why she withheld correspondence during her visit at Messina?—Why she had considered him not worth enquiry upon her return? was too apparent to be misconceived; and he felt assured that the truth of the anonymous communication which he had destroyed was perfectly unquestionable, and in the smiles of another she had forgotten his.

The Conte Golfieri, his friend, was still absent. To hazard the coolness of reception, or the insolence of denial to her presence, under existing circumstances, or to suffer it to be presumed that he had subserviently essayed to regain an intercourse upon such pityable terms as only could be offered, was not accordant with the spirit and sensitive feeling of a Leontini.

Twice by design had he thrown himself in her way; but her wish to avoid him was formed and executed in the same moment. He resolved to be thought indifferent to her behaviour; and at every place of public entertainment Leontini was seen in pursuit of its most fleeting enjoyments.

The proceedings which daily occurred at the Castelli di Romagno he was not ignorant of. Matters seemed to proceed in the same course for a considerable length of time; but what added to the surprise of Leontini was, that no appearance of a suitor to the hand of Rosalviva was discoverable; and no persons had marked the preference of her esteem to one individual more than another.

The Signor Compte Napoli, a young Sicilian, whose birth and fortune were more in repute than his wit or imagination, was the most constant in attentions to the Comptessa; but his known imbecility and barrenness of understanding readily convinced those who might have momentarily envied his seeming felicity, that a soul like Rosalviva's would abhor unity with one so incapable of sensibility.

Napoli was the favorite protegè of the old Conte di Cardoni and the respect paid to him during her father's existence she was not inclinable to discard; and if his pretensions and behaviour bordered upon the extreme of folly and insignificance, there was a show of splendour in his equipage, a supremacy in his entertainments, and a magnificence in his general appearance, which far exceeded either of the nobles of Palermo, and which Rosalviva could at all times definitively command.

It was considered indispensable, since that the solemnity due to the memory of Cardoni had expired, that the title deeds and inheritance of the domain should be consigned from the care of the Padre Vivaldi, to the legal and full possession of the Comptessa Rosalviva.

The Padre was waited upon for the discharge of his trust; and by the wish of Rosalviva he attended the Castelli.

The Monk bowed from his erect posture in lowly submission to her person, as he was introduced; and in a tone of reverential dignity; pronounced on her a blessing.

The character and person of Vivaldi was never social to the esteem of Rosalviva. There was an imperative and mysterious carriage that ever accompanied his demeanour, which to a female mind was far from gaining prepossession; and before her ideas had formed themselves in correctness of discrimination, the disposition and terms of friendship offered to her by Vivaldi, were by no means welcome or acceptable. Since that she had attained the age of maturity, the Monk had rendered his subservience to her rank more practicable—and appeared to regard it with the humility which she felt ought to be paid to her inheritance.

The tall figure of the Monk, habited in the sombre garment of his order, had retired in silent devotion to a recess of the apartment where the portrait of Cardoni was suspended.

The impressive stillness of the moment tended to convey a throb of unpleasant feeling in the bosom of the Comptessa, and which the advanced hour, and the obscurity of the apartment, appeared to increase.

The Padre bent to the painting of his late master, and Rosalviva waited during an elapse of many moments, whilst he inwardly murmured a prayer of invocation.

"The subject, reverend father, which required your attendance," spake Rosalviva, impatient at the loneliness of his mood, "had better be deferred until an earlier hour on the morrow, since the lateness of the evening will prohibit the conference requisite."

"The duties of my holy office, daughter," replied the Monk, as he approached towards her in respectful obedience, "are too numerous and too impervious to be disregarded; it is therefore only at a time like the present, when those avocations have ceased, that I can bestow leisure and opportunity to merit the confidence of that part of the community, which I trust I may number the Comptessa with my friends. I would hazard much, beauteous Rosalviva, to complete thine. 'Tis yet some two hours till midnight, and much may be discussed in that period—name then, daughter, thy wishes."

The Comptessa hesitated, there was a familiarity and a consequence in his manner that she did not expect, still she could have nothing to apprehend.

Turning to the Padre, she observed, "at the decease of my lamented parent, the documents of his estates and my claims were vested in your authority and possession; at least that of the holy brotherhood, of which you are the principal, until the arrangements of the funeral rites had been performed, and until whatever incumbrances which have accrued should be discharged."

"Yes, fair daughter, your memory is good; *until the incumbrances should be discharged.*"

"Time and obedience have fulfilled such bequests," spoke Rosalviva, not altogether mindful of the hurried voice of the Monk, "and the holy and honourable charge of the father Vivaldi, it is my intention now to cancel."

"Indeed," murmured Vivaldi and his dark eye was raised in earnest look to Heaven, "that were a task, my daughter, I shall be pleased to witness the completion of; but those *incumbrances* are not cleared, nor is it in your present power to get them cancelled."

Rosalviva was astonished, she could scarcely give credence to what she heard, she shuddered to think that some dark purpose was in agitation; but adverting instantly to the functions of the confessor, she conceived that he doubtless retained an erroneous idea of their arrangement, and a hasty opinion was the result; she imparted the nature of her belief to Vivaldi. His enunciation of her credulity was instantly opposed to the remark, and his voice, accompanied with a half suppressed smile, repeated his previous suggestion; adding—"I can assure you, daughter, there is more to be done before the domain of Romagno rests peaceably in the possession of the Comptessa Rosalviva."

For some moments the heiress of Di Romagno was absorbed in a painful silence. She meditated upon what possible ground an opposition could be made in justice to her claims; and as her reflections deepened, she felt the more convinced that the views and intentions of the Padre were injurious to her rights: and in the enthusiasm of her imagination upon his baseness, she resolved to defeat his attempt of persuading her as to the illegality of her heritage—she challenged him to produce whatever mandate that authorized his immediate denial of her property; and declared, unless it was restored to her, every document committed to his care by the Conte di Cardoni—the decrees of her tribunal should enforce it, and bring down disgrace and infamy upon every brother of the order allied to Vivaldi.

"This may appear probable," answered Vivaldi, who had calmly listened to her vehement harangue, "but you will repent the application, Comptessa; take counsel, and profit by it: be satisfied in the indulgence of your present luxuries, and seek not to enthral the memory, and let me add, the *poverty* of your dependance."

The injunction of Vivaldi sounded mysteriously upon the ear of Rosalviva; the emphasis which he applied to the words *poverty of her dependance*, was singularly impressive, and his expression of features at the same instant, was equally forbidding. The haggard, but stern menace of countenance, the angry flash of terror that his eye conveyed, and the infuriated tone of voice, severally struck upon the mind of Rosalviva a severe and fatal presentiment; and much as her spirits were usually buoyant, their solidity felt a shock at the sudden and strange evidence of the confessor Vivaldi.

"I should not be wanting," rejoined the Monk, "in rendering assistance to facilitate the utmost of your wishes—and moreover to shield you from the lash of adversity, did occasion require it. But

I cannot, in duty to the last words of the late Conte, in compliance too with the holiness of our Order, and with my sense of moral and religious obligation, willingly be the instrument for the indulgence of your vices."

"Vices," interrupted Rosalviva.

"The term may appear harsh, daughter, but I am not ignorant to what excess youthful passions will dive into when rushing upon the wide stream of pleasure; without an arm to direct, without a warning voice to impede. In the whirlpool of fleeting enjoyment, the mind is easily drawn from objects that demand the more grave and tranquil obedience, and the performance of a duty degenerates into a task so irksome, that the burden is gladly thrown from our endurance ere we pause to reflect on the probable enormity of the act. Setting aside, fair daughter, the frailties attachable to the weakness of thy sex, you must bear in mind that there exists a promise, nay, an oath, it is registered in the volume of eternity; which forfeits the fulfilment of the genial ties of nature in the sworn determination of avenging the insulted remains of your deceased parent. You must not suffer to slumber the injunction of his dying moments; you must not idly pass over the continued species of malevolence and reprehension, that slanders the name and rank of Cardoni.

"The Conte predicted its blighting voice, nor was his prophecy grounded on fiction. You, Rosalviva, are ignorant of its real terror, and equally unable to combat its wrath. It is said that the cause which terminated with the assassination of the Conte was not that of accident, but originating from a dispute persisted in by Cardoni, and that so forcibly, that rather than suffer his authority to meet opposition, he determined on the ruin of his aggressor. It was accomplished, but the offspring of the fallen party, indignant at the crime and injury sustained, publicly accused the Conte of the atrocity. Words ensued, their quarrel was heated malicious; strength and superior skill prevailed, and thus was vanquished the instigator of the broil, Reo Cardoni."

"False and calumniating assertion," vehemently uttered the Comptessa, "and to this tale devout confessor thou hast listened?"

"Appearances, alas! daughter, unhappily carry with them conviction in the present instance."

"And hast *thou*, Padre Vivaldi," warmly spoke Rosalviva, unmindful of the confessor's latter remark,—"also forgotten the pledge of assurance made at the same couch of my departing parent."

"Of what nature?" hastily questioned the Monk.

"That of thy *faith* on the *innocence and honour* of the Conte of Cardoni."

"I should have staked all I possessed in life against the dissimulation of a Cardoni at that period; but I have since learned the fatality of human confidence—but argument like the present is better avoided, daughter; you have the means of attaining peace, and obeying the bequests of your parent. It is given you simply in the solicitation, that you bend your knee to the throne of Providence, there supplicate his commanding aid to bring to light the assassin of your parent. Rosalviva, this advice must not be ridiculed, as you value the righteousness and forgiveness of that God to whom you bend, reject not the counsels of one who gains little by deceiving thee, and thereby suffer me to emblazon the rectitude and acquiescence of thy heart in characters that shall be exalted through the remotest generations."

The Confessor paused, and taking the hand of Rosalviva, made the sign of the Holy Cross on her breast, whilst his lips acknowledged a benison.

No reply was offered by the Comptessa, no resistance marked the detention of her hand, which was still in that of Vivaldi's; she was silent, save the brightness of her eye, and the fixed and settled countenance, which fully indicated the wandering of her mental faculty.

The Padre motioned to depart, and intimating his intention of returning to the Palazzi on the forth-coming evening, he concluded with—"retire, my daughter, to the repose of thy chamber—reflect upon the value of my counsels, and the beams of the morning shall bring with it consolation and happiness."

The Confessor quitted the apartment, and as his hollow footsteps resounded along the outer corridores, they conveyed back a new and strange feeling towards the object. She would have indulged in an apathy which had hitherto been unknown to her, and the more she ruminated upon the remarks of Vivaldi, the more susceptibly was her mind receding into a languor that she seemed ill calculated to support; she called to memory the last bequest of her parent, she retraced her vow made to his dying pillow—it might have, in the effervescence of her youth and gaiety, gradually obliterated itself without knowing its importance; but she now felt that it was re-kindled, she felt that exclusive of her own anxiety and resolution to avenge the ill fated death of the Conte—there was a spirit more impelling than her own, whose agency appeared to pursue with alacrity the hope that would lead to the perpetrators of the deed; she had already consulted her admirer Golfieri—she had purposed to offer large rewards for the obtainment of information relative to the unknown assassin; she had urged Golfieri to aid her in the endeavour to fulfil her parent's desire; but her solicitations, her anxieties were severally soothed, and the blandishment of his speech, and the felicity of his presence, charmed her into a forgetfulness of those unhappy circumstances, which he inferred, by cherishing, would only tend to injure her happiness. He prayed her to think no more on what Providence had ordained, avowing himself devoted to her future commands and wishes, and whatever loss she might incur from the decease of a parent, his life and prospects were pledged in the hope of reinstating the value.

She listened to his professions of truth and assiduity, and in their existence she ceased to think of her father's injunction. It might have rested peaceably in her soul, but that the charge was still unrequited in the breast of Vivaldi. He had marked too carefully the levities of Rosalviva, and for the reverence due to the late Conte, he appeared to be resolved not to suffer his offspring to be deluded into every maze of extravagance and dissipation. This was at length her opinion of Vivaldi's regard, and the asperity she had entertained was to a certain degree lessened.

Rosalviva had not remained many minutes in reflection after the departure of the Confessor, when the voice of Golfieri, in an accent scarce beyond a whisper, pronounced her name. It dispelled all her sorrows, and hurrying to the door of the apartment she gave him admittance.

The lateness of the hour, told her of the retirement of the Pallazzi; she cautioned him as to disturbance, and taking his hand within her's, conducted him in quietude to her chamber. The night was dark and cloudy, and the fitful light of the moon that at distant intervals shone through the apartment, betrayed the paleness of her cheek; the partly contending smile too, that seemed with reluctance to lend a lustre to its altered sweetness, told Golfieri that all was not serene, and pressing her lips with the utmost tenderness, he entreated the confidence of her inward dejection—he listened in silence to its intelligence; at length throwing himself at the feet of the Comptessa, in a tone of earnest supplication he cried—"Rosalviva tell me, tell me, without hazarding the least dissimulation or doubt, am I the man on whom you can for ever repose your heart, your happiness."

Rosalviva made no reply, but the internal sensation of that heart implicated the certainty of that which she hesitated to acknowledge.

"Speak, my peace, my existence depends on it. Yes, you do, you will love me, Rosalviva?"

The tear of sensibility bedewed the soft eye of the Comptessa, it rested in earnest gaze on those of her lover, and voluntarily falling upon his neck she rejoined.—"Question the proofs, Golfieri, that I have given you of my affection, and it needs no further scrutiny."

"Yes—then dearest Rosalviva, thou art indeed mine, and no earthly endeavour can disunite us."

"Never!" added the heiress of Di Romagno.

"You are irrevocably mine," again repeated the Conte.

"As Heaven is my witness," emphatically pronounced Rosalviva, and her eyes were raised to Heaven.

"Enough, till this hour I have kept in secret what knowledge I possess of the lamented catastrophe that deprived the Conte Cardoni of existence. I, Rosalviva, was by *chance* directed to the spot where the conflict ensued; I saw him fall, and, Oh! Heaven! the remembrance of the deed is still before me. The assassin's name, his family, are allied to mine own: quarrel had invoked the anger of my friend, and before Golfieri could interfere, his weapon had pierced the heart of his opponent. I was about to fly in horror at the sight, he prevented me, and bade me swear never to reveal the affair of this night. I did, I did, and when, Rosalviva, you hasten to bring to justice the destroyer of your parent, you immolate the peace, nay, the life of Golfieri, in the same moment for ever."

The Comptessa shuddered at the unwelcome recital—an icy coldness seized her faculties; her lover perceived its effect—he enfolded her to his bosom.

"Rosalviva, I will not think it is your wish that our dreams of joy should break so soon; it is in your power eternally to bind it, and whatever sacrifice those feelings may suffer, Golfieri will remember it is for him—he will repay it with unbounded sincerity."

Such an acknowledgment Rosalviva would have hazarded much to obtain—she felt its worth, and resolved to secure the felicity which Golfieri seemed equally desirous of sharing. She convinced him of her satisfaction of his ardour, and for some moments they mutually experienced decided happiness.

Rosalviva retired to her chamber, and the Conte crossed the staircase that brought him to a secluded outlet of the building.

The conduct of the Padre Vivaldi was foremost in his imagination, and unmindful of other matters, he meditated upon what pretext he could rid himself of the Confessor's interference. To secure the title deeds of the Di Romagno domain was at the present period difficult; he was convinced that were *he*, either by threat or persuasion, to make a demand of them from the hands of Vivaldi, suspicion and danger would follow. His intimacy with the Comptessa was a matter of privacy; he concluded, therefore, that by stratagem only could the means be effected, and on the approaching interview with Rosalviva he would counsel for its immediate adoption. Once in his entire possession, Rosalviva was irrecoverably his—with the wish of "morning's beam" he sought his pillow.

CHAPTER IV.

"Time o'er the virtuous cheek may spread,
Its traces of decay;
But when the rose of beauty's fled,
No love is ta'en away."

FELLOWES.

"No tie so near———
No bond so sacred, but the cursed hunger
Of gold has broke it; and made wretched man
To fly from nature, mock religion,
And trample under feet the holiest laws."

Old Play.

AGREEABLE to the wish of Viola De Morini, the Signor Leontini hastened to their proffered meeting; but his hopes were disappointed—he had fondly traced some pleasing theme in which his assistance, his friendship would be deemed worthy the use of Viola; he had imagined the recital of her future intentions. He was not insensible that she still loved him, and since the treatment he had experienced from the hands of Rosalviva had rendered him capable of at once forgetting her, he felt an inward sensation of regard for the unfortunate Viola: he knew of no opposition that could dispel it, and he looked forward for that period in which they both would be endearing to each other.

Her acknowledgment that she was still the wife [of] ———, disquieted in some degree the projects he was about to form; but meditation taught him to think of it with impunity. He remembered the ardor of her passions, he remembered her look, her manner, when she exclaimed—"I am still his wife; but do not discard me, do not break the remnant of a heart that is all your own." These were sentiments that cancelled every other feeling; he was not the man that would in secret enjoy what he knew to be the idol of another; his pretensions were honourable—he knew too well that illicit love brought with it ultimately misery and remorse, and these were not pangs he felt inclined to encounter, nor would he hazard their existence in the bosom of Viola.

He was perfectly aware that the laws of his country would

disannul the bonds of matrimony, under circumstances like those which had joined the inexperienced Viola, and to such an expedient might he resort; he would but entreat the sanction of her he still delighted in, and the certainty of his endeavours he held no fear of. It was in his power, both in inclination and wealth, to make her indisputably happy, he was anxious to secure its possession.

The last ray of the setting sun had receded some few hours ere the appointment with Viola demanded his attention; he had beguiled the time in perusing the epistolary correspondence of former days, and over their rapturous effusions he dropped at intervals a tear.

Amid the darkness of night he visited the temporary abode of Viola—he was received by a stranger, who respectfully inquiring if he were the Signor Leontini, placed in his hands a small packet; he broke its envelope—some hurried and wild stanzas from the pen of Viola—a letter addressed to the Signor, and a curl of her fine dark hair were the contents, each of which the eye of Leontini rested upon in amazement.

"And where is the Signora Viola?" he tremulously exclaimed, to an interesting female who was in attendance.

"The Signora quitted Palermo this morning early—from the nature of a communication she received last night, her departure was of immediate necessity."

"And the direction of her route," enquired Leontini, who had eagerly glanced over the tenor of her letter.

"Alas! Signor, I am ignorant, poor, dear lady, her heart was so full of anguish and her agitation so apparent, that I had much difficulty in restraining my own sorrows from keeping pace with her's."

Leontini's several interrogatories were but simply answered, but they were marked with so much candour and artlessness, that the possibility of being fraught with any meaning but that of sincerity was instantly dismissed.

The epistle merely solicited the forgiveness of Leontini, stating that reasons which might at some distant period be revealed, commanded her absence; she conjured him to believe that his image would ever be nearest his heart—she intreated his confidence to their recent interview, and intimated the hope of being eventually a contributor of his happiness.

The accompanying stanzas were seemingly executed in much taste; they were not submitted with the accuracy of refinement and study, but disclosing more the purity and language of her breaking heart.

There's a pleasure in thinking on days gone by,
  Tho' the thought alone be left to cheer us;
There's a pleasure in heaving the pensive sigh,
  To shades that once were belov'd, and near us.
'Tis a pleasure to know that whilst life shall last,
  Nought from the bosom, this charm can sever,
To live in the *sunshine* of scenes long past,
  Tho' we feel that the *sun* has set for ever!

I have witness'd the calm of long summer eves,
  When winds in their caverns seem'd reposing;
Whilst the soft air stirr'd thro' the falling leaves,
  And the bells of the flowers were gently closing.
I have linger'd to view in that silent hour,
  Which fills the soul with a pleasing sadness,
The sun's last ray on some hill or tow'r,
  Like the soothing shade of departed gladness!

And tho' the orb had long sunk from the sky,
  Its radiance linger'd there, warm and beaming;
It shines on another world thought I,
  On another sphere, its light is gleaming!
Thus, thus, though thy face thou hast turn'd from me,
  And thy smile, in another circle shineth;
A bright recollection remains of thee,
  The sacred flame, which my heart enshrineth.

Speed on thy bright course! I have known the time,
  When love shone in every glance you gave me,
And now, tho' that bliss is no longer mine;
  Of the sweet reflection, you cannot bereave me.
I'll not bid thee farewell,—'tis a sorrowful sound,
  And tho' we may meet again,—ah! never!
To know *we have lov'd*, flings a sunshine around,
  Whose light, shall illumine my soul for ever!*

* Note.—I have to acknowledge my obligation to Miss M. G. Lewis, Author of "*Gwenllean*," "*Zelinda*," &c. for the introduction of these verses.

The variety of sensations that alternately swayed the bosom of Leontini, were more acute than expression could pourtray; his smiling look, his manly form, contrasted with the motionless and sullen statue of despair, can readily excite a feeling of deepest commiseration in the heart of those who have felt the throb of ardent love. He was not sensible to the belief that a meeting with Viola could have created such interest—he was less so that her loss would leave so cruel an affliction; yet those few moments which he had passed with her the previous evening, had unquestionably excited him to the utmost warmth and admiration. He knew that love for him had brought with it all her sufferings; he knew how long she had wept in sorrow and sadness, and he was the spectator of the forlorn wreck to which the cherishing of such love had reduced her. He was convinced that no artifice had been used to render the melancholy picture more desolate, he was convinced that no motive of interest had led to the interview—he felt assured that the unsubdued flame of affection had lighted her onwards, though its momentary blaze should even destroy with its brightness.

These assurances appealed more sensitively to the softer feelings of nature, and he contemplated on their fatality in the most painful reverie; he viewed the path that was only open to his tread, it was dark and comfortless—there was no gleam that could cheer him on to emulation and delight—there was no star that would set to the splendour of his happiness, all the sweet delusion of hope and gladness had withered—he knew that few human beings arrived at the age of feeling, but had some pleasing wish—some charm in existence that inspired the heart and mind with heroism, virtue, and sensibility. He knew no bosom contained a heart so cold and sceptical, as not to feel a spontaneous glow towards the attributes of woman's love. Yes, all mankind had some interest that strengthened unity; but *he* felt proscribed, and careless to its tie—there was no human being that he wished to bind the hand of friendship with; he cared not to know of it. Rosalviva had blighted his confidence and his hopes, and what few embers the presence of Viola had re-kindled, were now faded, and extinguished for ever.

These were his reflections, these were the melancholy train of thoughts that crowded upon his forlorn heart.

He had not passed over many moments in the recognition of

his solitude, when he was aroused by the cries of danger, and from a remote corner of the street he perceived two men dragging the body of a monk, whose struggles contended hard against the completion of their purpose—that murder was its purport, Leontini held no doubt. The suggestion demanded his courage and interference, and without further hesitation, he rushed immediately to the spot.

"For the love of God and humanity, preserve me, stranger," faintly exclaimed a monk, still in the grasp of his adversaries.

Leontini drew his sword, and closing a desperate thrust in the arm of one of the assassins, caused his instant retreat. The other being exempt from any extraordinary skill or resolution, resigned his burden, and hurried away towards the direction of his companion.

Leontini found that the priest had received a slight wound in the breast—he staunched the blood which flowed copiously, and procuring assistance, had him conveyed to the convent of his order.

The wound was not dangerous, and after its examination, Leontini was about to depart.

"The Padre would return thanks for thy care," cried one of the fathers.—"Yes, worthy Signor," added Vivaldi, (who had been the object of attack) to my latest hour I have to acknowledge thee my preserver."

Leontini bowed in silence, and testified his satisfaction of being instrumental in defeating the designs of the assassins.

The Padre extended his hand to meet that of Leontini. A lamp that burned in a corner of the cell, emitted but a faint and uncertain light. A lay-brother revived its flame, and obeying the motion of Vivaldi, passed the light across the countenance of Leontini, which was directed to that of the Padre.

"Jesu Maria!" he momentarily exclaimed, and an icy dampness took possession of his limbs; his voice faultered, and with a look of strange, but enquiring meaning, he sunk down upon the pallet. Leontini beheld the change of his features with astonishment; his hand was still grasped by Vivaldi. One of the monks who had witnessed the emotion of the superior, urged him to signify the cause of his discomposure. "Speak," cried he, "and if sorrowfully, that it may be alleviated—these bewildering flights of imagination, Signor, (turning to Leontini) are not uncommon, you will therefore"—

"Oh no, my senses are no longer bewildered," interrupted Vivaldi—"'tis real, 'tis real; in him is marked the remembrance of Isadora too powerfully to be deceived. Speak, young man—your name, your family; but I am not deceived."

The irregular expression and vehement manners of the Padre was mysterious to the mind of Leontini, and for an elapse of some moments he was unable to reply.

"Speak, boy, thy name!—'tis"—

The Monk paused in expectation of the definition—"'tis Leontini," bowed the Signor. "Yes, Leontini di Nicolenzi," eagerly added the superior—"my son, my son."

A stupifying lethargy for some moments bound up the senses of Leontini. The voice of Vivaldi awakened him.—"Look up, my boy—look up, and give new life to thy no longer dejected parent."

"Have I, indeed, rescued from assassination the author of my existence," solemnly rejoined Leontini, and directing his look to heaven, added, "benignant Providence, that has given to me at once a friend and a father."

Leontini embraced the superior with duteous respect. He was anxious for the intelligence of his father's narrative, and to learn from what cause he had lived until this moment in ignorance of his being in existence. He expressed his hope that he might be in immediate possession of its several particulars.

The brother, who was in attendance, withdrew; and Leontini fastened the door of the apartment. Vivaldi, desirous of communicating the varied incidents of his past life, thus commenced:—

"At the age of twenty-one I was united to the daughter of a valued friend, with whom I possessed every species of wealth and felicity, and for several months I knew no pang of sorrow or disquietude. The termination of the year, however, deprived me of my respected parent. By his decease I became inheritor of property to a considerable amount. Due respect was paid to his memory, and in the smiles of my wife, and the anticipation of becoming a father, I was not rendered wholly disconsolate at his loss. My Isadora gave birth to the offspring who this night, by the all-wise decree of Providence is restored to me." The Confessor wiped away a trickling tear, and gazing full upon the features of Leontini, again proceeded:—"But O God, at what a price, and what suffering was the summit of my wishes realized; by a forfeiture of a life dearer to me than mine own, by the sacrifice of that of Isadora's."

"My mother," exclaimed Leontini.

"Yes, boy, in a few hours subsequent to thy first breath of life, her's was no more. With scarcely a struggle, she resigned her soul to the call of her maker. To the being like myself, whose heart and existence was cemented with the partner of his fortunes, it required a fortitude but few can command. Dissolved as I was, from every hope, from every blessing; the quality of that mind, the goodness of that heart, the sensibility of soul, and the warmth of affection, I lost with her, hung with such weight upon my imagination, that for some considerable time the efforts of the most skilful men were opposed, and tended towards the restoration of my former tranquillity; but I had too deeply impressed on my poor withering heart the image of Isadora—every change, both of time and place, brought with it her form—her look—her dying look—the last blush of health that tinged her cheek, dispersing itself for the pallid hue of death, was ever before my eye; and oft was I seen in earnest attention to catch the ideal sound of the last words she uttered to me; in silence and in solitude, through my cares by day, and my dreams of night, the memory pursued me; had I been wholly left to its influence, I should have inevitably fallen its victim; the only relation I was possessed of watched my sorrows with unremitting care, and ultimately succeeded in separating me from the spot where I had cherished my miseries. Under the charge of protection of this friend you were left, while I endeavoured to seek relief in the bustle and socialities of other shores.

"A small province in the south of Italy was my retreat, and in the numerous circles of splendour and gaiety with which I associated, I was diverted in some measure from that constant gloom and dejection; but here too I suffered. I had not long singled out one of my fellow men, with whose stamp and character I was prepossessed, ere my credulity lost me the whole of my fortune, and by the perfidy of my assumed friend, I found myself a beggar: yes, Leontini, the whole of my property was in his hands—one roof had for some time sheltered us, I entrusted him with my confidence, and in an unguarded moment he plundered me of every article that was convertible to cash and of value. All the horror of wretchedness and despair rushed before me, and only one bleak scene of desolation presented itself.

"The detail of my misfortunes I communicated to the protector of my boy, I commended to his guiding hand the safety of a Leontini; it was not my wish to hear his reply—I waited not for it, but hastily quitted the province that had familiarized me with trouble and beggary, and again set forth upon the world an unknown and heedless adventurer. It would be painful to bring forward the catalogue of a series of hardships and oppressions that I felt through a lapse of many years.

"I shall draw to the sequel of past events, my son, retain thy patient hearing until its close."

Leontini in silence signified his feelings, and deeply commiserated the occurrence which had blighted his father's career.

"Alas, Leontini, it would bring from thee tears of affliction, couldest thou have witnessed the weakness which sorrow and subjection so rapidly brought me to. I purchased obedience at a severe rate; but I supported it in the hope of the day arriving when I should retire from a world wrought up with so much of perfidy and ingratitude. I was not insensible that there was at least one individual exempt from the human race, but I too much revered his worth, and paused, ere I wished to have united him with my miseries; poverty had fixed her cold and iron hand upon me, why should I wish my child to be equally branded with its mark? It was too hard that he should be the witness of his father's struggles—I poured forth my earnest supplication to Heaven for its future care towards my boy, and felt resolved to hide from him the presence of a parent—'twas almost an unfeeling, an unnatural wish; but I hazarded all its infliction, and trusted to destiny for the future. Harassed at length by the continued and cheerless oppressions of fortune, I looked to some refuge where my sufferings would at once come to an end. My mind and heart had in their earliest state looked up to religion as its aid; it seemed now to approach me, bringing with it gleams of comfort, and under its renovating, and certain existence, I anticipated the cup of my sorrows to be brightened by piety and resignation. From that hour I became a diligent pursuer of the path of devotion; I benefited by my zeal and attention to its precepts; I felt encouraged and animated that I was labouring to some advantage; and ultimately, the reverence and respect every being devoted to the rites of holy religion could hope to enjoy. My studies and the integrity of my principles, gained me the appointment of Confessor to the Castelli di Romagno."

"Di Romagno?"—echoed the voice of Leontini.

"Yes, my son; but why this emotion?"

"Forgive me, father; the communion of feeling at the mention of di Romagno, I promise at a future period to reveal, proceed."

"Of the description of the man to whom I bowed, I have little to speak; splendour, and the brilliancy of rank, were his leading wishes. His riches served to promote whatever his ostentation could hope for; but little did I imagine, that, in the formation of such greatness myself had contributed so large a share.

"From the first moment of self-importance in the ideas of a Lucenza, he had cherished a fondness for every species of gaming and daring speculation, and for a continual period was he known to be a successful inheritor of its practices; but luring as were its benefits, and much as he profited, there was a "tide in his affairs" upon which the future fate of his circumstances turned, and in one eventful night the proud Lucenza was bereft of every ducat—his estates were staked in the endeavour of regaining some portion of his loss; but fortune seemed resolved to oppose him, and in a few hours further, his claims to greatness were valueless. His mortified pride, and suddenly reduced state, were too appalling to be brought to him as the every-day theme of conversation; therefore, in disguise and unknown, he quitted the scene of his ruin. Change from splendour, and disgust at poverty, broke the peace of the Marchioness, and her grief brought her to an early grave.

"On the outskirts of the province where I had selected my abode, was situated, rather obscurely, the dwelling of Lucenza; the quietude of the spot, and the apparent similitude in the habits of its owner, rendered it pleasing to me; and I became his inmate. He appeared generous and retentive, and taught me to believe that in his bosom was placed a sincere, honest heart. I made him my friend; and 'twas he—it was this serpent of ingratitude that stung me; he repaid my confidence with ruin, and left me the wretched object which the commencement of my narrative pictured.

"An elapse of fifteen years had worked so powerful a change in the manner and appearance of my betrayer, that when I was ushered into the presence of the Conte Reo Cardoni, whose domain bordered on the convent of our order, no trace brought him back to my memory—never was my suspicion awakened to the belief that I was the pious adviser and retainer of the recreant who had so deeply wronged me; to his death bed was my zeal enthusiastic. In his prayer for mercy he bore no resemblance to his former self, and to his latest moment he had my blessing."

"And what subsequent means," questioned Leontini, "brought forward a discovery?"

"In the written confessions of his past life, which, with the whole of his documents, and claims to these domains, were submitted to my charge during the minority of his daughter; and further, in conjunction with a pledge of that same offspring, to see avenged her parent's memorable death."

The circumstances of which he narrated to Leontini, to whose astonishment was evidently recalled that night wherein he had himself witnessed the engagement with Cardoni.

"It was on the eve of St. Rosalia," spake Leontini.

"It was, my son, and you equally remember the assassin," impatiently questioned Vivaldi, "say by whose hand did Reo Cardoni die?"

"That of Paoli Conte Golfieri, he was my friend, and I my father, assisted in the fatal rencontre; but to this hour was I ignorant of the title and family of his opponent; and I am still ignorant of the motives that induced the act; all that Golfieri imparted, was, that in a public assembly he had been insulted, his family traduced, and himself basely slandered; that a nobleman of distinction was his implacable enemy; and on the punishment due to such a man he had resolved: he intimated the certainty of meeting with the aggressor after the vespers of St. Rosalia. He urged me in friendship to accompany him—I did, and there found two hired assassins in the employ of Golfieri; we waited under the Piazza de Luiga for the approach of our object. I need not name the result; an obstinate attack ensued with Paoli and the Conte—he fell. I had also been in a similar occupation with a companion of Cardoni's, but his heels were more alert than his bravery; and the consequence was, that I was prevented the commission of a crime by the Signor's hasty emancipation.

"Paoli had no sooner disencumbered his sword from the body of the Conte, than we hurried from the spot to the society of some friends of Paoli's, in a distant part of the province, and from that hour I had ceased to remember the circumstance attending the eve of St. Rosalia."

A thrill of animation momentarily lighted up the features of Leontini at the conclusion of the sentence.

"Oh Providence, Providence! receive my thanks!" and his large expressive eye looked up to Heaven—"this will be food indeed for the soul of the discarded Leontini to glut upon!"

"What means my boy?" asked the Padre, ignorant of the knowledge of his offspring's former correspondence with Rosalviva.

Painfully did Leontini narrate his ardour and his intimacy with the Comptessa; he drew a strong, and not exaggerated picture of the sufferings which he had survived; they met with the sympathetic tear of a parent; he felt for the neglected and insulted affection of his boy; he reproved the specious art and dissemblance of Rosalviva; his mind was in a state of uncertainty how to act; he had pledged himself to preserve the rights of the Comptessa, and at the due period to see her reinstated in all her endowments; yet, when he had thus pledged, was he aware such an inheritance was the produce of unlawful and illegal possession? that it was the property he had been wronged of? no, he was not sensible of these particulars; he was not sensible till after the decease of the Conte, that in him had lived his betrayer. He held once more the documents of his former property, and which the authorities of justice must decree as his own legitimate rights; and how would that result terminate? In the poverty of Rosalviva! To Leontini this might be some triumph for the perfidy of his friend—the duplicity of the Comptessa. It was a sacrifice that the Padre's heart almost recoiled at the execution of; but the claims of his offspring demanded preference, and he yielded accordingly. Vivaldi was about to detail the substance of his mental contemplations, when the entrance of a lay-brother impeded the discourse.

"Thy purpose, Julian," cried Vivaldi, as the inferior made towards him.

"An infidel unbeliever, holy Padre, is borne to the grate of our convent—he entreats, with his seemingly fast dissolving breath, confession and the absolution of the father Vivaldi."

"Admit the wretched sinner, and see that care be extended towards him; such relief as can be administered let it be applied."

The Monk bowed, and withdrew from the apartment.

"Peace to the soul of the penitent, and forgiveness from its Creator," uttered Vivaldi, as the father Julian closed the door.

But few moments had been numbered, when the sudden entrance of Julian, under the appearance of alarm, attracted the mutual surprise of the Padre and his son.

"Jesu Maria!" breathlessly exclaimed the monk, and devoutly crossed himself—"Haste—haste, Padre Vivaldi, the walls of our convent is polluted with the murderer and assassin of Vivaldi! Haste, then, and give to the miscreant his eternal doom."

"Hush, hush," calmly replied the pious superior, and taking the uplifted hands of Julian within his, cried, "Tell me thy tale with less ardour."

Julian bowed with submission to the exhortation of the Padre, and proceeded.

"A being, whose wretched and haggard state denotes his near affinity to death, prayed for admission to the chief father of our community," here the father Julian again traced the sign of the cross upon his bosom—"by your authority it was complied with—convulsed and tortured—a deep wound near the heart *was* still bleeding; he was supported by our brotherhood, and placed in the cell adjoining the refectory; not the consolation of any of our order can calm him; his exclamations are wild, painful, but directed to the Padre Vivaldi, whose presence he implores for a few short moments, and then to die."

"Miserable man," plaintively spake Vivaldi, and followed by Leontini, he sought the pillow of the repentant stranger.

"Yes, yes, it is the assassin of the father Vivaldi," eagerly cried Leontini, as he surveyed the ghastly countenance of the man he himself had wounded.

"Hold, Signor, hold," in a tone of fearful tremor, cried the object of their compassion: "do not finally commit to everlasting torment the soul of one which lingers here for a little space, only while he sues to his holy father for forgiveness; and if lips, stained as much as mine are with the execrations of guilt and horror, can ask that of Heaven also, it is hoped none present will by their curse impede it."

The dying man half raised himself from his recumbent position, and begged for the presence only of Vivaldi and the Signor.

The monks severally obeyed the motion of their superior, and retired for the night.

"Involved, Signor reverissimo, in difficulties, and struggling amidst a thousand merciless oppressions for life and sustenance, see before you the wretch, who, for a few ducats, and the promise of more, hired himself for the execution of crime and murder." The father Vivaldi shuddered, and an involuntary sensation of icy coldness crept through his veins.

Leontini listened with minute attention to his confession, whose every sentence was narrated with painful difficulty.

"And the name of thy employer," questioned Leontini.

"I have not much to disclose—you shall know all. The night prior to the present, I was pining in the midst of my poverty, over a cheerless fire, in my scarcely roofed hovel, when the entrance of a signor closely muffled, but whose dress demonstrated the superiority of my visitor, disturbed my half distracted meditations; in a tone of haughty brevity, like one who seemed to command, he enquired if I were not Piozzi di Borji?" I replied in the affirmative. "I need not question your wants," added he; "thy wretchedness is fully pourtrayed in these black and broken walls, in this desolate and half human abode; you can serve me, fellow, and I can reward it with gold. Here, let this speak my intentions, and be satisfied that you are rescued from starvation; you can earn double the amount of this token." To all this, Signors, I listened, I was nearly overwhelmed with confusion and joy; I took a small purse from his hand, and was about to stammer out an expression of gladness; he prevented it, crying, "Hush, I need no repetition of idle thanks, your punctuality and obedience to my dictates, will best speak your gratitude—listen, some two hours beyond the present, in the evening of to-morrow, I shall require the fulfillment of thy services—the spot is adjacent, and at such an hour expect me here in this hovel, on no pretence be absent, nor let no excuse defy my prompt demands." To these several imperative announcements I bowed assent. "You have more gold to earn—remember, and it shall be duly awarded—at the hour, then, I state, expect me; I need not further add the necessity of your silence."—"Signor," cried I, somewhat revived, "you have purchased my vigilance, and rest satisfied in its security." "Enough, I *am* satisfied;" and withdrawing the bolt of the door, he departed. I was too well bribed to doubt the failure of his visit, nor ruminated I upon its purport; be it understood, that on the hour he named, I was in waiting for his summons. He entered, accompanied by a menial, securing my door—"Di Borji," said he, "mark this man—he is your companion and partner in the services I require of you," and taking the arm of the coarse masculine figure beside him, he presented him to me. The red glare of the fire threw its light upon the features of my new companion, and those of my employer; the one was rude and disfigured, those of the Signor were wrought with much expression, and commanding much diversity of character. "On your route, Strombolo here, will give you your lesson, heed it well; and be mindful that one more interested will regard its value." Thus saying, he motioned to depart, and following the steps of my comrade, we were soon in public streets; it was at the corner of one of them that we loitered. During our stay, I learned from Strombolo, that our employer was the young Conte Golfieri."

"Conte Golfieri," repeated the agitated Leontini, in an expression of surprise and horror.

"Yes, Signor, and the intended victim of his wrath, the Padre Vivaldi."

"Merciful Omnipotence!" exclaimed the father, and he again marked the sign [of] their holy faith.

"I need not further describe that event, Signor, you well know its sequel."

The life of the assassin was nearly exhausted: Leontini had taken the minutes of his last confession; to its substance was added the tremulous signature of Di Borji. Vivaldi interceded with his God for his pardon, and while yet in the act of administering alleviation, he heaved one heavy sigh, and with it fled the remains of guilt and repentance.—Vivaldi was too affected to muse upon the incident; he committed his peace to the care of Providence, and embracing Leontini, retired to his couch.

Orders had been given for the preparation of a principal chamber for the reception of Leontini, and to its solitude and reflection he consigned himself.

CHAPTER V.

"There is in the human heart a perpetual succession of passions,
So that the destruction of one is almost sure to establish another."

ROCHEFOUCAULT.

————————Let there be no honour,
Where there is beauty; truth where semblance; love,
Where there's another man.——The vows of women
Of no more bondage, be to where they're made,
Than they are to their virtues, which is nothing.
Or above measure, FALSE.

CYMBELINE.

THE venerable and homaged Napoli Ruggieri had enjoyed the dignities and privileges of his important rank as Duke of Palermo through a series of years,—he had maintained his electoral degree without austerity; he had commanded esteem and honour without enforcing it; he had rendered himself an example for domestic felicity and piety, and upon the noblest and most strict foundation of rectitude were his principles formed.

The death of the partner of his affection, and with whom he had derived every possible happiness, caused a sudden and singular change in the mind and disposition of Napoli—he was no longer the calm and social character nature had seemingly stamped—he shunned those societies where his presence had ever been revered—he avoided those friends who appeared to feel his grief, and wished to console him; and the mind and genial virtues that had hitherto adorned his manner, were exchanged for the churlish and reserved habits of one who had renounced the admonition and sympathies of every thing that endeavoured to offer him relief. He had long ceased to mix with the "bustling world," and in a life of seclusion within the walls of his own palace, his broken spirit and irritable temper seemed to have free range.

Paoli Golfieri, nephew to the Duke, was his nearest and only kindred, and by the earnest desire of the late Duchessa, (who having no issue) the young Paoli was received and educated as their own. To the elegant and prepossessing figure of Golfieri, which was pourtrayed in an agreeable stature, was engrafted a mind of peculiar qualities, and which had shewn itself even in his infantine years. Amongst the numerous companions, and young noblemen who were classed as his associates at the ducal palace, the disposition to controul over them was eminently manifest;—there was a vivid spark of ambition and design about him that materially differed from those in his friendship, and though he mingled in their pursuits, and attached himself to their habits, there was an artful enthusiasm that prompted him beyond a common enterprize. These were the traits of an early character which maturity made the more ardent and striking;—his strong inclination and desire for the love of gaming was attained the moment he had arrived to that fortune and property which at the termination of his minority was his inheritance. To its propensities he was nearly the fatalist, when the intermediate grasp of Leontini snatched him from the impending ruin. From that moment friendship had closely allied him to the interests and welfare of Leontini, and he felt a gratitude for the disinterested service he was sensibly aware of having received at his hands. Their interests and happiness became mutual, and there was at length no pleasure, or no pursuit, but theirs was an equal participation.

With the correspondence of Leontini to Rosalviva, circumstances at times rendered the confidence of Paoli necessary,—he was entrusted with it, and as the friend of Leontini he was received by the Comptessa with all the respect due to his character. But the interview with Rosalviva was fatal to that friendship; and in defiance to every rigid moral sentiment, his once firm and unsullied principles yielded to a passion which was uncontrolable, and with the possession of Rosalviva only could that passion become abated. It was the first feeling that woman's excellence had created,—it was too vivid to be extinguished with facility. He cherished an immediate regard for her—he envied the choice and felicity of his friend, and in the heat of his sensibility, his mind was hurried into a forgetfulness of that honour which had been pledged between them. There was every charm in Rosalviva that tended to delight him,—there was not a moment in her presence that he did not feel himself awakened to every delightful transport—its inspiration was not to be vanquished, and each succeeding interview bound him the more forcibly in the power of her reverence and adoration. He marked with intense acuteness of passion her esteem for Leontini, but his imagination was too much upon the alert to discourage his hopes of obtaining her esteem—he already had an opportunity of judging by her disposition and manner the buoyancy of her soul, and his penetration led him to believe its similitude with the opinion of an admired writer, Rochefoucault, "There is no art which can long hide love where it is, nor feign it where it is not." He shaped her lightness of heart and warmth of disposition, into a familiarity and an attachment by which he counted largely on the profit; such then was the mind and ideas of the man in whom was reposed the confidence of Leontini.

Leontini had studied many of the characters in the catalogue of human life,—he had initiated himself with the extravagancies and weaknesses of their nature, and had contemplated on the irregular depravity which the heart invariably falls into—he viewed it with pity and horror; but such feelings were not in sociality with his friend, and the fervency of his alliance in honour and estimation towards him, caused him to neglect the strict examination of those qualities in common with the rest of mankind. The appointments which at length committed the Comptessa to his attention, Paoli was not unmindful of.——Rosalviva on the same hand was enlivened with his vivacity; she was animated and instructed by his cheerful and engaging manner. The various pleasing and glowing attributes of his nature elicited her warmest admiration, and she failed not to encourage a more than usual mark of friendship and respect. She perceived how materially the habits and opinions of Leontini differed with those of Golfieri,—she felt the natural reserve attached to Leontini's conduct,—she considered him too, less communicative, and at every internal of reflection she found her disposition and wishes yield more towards the Conte Paoli than to his mistaken friend. It was not to be supposed that with such a character Rosalviva could for any length of time retain merely a cold and common-place intimacy; her passions were naturally strong, and she felt too much gratified in the daily proof of his attention and feeling towards her, not to be deeply impressed with its value. His constant command and flow of spirits elated and kept warm those of Rosalviva's—they charmed her to an extacy in his presence, and the exercise of her remembrance of it in his absence.

During circumstances like these, it may be expected that the heat of Rosalviva's affection towards Leontini was materially calmed. His appearance and his conversation combined, placed in contrast with his friend, appeared heavy to her, tedious, and uninteresting. Paoli became too successful, and she rewarded his ardour with all the warmth and impulse of a soul susceptible of pure enjoyment. It was at this period that she contemplated a visit to Messina, as narrated in a prior chapter,—and it was at this period that the intercourse and principles of Paoli and the lover of Rosalviva became disunited.

A mission of some importance from the Duke of Palermo to the Port of Syracuse, demanded the service of Golfieri, who, taking a hasty farewell of Leontini, proceeded on his departure.

The execution of Golfieri's mission was terminated. He had, previously to Rosalviva's leaving Palermo, been made acquainted with her intentions and the length of time she intended remaining at Messina. He feared her former regard for Leontini had manifested itself before her departure; anxious, therefore, to ascertain the fact of his suppositions, he determined to stay some short time at Messina, and there, unknown to Rosalviva, he might have an opportunity of witnessing her general conduct,—he communicated this to Leontini, with all the seeming assurance of friendship, and further intimated that he should be attentive to the care and interests of the Comptessa, upon the score of that confidence which Leontini had ever reposed in him.

It was upon the receipt of such an epistle, subsequent to that which was forwarded by an anonymous hand, that he felt the more indebted and bound towards his friend, and in the satisfaction and belief of the slander from his unknown correspondent, he was appeased and delighted that one like Paoli was willing to offer her his protection. To Golfieri his several epistles were forwarded, who dictated that kind of reply which at length brought Leontini to consider, that by some means he was no longer in possession of her affection.

The entire termination of the correspondence on the part of Rosalviva, and the being totally discarded from her notice, created no small poignancy in the bosom of Leontini, but he was ignorant and unwilling to believe, that to his friend was he indebted for all his moments of anguish. Time at length revealed, and pourtrayed in its genuine colour, the duplicity and ingratitude of Golfieri. This, and the contemptuous manner in which he had been treated by the Comptessa, (notwithstanding he had embraced every means and every opportunity that offered for his amusement and gaiety,) was too forcibly imprinted on his memory to be easily eradicated,—and though his mind appeared at intervals light and cheerful, there was a gloom, and a throb at his heart, which was fast blighting his other more genial and dependant virtues.—Change of scene was indispensable, and with the resolution to quit Palermo, he had endeavoured to prepare for its effect, when the incident which brought him to the assistance of Vivaldi defeated his projects, and brought him to the embrace of a parent. With Vivaldi's power, and from the confessions of Di Borgi, he cherished sensations that till then had never found place in his bosom;—instead, therefore, of his spirits sinking into despondency, they were newly strung with a passion and an exultation that were rapturously enjoyed,—he felt himself in duty impelled to avenge his parent's attack,—his soul spurned at the idea of bringing the object of his resentment to an immediate or disgraceful death,—he knew that there were tortures far more afflicting than the sufferings and fate of the common horde,—his heart beat high with the satisfaction of his hopes, and he looked forward to a period when Golfieri and the unfeeling Rosalviva should be degraded and humbled.

In the meanwhile, we momentarily return to Golfieri.

The utmost rage and mortification fired the breast of Paoli, as the comrade of Di Borgi, in almost breathless detail on the subsequent day, intimated the fatal consequences of the wounds which Piozzi had received.

"And thou, dastard," exclaimed the Conte, "left him to perish."

"My lord, dissolution immediately followed the thrust of the stranger's poignard. I was not fool enough to hazard a similar condition, fearful, too, of the number of my opponents, I judged it more expedient to give the direct information to your excellence, so that if you are still disposed, no time might be lost in giving me further aid, I then will pledge the worth of the Cassaro to a single Marvredi, if before morning the old Padre is not in other worlds."

"Psha," bitterly implied Paoli, "'tis too late, the Padre will not so readily leave the convent. Here, be satisfied with this until my further summons, and expect my wishes realised on the night of to-morrow,—something shall surely be determined," and putting into the hand of the assassin a purse containing a few pistoles, he abruptly left him, and hastened to the Palazzi of Rosalviva.

****

"Think no more of it, Golfieri," interrupted the Comptessa, as Paoli, in a tone of vehemence reprobated the fatality of the occurrence, "'tis the business of a weak and common mind, to entertain regret at trivial disappointments; Vivaldi cannot dream of the person of his antagonist, and doubtless will take the opportunity of an early visit to my Palazzi—what, if in your presence I demand the authorities and documents of my inheritance? his reply will instantly govern your fixed and decided resolution of acting; and to Paoli Golfieri there is little need of further counsel on such an occasion, his own dictates are his surest guide."

"They are, dearest Rosalviva, and be assured that I will not easily disregard their tenor."

The evening had already far advanced, but its soft and genial air invited the lovers to quit the Palazzi, and in the desire of enjoying the pleasing scenery of the surrounding scene, they slowly traversed the pavement of an adjoining terrace—through the shade of a distant cloister, the Padre Vivaldi was seen to pass in hasty step.

Rosalviva snatched the hand of the Conte, and hurrying through a near wing of the building, speedily attained her apartments.

The sound of footsteps crossing the suite of rooms leading to

Rosalviva's announced his approach, and directing Paoli to retire within a recess communicating with the next apartment, she awaited the appearance of the Confessor.

"The Padre Vivaldi," announced one of the domestics, who had conducted the Monk to the presence of the Comptessa.

Rosalviva received him with her usual respect.

The features of the Monk were closely hidden by his cowl, so much, that scarcely a trace of the countenance was perceptible. There was an unusual and faultering agitation in his step that engaged the attention of Rosalviva; but notwithstanding his manner was firm, and she fancied his stature more erect, and marked with a kind of mystery that made her doubtful of its real meaning. There was a silence too, about him, that she endeavoured, amidst surprise, to comprehend; till the event of the preceding evening occurred to her recollection, and this at once she considered accountable for his apparent gloom. She had not time, prior to his entrance, to have the apartments lighted with their usual effect; and the feeble glare of one lamp only reflected its sombre ray throughout the room, rendering obscurity more perceptible, and which seemed to be in similitude with the mind and dejection of the Confessor.

She was about to summon a domestic for lights, when the Padre advanced.

"Stay, Rosalviva, my presence here requires no splendour—its purport is brief and decisive; what communion we may have together, ceremony is not wanting to attend it."

The surprise of the Comptessa was strongly excited—the altered voice and tone of the Confessor struck upon her ear in dismay, and her eyes were fixed upon him with a suspicion, that she seemed to endure, yet felt incapable of expressing.

At length attaining some degree of energy, she disengaged her hand from that of the monk's, and in an articulation of imperious astonishment, uttered "Vivaldi!"

"Yes, such is the family of whom I am the last descendant, dissimulation is unnecessary—in the disguise and habit of your confessor, behold Leontini!"

"Leontini," shrieked the Comptessa, and her heart underwent a heavy pulsation.

"Yes, deceitful woman, I have condescended to practice a deception in this instance for admission to your presence; since my real character, my entreaties, my atonements have each been so insultingly and unfeelingly degraded; think, Rosalviva, what I have suffered by your cruelty—tell me of the wrongs by which I deserve it, and reflect upon the base and dishonoured character, such conduct has stamped you."

The soul of Rosalviva, during the enunciation of Leontini, had suffered various emotions; but pride and mortified feelings surmounted the conflict; and assuming the firmness of contempt, she replied, in a haughty and sarcastic tone, "Daring and insolent intruder, instantly leave the Palazzi, or thy specious and artful purposes will meet with their due award. Oh! this act, and attempt to break in upon my privacy with mean and sordid pretence, is worthy the honour and origin of a Leontini."

"Wretched and abandoned as *thou* art, to the feelings of *honour* and rectitude, I come not to triumph over the miseries that inevitably threaten you; I could have wished to have spared myself the pain of this interview; and would have left you to the destruction which your vices and pursuits will ultimately lead you to; but Rosalviva, I am not too proud to remark, nor do I blush at the confession, that I have loved you, and that there are moments in recollection still dear to me, gratitude for which has urged me to this step; and rather than reproach, I come to offer.—"

"Forbear, Rosalviva needs not your attention, nor regards your inclinations; she alone is responsible for her past and present actions; and be their impurity as it may, the interference of one so unmindful of that *honour* and *rectitude*, which he now so sensibly descants upon, is as weak as it is presumptuous; retire, then, without giving me the necessity of assembling my attendants, as in the event of such, force must compel what is in your power to avoid—exposure!"

"And this is the language of the Rosalviva, whom I once adored? Oh God! it can scarce be real."

The feelings of anguish overcome the scruples and intended contumely of Leontini; the determined idea of venting forth his resentment was subdued: his firmness appeared shaken, and unable to retain his fortitude; his internal sensations for some moments reduced him to a lethargy, and a wretchedness, which Rosalviva viewed with the utmost coldness and indifference. Had she ever felt for him the pure regard, her manifestations had taught him to believe, she could not, with such insensibility, witness the weight of suffering he with difficulty supported. His faultering voice, and even the tear that started within his sorrowful eye, created no throb of pity; but in silence and disdain she contemplated on his painful submission. He had called forth every essay that his strength of mind would admit, rather than his struggles should be betrayed; and great as was the victory which he knew Rosalviva must acquire over his weakness, still he felt that his confidence in himself was lost, and to the shrine of her violated faith his heart yielded its sacrifice.

Her bold and stern resolution seemed fixed, and not all the implicit tokens of his yet willing affection, awakened in her soul the slightest pathos of affection or consolement. His humility was still under the influence of her charms; and in the most mild and piteous accents, he importuned her compassion: "Tell me, Rosalviva, that I am not unworthy of you, say, that whatever may have been my imaginary offences, that you will forgive them, and I will yet hope that you will be mine."

"Never, never," harshly pronounced the Comptessa—"indulge not in a thought so futile, my heart is relentless, and were it even softened by your wish of atonement, its sentiments cannot be altered, since that it is eternally plighted to one who has deserved it."

Leontini was silent, the impression of the scene had totally unmanned him; stern and morose as had been his intentions on the engagement of this interview, they had separately weakened, and in the involuntary sensation of grief and despair, all his purposes had vanished.

"It is then your wish, Rosalviva, that we should never meet again?" interrogated Leontini, his tone of voice, after a pause of some length, assuming a more settled calmness. "Nay—such a question surprises me," answered the Comptessa, and her features were contorted into a derisive smile. "You might have spared yourself the task of requiring its conclusion, and me the necessity of replying—that it was, and is my imperative determination, you might have gained the full reliance of, had you but reflected upon the guide of my conduct, and to terminate a conference that cannot be in either way beneficial, I entreat you to retire; I have but to add, Signor Leontini, that your presence in my Palazzi is extremely irksome, and as it is in my power to remove any such unpleasantness, I must, in duty to myself, command its instant obedience."

"Yet, one moment, it is the last wherein we shall ever meet," eagerly cried Leontini, and he clasped her hand within his, thereby detaining her, before she had availed herself of summoning any of the domestics; collecting his utmost composure and effort of mind, he pronounced: "Rosalviva, could this meeting have rendered itself agreeable to a mutual conciliation, without wishing, or attempting the renewal of our correspondence, I could have parted with you in submission and content, as it would have been my hope that the felicity you were wont to exchange, would have been replete, and in the affection of another, that you should have forgotten me; but as you have inhumanly torn from me every tie that I had anticipated to render existence blissful—I will not shrink from the communication that otherwise should have fallen to oblivion.

"Ha! you tremble; but it is only your future acts that can affiance you with guilt—its prevention is in your power, and beware, Rosalviva, if you value the ordainment of Heaven's most sacred decree, that you hazard not its worth."

Leontini's dark and penetrating eye met those of Rosalviva—their brightness seemed fraught with an unusual degree of expression, and an inward pang of secret affliction fixed in the same moment on her heart, but it was of too powerful a nature to be easily moved; and in a voice of half frantic gesticulation, she uttered—"Speak fully, what these insinuations refer to, or I shall deem their apparently portentous remarks to be shaped merely for sinister motives, and in that assurance, will treat them as they deserve—my vows are plighted, and no earthly power shall ever cause their dissolution."

"And to whom?" enquired Leontini.

"To one whom thyself can only be thanked for the introduction."

"To whom," eagerly repeated Leontini, doubting whether

from her own lips the name of her paramour would be disclosed, "to whom?"

"Paoli Golfieri," answered the Comptessa, with an undaunted air.

"Be not too sanguine in the credence of thy pledge, Rosalviva."

"As the all-powerful God of Heaven is my Creator, so—"

"Hush, desist from thy oath, lest apostacy should stamp the covenant—hear me, it is needless to withhold the intelligence by which you may profit. I came to render you service, and notwithstanding the obduracy of your proud heart, my endeavours for your welfare shall not be passed in silence; in one word, I affirm that with Golfieri you can never wed. This may be some alleviation to the many hours of bitterness and misery that I have endured for you, Rosalviva."

"Insulting fool," replied the Comptessa, "can'st thy puny efforts forbid the decree, miserable and presumptious infatuation—never!"

"Never—you deceive yourself, thanks to that righteous Providence, this confirmation of my hopes will be a recompence for me in the hour of solitude, and reflection, to know that with such a traitor as Golfieri you can never be united; and that there will arrive a time when conviction and punishment will repay his deserts."

"These implications may sound important; but in the presence of the Conte I doubt their utterance," remarked the Comptessa with a tone of complacency and composure.

"Rosalviva, for your sake I dare do more than would almost be credible to human species—but if you esteem the character of virtue, and the desire of happiness, you will banish from your heart an attachment which can only end in your ruin."

"This is language which I will no longer be the auditor of; and that your boasted and incomprehensible designs may be put to the test, I shall summon the presence of the Conte Golfieri, he is now in my Palazzi—with him you can adjust matters as your inclination is most suitable;" and withdrawing to an apartment that opened to a further suite of rooms, she left the astonished Leontini confounded, and for a time insensible of her absence.

Many minutes had not elapsed when the door of the apartment was thrown open, and preceded by an attendant with lights, the Conte Golfieri presented himself. Surveying the figure of Leontini with an indignant menace, and with a kind of strangeness, he pronounced—"and is it by your request that I am directed hither—the Signor Leontini, if I mistake not?"

"Yes, callous and detestable miscreant, it is the deceived Leontini; arm thyself, villain, before my resentment charges me with thy murder—draw and defend thyself (and his conduct became nearly frantic), or this weapon will find a sheath only in thine heart."

He rushed upon the man who had been instrumental to his wretchedness, and but for the interference of the attendant, who had loitered in the apartment, his thrust at Golfieri's bosom would have been fatal.

"Hold, Signor," exclaimed the domestic, grasping the arm of Leontini—"the Palazzi di Lucenza must not be allotted for madness and assassination, retire peaceably."

"Aye, and thank thy better fate for so easy an escape," added Golfieri, darting a fierce and revengeful look at the suppressed turbulence of his aggressor—begone whilst thou hast the means, and incur not the serious chastisement of Paoli Golfieri."

"The Comptessa has acknowledged my protection, and it shall not with impunity be violated."

"Inhuman betrayer, can crime and sacrilege like *thine*, offer itself in conjunction with—"

"Peace, fool, ho there, Gioeni Orino—bear hence this maniac impostor from the Palazzi; and should he ever resume these practices, know that there are dungeons which can quiet them."

Several within the command of Golfieri instantly entered the room, though not without considerable difficulty, were they enabled to subdue the opposition and defiance of Leontini.

Overpowered by superior strength, with which he was surrounded, and breathless with the maintenance of so unequal a conflict, he sunk exhausted in the arms of the domestics.

They hurried him from the Palazzi, and fainting nearly with the pain of a wound which he had received in the struggle, he was conveyed almost senseless to an obscure part of an avenue; where, overcome with fatigue, the menials of Golfieri left him to seek his own safety.

CHAPTER VI.

"What? if one reptile sting another reptile?
Where is the crime?—the goodly face of nature
Hath one disfeaturing stain the less upon it."

COLERIDGE.

"To stab your friend were barbarous indeed."

YOUNG'S REVENGE.

"INSUFFERABLE weakness, Golfieri," cried the Comptessa Rosalviva, as she traversed in an agitated and unsettled step the length of her apartment, where the Conte had sought her on the termination of his affray with the Signor Leontini—"to what folly and danger withal have you not subjected yourself, and wherein I too must equally suffer—think ye that a soul and spirit like Leontini's, influenced and aided by hatred and resentment, can submit calmly to the treatment and insult you have offered! No Golfieri, he will avenge it—shame on thy womanish heart, not to have more effectually silenced him; had I momentarily premised that the conqueror of the Signor Leontini's love and hopes could have so leniently dispensed with the man whom he should most avoid and abhor—I would have undertaken to have *made secure* means that could for ever put the influence of thought, or the fear of danger, at rest; shame, shame Golfieri!" and taking the arm of the Conte suddenly within her grasp, she threw her angry glance upon his partly averted countenance, and, in an emphatic tone, added, "could not thy dagger have done its duty?"

Golfieri was motionless; he marked in silence the insinuation of Rosalviva—he could not mistake its real tenor, and so great was the controul by which her affection bound him, that, rather than lose one smile, or forfeit one moment's adoration, he would have waded through streams of guilt and misery to have prevented it. He perceived the weak feeling that had guided him in the instance of Leontini, but aware that it was not to be recalled, he instantly exclaimed, amidst the various emotions that crowded upon his intellect—"I will redeem this rashness of thought, Rosalviva, and prove that Paoli's heart and soul is your's; it shall be certified in the immediate obedience to your suggestions, and for this, he dies."

The Conte was hurrying from the room in compliance with his resolve, but Rosalviva detained him, intimating, "Golfieri, thy senses are disordered, that frenzied eye, and pallid lip should be perceptible in a visage marked only with crime: be calm, and if in your contemplative moments you may deign to consider that the existence of Leontini is irksome to you—forget not that there is a method of alleviating your anxieties."

"Divine and lovely Rosalviva," ardently pronounced Paoli, his voice and manner assuming a fellowship with the more composed and lively feelings of his nature—"this poor heart is scarcely an equivalent for thy unbiassed affection, but it will cease to retain the slightest throb, should it ever be considered unworthy of Rosalviva."

"I am sensible of it, Golfieri—or would not have yielded thus far to its influence."

A warm embrace testified their mutual feelings, and Golfieri signified his immediate departure, for the more ready enforcement of an efficient plan for the riddance of Leontini.

The acquiescence of the Comptessa was not wanting to render his designs replete; and in the promise of the morrow's meeting, he left the Palazzi di Lucenza.

Amongst the most distinguished members of Ruggieri's counsels, Visconti Carraccio, a nobleman of illustrious birth, but of decayed fortune, was estimated by the Duke with more than common associations, and participated more with his confidence than either of the nobles comprised in the suite of Palermo's dignities.

The daring habit, and sanguinary projects of Carraccio, had occasionally formed striking features in the records of his country; but though the remembrance of their dark and ambitious views was generally acknowledged, there were few individuals with sufficient temerity to recognize them, or seemed willing to hazard a remark upon their true construction.

To the Dukedom of Palermo had Carraccio, though a series of years, entertained an ardent and confidential hope of ascendancy. His desires were entrusted to a limited number of partizans, whose interested wishes found means to continually keep alive the heat of his enthusiasm, and urged by their devices and his own pretensions, a perpetual succession of imaginary pursuits were collected for the formation and establishment of his purposes—but each had been unavailing.—Golfieri seemed to stand before him in every hope, and with his inheritance was the prospects of Visconti lastingly blighted; his policy was too well directed, to let it be made apparent, that in Paoli he viewed the destroyer of his enterprize, nor did he ever receive him without the most seeming partiality and friendship. The mind of Visconti was composed of materials of too subtle and weary a kind to be readily vanquished; and disappointed by trifling calamities, the manifest ardour which he took upon all occasions to contribute towards the welfare of Golfieri (to outward appearance), was too glowing to be unnoticed. In the confidence, therefore, of such a man, Paoli had deemed his propositions at all times secure—and he looked for his assistance as certain, as it were desirable.

To Carraccio he unfolded his correspondence with Rosalviva, and enlarged upon the hatred and enmity towards Leontini.

Visconti listened with animated attention to the detail of the Conte; and in reply to his interrogatories upon the most probable means of success, he intimated that "a trusty dagger told no tales;" and the more to confirm the value of his suggestion, he offered himself in devotion to the deed.

The sudden impulse of Carraccio's disinterested regard, made him for some moments recoil at its safety. An inward emotion that simultaneously rushed through his bosom, caused him to declaim against the act and commission of murder; but when he recalled the reproaches and contempt of Rosalviva, at his sense of conscientious duty, he directly banished its weakness from his mind; and with the aid and counsel of Visconti, he resolved on the fulfilment of his wishes; and his conference with Carraccio left him little doubt of their certainty.

"The signor and myself," remarked Visconti, "are not wholly intimate; but I have twice done the honours of the table in his presence, and the name of Carraccio is not unknown to him. I have, upon the evening of to-morrow, a select circle of private friends; for the more effectual success of our prospect I will issue an invitation to the Signor Leontini, and on the score of a prior acquaintance, will take no denial or apology for the possible inability of acceptance."

"This act completed, will cement in one eternal bond the interests and views of Carraccio and Golfieri," exultingly shouted the lover of Rosalviva——

"It shall do so," muttered Visconti, with a half suppressed smile of malice; and momentarily relaxing his features into that of the utmost complacency, he flatteringly rejoined, "my Lord Paoli, inclination shall not be wanting to merit the honour you purpose me."

"And the present residence of the Signor Leontini," questioned the Conte, after a pause of much reflection? "Is easily discovered," replied Carraccio, "of that I can be informed speedily, therefore Conte Golfieri, let matters rest until next we meet—be mindful, my lord, that this Leontini, your rival, is destroyed, and your tranquillity reinstated."

"But one inspiration shall guide us, worthy Carraccio, and our next meeting ratifies the pledge."

"It shall my lord;" and in the midst of the variety of opposite feelings that lived in each other's heart, they separated.

The wound of Leontini was slight, and at an elapse of a few minutes, he found himself enabled to contemplate on the conduct of Rosalviva, and the baseness of his friends. He had been left prostrate on the ground. The interference of successive gusts of night wind revived him. Passion and indignant feeling roused his impaired faculties, and with every sinew strung with fury, he breathed a terrific and horrible oath, to avenge the deed, "Blood only can wash out its remembrance; and till it be accomplished, the sufferings of Leontini will never terminate. Merciful God! look down with forgiveness on crimes that my agonies create."—He was aware that there were baneful and lingering tortures, with which his victims might be inflicted, he felt determined to shape his mind and principles into vengeance, the most callous and remorseless. "This hour," he pronounced, "shuts out my soul from every sentiment of humanity, friendship, and feeling; this last act of treachery and contumely that I have been the victim of, can never be forgiven or forgotten; it has awakened me to the sense of a new creation, and farewell every softer attribute that has hitherto been the pride of Leontini Vivaldi."

The gloom of evening had nearly attained its midnight hue, as Leontini entered the Piazza that conducted him to his abode. "Yes, my mind is fixed, and not all the recollections of thy earlier fondness, can bring me back, Rosalviva, from the irrevocable resolution of my purposes," solemnly apostrophized the infuriated Leontini, as with indignation he dismissed from his attention the last epistle from the pen of the Comptessa, which he had selected from a packet of Rosalviva's letters some few moments after he had entered his apartments.—"Here is the countepart of thy faith, these vows were recorded on the rolls of eternity, what must not be the guilt of those who would dare to violate them? Rosalviva, *thou* hast done this—be assured, that there will come a time, when their penalty must be exacted."

He traversed the room in evident disorder, and the faint gleam of twilight had already superceded the shade of darkness, as he threw himself upon his pillow.

The perturbation of an unsettled mind had defied the calmness of sleep, and it was late the following day ere he quitted his chamber. He rushed from it, heedless of his course—his gait was hurried and irregular. During the various intervals wherein his reflection was tempered with composure, he noticed the appearance of a stranger richly habited, and who more than once endeavoured to attract his observations. At length, entering an obscure part of the town, near the outskirts, the stranger passed him, and not unpolitely remarked—"You are the Signor Leontini?"

"The same, and you, Signor?" replied Leontini, in a tone of threatening impatience.

"A stranger, but can serve you."

"Your name?"

"It matters not. When you hear more from me, it shall not be withheld. If there be time and place, Signor, I would commune with you. I can prove your friend, and our assistance may be mutual."

"The nature of your intelligence is easily detailed here," affirmed Leontini; his surprise increasing at the strange and important manner in which he was accosted.—

"It is of little consequence, Signor, where its detail is given. Save that at this moment, there may be other auditors even more attentive than yourself. You have nothing to apprehend from me. I respect your character too much to admit of its being injured; and from such a feeling I have thus with diligence essayed to seek you. Follow me, and you shall be satisfied of my integrity."

Leontini hesitated. The positive manner and command of the speaker had fixed his attention so deeply, that he stood for some moments in a kind of stupor.

"If you decline, Signor," resumed the stranger, mindful of his silence and apathy, and perfectly sensible of its cause, "danger threatens you. As a man of honour, I pledge myself that the purport of my communication is to your advantage, nay, your safety,—dismiss these doubts, Signor—a Sicilian shall never have the opportunity of declaring that a Neapolitan once wronged him; nor will Visconti Carraccio, hazard thy displeasure."

"Senhor Carraccio?" momentarily exclaimed Leontini—"the kinsman of Golfieri!"

"I am so considered. I have the Conte's friendship; and by it am in possession of the enmity he bears towards you. My hand, Signor, to your cause; and if engagements are not too necessitous, you shall accompany me to the Palazzi."

Visconti extended his hand in affiance to his sentiments of honour, and which Leontini received in token of his confidence.

Having crossed several avenues and magnificent arcades, leading from the palace of Ruggieri, the Signor Leontini was conducted to the abode of Carraccio, which terminated one of the furthermost wings of the royal building.

"It is here, Signor," Carraccio pronounced, when they were seated in a costly apartment, adjoining a saloon, where a sumptuous banquet was preparing—"it is here;" and his familiarity had lent to the mind and credence of Leontini, a prepossession by which he estimated his sincerity. "The intentions of Paoli were expected to be resolved—and here, Signor, he concluded upon your destruction."

Leontini startled—an inexpressible shuddering for the moment seemed to appal him. He almost doubted the honesty of Carraccio, and trembled to think whether he had not been ensnared into the complete power of Golfieri by the specious and well paid deception of his agent. His suspicions were almost verified—when the voice of Visconti hushed him, who in an enunciation of the most exulting kind, cried, "But no, his hopes are defeated!"—The announcement of some of Carraccio's friends silenced the conversation; and to the several visitors Leontini was respectfully introduced. Every possible luxury adorned the table of Carraccio, and the conviviality of the guests was supported with unabated ardour.

Leontini was buried in conjecture, as to what manner the scene would terminate. Several hours had elapsed in the celebration of their riotous mirth—every succeeding moment he anticipated the summons of Golfieri; and at every opening of the saloon entrance he looked for his appearance.—The friends of Carraccio were severally departing.

Leontini motioned to retire, but a prohibition whispered to him by Visconti, urged him to remain, and as the Neapolitan closed an outer portal, he found they were the only occupants of the apartments.

Time had scarcely been given for observation on either side, when a low knock at a small arched door, at the opposite end of the saloon, called the attention of Visconti, who pronouncing the leave of admittance—a countenance apparently superhuman thrust itself forward on the partial opening of the door, and looking around in mysterious silence, he entered, closed the porch, and deliberately approaching Carraccio, stood in a lofty attitude, and inquisitively surveying the Signor Leontini, which when concluded, he presented Visconti with a billet, and awaited his answer.

"The Conte may expect my prompt obedience," pronounced his confident.

The messenger rudely bowed and withdrew.

Visconti handed the written communication to Leontini, adding, "here, Signor, you may perceive the intentions of Golfieri." He glanced on the paper, where was legibly traced by the pen of the Conte Paoli, "If the Signor Leontini be in the immediate power of Carraccio, let him be conveyed to the grating which terminates the lower court of the palace. Golfieri and his confederate, alike disguised, will be in readiness to receive him, once within the dungeon walls of the Palazzi, he rests secure, nor ever again have the light of Heaven to gaze upon."

An almost total annihilation of faculty succeeded the perusal of Paoli's order—he was about to comment upon the horrible machination of the Conte, when the Neapolitan, in a tone of commanding confidence, cried,—"utter no fears, Signor, the pledge of Visconti is at stake and shall not be broken—obey with strictness my dictates, and be certain of their profit."

"But the dungeon where this atrocious and treacherous Paoli, would have his victim consigned," insinuated Leontini, almost bewildered in a train of doubts and apprehensions.—"How could Signor Carraccio effect release, if once within its power?"

"It shall be effected," imperatively replied Visconti, and looking sternly upon the countenance of Leontini, which was pallid, nearly by the oppression of a mind worked up with suspicion, and an appalling sense of his situation.—"It shall be effected," was again repeated by the confidante of Golfieri.

"But on conditions," interrupted Leontini, "which may be equally fatal."

"No Signor, this moment can mark thy friendship, and whenever the services of Leontini can promote the views of Carraccio, can they be secured?"

"My desire is to leave the Palazzi, nor hazard any plan formed by Golfieri—if then, my rank and services are respected, you will offer, Signor, no opposition to my departure; it was only on the score of confidence, and my belief of your honour, that I acceded to the association already known, beyond that I know not—nor will I conform to."

"Signor Leontini, you touch upon the feelings of a man of honour, when you frame resolutions, at present insinuated, had the purposes to which I were solicited by the Conte been put in practice, where would be the necessity of apprising you of their purport. If at your immolation I had aimed, there were other methods of effecting it, without offering a confidence which is founded on the most honourable motives; in giving you, Signor, the intentions of the Conte, and his determination to assassinate, I conceived that I had served you so much, that not a trifling debt of gratitude would have been due to me. I needed but its acknowledgment, and which would have been exemplified in the obedience and attention of those directions it was now my business to expedite."

"You can give no better proof, Signor Carraccio, of the value of your good will and friendship towards me, than by an acquiescence to my request—that you were willing to befriend me is fully pourtrayed in the disclosure of Paoli's diabolical arrangement, and which I shall never cease to remember. Profiting by it, is in having the opportunity of escaping from the ruin which is attendant."

"Signor Leontini, I cannot but admit the correctness of your observations—that the matter may retain its intended shape, will the service I have rendered you be worth a similar instance in return?"

"Unquestionably," answered Leontini, without the coldness of hesitation.

"It is now required, then, Signor—in conducting you to the public street from hence, and there with sufficient protection you reach your abode, my act of friendship is replete—to repay it, is to follow implicitly the actions of Visconti, and fearlessly meet the designs of the Conte Golfieri—on such conditions you can serve me, and the obligation is mutual."

"I accept of the terms," confidently rejoined Leontini, after a momentary pause—"you undertake that in so doing I hazard not the commitment of crime, but assist the designs of Carraccio."

"I do."

"You equally pledge yourself that my liberation from such sanguinary horrors is in your hands, and it shall be instantly effected."

"I do," repeated the Neapolitan, "and but few hours shall number your confinement."

The discourse was interrupted by the sudden entrance of Paoli's uncouth and scowling messenger, who, in an enunciation of savage expression, enquired the reason of Visconti's delay—"the Signor Conte," added he, "has awaited your appointment during the last half hour—how much more time will your excellenza be pleased to—"

"Silence, fool," roared the stern voice of Carraccio—and lowering its tone to that of a whisper, cried—"inform the Conte he has need of but few moments to complete his purposes," and instantly the ruffian again retired.

Carraccio intimated to Leontini that they must attend the summons.

"Stay, Signor, a bumper of Lachryma to our unity."

The pledge was mutual, and the Neapolitan furnishing Leontini with a large cloak, similar to one he himself was wrapped in, they quitted the saloon through the small porch by which the ruffian had gained admittance.

Closing the door, and preceding Leontini, the tall figure of Carraccio (bearing a lamp), they issued along the narrow avenue that branched from the apartment.

Proceeding some distance, they came to an aperture, where, with some difficulty they passed, and entered a wide and capacious apartment, leading to a spiral staircase, which was terminated by a pair of folding gates, but from their dismantled and delapidated appearance, some years had elapsed since any use or defence had been made of their pliability.

Not one word had escaped the lips of the Neapolitan during the descent.

The obscurity of the abyss that was before them, and the immense depth it appeared from any inhabitable part of the building, created a cold and agitated sensation on the heart of Leontini, and he almost reproached his credulity for being conveyed to the dreadful and sepulchral void that seemed to enclose him.

A swift current of air dimmed the light carried by Visconti—the gloom of the apparently immeasurable recess in which they halted, and the strange silence of Carraccio, hung with appalling sense on the mind. The deathly solitude, and vast obscurity of the expanse, increased with the pause in which Visconti revived the flame; he hesitated to break the silence, lest the tone of voice should betray his terror, and assuming the possibility of confidence and caution, he obeyed the motion of Carraccio's arm, which ushered him onwards; and in an accent that scarcely rose beyond a whisper, but which vibrated with dismal sound throughout the vault, he pronounced, "our progress will speedily terminate—follow, Signor, but speak nought."

They emerged further into the void of the darkness, passing

through an unroofed piazza, or kind of broken archway, closed by an iron grating, which Visconti unfastened, and opened into an opposite avenue of some length, which the gleam of a torch-light in the distance sufficiently pointed out, and served to trace its black and unfrequented compartments.

Visconti re-applied his key to the grating, and with slight assistance it returned to its threshold; their light, though not extinguished, afforded but a feeble ray, and in order to ascertain the approach of the figure that the flare of the torch faintly discovered, Carraccio shaded the lamp.

In anxious suspence the heart of Leontini beat with heavy pulsation at the infliction he might be doomed to.

"Breathe not, Signor," intimated Carraccio, "the Conte Golfieri and his attendant is near."

Leontini was silent, but in his imagination a series of singular constructions were in formation, as to the conduct and seeming mystery of Visconti.

The motion of the two figures habited in sable cloaks and partly masked, rivetted him to the solemnity of the spot, and in quick and distrustful tones, the Conte exclaimed to his companion,—"Carraccio might have been less ceremonious—in the name of St. Athanasius, what had he to fear?"

"I think, my lord, that the Signor was not so easily deluded as was expected; for their conversation seemed loud and debating. On my entrance, the Signor was pressing to withdraw to his Palazzi. Words ran high; besides, in the state of the Signor's reason, it was not probable that he would tamely submit to be borne to these regions."

"The drug that I remitted to Visconti," remarked Paoli, "could not have been administered—its suporific and invincible influence is certain."

The feelings of Leontini, who had distinctly heard these several ejaculations, may be more readily conceived than expressed; still the expression of the last speaker somewhat animated him, aware that Visconti had not applied the baneful drug; and the hope that he was still secure in his confidence, was not wholly banished. Such a failure in the obedience to Golfieri's design, augered the private and peculiar resentment he questioned not, but Carraccio must retain against the Conte, his exigencies was therefore somewhat alleviated.

There was little moment for diversity of opinion, as the voice of Golfieri directed his companion, in order to prevent further impediment, to throw open the grating of an inner dungeon.

They both proceeded to the extent of the vaulted area, and for some few minutes the entire space where Leontini and the Neapolitan had remained, was immersed in utter darkness.

"Now, Signor Leontini, further time need not be lost," replied Carraccio, and taking his hand, he retained it with muscular pressure. "In the distance there, through which the Conte had passed, is the dungeon intended for dissolution. Nay, do not tremble thus—it ill becomes a man of your worth to fear. Remember the pledge existing between us. Seem resigned to your fate without a struggle." "Harkye! Signor Visconti," interrupted Leontini,—further pronouncement of the sentence, was impeded by the words.—"Hush, desist!" from the voice of Carraccio, who had marked the return of the Conte from the grating, and perceiving his approach, in a tone of authority, reiterated—"Ho, there, Bertroni—Bertroni."

"They are here," in a low but reverberating tone, cried Golfieri, and desiring the assistant to answer the call of Visconti, the ruffian, whose name had been made to resound throughout the vault, in equal vibration, replied, "Here, Signor, here."

The hasty step of Bertroni immediately brought his masculine form to the spot where Carraccio and the Signor had rested; and throwing the reflection of the light full upon the sullen feature of Leontini, cried, "Come, Signor, there is no ceremony requisite for the introduction to this new abode—see, my comrade there has perfectly and carefully prepared it for your excellenza."

A rude and splenetic burst of laughter followed the expression, and looking with a scornful smile upon Carraccio, bellowed out—"Your lordship knows that we are pretty attentive in these matters."

The ruffian grasped the hand of Leontini, and snatching him with the utmost ease to his arms—he hurried into the inner dungeon.

The large dark eye of Golfieri flashed with an exultation—his victim was borne in the herculean grasp of Bertroni, and taking the hand of Carraccio, who had followed, exclaimed, "My rival is at length secure;" muffling the tone of his voice, he added,—"now Bertroni, to the completion of thy errand—aye, and with this," producing a dagger—"he sleeps for ever."

"Ruffian," replied Leontini, and at the same time drawing his sword—"dare to move thy arm, and my weapon pierces thy blood-thirsting heart."

The intention of Bertroni, whose arm was already uplifted in the execution of the deed, and which the menacing position and defiance of Leontini had prevented, admitted not of delay; and Carraccio seizing the hand of Bertroni, peremptorily desired him to withhold—"the Conte Golfieri," added he, "has placed the Signor in my charge, I know best how to retain it—the worthy Conte"—and he partly addressed himself to the figure that seemed to guard the grating of the dungeon, "will be quite satisfied of the safety of his prisoner; his presence could not have obtained better security, and being informed of this, the Signor Leontini remains here till further commission—but blood must not be spilt;" and without giving the opportunity of reply, Visconti instantly closed the grated door of the vault—and in silence they each proceeded along the chasm of darkness.

The iron portal at which they separated was heard to close, and in a few moments the dusky resemblance of their torches died away in total obscurity.

The pause, and the unearthly silence, were awfully impressive; and as the sight of Leontini still rested on the direction they had severally taken, a thrill of shuddering horror friezed his veins at the strange and indefinable circumstances of the night.

A period of some length expired, in which the sense of Leontini had been chained in unceasing wonder. The cold air of the vault, and the fixed and motionless manner that he had been absorbed in, impelled the free current of health and animation;—his blood seemed to trickle back on his heart in icy and heavy throb, and the damp perspiration that clings to the human form, generally the precedent of death, appeared to be settling on his limbs:—an instantaneous gleam of moon-light, that rushed through a narrow aperture of the cell, (which bore the appearance of a grated window) revived his sinking powers; and desperately extricated himself from the lethargic torpor that threatened him—he surveyed, by the bright ray that still lighted the spot, the space of his confinement.

END OF VOL. I.

ROSALVIVA.

CHAPTER I.

> She stood like form enrobed in shroud.
>
> PARGA, *a Poem*.

> Much there is wanting still to be fulfill'd,
> Much to my wish, but little to my guilt.
>
> OLDHAM'S *Trans. of Ovid's Metam*.

LEONTINI could with difficulty support the varied thoughts and apprehensions that chased each other, in quick succession, across his mind. Carraccio would never, after the attestations of his honor, betray him, and leave him to the execrable power of Paoli. No! he dared not think that he was in treacherous hands, but looked with anxious eye for the approach of the Neapolitan. The night was waning fast; the dark and chilly region in which he was bound, and the thick air, that seemed to hustle near him, required a desperate fortitude to withstand its paralyzing effects. He moved round the dungeon with a heavy but hurried step, his bosom poignant with the state of its sufferings. The cell was spacious; its vaulted roof and dark projecting walls, rudely shaped from its immense rocky basis, fully pourtrayed the strength, as likewise the horror of its situation. To be immured in an abode of almost superhuman contrivance, and probably under the momentary threat of death, was a contemplation that heightened his mind and feelings to a sense nearly of madness. He staggered, weakened by sickening emotion, along the side of the dungeon, in hope that some cavity might form an egress to his escape; but search was fruitless, and he threw himself along the flooring of the cell, stupified with the weight of his anxieties.

The removal of the iron grating, which secured the entrance of the area that branched from the cavern, awakened him, and looking towards its direction, from a crevice which Time had mouldered, he beheld the figure of a female, closely wrapped in a dark cloak, and seemingly conducted by two men, equally disguised. They advanced along the avenue in cautious silence, and paused, with some degree of emotion, as they attained the door of the cell.

"And is there another victim added to the sacrifice of Golfieri?" meditated Leontini.

His ideal suggestions were impeded from further dissertation by the known voice of Golfieri, who, in a tone of partly suppressed inquiry, cried,—

"This step, Rosalviva, will unhinge you;—I regret that it has gone so far."

"Peace, Conte Paoli, or you will teach me to consider *you* fearless. How can the attainment of an act like this be conformable to fear? Rather that of gratification and triumph. Stromboli, unbolt the door, and to the fulfilment of thy present mission!"

"Stay," interrupted Paoli, "first be assured of the attendance of Carraccio and his follower. Stromboli, see who waits at the grating near the lake;—yonder passage," pointing to a narrow extremity of the avenue, "breaks itself into the subterranean vault. This key opens the grating. On the swelling surface of the waters floats the barque of Carraccio."

The confidant, lighting a torch from the small lamp carried by Paoli, proceeded along the route marked by the Conte, and was momentarily lost from discernment.

Rosalviva concealed the lamp which the ruffian had left.—The Conte carefully removed a small pannel of the door, and whispering to Rosalviva, exclaimed, "Unobserved we may here behold the last moments of the object of our mutual abhorrence."

"Great God!" involuntarily escaped from the lips of Leontini. His strength and power of animation seemed almost convulsed; he sunk beneath its pressure; thought, feeling, power of speech, all his faculties defied their natural function, and he was fixed to the spot, an almost lifeless victim.

The return of Stromboli announced to the Conte the punctuality of Carraccio, and at the same time signifying that the Signore was sufficiently under the influence of the drug wrought up by his direction.

"'Tis his death sleep!" vauntingly shouted Paoli, while he snatched a pistol from the belt of Stromboli, and descended to the cavern.

Carraccio awaited him, and pointing to the motionless form of Leontini, the Conte fired upon his already subdued rival, and grasping the arm of Rosalviva in eagerness, mixed with excessive tremor, hurried from the dungeon.

The echo heightened the explosion of the pistol, and its peal vibrated incessantly throughout the surrounding vaults. Leontini stood aghast with the terror of the moment. Carraccio was beside him; he perceived the sensations of his mind; he essayed to soothe rather than provoke their irritation, and, in affiance to his fidelity, his hand was extended as the pledge.

"Signore Leontini! these incidents amount to mystery. To the Conte Paoli I have done all that his thirsting vengeance designed, and still have preserved the bond of faith to you. Follow me, in silence, and you may again draw the breath of liberty. We part then! Our mutual obligations are alike cancelled, and the wind of Sicily must waft you from its shores for ever. Follow, Signore!"

The voice of Carraccio was audible and impressive; it was not the tone of fellowship, but that of command; and without one word uttered in reply, Leontini yielded to its authority.

They left the dungeon by way of a cavity ingeniously contrived in the wall, which opened to a passage of narrow and low interior. It was with much difficulty considered passable, but Carraccio seemed familiar with its intricacy, and repeating his directions to Leontini, they were speedily in the midst of a path more capacious and lofty. The current of air that seemed to rush near him, indicated that their approach was towards the exterior of the building; the next moment brought him to an archway that fronted the stream.

The dark wave upon the bay was rolling swiftly, and he could perceive, with trifling endeavour, the spray of the water which appeared to dash against the outside of the cavern. Carraccio applied a key to a circular grating, and yielding to its power, the almost starless sky and the serpentine track of the lake were at once before his gaze. In the distance was floating a small boat, in which two men seemed in waiting to the summons of the Neapolitan. They advanced, Carraccio entered it, Leontini followed, and amidst the nearly total silence of the scene, the boatmen rowed from the pallazzi.

The night had become completely tranquil, and the little vessel glided along the surface with scarcely the power or appearance of motion. Leontini turned his eyes to the features of his conductor, they were wrapt in meditation; he threw at length a penetrating glance upon Leontini, and breathed, almost inaudibly, "Signore, from Paoli's malice you are irretrievably removed." Leontini was about to reply, but the Neapolitan signified the expression of silence.

The grey tint of twilight was perceptibly superseding the darkness of the evening, the mind of Carraccio seemed vacant: a kind of passive submission to the influence of sleep inclining him, and which the surrounding quietude and serenity encouraged. Leontini looked anxiously at the strongly marked lines of his countenance, he fancied there was no trace of artifice or duplicity in its outline.

The direction of the boat, and the course of conduct Carraccio was expected to exhibit, were, amidst a variety of reflections, upon the mind of Leontini. He was about to indulge in their formation, only the voices of the boatmen, pleasingly united in singing a descriptive piece of melody, which the stillness of the water rendered more harmonizing and clear, diverted his thoughts, and he attentively listened during the execution of their

SICILIAN BOAT SONG.

FIRST VOICE.

Ply the oar, and swiftly glide
O'er the calm unruffled wave;
Ply the oar, and swiftly glide,
For soft and clear the waters lave.
Sing the night song! trim the boat!
Winds are sleeping,
Moonbeams creeping;
Sing the night song: now we float!

SECOND VOICE.

The moon, with bright and silver gleam,
Is stealing from her cloudy way;
The night-star falls upon the stream,
And sparkles in the rising spray.
Sing the night song! set the sail!
Dews are breaking,
Sea nymphs waking:
Sing the night song! set the sail!

DUETTO.

List! list! what is't we hear?
'Tis Echo! Echo near!
'Tis the murmur of night,
In its slumber reposing;
'Tis the minstrel sea sprite,
Her music disclosing!
Ply the oar, and swiftly glide
O'er the calm unruffled wave;
Ply the oar, and swiftly glide,
For soft and clear the waters lave!

The mellow tone of the voices gradually receded from the ear, and the boatmen were seemingly employed in the arrangement of landing. Leontini surveyed the appearance of the beach, but the dim and imperfect light of the atmosphere prevented the extent of his view.

The boat was guided into a small inlet: a sloping eminence or bank formed the spot where they halted. The Neapolitan alighted from the vessel, proffering his assistance to Leontini, and after the lapse of a few moments, during which Carraccio conversed with the boatmen, the barque was speedily pushed from the shore. There was a silence and an appearance of gloom, that, to a weak mind, was far from consoling sorrow, or subduing fear. Visconti had caught the arm of his companion, and hurrying through an arched portico, knocked loudly at the entrance of a small isolated building, which the light of a lamp affixed to its exterior, rendered just discernible.

The demand of admission was scarcely repeated, when the grating was withdrawn, and the visage of an old attendant, upon whose brow the silvery hair of age and debility was scattered, protruded itself.

"Now, Melfi, the door!" impatiently commanded Carraccio, as the old man was attentively surveying the appearance of his visitors.

"I'faith, by the holy San Pietro, 'tis the Signor Visconti!" pleasantly spake the dependant of the Neapolitan; and lighting up his furrowed features with a smile, he unbarred the door.

Leontini and his guide were conducted into a spacious hall, from whence a half-dismantled stair-case gave ascent to a circular corridor, leading to a number of apartments, which formed a gallery, or rotunda, around which the Neapolitan throwing his eye, enquired if the apartments had been prepared?

"Aye, right welcomely, Signor; and saving your worshipful presence, I'll bestir me to give ye admission."

The attendant was preceding the Neapolitan and Leontini, when the former, detaining his arm, cried, "Save thine old limbs the toil, and retire."

"E'en as your worship wishes it," replied the tottering Melfi; "the saints commend you, as I always importune:" and facetiously bowing to Visconti and the Signor Leontini, he descended from the hall.

"To this implicit confidence," remarked the Neapolitan, when they had gained the interior of one of the apartments, "is indebted much protection. We are here alone, and uninterruptedly may commune as our business needs. I have hazarded much, Signor, in this proof of my assistance, but I have little to require."

The voice of one of the attendants at the door of the apartment, checked the discourse. The Neapolitan, in an authoritative but not angry tone, desired his absence, and the heavy footstep of the intruder was gradually lost in absolute stillness.

"Signor Leontini, we are now upon terms of equality. Speak, if ought be required ere you leave this province; we sit here surrounded by a hundred as brave men as ere drew breath in human frame. You startle; but I do not dissimulate. Think not that in Visconti Carraccio you see a brigand leader, and the proscribed of his country: no!—yet this part of my detail cannot be interesting, let it be silenced."

"And this building!" ejaculated Leontini, under an impression of evident surprise and dismay.

"Is their abode! It adjoins the rocky dormitory, sacred to St. Rosalia; and the staff, the crucifix, and the pilgrim's exterior is no less familiar to the achievement of Carraccio, than is the full flagon and trusty carbine of his comrades. Hither, Signor; you may on the latter score judge for yourself."

Carraccio took a lamp, and conducting the Signor through an antichamber, they descended an almost perpendicular flight of steps, into a region that seemed the receptacle of death and misery. He was prevented from contemplation, by the clamorous shout of laughter that burst from the extremity of the vault, and he followed, in silence, to whence the boisterous mirth seemed to proceed.

The Neapolitan paused, and, extinguishing his light, he placed Leontini near a small cavity, where the nocturnal group were in the same glance before him; it was an interior cavern, capacious, and lighted with various suspended lamps from the arched and canopied roof. A number of individuals in appearance and character something beyond the common description of men, were collectively seated round a massive table, profusely spread with viands, an unusual description of wines, and other refreshments in the utmost abundance. A smaller table was placed at the further corner of the vaulted apartment, and about half a dozen coarse figures, whose countenances and manner told their inferiority, were closely engaged in a species of gaming in which they seemed to participate with general delight.

"The curse of Sicily follow the winner's joy," savagely exclaimed one of the party, as he threw down a ducat and a few florins, the amount of his ill success.

"Paltry fool," replied another of the party, and he rose from the table in an articulation of frightful malice—"may I be broke upon the wheel and hanged in chains till eternity, if I avenge not this insult."

"Peace, Ghoto," vociferated a voice seemingly in command, "how oft is the community to be disturbed with your cowardly broils; by the cross of St. Januarius, and you shall both find your level upon the earth if more of this quarrel be repeated."

Silence was again restored. The mind and sensations of Leontini were disturbed and agitated; he feared to anticipate where the scene of his present circumstances would end.

"Let them revel in their mirth," spoke Carraccio, "time will not admit of our presence among them; you perceive, Signore, the strength of my arm, or as I should infer—*that* which it can command; but to our apartment, I have one request to secure and which is dependent only with you."

He pointed to the directed course in apparent caution, and preceding the Signore Leontini, they gained the gallery chamber.

"I hasten, Signore, to put you in possession of a few incidents whereby you may collect the circumstances of him who has some claim as your friend—you, Signore, can forward his views, and promote in some degree his peace; listen: Under an early passion and prospects of a brilliant fortune, I became enamoured with the charms and person of the offspring of a Sicilian noble. We were united, but I did not then know that I conducted to the marriage vows, one whose ideas were more of eternity and loneliness, than of the bright inspiration and joys of a young and handsome bride. Time, and the constant succession of every variety, failed in its efforts for the procuration of her happiness, and in less than two months I scarcely knew the sacred tie of matrimony beyond its name. It was obvious that the feelings and principles of my wife were withered, or had wandered into another creation, and though at an age when the spirit of activity and imagination is most buoyant, she seemed too much allied to apathy and weakness, to be considered a lasting image of this world. Of her endeavours and attainment at happiness, I might speak some few words, since she essayed to deserve it; but the cankerworm of disease and malady was fastened upon her constitution, and she was borne along the wearisome stream of life by its slow and painful impulse.

"It is not to be wondered that my hopes and projects had failed me; that I was ignorant that the star of my illusion was likely to set in darkness and disappointment; she became a burden upon my mind and an interruption upon my path, I was resolved to,—stay, Signore, do not misinterpret my meaning," suddenly exclaimed the Neapolitan as he perceived a slight agitation in the manner and features of Leontini; "I did not crush this withering flower, I did not press it more heavily with sorrow, I have but given that grief and dilapidated heart to indulge in its own communion in a world of itself—for ever."

"She is dead?" interrupted Leontini.

"Not so, Signore, she lives, but in poverty, for our fortune and family alike deserted us."

The Neapolitan brushed away a tear that was approaching, and assuming his self-composure, added, "You will not refuse me what I have to ask, but I will detail the sequel. The disposition and love of liberty which I have cultivated from my childhood (perhaps unfortunately) with too vivid a feeling, has led me to acts I scarcely know or dare to pause upon; the government of Sicily, at least that portion of it centred in Palermo, rushed on my imagination with all the ardour of greatness and reality; I became eager for the engagements and duties of public life, ultimately I obtained them; I was surrounded by a set of beings of almost undefinable character, with new associations, with new dispositions; but it can afford trifling entertainment to enlarge upon their contracts; their habitation was upon the same public stage of life which I studied from, and I soon became familiar with every habit, every pretension, and every civility essential to the qualifications of a statesman: by progressive gradations I arrived at honour, and subsequently, what I had industriously laboured for, the confidence and friendship of Ruggieri. I possess it, and must hope to use it with advantage; a select band of partisans in the cause of liberty and independence, are ready to die for its rights; to be brief, Signore, it is the voice of these, my friends, that rouses me to the dukedom of Palermo. Zestrozzi, a Sicilian captive, and the descendant of a noble race, of Greek independence, is the enthusiast of our party; and the dormant spirit of his ancestry will, in the eventful and coming day, again burst forth with all its vigour. To this hour they look with ardour and devotion. The Conte Golfieri has been deemed the barrier to all our hopes, but this act directed, Signore, to you, removes him from Palermo, or death will release its demand.

"As I have been the willing instrument of your preservation from a death unjustly merited; as I have renewed an existence which ere this is considered annihilated, you will not, for a period at least, refuse to hold it in secresy and honour. Signore, I can almost project your reply, but await my conclusion. There will come a time when your injuries may find atonement; might I deign to advise, I could picture such torments and such horrors, to pursue the every step of thy betrayer, that all the collective miseries inflicted on the heart and feelings of man should be parallel in his. Continue true, Signore, to my counsels, and you will never cease to regret them."

"I will, I will do all you may impose on me; and am thy debtor for ever."

"Enough; now, Signore, for the performance of that duty I would have devolve upon you."

The Neapolitan took from his bosom a letter carefully sealed, and delivering it to Leontini, added, "This, Signore, I entrust to your charge, to be given to the hands of my wife; the abode and scene of her misery is some leagues from hence, but it will not discourage you, Signore?"

The tone of the Neapolitan at this moment was so pathetic and so earnest, that had the request been made to one of less obligation than Leontini, it must have not passed unsuccessful; he took his hand, and pressing it, further proceeded, "You will be the spectator of a cheerless portrait, a valueless relic from the hand of Nature; but it was not my means that made it thus; my wife was destined to another sphere—it was that which pointed to heaven;—but I digress. In a remote and humble part of the province of Reggio, upon the coast of Naples, is the abode of Signore del Capucio; he is the foster brother of my maternal parent, and to his protection is committed the wife of your narrator; this letter contains an order upon the Viceroy's Court, for the payment of one hundred pistoles. On your fidelity, I cheerfully rely. You will avoid Palermo, till the communication of Visconti hails your return; in the mean time, the flame which lights up my ambition brightens also the prospect of your's."

Leontini was pleased with the task, and the ensuing day was named for his departure. He retired to the solitude of the building to dictate a communication to his parent, and contemplate on the occurrences of the past.

CHAPTER II.

Where is thy son? Oh, ask not where——
HENRY DE COURTENAY, *a Poem.*

O tell me all; to soothe thy mind,
Friendship, its aid shall soon impart.
No answer; yet too well I guess
Thy grief, and well thy eyes reveal
And tell, what thou wouldst fain conceal.
ANONYMOUS.

"THE struggle is past, and cheerful fortitude, with lasting ages of blest felicity, shall follow our united step!" triumphantly spake the Conte Golfieri, as he drew to his embrace the paramour of his illicit affections;—"Speak, Rosalviva, hast thou aught to ask?—is there aught that Paoli can more perform to speak his ardent and endless love?—Name thy commands."

"I have nought to ask, but in loving thee to receive its full reward," warmly replied the Comptessa, and her full brilliant eye spoke at once all the internal gratifications of her soul.

A splendid banquet was served up in the principal suite of apartments of the Romagno Castelli, in all the magnificence and showy splendour which the Comptessa was capable of affording.

The evening was passed amidst every enjoyment human appetite could desire, or the fancy create. Rosalviva and the Conte were its sole participators, and in each other's fervent caresses they received the supremacy of earthly bliss. The night elapsed before Golfieri reached the ducal pallazzi of Ruggieri. An attendant signified that the Duca had in earnest inquiry desired the presence of the Conte.

Paoli retired to his own apartment, and, with the earliest beam of day, awaited the command of Ruggieri. He had traversed the chamber some minutes prior to the appearance of the venerable Duca, whose cold salutation upon his entrance called forth a mingled degree of surprise and apprehension.

"The request of my uncle and protector I have with pleasure

obeyed," interjected Golfieri, anxious to break the suspense his mind had encountered.

"Paoli," answered the Duca, "the period is arrived that opens a new and interesting page in the volume of your existence."

"What means your Highness?" emphatically rejoined the nephew of Ruggieri.

"Son of my adoption, need I pronounce how progressively the ray which lights this feeble existence is drawing towards its close; the last important wish my heart contains, is to witness the happiness and honours of Paoli."

The Conte bowed in implicit and submissive respect at the Duca's signification of his warmest wishes, and looking earnestly upon his venerable features, he almost anticipated their meaning.

"Though weakened by age and infirmity," resumed the Duca, "I am proud in being enabled to witness its completion;—I am proud in being the harbinger of intelligence that must be exulting to the son of mine inheritance; briefly, Golfieri, your union with the lovely Francesca, daughter of the Marquis Di Branciforte, is the prevalent topic of Palermo's boundary, and the envied one within its walls."

"Francesca, daughter of the Marquis Di Branciforte!" deliberately exclaimed the nephew of the Duca, and his countenance was relaxed into a thoughtful gaze. "Pardon me, my Lord Duca, but this must be an error, from what source I am at a loss to conceive, but that the subject is unfounded, I call my honour to witness; nay, I cannot recollect, beyond the attention and respect due to the Signora, as the favoured object of your Highness's patronage, to have made the most distant profession of a regard that could lead to the enthusiasm of an union; indeed, therefore, my Lord, you have been misinformed."

"Impossible; the Marquis was closeted with me during several hours, and so much am I in possession of the decided and absolute facts, that the necessary preliminaries attendant upon the nuptials are in preparation, and mutually signed by the Marquis and myself."

"Strange and indefinable circumstance! Am I in the credence of my senses?" wildly uttered Paoli, "or do I doubt, my Lord, those of your's."

"Paoli!" and the voice of the Duca had attained a peculiar tone of harshness, "I am not inclined to an useless parley, nor do I advance fictitious motives: to be decisive, if you consider the future happiness and welfare of yourself in the least at stake; if you can look forward with pleasure to rank and sovereignty; if you value the determination and plans of Ruggieri, you will not consider the present moment one of levity: the charms and accomplishments of Francesca Di Branciforte is the acknowledgment and delight of Palermo; nor less so is the attraction of Golfieri in her consideration: this confession, made known to her father, has elicited the resolution, and the hand with the noblest fortune coupled in Sicily, is now in your acceptance; you must not, cannot refuse it."

"Must not, my Lord!" hesitatingly expressed Golfieri, "in mercy do not strive to bring about what may end in perpetual misery and wretchedness; suffer me not to perform vows before the altar of heaven, which a trifling interval obliges me to renounce and become an apostate. You must be aware, my Lord, that hearts, unless in unison, beget horror and irreparable torture; cease then to bring about, thus precipitately, an event which only time, reflection, and confidence can or ought to determine. Oh no, my Lord, you will not act thus dissonant to the feelings of nature;—spare me the pain of a refusal, and urge not an alliance which may bring with it distraction and sorrow."

"Paoli, I must insist upon your silence, and dismissal of this tissue of absurdities. With qualifications associated together like those of Francesca, he must be insensible, indeed, who could not admire and prize them."

Golfieri was silent; amazement had sealed his lips, and he stood the involuntary statue of indignation and despair.

"This obstinate silence, imperious boy, merits chastisement; beware how you excite the wrath and power of Ruggieri, or I shall forget, in the duties of authority, the ties of kindred.—Francesca is your destined bride, and no other."

"Oh never—impossible—impossible!" ejaculated Paoli, with half frantic vehemence, "the claims of Rosalviva can never be cancelled; to her am I irrevocably bound, and no human aid can or must divide us."

"Peace, infatuated and abandoned fool! mine ear must not be polluted with the familiarity of a name so disgraced."

"Disgraced! pardon me, my Lord, but I will not listen to the profanation of a character so dotingly dear to me."

"What, is not the profligate Rosalviva scorned and reproached? Bears she not the censure, and almost the curses of every honest heart?—How was the tomb of her murdered parent violated? Behold her degenerate and vitiated habits! Where are the ties which innocence and filial affection should have cherished?—Where the pious rectitude and demeanour her character and sex demanded?—Banished! and in the paths of sensuality, deceit, and disgust, the basilisk pursues her present career; time will show you her in perfect colours."

Golfieri seemed almost petrified with the harangue of the Duca; by what information he had become possessor of the means for such insinuations which had been made, and from whom he could have gleaned facts which, amidst his own disquietude, he could but acknowledge as plausible; and the more he contemplated, the more agitated were his thoughts. The power and charms of Rosalviva were too firmly fixed on his mind to cause a moment's thought contrary to her pleasure; and, however fatal the consequences, his soul was resolved to forfeit every hope—every prospect, rather than the hand and affection of the Comptessa. "Yes," he pronounced, in the delirium of his imagination, "thou art mine only, and no human interference, divine Rosalviva, can or shall part us."

"Cursed and obdurate boy, unworthy the claim of relative! Dare to disregard my injunctions, and my resentment shall light upon your desolate and blighted hopes for ever!"

"It must then—it must!" solemnly ejaculated Golfieri, and he stood absorbed in the wreck of his feelings.

"Away, then, mistaken and relentless fool! Hide thyself and thy name from my recollection for ever; let no hope of pardon wanton in thy breast, nor suffer the calamities which must inevitably overtake you, to plead thy future atonement. No, the feelings which my old and care-worn heart so long has cherished, will, by this act, be vanquished; and with felicity will I erase from memory my paternal care for Paoli Golfieri. Away! away to the arms of your paramour, and revel in thy course of infamy."

The social sentiments of [Golfieri] were overwhelmed; he scarcely knew how to reply. Conscience, and the recurrence to the untimely death of Reo Cardoni, impelled his silence; he already felt the stain upon him, that proclaimed him assassin; he thought he perused its mockery and reproach, in the stern brow of the Duca; he dreaded lest still more of his pursuits were known by him, and that the fate of Leontini was alike of their number. Was Carraccio sincere with him? Had he not whispered to Ruggieri every transaction linked with the ill-fated correspondence and destruction of his friend? Might he not provoke the wrath of Ruggieri to yield him to public justice and punishment, and what was then his doom?—the scaffold. He paused. No, Carraccio could not have betrayed him, and in its confidence he enjoyed a momentary release from the wildness of his ruminations.

During the chain of reflections which had so wreathed itself around the mind of Golfieri, the Duca had retired, and the Conte was for some minutes insensible to his absence. "Now, Rosalviva," he cried, on the recognition of his situation, "is the period when the proof of thy attachment will be given. Golfieri is an outcast! Wilt thou shelter him? He stands alone in the vast world, unfriended; will thy arms be open to him? will thy embrace testify that he still is your's?—Oh, be it so! and his life, his death, are wholly thine; thou art his future world!"

These were the touches of imagery his fancy traced, and he hastened to effect its colouring; every soft and endearing moment he had received with Rosalviva, every art that he had contrived to ascertain her regard for him, and every sacrifice he had known her to be capable of submitting to, came forcibly to his recollection, and he felt too strongly persuaded that his appeal, and his willing deprivation from splendor, rank, and riches, that his sudden change from thence to poverty, would not be reviewed by her in vain, and he rested assured that he still should be retained within her heart, with every earnest and willing pressure.

He found the object of his adoration, in anxious thought, awaiting his approach. Her eyes and heart hailed him with a lover's joy, and another moment marked her rapturous embrace.

He was silent;—it was an unusual quietness; Rosalviva could not fail to notice its apathy, and questioned its influence. She kissed, in repeated fervour, the cheek; she perused there the lines of care and anxiety: and she solicited with persuasive eloquence, its derivation. "Speak, Golfieri, thou must not know concealment with Rosalviva."

"I would not, dearest girl; and 'tis thus I meet the idol of this wretched heart, to speak our last farewell."

The Comptessa was abstracted in silence; he pressed her hand within his, and fixing his eye full upon her changed features, uttered,—"Rosalviva, lose not your firmness! I have shown mine, and if I can suffer your loss, it will be only in the satisfaction, that I have repelled the cause of your unhappiness."

The voice of the Comptessa faltered, and with excessive emotion she almost inaudibly asked, "Wherefore, Golfieri, this sacrifice? to what am I doomed?"

"Happiness, dearest Rosalviva, must be your's; but I—I am not so lost to the feelings of humanity to seek its destruction, nor will I. In less words, the wretched Paoli is a beggar; he kneels to you, humbled, friendless, and destitute. You, Rosalviva, are too valuable to be made the partner of such a desolation of my hopes, and, whatever, may be the conflict, I resign you with the prayer for your real and everlasting felicity."

An inward pang of terror coiled round the heart of the Comptessa; she conjured Paoli no longer to torture her in the darkness of a horror which his intimations conveyed, and assuming an apparent calmness, cried,—"Speak, I will be obedient to all thou canst demand!"

"I know it, Rosalviva; I am convinced of it," he kissed her lips with ardour, and detailed, during the collection of his spirits, the narrative of the Duca's confession and treatment. "And to the utmost extent," added he, "of the Duca's malediction will I cheerfully subscribe, rather than bring down one afflicting hour upon Rosalviva. This night proves the fortitude I can command, and we separate for ever."

"The God which created us, prohibits such an act!" in emotion of courageous and energetic feeling, exclaimed the transported Comptessa;—"no, Golfieri, if love can separate like our's, this instrument alone can ratify the decree. Here! behold a bosom daring as it is fair! Paoli's loss can only be endured, when the life blood that warms its current ceases to flow; strike, when you would leave me, plunge that weapon deep and fearlessly rather than part from me; nay, falter not in the task, since it will convince you that with Rosalviva only Death can divide you."

"Hush!" tremblingly whispered the Conte, "this frenzy alarms me; peace, Rosalviva! or my brain will burst with the madness which already fires it."

"Then we are inseparable? Quick, or I will shew what thy fears pause to complete," and snatching the dagger which she had thrust into the grasp of Golfieri, she bared her bosom in almost preternatural boldness to the execution of the deed.

"We are indeed inseparable!" shouted the Conte, "Rosalviva wishes it."

"She does! she does!" the overpowering sensations which her spirits had struggled with, at length gave way, and she sunk in the arms of Paoli, in a state of total exhaustion.

For many moments she was insensible to her situation; returning sanity at length appeared, and in the tenderness and solicitude of Golfieri, she was removed to her chamber. Paoli still continued his attentions towards the Comptessa, and he gazed upon her sleeping but disturbed form with eyes of tributary fondness.

The animation of Rosalviva was fully restored;—she looked earnestly upon the features of her lover; in the melancholy but half brilliant lustre of her eye was depicted all the intelligence of her heart, and she wept upon the bosom of Paoli with tears of mingled adoration and sadness. She essayed to declare what her soul contained; the suppressed sigh, and the tremulous tone proclaimed its weakness, and stern as had been her nature towards the being she had first taught to love, (the unhappy Leontini,) and whose hopes she had destroyed, her dread of Golfieri's loss was subservient to every other.

Paoli was satisfied of the proofs of her fixed affection, and felt confident that their mutual remembrance would terminate only with life.

The entrance of an attendant, who announced that the Padre Vivaldi claimed an audience with the Comptessa, aroused the lovers from their dreams of romantic delight, and for the moment created a sensation in the breast of Paoli far different from unison with his prior feelings.

The time had rapidly passed during the exchange of sentiments of the lovers; the lateness of the hour gave them cause to conjecture as to the purport of Vivaldi's visit. Paoli signified his intention of retiring, at the same time stating, that in the adjoining apartment, he would remain, obedient to her summons.

The appearance of the Confessor brought with it a cheerless and unpleasant reflection in the bosom of the Comptessa;—the recollection of the assumed garb by Leontini, and its fatal effect, tended to augment her visions and apprehensions of some new and eventful catastrophe; and as his almost shadowy figure was conducted to the apartment, her bosom throbbed with a swelling emotion known only by those whose deeds proclaim their familiarity with guilt and treachery.

"Signora Rosalviva," spake Vivaldi in a voice of much impression, "I come, probably for the last time, for a conference with you alone."

The Monk paused, and the chilling silence which his introduction created, seemed to render the terror of her mental faculties more predominant; his glance was fixed upon her; the filmy hue of dissolution she fancied to reveal itself in its hollow light, and she averted the gaze with tremulous impatience. "Signora," resumed the Monk, "I will beg, for the present instance, to throw aside the terms upon which we have hitherto been known. I approach you in a character more indulgent, more appealing,—that of a parent."

Rosalviva started; she turned to the visage of the Padre, its features were moistened by a tear; it afforded her a strength of mind she had not calculated on, and in more collected thought and positive emphasis, she requested him to proceed.

"Tell me then, Rosalviva, the fate of Leontini, my son."

"Thy son!" instantly interjected the Comptessa. "Leontini, the offspring of the Padre Vivaldi? Mysterious confession. Oh, thou indefinable Creator, to what strange discoveries thy might and power leads us!"

The Confessor piously crossed his breast, and awaited the reply of Rosalviva. She shuddered, and the untimely destruction of

Leontini rushed across her mind, with the accusation of murderess; she felt almost paralyzed with the variety of sensations her sensibility encountered.

"Speak, Rosalviva!" urged the Padre, "the anxiety of a father demands it; tell me what authority secrets him from my presence, and if my hopes of paternal joy should depart so soon? I ask in mercy, Signora; the language of a father's breaking heart is not a common appeal."

"Padre Vivaldi," replied the Comptessa, her self-possession having overcome her painful ruminations, "I am not answerable for the singular vicissitudes attendant upon mortality."

The Confessor was silent; Rosalviva beheld with gratification the distress his mind seemed to partake of, and, amidst its contest, she triumphantly assumed all her accustomed spirit and greatness.

"Speak, my daughter, if there be ought you can communicate, in justice to what I ask, and believe me, the act of kindness shall not go unrewarded."

"In what instance can I look for requital at the hands of the Padre Vivaldi? The Signore Leontini's conduct has warranted the authority of my resentment; but, setting aside my disposition of parleying at this unusual hour, I answer, that the Signore Leontini has received the punishment due to meanness and cowardice; actuated by motives known only to his own breast, he sought to practise them, by fictitious garb, and an artful introduction to my presence. Could those intentions and endeavours be less than those of an assassin? No! it reflects, worthy Padre, infinite credit and honour upon thy doted offspring, to be thus attired, thus armed, and in the dark and lonely hour of night, to break in upon my solitude, with taunts and threats, to my dishonour! Oh, base and dastardly imposition! But heaven rewarded the design, and in my own protection was *your son*—this scion of your race, hurled to his own sought-for oblivion."

"My son destroyed!" and the countenance of the Padre underwent a total change; his black and sunken eyes were raised in fixed exclamation to his Creator, and the pallid and trembling lip, the flushed and damp cheek, severally told the internal pang, the horror of such an enunciation cost him. "Inhuman woman, and was it at thy decree he suffered?" frightfully pronounced the Confessor, and an almost preternatural strength of voice and action seemed to inspire him. "Great God! do I stand here unappalled in the confessions of a murderess! do not the heavens listen to thy crimes? doth its lightnings fly, and not sear you?"

"Peace, wayward old man, or thou wilt repent this! Know, that had not his temerity carried him beyond his discretion, he might have still existed, the deluded offspring of the *pious* Vivaldi. But no, he needs must seek in quarrel those who would have willingly held forth the hand of peace; the strength of his sword haplessly failed, and his presuming and wicked intent was crushed with others for ever."

The Padre sunk upon his knees, his features were hidden within his extended hands, and during some moments a solemn ejaculation passed his utterance, and which the entrance of Golfieri interrupted.

"Now, babbling and officious Monk!" cried he, "what has thy resolution framed? Look up and see the antagonist of the fierce and avengeful Leontini; see in me the man who, drawn by this heated Signore to open combat, has decided his doom; and see in me the avowed protector of the Comptessa Rosalviva—Yes, look at me well, Paoli Golfieri!"

The Padre fixed a look of keen anguish upon the erect and haughty figure of the Conte; the mingled sensations of horror, grief, and revenge, all lighted up his bosom with the most poignant feeling, to the being who stood in bitter and cruel menace before him. His existence had been changed with him; he saw in him the destroyer of his hopes and his offspring; his withered sinews seemed strung with tenfold vigour, and he fastened upon the throat of Paoli, writhing in acute torture.

The Conte with facility dashed the Padre from his hold, and darting a look upon him of the most vindictive wrath, cried, "Frantic priest! what presumption blindly leads you to this attack? Wretched old man, but I pardon it, since it moves my pity, rather than my resentment."

The Comptessa witnessed the scene in calmness.

"And thou art the Conte Golfieri?" pronounced Vivaldi.

"The same, Padre, and the betrothed of Rosalviva!"

"Impious and heretic acknowledgment! Oh, murdered spirit of

the deceived and fallen Cardoni, even though shrouded in guilt will thy remains repose beneath the tomb? will thy unearthly form not appear, and blast, by its horrific presence, the profanation of this moment? when shall innocence sleep, and oaths, that are registered in eternity, be blotted from the recollection! Nay, turn not from me, Signora, in contempt. Remember thy oath. Hark, thou recreant and perjured criminal!" and taking from his bosom a small scroll, pronounced, as he seemed to read it,—"*swear that to no human being shall thy hand be given, until thy father's murder be discovered.*—Hush!" and the Monk appeared to denounce their reply, proceeding in a distinct tone,—"*record, too, that on whom this blood may rest, you will, with hatred and revenge, pursue, and when the mask be removed, that you will lead him to the scaffold!*"

"I did, I did!" shuddered Rosalviva, and the large drops of perspiration stood on her forehead, with trembling sensation.

"And when that oath was forgotten," resumed the Confessor, after a short pause, in which the appearance of the Conte seemed equally disordered, "thy soul was condemned to *endless destruction.*"

"No more of this, infatuated lunatic!" as he threw aside the Padre, and clasped the fainting form of Rosalviva; he held her in his arms, and commanding the Monk to retire, added—"This, most holy and *devoted man of God,* is thy creed; and thou wouldst brand the name of the Comptessa with perjury; liar and reprobate, hence, or my words shall benumb you. Where is the guilt? Who can speak to the guilt of Rosalviva?"

"Aye Padre," and the eye of the Comptessa was directed to the Monk, on whom she fixed it, while returning sanity and composure relieved her, "Aye, what has Rosalviva to fear from thee?"

"Thou hast much to fear from thine own conpunction, in acknowledging the bonds which can ally that heart with thy father's assassin."

The voice of Vivaldi was firm and unshaken, and as he uttered the bold insinuation, he pointed to the Conte Golfieri, whose tremor and agitation would have almost confirmed the charge. Rosalviva was overwhelmed with agony at the accusation; gladly she would have closed her eyes from the dark meaning, had its sense have alike failed in the power of suffering; had she to think that the being on whom her soul and happiness was hinged, had she to think that her dreams of bliss and hours of ecstacy were numbered, and in the acknowledgment of so lamentable a catastrophe, was interwoven the guilt and character of her father's murder. Was she prepared to forfeit all her joys of futurity, and send to the scaffold the possessor of her whole heart? No; she would not pause, even to think of its horror; rather her mind should suffer all its other reproach, than that resulting from disaffection to Paoli. She felt his lips press warmly on her cheek, in that moment how weak were her efforts to repel his embrace; she did not, but essayed to maintain the artifice and duplicity which must have warranted the assertion of Vivaldi.

The Monk was extended on the floor, the black blood had rushed into his countenance, and in an afflicting groan was seen the last pulsation which lifted his heart; she turned to Paoli, and hiding her head in his bosom, forgot for a temporary period the sense of her sufferings.

CHAPTER III.

The pale assistants on each other stared,
With gaping mouths for issuing words prepared.
The still-born sounds upon the palate hung,
And died imperfect on the falt'ring tongue.

DRYDEN.

Fathers, your presence seems to move the Count
More deeply than it might beseem a man,
Strong in the consciousness of armed innocence.

THE MAFFEI, *a MS. Tragedy, by Leigh Cliffe.*

GOLFIERI perceived how much the senseless and inanimate form of Rosalviva was a victim to the Monk's assertions and exposure, and while she had lain, locked as it were beneath its stupor, he had rushed upon the Padre, and, grappling with him, his more powerful strength brought him to the ground; and, in his grasp, no time had scarcely elapsed, when the evident marks of strangulation caused the Conte's desistance.

The body of Vivaldi remained stretched in the cold state of death, and the discoloured and swollen features too plainly spoke the effect which produced it. The Conte disengaged himself from the remains of the Monk, and endeavoured to force Rosalviva from the appalling spectacle.

The Comptessa shuddered at the deed; yet her heart seemed to feel relieved from a burden of torture, which the presence and expressions of the Padre unquestionably created. She gazed upon the corse, and her lips were fixed in ashy paleness;—she turned from it in disgust and terror. Paoli's heart grew cold within his bosom, and his agitation encreased with each moment; its guilt and apparent fear served to influence the mind and courage of Rosalviva, and, turning her eyes to his, she cried, "Paoli; thy unsteady and tremulous heart would fain hold alliance with remorse;—away—return to thy pallazzi;—kneel with penitence to the Duca's relenting heart; say that you are obedient to his will, and have renounced the unfortunate Rosalviva.—Do this, and give thy bosom a returning throb of felicity."

The Conte directed a look of penetrating inquiry to the half-scornful visage of the Comptessa; and, taking her hand, in an unusual tremor, pronounced,—"Rosalviva; this from thee!—Has my conduct," (and he unconsciously turned towards the body of Vivaldi,) "merited thy suggestion?"

"Lose not then the spirit of a man, Paoli, or I must think that shame and dread of danger will announce to me your loss."

"Oh, never—never, so long as you exist to bless me."

"But the corse?" whispered the Comptessa, "to *whose* charge, Paoli, *can* it be entrusted?"

The Conte paused; concluding his resolves, he replied, "To nought but ourselves. The knowledge of this act, Rosalviva, must not be extended. Dare you but summon fortitude to assist in the removal, and on the dark wave of the Mediterranean, it shall float to distant worlds."

"Be it so: I have courage, and desire to effect all that you may propose.—The secret, then, dies within our own bosoms."

The night, though far advanced, was impenetrably dark, and the castelli appeared hushed in the most profound repose. Paoli suggested that, by means of the small gate leading from the terrace, he could with safety, and without fear of observation, convey the body of Vivaldi, "From the platform beneath the terrace, the swelling surges will readily receive its burden."

Rosalviva, throwing a cloak loosely about her shoulders, motioned the Conte to cautiously accompany her through some of the principal avenues, to ascertain their loneliness; removing such obstacles as impeded their progress, they speedily attained the gate on the terrace.

Rosalviva reconducted him to the private staircase leading to these apartments, and, signifying her intention of remaining in attendance at their ascent, in case of alarm, she directed him to hasten the completion of the task. Paoli took from an adjoining avenue a small lamp, and ascended towards the chamber. He passed the range of apartments, open to his tread. The reflection of the Comptessa's light in the hall receded from his sight. He approached the apartment which had solemnized his further accession to guilt.—He listened; but there was not the slightest breath or motion;—Nature seemed bound in almost an awful and mysterious silence. The sensations that coiled round his heart at this moment, at the reflection of the act, seized him with terrifying vigour, and his limbs scarcely performed their office of supporting him.—He heard the voice of Rosalviva hastening him, and he rushed into the chamber. Fear of detection had rendered his determination desperate, and he grasped the livid corse of the Padre, and hurried to the stair-case. The light retained by the Comptessa welcomed his eye—he descended.

"I have waited with an impatience scarcely describable," murmured Rosalviva, "follow—hush."

Directing his steps with deliberate coolness, the Conte proceeded with the corse; the reflection of the light traced their shadows distinctly along the pavement; concealing its flame, they both maintained a perfect and cautious silence; the black foam of the waters splashed beneath their feet; the body was lowered into its deep, and the next spray seemed to wash it away for ever. Securing the various passages through which they passed, they regained the Comptessa's apartment in safety.

"Rosalviva," impressively cried Paoli as he sat beside her, his eye conveying a mixed expression of terror and sympathy, "for you is this deed performed—for you Paoli is registered in the list of murderers."

"Hush, Golfieri, hush, it binds more firmly our embraces, which now can never be separated. Paoli, our happiness will indeed be replete now; Heaven is my witness that all the pleasure, all the hope, my warm heart ever received was with you; each tumultuous pang my bosom could have suffered would have been borne with gladness, did it obtain but one smile from thee in return. Oh, Golfieri, convinced that you love me, I am eternally your's. How shall I declare my joy! how detail my gratitude!"

"It is breathed, Rosalviva, every moment; and for such acknowledgments, what could your Paoli not forfeit?"

"You have forfeited much for me; I will never cease to be mindful of its value." An affectionate embrace testified their sense of mutual adoration.

The Comptessa pleaded excess of indisposition and retired to her chamber.

Golfieri passed to a further apartment which had been appropriated for his use, and hastily closing the door, threw himself in disorder upon the bed, eager to forget events gone by. Sleep was far from affording her influence, and his mind encountered a revolution of guilt and horror; he felt his heart throb heavily, and the scenes of the recent period, of which he had been the hero, came before his imagination with gloomy retrospect. "Miserable old priest," exclaimed he, "why didst thou step in my path?" he paused, and a tear almost fell from his streaming lashes, a goblet of Greco stood upon a side-table, he snatched it with avidity, and in its exhilarating effects he became progressively impressed with new and fearless resolutions. After an interval of some length, his meditations were thus expressed: "Psha, 'twere cowardice to fly! why fear detection? where is there the accusing voice? No human eye saw the deed, no human tongue can pronounce Paoli the culprit. What then has this bosom to do with fear?—this bosom where a deity inspiring as Rosalviva governs, with sweet controul. Hence, vain and imaginary terrors, I defy thy vengeance, and am free." He drank deeply of the beverage before him, intoxication soon followed, and he sunk into a heavy but unsettled slumber.

The mind and soul of Rosalviva were moulded from more

stern and impenetrable materials than those of Golfieri; left to herself, she felt no shame, no terror, no remorse; she paused not to think on what condition her iniquitous and daring acts rested; her soul was wrapt up in one spell only, and to its influence she was irrevocably bound; she cared not to be drawn from its illusion; she felt that with Paoli her life was wholly hinged; it was so indissolubly chained, that even should destruction follow the unity, she would rather look forward to its triumph than shrink from one moment's loss in Golfieri's love. With Leontini she remembered to have breathed totally an opposite passion; it was the gleaming of a first and uncertain love; her own bosom knew not its legitimate feelings; under its then false and delusive sensibility she had encouraged the addresses of one whose esteem strengthened as it journeyed onwards. In the artificial warmth of her bosom she had proffered the repose and happiness of a heart devoted to her controul; she suffered it to remain there until a new object envied its felicity, and for the promised sincerity, goodness, and ardour of affection she had taught him to hope for, she dealt out the shafts of duplicity, and Leontini became its first victim; his remembrance now was wholly obliterated, and she looked forward to new and interesting pleasures. Golfieri loved her, his proofs were invaluable, and since he had the more earnestly shewn it by a refusal of the divine Francesca, her fortune and favours were devotedly his. The gray tint of morning had appeared before her ruminations became tranquillized.

Paoli awoke from a restless pillow, and joined the Comptessa in her apartment. The sun had obtained its meridian height as they repaired to the morning repast. Their discourse was intruded upon by the entrance of a domestic, announcing that an official of the Jesuit order requested admission to the Comptessa. She had scarcely opportunity of reply, when a confused mixture of voices caught her attention in the adjoining apartment. She perceived the messengers from the legal authorities in close appeal with her various domestics, who had in surprise and astonishment surrounded them. There is something so appalling in the terror and suspense which a bosom, fraught with error and guilt, endures prior to its arraignment, that the very countenance speaks a volume in the confession of its criminality!

Paoli preserved a silence and composure which he could but ill support; while the Comptessa started from her seat in an emotion of wildness, her cheek alternately flushed with guilt and haughty indignation.

"Signora," cried one of the official attendants, after the particulars of their presence were made known, "I am compelled to announce that the Cardinal Guiseppe, our Holy Superior, holds your appearance indispensable, to account in some measure for the absence of the Padre Vivaldi, inasmuch as the Confessor was conducted hither by two fathers of his order. An affair of importance, it is supposed, urged him to visit this castelli at the cessation of his pious labours; this intimation was made by him to the members of the order who attended him, and whose evidence upon the salvation of the cross has been given to the Superior. They further state, that no human being passed the portico of the castelli, where they, by the Padre's earnest order, awaited his return. The clock of the St. Colombe monastery told the hour of morning as they hurried back to the convent, judging that from the detention, the Padre intended to embrace the light of day for his re-appearance; search has been anxiously made throughout the limits of our convent, but without effect, and on the depositions of the fathers accompanying the Padre to this castelli, by the Prior you are summoned, Signora, to declare such knowledge as will admit of the circumstance."

"Holy Providence! what testimony can I adduce? what ray of light is it possible for me to throw upon the mysterious affair?"

"That may be questioned," answered one of the officials, "in the presence of our Superior. You will be mindful, Signora, that as the possessor of this castelli you are bound to appear within one hour of the close of vespers, provided the father Vivaldi is still missing."

"Vivaldi!" "Me culpable!" severally interjected Paoli and the Comptessa, and their mutual attempt at consternation and ignorance was exceeded only by the dismay and agitating tremor which their manner evidently betrayed. A strange and unmeaning look of wonder was observable upon each of the domestics, whose innocence the excessive vacuity of mind and conduct rendered colourable.

The official visitors were retiring, Rosalviva caught the arm of the principal speaker, and assuming a confidence of tone and courage, which excess of fear had made desperate, cried, "How, insolent intruder, darest thou, in the presence of my household, thus rudely proclaim insinuations which, for motives unknown, the name and character of the heiress of Romagno suffers under? Is the title of Reo Cardoni to be made the every-day theme of the vulgar herd, in even supposition only of being accessary to the absence or loss of a foolish wretched old priest? Leave my castelli instantly, and recal thy magisterial command, or Palermo's Duca shall be apprized of the unwarrantable and ignominious insult."

"Signora, we do but obey the direction of the Superior," answered one of the officials, surveying with a look of scrutiny the yet maddened Rosalviva. "If, Signora, you are ignorant of the circumstance attendant on Vivaldi's departure from hence; if, too, that you *fearlessly* make oath that in no way the inmates of the castelli are concerned, and no possible traces or elucidation of the mystery can be given, then will the illustrious house and rank of Cardoni be exempt from the talk, or even the hearing, of that vulgar herd which you seem thus to scorn; however, Signora, be mindful of the summons or you must dread the result." Leaving the petrified Comptessa and her paramour in absolute amaze, the Jesuit professors withdrew.

For several moments the Conte was silent—his eyes involuntarily caught those of Rosalviva—they conveyed a fearful and expressive confession, but a momentary flush of passion and anguish crimsoned her cheek, and in a voice almost frantic, she cried, "Paoli—we are lost." The Conte was absorbed in meditation, and scarcely did his sense recognize the exclamation,—"Speak, Golfieri, this is not a time for silence—expedients are necessary, and some instant resolve must be our's."

Paoli trembled, he almost dreaded to think of the act—he seemed to feel the curse that was marked out for him—his feelings were wrapt beneath a stupifying distortion, and the more he reflected the more gloomily his mind depicted its horrors.

Rosalviva snatched the hand of the Conte within her's, and gazing earnestly upon his features with a smile denoting a contempt of his weakness and apathy, and which the sullen Paoli clearly pourtrayed, remarked, "How! Golfieri, lost in despair!—Shame!—dost thou bend to the poor attributes of penitence and misery?—has Rosalviva no charm, no influence, that can remove these gloomy presages? What has she to fear, so long as she possesses Paoli's love? In retaining that—the lightnings of heaven would fail to startle—its thunders only would seem harmony to her soul—she has done much to prove its value—she will do still more—away then with idle apprehension—love like our's will not admit of interference, will not admit of alloy; and for its full enjoyment, Golfieri, let every other thought, every other dependant be cancelled." She kissed his lips during a pause of intense silence—passion and tremor had almost scorched them, but the warmth of her kisses restored, in some degree, his animation; and amidst her rapturous caresses and her ardent professions of attachment, he became cheered. He felt that in her affection all his hopes of happiness were decidedly registered; he saw that whatever might be his fate in life, Rosalviva would be a willing participator; he looked at the sacrifice he would be compelled to make; he had signified to her the ruined outcast that he was—from Palermo's dignities and splendour he must be at once proscribed—but Rosalviva's heart gave him a shelter, a protection. Could she fly with him, and in that spot where themselves would probably be its only inhabitants, dared she forfeit all the felicity and honours her birth had entitled her to?—this for Paoli, and still to love him—oh no! the task would be impossible!

"Yes, yes," she interrupted, in a tone which fully indicated the genuine and sincere spirit of feeling that lived within her soul, "Rosalviva can do all this; she is Golfieri's for ever! The voice of God only," and she paused for a moment, "can forbid it."

"Endearing woman!" breathlessly answered the Conte, and his bosom vented its ardour in exulting embraces.

"Now, then, Golfieri, to the considerations which are connected with our future prospects. Our present aim is to triumph over circumstances gone by; listen to what remains to be done. No evidence can be adduced to speak to the deed, and prove the Padre's death by our hands. Still the heiress of Di Romagno must not trust to investigation or chance, or even the suspicion attached to such an occurrence;—flight, Paoli, is our only refuge, and with the darkness of the coming night, we must leave Palermo, for an abode more secure. Nay, do not tremble; my heart will lose all its fire, its dotage, if Golfieri hesitates and pauses at the whisperings of fear."

The Conte was silent. A trifling lapse of time witnessed the contemplation of the incidents passing in his determination, and he replied,—"Yet, Rosalviva, will not this abandonment, of our's carry with it conviction the most glaring?—Will it not subject us to reproach, and the character of the guilty? Think if it were not better with confidence and decision to meet the investigation. Where is the voice that will speak of Vivaldi's death? Yes, it must be so; I have well considered the matter, and my mind tells me, Rosalviva, that our best hope will be in forwarding this examination. Acquittal must be the result, and then the house and family of Cardoni remains unsullied."

"I yield me, passively and gladly yield me to thy better judgment," answered the Comptessa. "I will await the hour with firmness; one throb alone disturbs my heart. Can Golfieri maintain his boasted courage and self-possession?"

"He will, he will; 'tis Rosalviva demands it;—her goodness will ensure it." Mutually elate with their resolve, they willingly separated until evening.

The pangs of a conscience chained with guilt was the only evidence that could be adduced of the crime of Vivaldi's death to the name and character of Golfieri—its affection once quieted, who had he to dread? His intercourse and intimacy with Rosalviva was hitherto only partially known, and for her himself might become bound as to the Comptessa being free from the Padre's destruction; his hands alone committed the deed! on his head alone rested the guilt! Rosalviva might have been instrumental to its cause, but then her love, her sympathy, her sincerity to Paoli, each grounded it. The madness of his enthusiasm had urged him to the deed, and in an eventful moment the passions of his bosom hurried him beyond reflection; Vivaldi was its victim; any accusation possible to be placed to the charge of the Comptessa must evidently fail; no testimony could support it: and for Golfieri, for the illustrious name and rank allied with it; the kindred of Ruggieri, who would be daring enough to couple it with murder? even where suspicion might be harboured—he felt satisfied that its expression would never be propagated, and in the security of his own and Rosalviva's apparent innocence, he had little left to despair of. Carraccio too might be commanded for the aid of his responsibility in competition with Paoli, which must at once forestal the complaint, and nought but the most impartial and most impressive sense of the erroneous foundation of the charge would influence the bosom of every individual; he felt then anxious for the ordeal, and hurried to his confidant, Visconti Carraccio.

The mind and attention of the Neapolitan was too deeply impressed with the arrangement of future plans at the moment of Paoli's application to admit of interruption. To the announcement of a domestic of the Conte Golfieri's visit, he directed that an engagement of a limited interval had taken him from the palazzi, and his return would be one hour previous to the evening vesper.

Paoli was disturbed lest the counsel of Visconti should be precluded from him, and anxious that he should be in possession, upon the earliest moment of his arrival, of the tenor of his visit, he sat down in an ante-chamber, and addressed to him the following sketch:—

"An affair of the highest moment to the happiness of the Signor Carraccio's devoted friend demands the speediest conference; communicate then with Paoli the instant this epistle is perused, and suffer him to add another pledge to those already numbered by Visconti towards his friend GOLFIERI."

The billet was carefully folded, but breaking open the envelope, he further added,—

"It may be indispensably necessary to add, in few words, that the Padre Vivaldi is missing; the Comptessa Rosalviva is suspected of being aware of his detention and his absence, and at the termination of the ensuing vespers is summoned to the presence of the fathers of the order of St. Ignatius, where the holy fraternity are prepared to meet her; need I detail the importance of such a meeting, need I declare to you her innocence; on my head the deed rests, but who can accuse Golfieri; thy judicious advice, Carraccio, will best guide me; I owe thee much in gratitude; this act completed, the debt is still greater."

The instant the Conte quitted the pallazzi, the epistle was conveyed to the already waiting Carraccio, whose eagerness to know the purport of his sudden demand was instantly satisfied. Enthusiasm lighted up the countenance of the Neapolitan, as he perceived further instances of Golfieri's dependance.

"The Padre Vivaldi then is murdered! and by the Conte Golfieri!" proudly apostrophised the Signore Visconti, and his heart seemed to share an additional glow of triumph, as it acknowledged the information. "Yes, thou wilt indeed add another pledge, daring Golfieri, and one day I will claim to the full extent, all my demands. The Comptessa must not be vanquished; the time is not arrived when her catalogue of offences can be considered replete. This incident must be a successful one; it can be accomplished with ease to myself, and exultation to Paoli. Gold, thou preponderating and certain deity, thy influence now will be supreme. Zestrozzi, this is food for thy hopes, and fuel to the fire still brightening in the proud heart of Visconti Carraccio."

He took the opportunity of making immediate communication to the Conte Paoli, intimating, that his return to the palazzi was much earlier than he calculated, and, in obedience to his most pressing importunity, he awaited the mutual conference. Golfieri lost no time in attending his confidant, and during some few minutes he indulged in the declaration of how much he felt in the value of Carraccio's attention and respect.

The Neapolitan bowed with a familiar yet respectful dignity, adding,—"This confidence sufficiently repays me, my Lord, and for the distinction I cannot think myself too much bounden in those services you may deem worthy of acceptance. But we lose time in referring to the retrospect of events, name such of the present most desirable to be accomplished, and if the efforts of Visconti can render them effectual, the result is certain."

"Thanks, thanks, best of friends, in your hands my wishes are replete."

Paoli briefly narrated the several circumstances attached to the proceedings at the Castelli De Romagno, and unhesitatingly recited the incident which terminated with the Padre Vivaldi's life. "To speak of it in terms of reflection," remarked the Conte, "were folly; the mischief is done, and to remedy the evil arising therefrom, is our present study; say then, Visconti,—how it is to be accomplished."

"Fear nothing, my Lord; an acknowledgment of a thousand pistoles, with your signature, puts the affair to rest; this, and further marks of respect promised to the rank of those to whose official authority the investigation is consigned, will be sufficient; my life then upon the completion of our hopes."

The various requests urged by Visconti were put into negociation by the Conte. Paoli flew to the embrace of the Comptessa; his countenance pourtrayed the joy his heart had received, and he threw himself in the embrace of Rosalviva with peculiar warmth and ecstacy of feeling; smiles of mutual gratification played upon the cheeks of the lovers, as the account of Carraccio's zeal was stated by Golfieri.

The few hours flew with agreeable celerity, till the vesper bell of the St. Esprit Convent told the coming time for their departure. The spirits of Rosalviva were light and buoyant, and the intermitting gloom and despair which had occasionally attacked the mind of Paoli, receded amidst the kind of artificial rapture which his spirits had experienced from the entertainments and enthusiasm of the evening; the exhilarating effect of the various wines he had partaken of chased away reflection, and in its illusion every care or thought of sadness was at once dispelled.

The Signore Carraccio, punctual to the performance of his undertaking, awaited the appearance of Paoli and the Comptessa; and under their joint protection she surveyed the solemn and almost cheerless scene with apparent familiarity and calmness. The hall of the Jesuit order was in perfect unison with its disquisition, its cold and blank appearance fully denoted the kind of occupation it was generally open to. The partial light shed by a few dim lamps, beamed through the colonades, composed of dark granite, and the shadowy reflection from its stupendous columns was rendered visibly gloomy to the mind of the spectator, and conveyed a chill of apathy and alarm. At the extremity of the pavement, the fathers of the order were seated upon an ascending range of benches fixed on each side of a recess, in which the statue and tomb of their patron saint was erected. Central of the aisle was a temporary throne, surmounted by an antique canopy, covered with the sable cloth, displaying the emblems and inscription of the fraternity, before which was fixed a long massive table, ornamented with similar designs, and closed in by railed seats with the same black covering.

A lay brother announced the entrance of the Superior. The officials arranged themselves in their appropriate stations. A few individuals dispersed along the galleries, whose rank and interest had procured them admission, and the attendants of the Comptessa, placed within an adjoining corridor, seemed to comprise the entire assemblage.

The chief Padre, in a tone of profound respect, impressively and audibly read the indictment, by which the Comptessa Rosalviva was summoned; two of the Monks, at some distance from the brotherhood, kneeled in passive obedience to the shrine of their saint, while the occurences relative to the disappearance of the Father Vivaldi were recited. The oath was administered to the Monks, upon whose evidence such accusation as could be collected was founded. The Comptessa was ordered to approach;—with a firm and dignified step she attended to the order.

"Speak, Rosalviva, Comptessa di Romagno, as to the knowledge of such circumstances that may lead to the recovery of the Padre Vivaldi."

"I have none to offer," distinctly and without hesitation pronounced the Comptessa. "That the father Vivaldi was seen to enter the portico of my castelli is readily admitted; his subsequent interview with myself is likewise; but the purport of his singular visit at such an hour I know not; his wished-for conference was solicited at too unreasonable an hour to be acceded to, and, excusing myself, I retired to my chamber; by what motive I am thus arraigned, for incidents beyond my power of elucidating, I have yet to learn; the enviable and poisonous tongue of prejudice and slander has raised this inquiry; but its instigators, for the daring and insolent attack upon my house and honour, will uniformly meet with their deserts, and which, by the aid of immediate and legal authority, I shall pursue with the utmost rigour. Here, too, are my domestics, let them be questioned as to any information of the unfortunate Padre.—More than I have detailed is not within my power—let them, if possible, speak more favourably. If *my* veracity is questionable, probably that of the Conte Golfieri, and his friend the noble senator Carraccio, may better speak it. I have to thank them for this voluntary assistance in the present dilemma; I shall not forget its ultimate value."

The looks of the assembly were directed to the Conte and the Signor Carraccio, who had till now awaited in a more obscure part of the court, and who readily bended in obedience to the dignity and reverence of the Consistory President and Superior.

Their introduction had its effect. The Comptessa was entreated to pass over the hasty manner of their regret and interest of the fate of the Padre Vivaldi. The first means which had been adopted to endeavour to trace it, in summoning the presence of the Comptessa, they had conceived, from motives and principles, likely to deduce information agreeable to their hopes, and not from the influence of prejudice or the most distant intention of insult or degradation to the feelings and rank of the Comptessa. The official authority had acted under a conscientious discharge of an important duty. For the injury or affliction done to the feelings of the Comptessa they trusted they would be forgiven. The known responsibility of the Conte Golfieri, and the rank of the Signor Carraccio, if even conviction had been almost supportable, with the conduct of Rosalviva, would have been enough to have cancelled the further inquiry.

Since then it was evident that erroneous conclusions had been drawn, the chief Padre rose, amidst the silence of the fraternity, and announced with much solemnity,—"Since then it is no less certain than fatal that Vivaldi's death has been premeditated, or the Comptessa would have heard the cause of his absence, and that it is most positive that some implacable enemy had awaited the opportunity for his assassination, and his departure from the Castelli di Romagno——"

"Doubtless," interrupted the Signor Visconti in a commanding tone, "as it is well known that but recently the father Vivaldi had been attacked, and even dangerously wounded, it is not improbable, that by the *same hands*, whose attempts had hitherto been so feebly accomplished, were now but too successful, and to prevent detection must have committed his body to some impenetrable abyss, nay a dungeon might even exclude him from the world, and all hope or chance of discovery."

"The suggestion, alas! is apparently probable," replied the Superior, "yet search must still be maintained, and no opportunity lost that may lead to some tidings of the ill-fated Vivaldi."

The officials bowed in obedience to the command, and the Superior, embracing the holy cross, while he was prostrate to the shrine of the patron saint, murmured a few words in prayer, and attended by the monks withdrew.

The Conte Golfieri, in unity with Carraccio, conducted the Comptessa from the "abode of gloom," and were speedily conveyed to the Castelli di Romagno.

CHAPTER IV.

From fields of blood
And the wild havoc of ambition, Fame
Has turn'd aside, and wondering at her course
Pursued thy noiseless path, while tyrants quaked
Before thee.

SOTHEBY.

Look upon these wretched men,
Behold this human misery,—then think,
Think that these deeds of horror are your own.

BELLAMIRA.

"EXULT, my anxious beating heart," proudly cried the Neapolitan Carraccio, as he withdrew from the Castelli di Romagno, "this night has formed the foundation of my future hope. Golfieri, thy pursuits after crime have been daring indeed; the supposed destruction of one human being, thou hast made me a willing confidant to, the murder of a second, and *that* being, the parent of thy first victim, is equally in my charge; yes, to this do I bear convicting proof; tremble, cowardly and subtle miscreant, for one day the sting that sleeps here in my bosom will burst forth, and pierce the heart that has threatened to avenge it. Think not, mean and cold-blooded enthusiast, that I have forgotten the injury thy young ambition inflicted upon me; whose arm, neglectful fool, in the hour of peril, when the sabres of almost a countless band of Saracen invaders were lifted to thy destruction—whose arm repelled the blow? whose voice proscribed the deed? and who led ye in triumph to Palermo's gates? 'twas I.—From whom was the victor's wreath gathered to bind thy heated temples?—'twas the laurels of Carraccio which composed it. And what were the disgrace of the poor deluded infidels to whom I became the willing pledge? Think of thy broken promise, half the wealth and half the honours of Palermo were to have been at my disposal—where is it? where is the remembrance?—only in this brain; thine rejected it when thy purpose was replete, and thou hast temerity enough to think that it was as easily forgotten by me; oh no! this honour was purchased at too high a price, it was thine own price; but thou hast not paid it; thou knowest not, proud Golfieri, the feelings of the men thou hast injured; the fury of our bursting Etna may be transient compared with the anguish of derided and insulted honour; live, base boy, enjoy thy illustrious hope of subservience and power a little longer, till when my measure of vengeance be filled." The Neapolitan in hasty step crossed the piazza of the building, and was speedily in the ducal pallazzi.

It was at the close of a perilous contest between the Greek and Saracen camp and the protectors of Sicily's rights, that registered the debt of gratitude made by the Conte Golfieri to the Neapolitan Carraccio. The Sicilian troops, worn by fatigue, and overpowered by increasing aid from bands of Greek and other renegades, whose strength was still receiving additional supply, when a detached brigade, commanded by one of the Ruggieri, and in whose lists the Conte Golfieri was second in command, were securing a retreat to an opposite shore, that in the most guarded and well defended ambush was secreted a powerful body of Greek soldiers—Carraccio was their leader—hundreds of Sicily's bravest men fell at the first attack—to continue further resistance was madness. Already had the Ruggieri commander bled and expired in the struggle; Golfieri was singled out as the representative of princely power and usurpation, and the swords of a ferocious horde crowded to drink their oppressor's blood. The sword of Carraccio was foremost; the young Conte sunk upon his knees—"Hold, Neapolitan," exclaimed, "this is but feeble conquest for one of thy race; yield me a life so humbly won, and Palermo's highest dignity is your's for ever."

The band were silenced, and Carraccio, sheathing his weapon, replied,—"Take it, young prince, and be the pledge exchanged."

Few survived to tell the slaughter of that day; such as were of the victorious shared the spoils of the field. Visconti, and a party of their most distinguished leaders, were proffered reward and protection by the Conte Golfieri; and, with the residue of his followers, they embarked on board a vessel, which, after a few days' uninterrupted sail, anchored in the mole of Palermo. The pride of conquest had swelled the bosom of Paoli, and he thirsted with pride and joy, fatal as had terminated the enterprise, to be the hero of that eventful period. To the Neapolitan his desires were communicated; they were sanctioned, and the friends of Carraccio echoed his exclamations, which announced Golfieri as their conqueror; half the wealth and half the dignities of Palermo's dukedom was the award; honour decreed the pledge; in obedience to such a dictate, Carraccio and his partisans held themselves as dependant upon the bounty and *protection* of the Sicilian, and with the same feeling he undertook to realize their most prominent wishes.

The Conte Golfieri's escape from death and slavery was hailed with enthusiasm by the old Duca; it lived for a time in the bosom of his countrymen; but few there were who had not suffered too much in the loss of their kindred to acknowledge the festivity of such a day.

Upon Carraccio and his "partners in toil," as the courageous refugees to the Sicilian standard, various honors were allotted, and to a certain degree, and for a time, they severally enjoyed the sovereign's munificence. Seven years had elapsed since the memorable era, since then the patronage of royalty had diminished. Carraccio only had been fortunate enough to secure its greater portion; the repining of his fellow refugees was construed into rebellion, and for the crime had suffered condemnation to the gallies; their act of mercy was forgotten; they were held in contempt; on the dependance only of the Neapolitan had they endured an existence; a wretched abode in a remote part of the Province sheltered the remnant of once noble conquest; in bitter contumely they lamented the tie that bound them to Sicilian treachery; but there was a spirit lurking still beneath the ashes of their faded glory, that warmed the heart amidst despair, and buoyed them up with hopes of wealth and liberty. A small secluded cloister was the scene where their woes and captivity were alike deplored: they had assembled earlier than usual, a communication from Carraccio had thrown fire into their bosoms, and they looked for his approach.

The dark wave of the Mediterranean was attaining its brighter hue; the blue streak of morning gradually proclaimed its empyreal sway along the vast space of atmosphere, and the almost unruffled breeze told in the murmuring accents the softness of the hour. Thrice had the refugee, Zestrozzi, ascended a projecting pier to watch the rippling of the current on which was expected the barque of Visconti.—"He comes not," exclaimed he, while his full eye seemed fixed upon the distant shore. "My country, for thrice three burning summers I have beheld thine heights rising from the deep ocean which surrounds thee; oh, what are these eyes doomed to be seared with?—Curse upon this yielding heart, for that hour that marked my tread upon Sicily's margin; realms of pride and scorn, when will the spirit of my country subdue thy haughty tyranny? Visconti, thou hast to answer it. When will the shrieking voices of my comrades hail the conquerors of Sicilian usurpation? Never, never!" The refugee shuddered, and his dark and swarthy countenance endured a painful and submissive smile. He retraced his steps to the colonade, and mingled with his companions.

"Cheer! cheer! Zestrozzi!" warmly articulated Kaled, a Greek partner in his slavery; "this day brings us new intelligence, and new hope, from the trusty Carraccio; see, his letter teems with joyous congratulations; the God of our country forward his prospects!"

Zestrozzi motioned not, but paced in sullen meditation the length of the cloister.

"Zestrozzi, wherefore this silence?" questioned Kaled, "it ill becomes thee; friendship, in bonds like our's, should refrain from mystery, from secrecy, save that of our cause; speak then in affiance to our sacred title, and let the heart of Kaled know at once thy more than common sorrow."

"Insult and scorn have so goaded and overwhelmed my once adamantine bosom, that I scarce care to hold fellowship with existence."

"You are altered much, Zestrozzi, 'tis true; but a soul like thine has yet to triumph in the fall of that captivity which has been our's; the vengeance of heaven has still one shaft remaining, which must, in some eventful hour, be thrown at the proud heart and treachery of Sicily."

The refugee frowned in horrid menace, and his teeth gnashed in maddening rage; the large glistening eye was moistened by a tear.

The heart of Kaled was warm and zealous, his sympathy was awakened at his fellow captive's weakness, and in earnest supplication he demanded its origin.

"'Tis detailed in few words," replied Zestrozzi; "this day numbers the 18th year, Kaled, since my wife gave birth to an infant; its first breath in life solemnized the last of its parent's; three subsequent years called me, in the occupation of my duties, to a distant port; on our passage the vessel was captured by a brig of superior strength, manned chiefly by Sicilian renegades, its valuable cargo plundered, and, with scarcely the means left to satisfy craving nature, we were left on the seas to perish. My child, for the sake of a few rich ornaments attached to its apparel, was torn from me; we survived our fate, but from that day, Kaled, in vain have I sought the form of my offspring; in vain have I endeavoured to trace the little spot which may contain its mouldering resemblance, or receive its human breath."

"Providence, Zestrozzi, by whose everlasting and omnipotent command all things are decreed, may yet bestow upon thee a father's blessing; hope in its righteousness, and in its mercy there yet——"

The sentence was interrupted by the shout of his countrymen, who hailed the presence of Carraccio.

"Welcome, Visconti," vociferated from the lips of the captive band. "Speak, Neapolitan, do we breathe the air of liberty, or has Sicilian pride further torment for our miseries?"

"It will be speedily terminated; the moment dawns that opens a chasm to liberty and independence."

"Carraccio," spoke the Greek Zestrozzi, and he threw a glance of deep inquiry upon the features of the Neapolitan, "speak to us in truth and firmness, nor suffer the hearts of your comrades to moulder through ages of lighting and agonizing hope. Speak, does Palermo's Senate contain bolder men than these around you? Hast thou power to bring it to the trial? Dares Carraccio wield the sceptre of Sicily? Speak, nor hesitate; that even yonder spreading waves may echo again with thanksgiving to Heaven and Visconti."

"Peace," calmly dictated the Neapolitan, "peace, Zestrozzi, nor mar the tidings that breathe of freedom. The dying spirit of Ruggieri is now in haste to unite with its common earth. The proud Golfieri lives successor to Palermo's dukedom; but mark, friends, the covenant to which this man is bound."

"He has forfeited more than Nature can ever create again," roughly remarked Zestrozzi, "what have we in him to look forward to? what have we from him to expect?"

"Wealth and honour," shouted the Neapolitan, "the wretched remembrance of your years of toil and captivity must now be repaid; yes, the pledge must be redeemed."

"True," replied Kaled, "in the hour of danger his life was granted on such condition, but how have we borne it, Carraccio? in torture and horror—the chains of the galley slave—the bleeding lash of its oppressor; and from whence can spring the slightest chance of blessed liberty under the yoke of tyranny like Golfieri's? Luxuries and hypocritical smiles, Carraccio, have weaned you from the interests of your once exalted followers; you have reposed in ease and splendour, and thereby forgotten the iron couch to which we, degraded outcasts, have been pinioned; yes, Visconti, you have indeed forgotten them!"

"Never, by the living Creator of this world's greatness," interjected the Neapolitan, "no bosom that feels like mine contains a heart hotter for vengeance than Carraccio's; let him who doubts, stroke his poniard to its hilt, and reeking it will tell its wrath."

"Rejoice,—rejoice!" unanimously shouted the confederates, and instant silence again marked their attention.

The Neapolitan detailed the various circumstances latterly connected with his confidence to the Conte Golfieri; the commission of crime that had singled out Leontini's destruction, and subsequently the deed which had bound upon his brow the murderer's guilt, in the assassination of Vivaldi. "Revives not this within ye beams of comfort?" exultingly interrogated Visconti, "yes, let it serve to dispel the lethargy which has hitherto closed up the freshness and bloom of souls like thine. In the arms of the rich heiress of Reo Cardoni's unparalleled wealth, he dreams not that the reward of perfidy and insult is so near at hand; this is not all;—his accession to Ruggieri's title is not secure, till the hand of the young Francesca binds it—this was his latest command; the girl was rescued from an untimely grave by the Duca, falling from his gondola, on return from a splendid fete; Ruggieri, at the peril of his life, saved her—the act was never forgotten; a fondness, equal to that of an offspring, was the result, and the Duca received it with a parent's joy; he resolved to perform even a father's duty towards her—he has done it—and the sovereignty of Palermo, and the alliance with the lovely Francesca, are inseparable. To this Golfieri can never arrive, since to the Comptessa Rosalviva he is too irrevocably bound to share Sicilian royalty without her."

"And this, Carraccio, leads to freedom and independence?" doubtfully questioned the half-suspecting Zestrozzi, who had listened with most earnest ardour to the narrative of Visconti.

"It will, it will," he hastily repeated, "listen to its sequel. The soul of this Golfieri is steeped too far in sin to be cleansed. In my charge is deposited the catalogue which tells his progressive list of crime; already is he aware upon what terms only the Dukedom of Palermo can be his; his shallow heart has not strength enough to cause the destruction it pants for, and what is wanting in demoniac contrivance and subtlety of invention the creature that governs his heart essays to effect.

"Seated in uninterrupted enjoyment during the midnight mirth of some since departed hours, the subject was discussed; 'Francesca must be removed,' vauntingly spake the Conte, his brain and senses half stupified with the wine he had swallowed, and turning to his *devoted Carraccio*, as he facetiously termed me, added, 'This can only be successful but under prudence discreet as thine; say then, Visconti, next to sovereignty, can Palermo's proudest title and rank be worth thy keeping?'

"'It can, my lord,' I instantly answered, 'and the light that blazes in thy path shall be extinguished.'

"The Comptessa indulged in a wild and rapturous exultation,

and, throwing herself at my feet, cried, 'Carraccio, thou art our redeemer!!'

"I intimated my command of the hearts and principles of a few trusty associates, and signified that on the grant of *their wishes*, so might the peace and enjoyment of the Conte and Rosalviva be made lasting. I motioned as to my departure to summon the aid of my friends; the resolution charmed them, and we parted. Ruggieri's remains are slumbering in the tomb, and the setting of to-day's sun lights the Conte Golfieri to this our silent retreat."

The refugees looked with eagerness upon the Neapolitan; his air and recital seemed to them alike mysterious. On the mind of some, suspicion of his faith held a trifling sway; other knew his heart too well to wrong him with unjust suspicion, and passively awaited the termination of his harangue.

The Neapolitan resumed,—"On the Conte's introduction to these secluded walls, but a limited number of our partisans must be observable; such of whom the misery and care of nine weary years have rendered haggard and emaciated only must meet the eye of Golfieri. Zestrozzi, you bear but too fatally the marks which the tremendous grasp of wretchedness his inflicted upon you, and to you shall the charge be given of effecting the Conte's purpose."

"What, Carraccio, and is the way to freedom to be gained only by an assassin's deed? My scorched and seared heart revolts even at the crime."

"Hush, Zestrozzi! desist thy fears, nor wrongly anticipate my great and glorious design; no blood shall be spilt, no stain of guilt shall imprint the brow of Carraccio, or one of his friends—the cause ends in triumph—in the face of Heaven it will be acknowledged, and we shall be hailed the annihilators of guilt and atrocity. Witness, great Heaven—witness every power earth can humanize, that to no deed but to liberty and your rights, has Carraccio held himself in justice and honour bound."

A loud and gratifying burst of approbation followed the energy of the Neapolitan, and the bosom of each confederate attained a new and joyous feeling.

"Francesca's supposed death places Golfieri in security over Palermo's dukedom. This is but the work of a few days, and then breathes the blest spirit that welcomes us to happiness. Golfieri once in our power, and Sicily's government is wielded with no other interest but what this shattered and humble roof in the present hour shelters. Remember, confederates, my life and honour is dedicated to this great and justifiable deed; and as I perform my pledge, so may the Creator of man dispose of me! Is there one here who doubts the fidelity of Carraccio?—Is there one whose heart and hands smile not on the cause of redeeming freedom?"

"None! none!" vociferated the whole band, and tumultuous shouts again resounded through the broken arches and avenues of the building. A banquet was served up in an adjoining spacious but dilapidated hall, and Carraccio did the honors of the table. The wine was circulated in abundance, cheered by the melody of those whose voices laid claim to distinction, during which was hailed, in successive repetition,

THE SONG OF FREEDOM*

We have fought for Freedom's boon;
  We have bled, and will be free;
Tho' adverse fortune clouds our noon.
  We will not bow to slavery.
Let us sing, and quaff the wine,
  And make our vaulted cavern ring;
Here we bend at Freedom's shrine!
  To freedom Io-Peans sing!

Time has been when tyrants bled
  By the daring patriot's arm;
Time shall come, when with the dead,
  Golfieri sleeps in endless calm.

Let us sing, and quaff the wine,
  And make our vaulted cavern ring!
Here we bend at Freedom's shrine!
  To freedom Io-Peans sing.

Courage, brothers! tho' we sleep
  Pillow'd on our trusty swords;—
Courage, brothers! tho' we weep

---

* I have to acknowledge to Leigh Cliffe, Esq. Author of "Parga," "Supreme Ron Ton," "Knights of Ritzberg," &c. &c. my obligation for these stanzas, written at a momentary warning.

For broken faith, and blighted words!
Let us sing, and quaff the wine,
And make our vaulted cavern ring;
Here we bend at Freedom's shrine!
To Freedom Io-Peans sing.

Soon will rise the glowing sun
Of liberty, with brighten'd beam;
We are firm, there is not one
Whose slumbers sink in slavery's dream.
Shout and sing, and quaff the wine,
Make our vaulted cavern ring;
Here we bend at Freedom's shrine!
To Freedom Io-Peans sing!

The loud reverberation of applause had scarcely closed, when one of the band announced the approach of Golfieri's gondola. Carraccio hastened to give him escort, and Zestrozzi, with such of his companions as were chosen for the meeting with the Conte, awaited his presence. The name of Golfieri was repeated throughout the abode, as the Neapolitan conducted him to the apartment of their revelry.

"Health and honor to the Conte Golfieri!" shouted Stromboli, who arose, in conjunction with his companions, on the entrance of Paoli. "The health of Golfieri!" resounded the other voices, and, for some few moments, silence was wholly banished. The Conte smiled, and returned a few acknowledgments for these tokens of zeal and respect.

"Sicilians and countrymen!" earnestly exclaimed Visconti, standing amidst their number, "it has already been stated what is the cause that originates the present visit of the Conte Golfieri. His Highness, (for soon will fame and rank so entitle him,) deigns to mingle thus familiarly among you, and to receive from your own lips the promise of allegiance, to the will and desire of which one and all of you will unquestionably profit by. Say then, confederates, is there an arm prepared to do the deed required?"

"There is, illustrious Neapolitan!" rejoined one of the number. "That of Zestrozzi is nerved to acts the most daring."

"To Zestrozzi be the deed consigned," observed Visconti.

The refugee bowed in silent submission.

"But the weapon that can inflict, and not betray?" questioned Golfieri.

"Means more effectual must be adopted, my lord," insinuated Zestrozzi, after a momentary pause. "Linked as you must be," and he surveyed the erect figure of Golfieri with an independence which told the greatness of his soul, "to the existing circumstances, the death of this girl, this Francesca, effected in too sudden and mysterious a manner, may throw even suspicion upon the highest of Palermo's dignity,—yourself, my lord. In order, therefore, that even the corse of the hapless Signora might bear minute inspection, a poison, worked in the most subtle and careful manner, must be administered. Its effect will be gradual and decided;—progressively the fair tinge of health is seen to fade; sickness follows, and in a few subsequent days, death will be triumphant. And so tranquil and mildly will terminate that existence, that no visible trace or livid mark can bear testimony to the act which called the fleeting soul of the young mourner to Heaven. Excessive grief at the lamented loss of Ruggieri must be the presumed cause of her early dissolution, and this once disseminated, the circumstance will soon be as forgotten as the object it is buried with."

"And of all this thou art capable?" demanded Golfieri, and his eyes sparkled with a brilliance that testified every exulting sensation of his heart.

"To all this I bind myself, my lord, and that within forty-eight hours from the period of your command, will be fast lingering the pulsation of the Signora Francesca's heart."

"Excellent inventor!" cried the Conte, "name to Carraccio its worth, and from his hands receive thy reward."

"It shall be so!" muttered the refugee, "we will ultimately share it in thy heart's blood!" Zestrozzi paced the length of the apartment.

The Conte and the Neapolitan stood several minutes in discourse; and at the desire of Golfieri, an order for the payment of five hundred pistoles, was presented to the Greek captive, in token of the estimation of his services. Two other companions were nominated in conjunction with Zestrozzi, and, as the attendants upon Golfieri, they were directed to be habited in the *costume of his household*.

A day was named for their presence at the ducal pallazzi, under the guidance of Carraccio; and with a heart made lighter from care, but more deeply crusted with infamy, the Conte Golfieri, accompanied by the Neapolitan, quitted the refugee abode, and steered for the pallazzi.

CHAPTER V.

There are some moments when the heart stands still,
As if the mighty touch that deigns to fill
Our sands, had left them where they last ran down.

That young lip *must* be lovely; soul, high soul,
Was in the sigh that o'er its ruby stole.

CROLY's *Angel of the World.*

TOO securely in the chains of vice and crime was the soul of Golfieri linked, to start from those ties which had marked him the creature of infamy and destruction. He had pursued the maddened career of his passions, void of reflection, and when he now hesitated to pause upon it, felicity left him no hope, and he rushed still further into the dark void of the future, to hurry from the scenes which hastily had crowded before him. The nuptials with Francesca di Branciforte had become the every-day conversation throughout the province; intended fêtes, public rejoicings, were already in "fancy's eye," for the commemoration of such an event. His mind sickened at the delusion. There was but little left him to resolve upon, and its result thereby required instant conclusion.

To the guidance of Carraccio he held himself wholly subservient; the alliance, then, with Francesca was his first object. Visconti, too, had urged it; by him was pointed out the success attendant, and under such an authority he determined finally to act; yet when he considered upon the resolution of intimating to Rosalviva his intentions, and the prospect of his plans, his heart endured a kind of dread, lest her will and influence would dictate to him to relinquish his designs. He saw upon what precipice circumstance had thrust him; he was too indissolubly united to the embraces and affection of the Comptessa, to execute a single act, or to form a design contrary to her wishes. He was equally in the power, and at the mercy of Visconti, to follow any pursuit opposite to that which he had dictated. By obedience to the latter, he not only reduced the weight of obligation due to Carraccio, inasmuch as he had sworn to realise every promise and every pledge hitherto exacted by the Neapolitan, for the accomplishment of their mutual purposes. He had closed the eyes of the lamented Duca, bound with the most solemn assurances towards his immediate union with Francesca. He felt determined that no obstacle should hazard its completion. The arrangements designed upon for the subsequent removal of Francesca, by the Greek Zestrozzi and his companions, emulated his hopes: and he looked forward to the ceremony that pronounced him at once Duca of Palermo, and Francesca's lord. The time hourly approached, and the funeral torch that lighted Ruggieri to the grave was scarcely extinguished, as the acclamation of Paoli's nuptials were wrung in every ear that hoped for its happiness. The Marquis di Branciforte was distantly related by marriage to the family of Ruggieri; interests and amity had strongly cemented their unity; and in the senate, as well as the confidence of the Duca, di Branciforte had long held the most distinguished rank. Francesca was his only offspring. She was one of Nature's purest stamp. Her mind was wrought principally with those expressions, which ardour and simplicity generally attain at the period of its susceptibility, and what may be termed at the age of its suffering. Her figure was light, easy, and graceful; the etiquette of splendour, nor the vanity of person had not, in the slightest degree, affected it, and her manners and disposition were as amiable as the features through which they were delineated. She had attained her 19th year when the bright ray of conjugal affection had warmed her into the feelings of becoming a wife. It was universally known that Ruggieri had loved with every fondness, and on decreeing her union with Golfieri, he considered that he had bestowed upon her the reward which her merits were entitled to. During a period so lengthened, in which she lived under the smiles of the Duca, she had ample opportunity of tracing the characteristic qualities of his nephew. He was the first object to whom her young heart attached itself. Circumstances but seldom brought them together, and even the interval of such opportunity was brief and limited. Golfieri had ever shewn to her the most marked respect; he had paid her many tokens of kindness and attention, and at times he had seemed to feel in her society a more than common charm. Francesca imagined it so at least; her sentiments conveyed much sympathy towards him, and she conceived they were likely, at some distant period, to meet with an equal return. His fine commanding figure, elegance of manner, and peculiarity of disposition, were the first attractions that lived in her bosom. She cherished in her imagination that his heart, by the influence of time and sensibility, would be wholly her own, and, with its ideal enthusiasm, she encouraged every feeling towards its possession. It was not difficult to trace, after that distance of period, which had first rendered her growing affection perceptible. It was easily perceived the effect which the levity of his manner, or the sullenness of his character, alternately had upon her. She would revel in the luxuriance of the one, and suffer her feelings to be borne away by the melancholy and sadness arising from the other. His dissipation and wildness of character were ultimately not unknown to her, but her soul was too resolutely fixed upon the object of its adoration, to admit of the smallest reproof to deteriorate in the opinion of his value. For months she "pined in secret," keeping her sorrows confined to her own bosom; she little thought how deeply her heart had been lacerated in the struggle. She little supposed that on Golfieri her affections were idly lavished; she did not utterly despair; there was a triumph still in her heart when she caught his smile, and when the effort of opportunity produced even a temporary meeting; her felicity then was too great not to banish the recollection of the wretchedness which his follies (she knew not a term more appropriate, or of a more harsh description, for his failings), and his indifference had repeatedly inflicted.

To a mind gifted with less acuteness of feeling, the various occurrences of life, society, and its pleasures, may effect a kind of renovation; but to a soul beyond the ordinary sphere, there is an attainment of sensibility at once fatal. To this species of sensibility is linked a perpetual chain of miseries and misfortunes; ambition has no lure for its recovery; joy has no charm to wean it from its pent up, and blighted disappointment and hope; its pang and its desolation yields to an apathy and an indulgence where it lingers a victim, a dreadful victim to every sensation of sadness and severity. The sunken eye, the emaciated cheek, and the colourless lip, each proclaims its destiny, and points out the decided termination of its painful existence—to this end the heart and sympathies of Francesca di Branciforte seemed fast approaching. For a time it was supposed that her anxiety, in the hope of Ruggieri's convalescence, and her very ardent care and watchfulness throughout the progressive stages of his malady, had wrought upon her the change visible to every eye. Her parent sought, by every means, to work a recovery, but she was too well aware that the attempt was futile. The charms of variety held out no prospect that seemed to cherish, and when the last remains of the Duca were consigned to its earth, her happiness seemed to fade for ever. Its cause was at length discovered, it was strikingly reprehended. In colours the most darkened was the conduct and depravity of Golfieri painted to her view, every appeal to the sense of her understanding was equally in vain; its indignation and aversion towards the being intended, failed in its attempt—her heart had received its first impression, it was strong, it was not easily to be erased. With Golfieri she had treasured up every fairest hope; in its loss, there was nought else left to desire. This was her situation when her approaching alliance with Paoli became the public theme; its sudden transition was wondrous—her passions were rekindled, the eye brightened, and the heart throbbed with new ardour—the impression upon her spirits was powerful—its effect almost produced delirium—medical aid restored her, and with its tranquillity she welcomed the arrival of that hour which joined her hand with Golfieri. Paoli, during the interval which intervened before the performance of the ceremony, had felt how essential it was to his future prospects, and therefore not only treated her with peculiar respect, but had signified how unmindful he had been of the happiness which Fate, and the blessing of Providence, had at length conferred upon him. "Beloved Francesca," he exclaimed, at an interview in which she seemed to participate with rapturous acknowledgment, "what an age have I not lost in being neglectful to one so kind, so amiable, as yourself; one so devotedly formed to make existence cheerful and happy?" Her heart beat in tumultuous gladness at the confession, and her bright eye turned to his with an expression of sweetest feeling. He kissed her lips with an apparent fondness, and, while he held her to his bosom, rejoined,—"This heart, Francesca, has been shattered indeed, but it is not so thronged with human frailties to be exempt from every claim worth keeping—oh, no!—there is a portion still left deserving the attention and warmth of my Francesca."

The bosom of Francesca was too full to allow a freedom to her happiness.—Tears relieved it from anguish, and she clung more closely to the kind embrace of Paoli. He led her to the altar, an intended sacrifice; to her nuptial couch, without an interfering throb, without a relenting pang.

At the period intended for the funeral rites of Ruggieri, the Comptessa Rosalviva had determined upon a limited visit to a distant part of the country; it was acquiesced in by the Conte, and, under promise of constant correspondence, their temporary separation was considered less important. Three months had gone rapidly over since Paoli's accession to the Ducal dignity; the heat and fondness of Francesca's affection had produced an unexpected and singular feeling in the heart of Golfieri; he essayed to pourtray it with all the warmth and devotion of an earnest sincerity. It was the first moment, during some few recent years, that he had stayed to reflect, or question the innate wanderings of his heart. A kind of releasement from the constant society of Rosalviva, and a portion of indulgence in solitude, up to a certain point, during her absence, had seasoned him, as it were, to a kind of reflection, which, as he entered upon, the more forcibly brought his imagination to that description of sentiment which, till then, he had never known; at least, he had not felt disposed to encourage.

Among the frequent instances of his leisure, he would find himself absorbed in passions the most agitating and oppressive; he would collectively review the dark pages of his past career;—madness marked the recurrence of his crime, and he would rush from the poignancy of his horror, to seek consolement in the pure embrace of Francesca.

On one occasion, he sought her soothing aid with more than common cause. She had reclined in her apartment under the "power of sleep;" her form and features were strikingly impressive and Golfieri gazed upon her with conflicting emotions of sympathy and pity.

The remembrance of Zestrozzi's plan for the termination of her existence, flashed strongly through his brain; the extremes of torture and rhapsody alternately attacked him. In one moment he seemed to cherish the idea that with such ease and certainty the object of his unhappiness could be removed; in the next, his blood would recoil and shrink back through his soul with icy pressure, in thirsting to single out Francesca as its victim.

To these unsettled degrees of misery he was at various times reduced, until he was recalled to those oaths which had been made to Rosalviva. Again he would consider how much she had endured for him, and how much she still doated upon him. Could he breathe a thought that denoted a separation?—No; he still fondly, and with enthusiastic feelings, loved her. He appeared sensible of the impossibility ever to live without her, and he uttered her name with symptoms of the most extravagant affection. His heart throbbed with delight at the announcement of her return to Palermo; he felt resolved that no obstacle should prevent or diminish his love towards her.

The mind of Paoli became at length gradually calm, and he sat down amidst its repose to acknowledge the receipt of Rosalviva's last communication. He knew that the intelligence of his union with Francesca had not reached her; he had neglected, through each of his replies to her epistles, to intimate the event; but, in the present instance, he felt necessitated to make known the occurrence. In the assurance of Rosalviva's concession, as knowing under the existing circumstance by which he was bound, he at once endeavoured to confirm his belief that her smile would not be wanting to render his felicity wholly complete. Free from intrusion, he sketched the subjoined epistle:—

"The moment is awaited with a lover's impatience, that brings with it Rosalviva to the arms of her devoted Paoli;—yes, devoted—and still must ever be, even though circumstances may seem to prohibit such a declaration. Of Golfieri's union with the Signora Francesca, till this moment I have withheld the announcement; start not, Rosalviva! nor suffer a reproach to pass your utterance.

Remember, to you alone am I bound by every tie that can constitute happiness—by every pledge, human or divine! These bonds can never be broken; the heart given to Rosalviva is all her own; his hand was the utmost he could offer to Francesca. Yet, by such an act, Paoli has secured the dignity of his ancestry—the honour of his country. Rosalviva will be proud to acknowledge it; she will prove to him her sense of the felicity which shall mutually live in their bosoms; she will look forward to worlds of purest delight and enjoyment. The appointed moment named by Rosalviva, will meet with an anxious attendance.

"PAOLI."

He dispatched a messenger with the epistle to the Comptessa. On retiring through an obscure piazzi of the palace, the dark figure of the captive Zestrozzi arrested his attention, and he halted some few moments unperceived, to mark its progress. The known features of Kaled were soon after recognized. The refugees hailed each other in stern and unceremonious compliment.

The dim light of the lamps just rendered their motions perceptible, and the Conte awaited the result in suspicious anxiety.

"Hush!" murmured the voice of Kaled, "speak not; a human step has tracked that of mine along the avenues here, with some caution;—hark, Zestrozzi!"

His compassion listened, and a silence, void of the slightest interruption, followed the denunciation.

"The cloister is secure;" pronounced Zestrozzi, first breaking the stillness of the moment; "speak, Kaled,—we may commune in safety; you are resolved?"

"Immoveably—our sorrows are but derided; look at the world of woe that has rolled over our aching brows since the recreant Golfieri deluded us hither, to the commission of a crime he fears to execute. Day has succeeded day, and we see him not, he avoids us; for what is its intent? It is madness to linger further in the uncertainty of a fate humbled like our's. Carraccio, too, is touched with something of human weakness, and heeds not the freezing recollection of our disgrace and injuries."

"Shame! Shame!" cried Zestrozzi, and his voice faltered with convulsed agony; "oh, the years that the spirit of my country has laboured to level the proud boast of Sicilian conquest! It had well nigh attained its long struggled-for glory, but, in the hour of blindness and intoxication, was bartered the honour and achievements of three thousand warriors; the blood-shedding lash, and the cankering fetter have been the reward.—Great God! Do we stand here unmoved? Has heaven no lightning to scathe their walls, and with its appalling vengeance crumble the heart of every Sicilian within its flaming ruins?"

"Peace, peace Zestrozzi! the distant gleam of light speaks the approach of some of the attendants; retire awhile.—Stay, this avenue leads to the citadel—away, away!"

The figures of the two captives were perceived winding through a narrow passage, and the astonished Paoli was left to his own reflections.

"What sacrifice," meditated he, and he gazed fearfully round the cloister, "does the hatred of these refugees design?" His mind again recurred to the foundation of that pledge, upon which the renewal of his existence was gained. He remembered, too, the task by which himself and Carraccio had held them in the fulfilment of; but it had slept in his mind, and the reasonings of honour and humanity had since that period diverted his heart from the pursuit of its intended crime. He seemed to feel some touch of feeling and horror, when he considered that with those creatures he had bartered the blood of Francesca; and as his contemplation was roused from the gulf that yawned for his further perdition, his bosom was not insensible to a throb of gladness that he had escaped its terror.

To pause upon the incidents of the moment was dangerous; the heated enthusiasm and revenge of the refugees was kindling into a flame, that spread itself with contagion and destruction. Paoli's figure was not wholly distinguishable by them; the darkness of the spot, and the appearance of his habit, would render it less so; but then it required a nerveless effort to effect what his ideas were suggesting;—however, he determined to hazard it. Hastily following the direction they had taken, he had not lost many moments when, in a colonade most opportunely obscure, he pronounced the name of Zestrozzi.

"Speak, stranger, the name of him who seems to hold acquaintance with one so dishonoured," harshly spake the refugee, as he turned to the figure of Golfieri.

"'Tis needless, captive; but from the Neapolitan Carraccio, I——"

"Hold, Signore, thou art his friend," interrupted Kaled.

"Or would not have borne this mission," unhesitatingly, and with steady calmness replied the changed voice of Paoli.

"True; and its purport?" angrily muttered Zestrozzi.

"Is to give thee instant revenge."

"Revenge!" shouted the captives, and even through the almost total darkness their large bright eyes flashed with unspeakable fury. "On whom?" questioned they.

"Ask not thus idly," remarked Paoli, "it falls upon him who has done the greatest injury; but, come, the orders of Carraccio must not admit of delay: beneath the portico nearest the palazzi terrace the Neapolitan expects you. The man who arrives first, will await the coming of the others. Much will be done; it will be a moment, refugees, that accomplishes an event which has long been frustrated. Quick! to the portico, and with Carraccio we must counsel. Yonder is the entrance, I will but retrace my steps, and hasten the trusty Neapolitan."

"Be it so," interjected the captive Zestrozzi, "to this meeting with Visconti we yield. Nature, and the feelings of insulted honour, had well nigh taught us to forswear further communion with Visconti. However, this shall be our last." *"It shall be thy last!"* mentally suggested Golfieri, and he enjoyed a kind of triumph that he had so far secured the perfidy of the deluded captives. He pointed the direction onwards, and turning through an opposite angle, he hurried for the obtainment of that power and assistance which would doom them at once to the torture of the traitor's dungeon.

CHAPTER VI.

What proof, alas, have I not given of love?
What have I not abandon'd to thy arms?
Have I not set at nought my noble birth,
A spotless fame, and an unblemished race,
The peace of innocence, and pride of virtue?

Rowe.

THE heat of frenzy which flashed across the brain of Rosalviva, when she perused the communication from Paoli, was immoderate. A myriad of projects and surmises chased each other in perpetual rapidity through her imagination. The union with Francesca, and that during so short a period, and even while the smiles of the Comptessa were cherished by him, was almost a delusion which in vain she essayed to dissolve. Sincere as appeared the language which he had written to her, and much as he had done in the way of proof of his love, the pride and enmity of Rosalviva was too great, of too rancorous a nature, to suffer the heart she had with such sacrifice gained, to be in the keeping of Francesca. She prized the affection of Golfieri beyond every other blessing; certainly, she could forfeit every hope and every felicity rather than lose his attachment. She read every sentence his letter contained with the most profound attention; its tenor breathed every semblance to honour and love; still she feared its association with a heart warm and young as that of the Duchessa. By such a step he had inferred that he had secured the *dignity of his ancestry*, the *honours of his country*; and was Rosalviva unworthy of its participation? Was the illustrious title of Di Branciforte more distinguished than that of Reo Cardoni?

The suspicion of his integrity, and the jealousy of her passions, worked upon her mind most forcibly, and she felt all the taunt of created and unforgiving insult. To live the acknowledged mistress of Paoli Golfieri, her soul would never stoop to. "Unkind and unfeeling Paoli!" added she, "what a mind and sensibility have you not wounded! What a soul of love, passion, and enjoyment, have you not heedlessly crushed! Oh, shame! shame! that it should come to this! that it should be known that Rosalviva had placed her heart's doting existence upon the caprice of such an imbecile. In poverty or in disgrace she would have snatched thee to her bosom, and cherished thee fondly there, reckless of the threats of a world! Thus we would have lived happily, and our bliss should have been a foretaste of that of eternity! Paoli, what hast thou done? Peace, peace, my lacerated heart! yet break at once, rather than beat with such direful anguish."

Tears gave a temporary check to the impulse of her passions. What a desolate and blighted scene presented itself to her view. In vain she tried to soothe the violence of her agitation; in vain she tried to believe that his heart was indeed wholly wedded to her, and that Francesca could never hold the least control over it. The tenderness and genial disposition of a female like Francesca, the domestic endearments, and the ardour of a woman whose first love was given to the man to whom she was united, were too powerful appeals to meet with resistance; and however enthusiastic might continue the affection of Paoli towards the Comptessa, she knew there must be *some* moments in which his mind would wander; and in the arms of his wife, her sweetness and her fondness, he would find an irresistible charm. She shrank from the reflection; her whole soul and faculties seemed to be absorbed in the agitation and alarm she endured. When she glanced upon the ruins of what might have been her future happiness, necessity, and the poignant feelings caused by slighted affection, rendered her almost desperate.

She sat herself down upon a couch, and wrote to Golfieri the following epistle:—

"Duca Paoli,—What pangs of horror hath not thy cold and merciless conduct struck into the bosom of Rosalviva! What have you not inflicted upon her heart, which is inseparable from your own! Is this the reward due to dotage like mine? Is this the fate it merited? Can you speak the name of Rosalviva, without feeling emotions of tenderness and compassion? How can you add insult to injury? How think to tempt me with the empty sound of an affection you feel not for me in your heart? Mine has been too sacredly reserved for thee; thy faith thou hast cruelly broken.

What! and since Rosalviva cannot hold thy heart in defiance of another's claims, shall she pamper it with temporary gratification?—never! Didst thou think that, lost as *she* has been to reason and the dictates of prudence, she could further abandon her dignity, to acknowledge herself publicly the mistress of Paoli? Weak and misguided man! you ought to have estimated somewhat more correctly the worth of her you think thus to delude, and to have known the pride of that soul you have conquered with such facility. Foolish infatuation, which compels me to speak what I feel, under circumstances like these which I endure through your duplicity;—yes, foolish indeed, that even amid torrents of tears, extorted from my heart, it bleeds for thee still. Shame on this insufferable and wretched weakness! Let me console myself with the thought, that my heart can cherish hatred as powerfully as once it did love. Yes, this will, in some degree, repay me for the broken faith and forfeited honor of one who knew not its value. Receive this letter as the last communication between us, until the period arrives that my vengeance degenerates into calmness; till then, we meet no more! You ought, at least, to have known that Rosalviva is not a being easily to be trifled with; you ought to have been the last in existence who should have attempted it; you have succeeded so far, but its result is yet to come. Revel, then, in the more chaste embraces of thy wife, but believe me, Golfieri, the day will arrive which will bring atonement for the insults and injuries lavished on

"ROSALVIVA."

The husband of Francesca was indulging in her caresses, when the unexpected reply of Rosalviva was presented to him. His eye but for a moment glanced upon the superscription, and tremblingly he hurried to his closet. He perused its contents; his bosom was torn with the severity its sentiments conveyed; he endeavoured to restrain the burst of passion that blazed within him, and in a paroxysm of rage and despair uttered,—"No—she will not hate me!"

"Hate thee!" murmured Francesca, who had, at the moment of Paoli's agitation and mysterious departure from her presence, pursued his steps, desirous to learn its cause. "Hate thee!" and her soft and delicate hand pressed that of Golfieri, "who could hate thee?" The artlessness of her manner, and the divine countenance that was bent upon his, softened for a moment his bewildered ejaculations.

"Peace, Francesca!—I am not unused to these touches of frenzy; forgive me," and the visage of Paoli became fixed in mental and gloomy abstraction.

The tender Francesca endeavoured, by every affectionate and gentle means, to soothe the discomfited feelings of her husband;— "Nay, 'tis cruel," she added, "to withhold from me the cause of this unhappiness; tell it me, and I will bear thy suffering with patience and resignation, be it but contributable to your comfort."

"Oh, thou art worthy a better heart!" inwardly rejoined Paoli, and his sorrowing eye was fixed on her smiling and cheering countenance.

"Come, do speak to me, Paoli," endearingly solicited Francesca.

"I will; but think not of these wild remarks; I am calm. I will but retire awhile, and all will again be happy. We shall meet, Francesca, at supper, in the saloon; till then, do not consider my absence irksome."

"Francesca cannot help feeling it so; but as it is your wish, Paoli, she will not oppose it."

Golfieri faintly pressed her warm lips, which were offered to meet his kisses, and with an air of apparent tranquillity, he quitted the apartment.

The distraction of Paoli's mind may easily be imagined; his brain seemed racked with its weight of anguish, and the blood rolled heavily across his heart in painful and contending throbs. He rushed from the pallazzi to Rosalviva. He threw himself at her feet, and, pressing her hands with much ardour, while tears escaped from his swollen eyes, pronounced, "Rosalviva! how have you wronged me; how harsh are thy resolves to him who cares not for life were it not in your keeping; indeed, I am not deserving of these charges."

"Hush!" indignantly replied the voice of Rosalviva; "this is not a time for the display of passion and feeling so little cherished; have some commiseration for the sufferings of a heart-broken woman, and let this interview be at once terminated—leave me."

"Never, Rosalviva; no power can part us."

"Insensible being! thy conduct has done it, and thy vaunting is but folly and insanity."

"Oh, no; at your feet, Rosalviva, in the sight of heaven, I renounce it; I am your's; death only can prohibit our eternal amity; how have I not sworn?"

"And how hast thou not annihilated its allegiance? What canst thou offer now to one like Rosalviva? Thinkest thou her caresses could be mingled with the feminine blandishments of the object that is termed thy wife? Could Rosalviva's kisses waft away the sweetness imprinted by those of Francesca? Never would she stoop to hold affection on such pitiable terms.—Rise, Duca Paoli; nor all thy newly acquired splendour, nor all thy honours, can give a charm to a heart like Rosalviva's.—Retire, then, and give me cause to forget the name of one so worthless; hence, perfidious fool!"

The voice and countenance of the Comptessa attained an almost appalling emotion. The Duca interrupted her, at the same time feigning a kind of command and courage, in the which he had hopes to profit, and, under its mingled feelings, he clasped with vigour the arm of Rosalviva—a look of resentment aided his efforts, he added, "Beware how you also wound the sentiments of a man who has known what it is to distractedly love you."

"Wouldst thou threaten me?" scornfully replied the Comptessa; "how dost thou think that the menace of a being capable of forfeiting the ties of honour and affection, can be in the least dreaded?—Miserable supposition! 'Tis thou who hast most to dread; 'tis thou who, although now vainly dressed with bridal happiness, may, by the morrow's eve, be wrapt in thy winding sheet."

"The will of heaven can extend the same interposition towards yourself, Rosalviva, was it so ordained, and to all of earth's creatures; therefore seek not to sound alarm in such seeming phantasies."

"I indulge not in phantasies; what voice can speak of the murder of Leontini? what tongue can relate Vivaldi's death? would not this public detail rob the bride, Francesca, of her recently enjoyed festivity? would not this be the summons to thy grave?"

"It would, indeed!" mentally exclaimed the disconsolate Paoli, and the remembrance of those events, the remembrance, too, of the deed which brought Cardoni to the tomb, hurried across his mind, and for some few moments it was overwhelmed in abstraction and horror. His heart seemed to sicken within him when he looked at the power of Rosalviva's malignity. His eyes seemed to swim in terror and embarrassment; they turned from her gaze, and while her impressive and avengeful menace rang in his ear, it was in vain that he tried to dispel the throbs of anguish that thronged tumultuously upon his swollen heart; his soul perceptibly acknowledged its subservience, and his only refuge was to seek conciliation, rather than oppose it. In a transport of agony and enthusiasm he threw himself upon her bosom; the tone of his voice faltered, his spirits seemed wholly broken, he plaintively uttered, "Rosalviva, that the hour should be known in which a meeting like the present should be our's. Oh God! can it indeed be possible?"

"It is possible," replied the Comptessa, "but you have been its accomplisher, Golfieri," her resentment somewhat lessened as she already witnessed the tears fast rolling down the cheek of Paoli.

"Indeed you wrong him, Rosalviva, in this cruel suspicion of his fidelity."

"Psha! does it not speak its own tale? needs there further conviction than what has hitherto unfortunately been deduced? What can thy alliance with the Signora Francesca otherwise pronounce! all that can be done by a man of honour has been done; sufficient proof of sincerity towards the woman he reveres! Of what avail can it be to Rosalviva, to boast that the heart you have pledged to her cannot be redeemed? Insensibility of human weakness! how doth it affect me, when I pause to think on such duplicity."

"Duplicity was never intended towards thee, Rosalviva. A proof of my sacred and still unbiassed affection for you may be easily recorded; name but one act which thy will can desire, and if the ability of man can render it effectual, such an act, Rosalviva, is your own Paoli ready to undertake."

A pulsation of secret joy animated the bosom of the Comptessa, as she heard the sentiments of Golfieri. Feelings which she had distantly cherished, and which only wanted some perfect colouring for their existence, now dawned upon her imagination with a sensibility she had hitherto but feebly experienced. Passions that pictured the extent of her anticipations were now before her in the shape of reality.

The rank of Palermo's Duchessa was a gratification her pride would have endured any penalty, any suffering to obtain; it had constantly been the utmost of her hopes. Amidst all her hours of pleasure and dalliance with Paoli, there was ever earnestly kindling within her bosom sparks of ambition that would eventually be lighted up, and as the Duchessa of Paoli she had looked with strengthened confidence. The terms which Ruggieri had drawn for Paoli's security of it were at once the annihilation of Rosalviva's prospects; this she heeded not; Paoli loved her, and every other attainment was a mere trifling consideration. But what was her astonishment on receiving the intelligence, and from Paoli too, that Francesca shared his nuptial couch. The feelings of an insulted and neglected woman are of but one kind, and such feelings were cherished by Rosalviva to their utmost inspiration. The flush of enterprise exhilarated her mind and spirits with unusual joy, and in her dark brilliant eyes shone all the fire and enthusiasm of her soul. The present moment was a triumphant one. She had feared that since Paoli had evinced strength of resolution to seek unity with the hand of another; he would also cease to acknowledge the power which, up to such a period, had cemented them. Her wishes seemed to be approaching towards their attainment, and she hesitated not to turn them to the best advantage. "There is but one condition," she pronounced, detaining with a slight pressure the hand of Golfieri, "on which our future intimacy is dependant."

"Speak it, Rosalviva, and it is done!"

"Stay, Paoli, this exclamation implies too much of wildness, and I may add weakness, to be admitted as the inviolable sentiments of your heart."

"Nay, believe me, Rosalviva, it is indeed sincerity; hasten to put it to the trial."

"I will," exclaimed the Comptessa, and a smile of the most expressive meaning seemed to give her beautiful features an additional lustre. She bent her eyes attentively on those of Paoli, and, in accents of firmness, she uttered,—"and Golfieri will not repent of his promise?"

"He cannot, if Rosalviva still will love him."

"Enough—in few words, Paoli, your wife Francesca must yield her rank to the claim of Rosalviva——ha! you hesitate. I imagined how readily thy proofs would be given," tauntingly concluded the Comptessa.

"And how," apostrophised Paoli, heedless of the scornful remark, "is Francesca to be removed?"

"Canst thou propose no plan that will decidedly realise it?" insinuated the Comptessa.

A pause of some moments ensued, and she surveyed his varying change of countenance, during its silence, with perfect calmness. "Speak, Paoli, does it require so much deliberation?"

"Indeed I am ignorant of such power that can, for the present, secure our hopes," expressed Golfieri, his heart encountering with various acute sensations, as to the purport of Rosalviva's designs.

"What! and has the angel form of thy Francesca so warmed thy heart that it ceases to pulsate, unless in communion with her's? *Thou*, Golfieri of all mankind, to be *ignorant* of the means which could render happiness lasting. I must think that the affection of your wife has already bound you too firmly within its embraces to study ought beyond it. There was a time when every difficulty vanished to the obtainment of Rosalviva's desires; but I will terminate a discourse so unworthy, so unprofitable—listen, Paoli—to this resolve you have brought me—to this hardness of heart your conduct, and your sense of *sincerity* has bound me—thank thyself only for the duty I would impose upon you, either it must be indisputably fulfilled, or this moment separates us for eternity."

A few moments delayed her utterance; the imagination and sympathy of Golfieri were mixed up with painful apprehensions, and he awaited her conclusion with sensible emotion.

"Yes, for eternity," resumed the Comptessa, "and then our suffering shall be,—but I deviate. Francesca must die!"

Paoli started with horror, a convulsive tremor seized him, and he stood for some length of time unable to reply.

Rosalviva gazed upon him with savage feelings; she could but despise the hesitation of the soul which, she had believed, accorded wholly with her own; "yes," she repeated, "Francesca must die!"

"No, no, Rosalviva, I shrink from the sound of murder; you *must* lose me,—we part for ever!"

"For ever!" and the interjection had rendered her desperate, "Golfieri! forbear this ribaldry, suffer me not to think that the spirit of your country hath lost its lustre. Oh, no, surely not; in you there still must live a soul, capable of feeling towards me, or we could not have so fondly loved. See, Golfieri, if example be wanting, to stir those latent sparks within you, I,—Rosalviva,—the once envied heiress of Romagno, will dare the menials to the task; and although the wheel should break each joint her Creator moulded, she would smile only at the feeble attempt of punishment,—punishment formed for cowards only, whose souls never knew the bliss we have shared!"

The Conte Golfieri shuddered.

"If that be not enough," resumed the masculine voice of Rosalviva, "ask me to sheath this weapon," and she snatched a poniard worn by Paoli, "in my heart. Ask me, alone and unprotected, even amid the horrors of night, even when angels guard the innocent, to hasten to the pillow of the Duchessa, and at one blow destroy my cares, my hatred, and I will do it; aye, tremble not, I will do it. The love of Golfieri inspires me to acts the most daring; remember what it has already done, and say,—say, am I not more than woman?"

"Fiend! fiend!" mentally shouted the Duca as he fell irresistibly in her embrace, amid the wild unmeaning strain of laughter that concluded her daring sentiments.

Rosalviva, fixing her dark eye on the object of her enthusiastic adoration, whispered,—"Golfieri, how frigid is thy disposition, how indifferent thy manner towards the woman who has sacrificed every feeling to prove her doting fondness; think on the eve of——"

"Hush, hush," vaguely interrupted Golfieri, "I have still a sense of shame within me; do not awaken it: your own conscience may recoil!"

"Conscience! think me not the timid fool to start at such fantasy; no, love like mine has no compunctious throb, and any thought of fear is momentarily hushed in its pleasures. There was a time when my bosom shrunk from pursuits dissonant to what is idly termed morality and virtue; and, in such a time, I adored with an affection pure as 'twas ardent; you, Golfieri, was its object, its sole, decided and envied possessor; the ripening bloom of its sensibility was nearly blighted, and a short period taught me to regret its fallacy. In that interval, what did I not suffer? Oh, I still feel all its horrors, yet again would I endure their pressure, to merit one smile—one hope of thy confidence. What, Golfieri, do I ask, that you cannot bestow? What have I not undergone, I repeat, but to live for this moment? and where,—where is that soul I had believed was so indissolubly entwined with mine? In mercy, speak! Your coldness, your silence wounds me more deeply than all. Speak, Golfieri!"

"Review my situation," exclaimed the Duca, "behold the circumstances Fate has riveted upon me. How, Rosalviva, are they to be dispelled? How repay thy ardour? the unquiet spirit of my wife would haunt me for ever!—oh, I cannot be *her murderer!*"

"Cursed ingratitude! memory blot its baseness, erase it from the events of the past, and let me not think on the wretched heartbroken creature which Golfieri has made me. Great God! and even my unmeritable woes will not claim his pity; miserable, degraded Rosalviva!"

She had appeared unmindful of the acknowledgments of the Duca; tears flew rapidly along her cheek. He was still in her embrace, his head and heart numbering unceasing pangs, and while he gazed on the same features that early days had given her, but pale and marked with anguish, he felt her misery in acute vibration with his own. The tears stole insensibly from their concealment, and he pressed the parched lips of his still-existing love, with agonizing fondness. He stated his desire to secure her happiness, his wealth might fully warrant it; and he rendered to her its sole use.

"Hush! when you speak in language like the present, you must be forgetful to whom it is addressed. Can fortune bind up the torn heart of a Rosalviva? Pitiable suggestion! Even did my necessities require pecuniary aid, the supplies of a Golfieri would be their last acceptance; but, thank heaven, I need them not; the death of Cardoni gave me all that my soul could wish. An age has revolved since your vows and promises won upon my belief, some portion of them must be repaid, and on such an expectancy I again extend my claim."

A considerable length of time had passed since the St. Rosalia Convent had closed her vespers, and the gray mist of morning seemed fast approaching, before the Conte was mindful of such an elapse.

He intimated his wish of departure, with a promise that the subsequent day should be devoted to her alone. The agitation of his mind was excessive, and it was with faltering accents he submitted to her the necessity of his quitting the palazzi. He was conscious of the uneasiness that would exist in the bosom of his wife, for so unusual an absence; he knew that her affection for him was too ardent to be disturbed by a thought of inattention, and the more acutely he knew she must feel her situation.

"I *must* leave you," emphatically spoke the Duca, "some trifling sense of duty and respect require my presence elsewhere; the domestics will have retired, and——"

"Evasive and paltry apology!" uttered Rosalviva, in a tone of absolute sarcasm, her action prohibiting the conclusion of Golfieri's sentence. "I can read the artifice sufficiently correct, believe me. It is your wish, then, that this should be our last meeting."

The Duca was silent.

"You still hesitate. Fear not to reply; I can imagine its purport, and since it is your decided wish, go to the arms of your doting bride; in her kisses banish the remembrance of mine; but hold their existence not wholly pure, nor think them lasting; I can destroy them!"

"Rosalviva talked of love and happiness," replied the Conte, "a few prior moments notified her hopes of felicity for ever, with the object she now threatens to destroy. Is it worthy of her superior soul to act with such severity?"

"You voluntarily encounter with it. If ingratitude can shew itself so manifest in the heart of Golfieri, he surely cannot think Rosalviva cruel, when she gives to justice its victim.

"Can you be speechless?" again resumed Rosalviva, after a pause of mutual silence, "think, Golfieri, of the disgrace that surrounds ye; be not callous to its sting, but avert it, or speedily behold thyself the fallen, debased, and ruined descendant of thy once illustrious ancestry; think, too, of the curses of your wife, the shrieks of your degraded offspring, which will hiss upon the very scaffold, and——"

"Spare me! spare me this reproach!" franticly pronounced the Duca, whose inward feelings were harrowed at her revengeful menace.

"Fool! thou hast merited its utmost pang; it will in some degree solace the pain my pride has suffered, in loving one so weak, cold, and unmindful as Golfieri. Oh, it will indeed be happiness, to know that for *virtue's* sake the dukedom of Palermo must be consigned to possessors more worthy; for *virtue's* sake thy wife must bear the contempt of pity, the sting of scorn."

"And these are *thy* sentiments, Rosalviva?"

"Yes, Golfieri, and so long as your heart may retain its present pulsation, you will deceive yourself in thinking contrary of mine; my sentiments, baneful as you may consider them, are begotten by your obstinacy, your weakness, your ingratitude; thank thyself only for all thy sufferings, present or future."

Rosalviva found that the terror of her language, which had marked their early meeting, was of no avail; she found it difficult to extract from him the slightest observation of renewed attachment; her soft and languishing intercessions for his future esteem were lost upon him, and not until she had recourse to the daring principles which her heart maintained, and which she fearlessly expressed, could she awaken the soul of Golfieri from its apparent lethargy.

The perturbed state of Golfieri's mind was witnessed by her with gratification, too certain how much he valued Francesca, and equally sensible how anxiously his heart seemed to yield in sensitive throbs for her.

The solemn and meditating manner in which he traversed the apartment, fully pourtrayed his internal sensations; and though Rosalviva breathed curses on the object that elicited them, still she felt a secret delight that Golfieri was so firmly in her power. "Yes, yes," she uttered, amid the ebullition of her feelings, unable to give them concealment, "thou art truly in the power of Rosalviva; *her* voice can load you with infamy; by *her* authority a Golfieri perishes upon the scaffold."

The Duca heard the remark in painful silence, his heart was

overwhelmed. "True," he mentally apostrophised, "I am indeed the sunken wretch she pictures; oh God, what will be the torture of Francesca's heart, on finding it wedded to such misery!" his hands pressed his aching head, and he staggered to a couch in distressing anguish.

Rosalviva feared lest her impetuosity should be too harshly received, and, instead of her threats appalling him into a concession to her wishes, they might act with a contrary effect; she, therefore, softened her tone, and, in a voice of affecting tenderness, a smile playing on her lips, and taking his hand, cried, "Golfieri, this grief affects me; why should hearts moulded as our's are, feel one rending throb? Desist from the indulgence of this anguish. I will be all that you would wish; it remains with yourself to command *your* happiness—to command mine. If the heat of passion has betrayed me to give utterance to sentiments which calmer moments would bid me to destroy, Golfieri will surely pardon it; a heart wreathed as your's must ever be with Rosalviva's, cannot long suffer, without a mutual sensibility, and such a sensibility is far from my desire to excite; speak to me, and let all be forgotten!"

"Rosalviva, that heart is breaking; you have disclosed too much to admit of its again hoping for one gleam of quietude."

"No, be Heaven my sacred witness," replied the Comptessa, "thy offences shall repose in this heart for ever, and with it moulder—promise me but your's and the Duchessa's friendship."

"The friendship of my wife!" in hurried accent questioned the Duca, surprised at the request.

"The friendship of thy wife," repeated Rosalviva, and her large dark eye flashed an unusual brilliance on the timorous gaze of Golfieri,—"is it so incomprehensible, or is the title I wear unworthy of the communion?"

"No, no,—but——"

"Wherefore such evasion? I ask, since I cannot hope for more, I ask a mutual friendship. Francesca is unacquainted with your present victim to receive her with coldness and animosity!"

"But that of your's?" interrupted Golfieri.

"Shall be forgotten; yes, my heart will relent, and I shall live to promote your mutual happiness—in your confidence of such, Paoli, the contract of our amity shall be lasting."

"I could be happy were such a declaration sincere," pronounced Golfieri, with a sigh of mixed feeling.

"Golfieri, add not insult to my sufferings; when was Rosalviva known to practise duplicity?"

"True," murmured Paoli, "it is thy wish, then, that from this moment our joint felicity should be registered!"

"Firmly so!" and, in the assurance of his visit being repeated on the morrow, she suffered him to depart, exulting in its hope that seemed to cheer it onwards to the completion of her invidious purposes.

Golfieri, amid the throng of mingled sensations, hurried to the ducal pallazzi.

CHAPTER VII.

"Her soft voice sunk in broken sighs,"
Half rapture, and half agonies;
Her moist blue eyes were shut in tears.

THE CELT'S PARADISE.

O, melancholy love; amidst thy fears
Thy darkness, thy despair, there runs a vein
Of pleasure like a smile, like a smile 'midst many tears.

BARRY CORNWALL.

THE arms of Francesca welcomed the restless and uncalmed bosom of Golfieri; she kissed with connubial joy the cheek which already wore the character of sorrow, and, as her rich beaming eye was settled, in earnest gaze, upon his, she tenderly inquired the cause of his sadness.

A profound silence marked the interrogatory of Francesca. Paoli seemed absorbed in his cares, till at length the incessant entreaties of his wife extorted from him some few vague expressions. "Fear nought, Francesca; fatigue, in the discharge of public duty, has depressed, in some degree, my usual spirits; rest and quietude will compose them, and all will again be well."

"It will, it will, dearest Paoli;" the virtuous and unsuspecting girl testified her hope and rapture in the full warmth of her fond heart.

How pure, how adulating was the mind and perfection of such a woman; how opposite to those of Rosalviva. With Francesca Nature had diffused every charm to inspire love and admiration; since her alliance with Golfieri she had improved both in spirits and sympathy; it was almost a cherub countenance, moulded with such sweetness, such mildness and resignation, and there beamed so much of truth and simplicity about it, that no being capable of susceptibility could have marked those features, without acknowledging the value of the soul through which it shed its lustre. Equal to her personal attractions were those of her heart; it had been educated under too delicate a tutorship to be impaired; it had been warmed by every moral and religious tie, and to Heaven and her father she had divided, during the years of her infancy, her most attentive duties. The victim of a malignant disorder, the Marquis de Branciforte mourned, at an early period of his alliance, the death of the mother of Francesca; he survived her loss, and to his child he looked forward with a parent's fondest hope, when all other objects and allurements seemed cold and worthless to the heart. Francesca was his only offspring; it is not to be calculated upon otherwise but that he pursued every method that could instruct and instil into her young mind the reverence due to her God; he knew that her other qualifications, which must follow, would spring from a tendency to every goodness. During her abode at the ducal pallazzi, she was scarcely known beyond the child of solitude. She had felt but little charm in the pageantry and gaiety of the court; her mind willingly exchanged its pleasures for scenes of retirement and duteous affection, and, until an advanced age towards maturity, it had never felt one throb dissonant to its earliest feeling. The mind and sympathy of Paoli at that period appeared joined with her own, and she looked upon him as a brother—a companion; age mellowed that disposition, and she became sensible of a passion devoted only to him.

She gazed upon him, as he still lay reclined on her bosom; she viewed him as the sole monarch of her existence. The storms of fate, the clouds of misfortune, would have held no controul over an affection like her's; whatever were his vices, they were of too light a nature to be placed in competition with his personal merits. Slander had no voice for her belief, and whenever his heedless career struck upon her fancy, her soul vindicated his with all the nobleness and fondness of the most distinguished and careful susceptibility. Had fortune forsaken him; had crime aspersed him; had all the horrors of poverty and disgrace hovered round him, it would have been then that her heart could have felt, and would have shewn the more tenderness towards him. The idea that Paoli could be capable of a depraved action,—an ignoble project, never was known to enter her imagination; he was too good, she would exclaim, to give encouragement to vitiated principles; and if he failed in shewing the warmth her confidence merited, she considered it want of opportunity, rather than inclination, that prohibited the feeling; she seemed to feel satisfied since their union; that he was, indeed, all she could wish; and she looked over the few petulant incidents that would occasionally ruffle his spirits and temper, with patience and resignation.

At the commencement of their alliance, Paoli certainly had wandered beyond the sphere in which Francesca reigned; it is known how much his attentions and kindness were bestowed upon her; progressively, however, the influence of Rosalviva again prevailed; he would at times consider that, to a soul like Rosalviva's, and to the enthusiasm which she had manifested, the excellences of Francesca formed but a slight comparison; indeed, he viewed her as the daughter of simplicity and artlessness, and however apparent as might seem her most engaging qualities, they were of too different a nature to take lasting impression in the bosom of Golfieri.

In the meantime, Francesca had the more assiduously devoted herself to the task of insuring the security of his more social and genial virtues; it was not altogether unsuccessful, and, contrary to his expectations, his heart yielded to a sort of emotion that felt some animation in her presence, and some sense of pleasure in her attachment. The mild and endearing sentiments of Francesca, contrasted with those of the Comptessa, were denoted in such incalculable extremes, that Paoli would frequently, in the midst of his cares and occupations, feel nearly overwhelmed in contemplation upon that disposition which might be estimated as the most pleasing to the fine feelings and happiness of human nature. His soul and existence was irrevocably chained to that of Rosalviva; to think slightly of her extraordinary and energetic habits and principles; he was likewise equally sensible as to the kind of regard and feeling towards Francesca, to admit of the perpetration of any act that could threaten her felicity. In this state of uncertainty was the mind and decisions of Golfieri bound. Different were those of Rosalviva; the sensibility of her heart was awakened to new and implacable sensations; there was the keen framing anguish of vengeance and hatred coiling round her bosom; the thought that Paoli could have entertained a momentary wish towards the happiness of another object, she never conceived would have been cherished by him. She was slighted, and now questioned her panting soul, "To what scornful and degraded rank does he not seek to point out for me? Fool! dost thou think Rosalviva has so little pride as to acknowledge subservience to Francesca?" The idea maddened her, and a wild chain of resolutions were drawn across her imagination.

There was nothing now seemed capable of restoring the affection of Paoli in terms of its former value; the only chance of redeeming its early state was the ceasing to know that one like Francesca existed; but she thought his heart was cold and benumbed to any act that could produce it. Images of frightful and malignant tendency sought creation in her brain, and, dreadful as many of them appeared, she felt an animated throb of joy and satisfaction at the probable hope that such as were most transporting would, at length, have free limit. Again she would reproach the coldness of Paoli's attachment, and her soul spurned at the idea that yielded to her even his most refined sensibility at the expence of friendship with Francesca. She was weary nearly with the burden of her imaginary and avengeful schemes, and chose to give them repose in the welcomed wanderings of sleep.

Matters of import had, during the few latter weeks, engaged the attention of the Neapolitan Carraccio, and, for a time, the completion of his designs were, in some degree, abandoned. The termination of his engagements brought with it the prospect of his wonted glory; he sought the captive Zestrozzi and his companion. Their absence confused him, and he feared lest they had been converted to a "more righteous cause," or had suffered for the probable heat and rashness of their schemes. The pallazzi was carefully searched, but no traces of the refugees offered. Paoli had confined the secrecy of their confinement within his own breast. Carraccio endeavoured, by distant meanings, to extract from Golfieri the fate of Zestrozzi; it was evaded by the Duca, and not until a period of some length, did he obtain the slightest clue to their suffering. His bosom yielded to an agonizing throb, at the reflection that, to his charge rested all the injuries of the unfortunate captives. His blood rushed in torrents through his veins, at the indignation he felt heaped upon them, in thus neglecting, even unwillingly, the liberty and honour of his once exalted companions. To no being was entrusted the keys of their dungeon. The daily portion of subsistence was conveyed to them through an aperture or iron grating, and beyond the visage of their keeper, nor light of heaven nor human eye ever beamed upon them.

The wretched Kaled had sunk under the burden: he died with the curse of Carraccio upon his lips. His fellow-captive daily breathed the same imprecations.

The silence of death reigned through the vast abyss, which still immured the wasting remains of Zestrozzi. The Neapolitan hurried to the cell. In the hour of conviviality he had introduced the subject of the refugees' absence to Paoli; their real fate was detailed. The Neapolitan willingly subscribed himself devoted to the termination of their existence.

Paoli feared him too much to express his doubts; but his suspicions had been awakened already, and he looked upon the wary Neapolitan with eyes of distrust and dissatisfaction. Arming himself with a poniard, he moved closely in the steps of the once worthy confidant.

Zestrozzi's dungeon was gained by Carraccio, and applying the key to its immense grating, it slowly gave him ingress to the horrible and almost superhuman abode. The cell was spacious; at the further end a flight of stone steps branched into an inner dungeon. The Neapolitan surveyed it with terror. Stretched and mutilated with the convulsions of a struggling death, lay the body of Kaled. From the appearance of the corse, its decease had been of recent date. A cold insensate thrill of disgust and stupor clogged the blood flowing on the Neapolitan's heart, and his eye measured the opposite angle of the cell with gloomy horror. Nearer towards the entrance of the dungeon, extended on an iron pallet, was the once powerful figure of Zestrozzi. Sleep had given a temporary relief to his cares.

Carraccio mused upon the withered and dejected appearance of the captive. "This also adds to the list of thy crimes, reckless Golfieri," uttered he, still bent over the body of Zestrozzi. "Look, look at another of thy deeds, and ask thyself what must be their award?—Death, Paoli, and damning tortures."

The exclamation, pronounced with all the feeling and bitterness of Carraccio's wrath, echoed in dismal but loud appeal throughout the cavern; its tones awakened the dreaming Zestrozzi; he moved. Carraccio retired behind a massy column, and shading his light, listened for the captive's emotion.

Fear, reproach, shame, and horror, had bound up the feelings of the Neapolitan, and he shrank from his presence with a momentary sense of awe.

A hollow and heavy groan escaped from Zestrozzi, and in solemn and distinct accents he murmured,—"Dark, dark still; speak, Kaled! No, that breath, that soul, is gone now; I only remain to own fellowship with a world, a perfidious world! Oh, come, minister of death, and claim the hovering spirit of one so accursed and betrayed; welcome, thou paragon of terrors!—None can give thee more welcome than Zestrozzi! Yes, friendly terminator of wretchedness and suffering, hither tread through these black shades and we will part not. Thou canst not cheat me,—thou *wilt* not; I will join thee through worlds of indefinable and unfathomable creation!"

The captive paused, and the oppressive struggle his breath seemed to endure, pronounced his near approach to eternity.

"And yet methought I dreamed; yes, methought that after worlds of pain and torture had made their pastime, and hurried me to the extended rack, methought even then the recreant Carraccio burst forth to my rescue; my chains were broken, and with his nerved arm he dragged me through heaps of slain, mangled and half emaciated victims! My brain scorched, and I shouted, Where, monster of iniquity, am I doomed?—what new horror awaits the deceived and degraded Zestrozzi? Ha, my brain seems bound with bands of unquenched fire!—Oh, oh!"

The dying refugee groaned in dreadful anguish. "The hard

iron grasp of death now clutches me.—Hold!—what art thou?" The strained eyes of Zestrozzi were fixed in intent gaze upon the Neapolitan, who had advanced from his concealment, and threw himself beside the pallet of his dying companion.—"Speak!" the captive reiterated, and the convulsed flush of madness lighted up his emaciated cheek.

"Cheer thee, Zestrozzi," exclaimed Visconti, "let the voice of Carraccio awaken thee to life, to joy and to liberty!"

Zestrozzi was silent. His large heavy eye surveyed the features of Carraccio. "Oh! do not mock me;—look at me, Neapolitan.—Thou hast done enough;—shame, ignominy, and torture, have triumphed. Come not to taunt the few moments which my soul lingers upon. Away! away! and tell thy tale of falsehood to other ears;—leave me to die in peace!"

The voice and strength of the captive appeared to fail within him, and he sunk back, exhausted, on his pallet.

The sympathy and pity of the Neapolitan was nearly touched; he took the hand of the refugee within his, and fervently exhorted him to the belief of his ignorance of his sufferings. "As the God of man can witness, so am I free from thy imputations of being treacherous;—but come, Zestrozzi, thou hast yet life to support thy step. Thou must fly this abode of death, and in calmer moments I will convince thee of thy erroneous credence."

"'Tis too late, the shaft has struck here!" and he guided the hand of the Neapolitan to his scarcely pulsating heart. "It has festered there; its result is speedy and certain."

"Nay, banish these frightful images; an hour yet will be thine, in which the hated Golfieri kneels to thy mercy; there is a passage open to his soul, it has long been crowded with infamy. Here, Zestrozzi, this poniard penetrates through it with safety, and lets out the guilty fiend which has lived there triumphant too long."

"Hush! hush! The friendly arm of death hurries me along. I called on his aid with a voice of earnest prayer; he has heard me, and not all thy proffered joys can tear me from him. Hark! 'tis his known shrill! Didst thou not hear the echo along these mouldering vaults? didst not hear the loud cheering yell? look there, in yonder recess, and you will see one form that sleeps, bound up beneath the spell. We hold a solemn pledge to meet soon. Look, look, 'tis but past the sepulchre in the other vault, and we meet again!"

The Neapolitan trembled; he felt the grasp of Zestrozzi more firmly in its pressure; the cold damp dew of dissolution struck to his; the eyes of the captive rolled in their sunken sockets, and a shivering, almost appalling to human sight, agitated his whole frame. He grappled the arm of Carraccio, and his sentences were breathed with dreadful incoherence.

"Hark! 'tis Kaled calls; seest thou not yonder tomb, which opens? He beckons me; unhand, unloose me. I will not forfeit my pledge!"

"Madness! madness!" exclaimed Carraccio, and his mind shuddered, as he witnessed the affecting state of the frenzied Zestrozzi; "Heaven pity thee!"

"Heaven has pitied me," and the features of the dying captive assumed a satisfactory and exulting smile. "I prayed for its help; and though from the dark, silent, and buried recesses of these dungeons, my voice spake not in vain. Heaven did hear it, and pitied me!" The refugee ceased, and fixing a wild and terrific look upon the distant opening of the cell, his gaze remained there for some moments, and at their close, an inward but difficult sigh escaped him,—with it, his spirit fled to its Creator!

The faculties of the Neapolitan were convulsed, and he stood the motionless statue of alarm and horror.

The stream of light, which had given ample reflection throughout the cavern, had served to conduct Paoli to a spot of such security, that he was the spectator of all that had passed. The mask, that had hitherto concealed the features of Carraccio, needed no further effort for its removal; he saw in him his most subtle, dangerous, and destructive enemy; he saw through the whole career of his latter schemes, and he dreaded to think upon what a power his future quietude rested. The knowledge, too, that to Visconti had been entrusted every act that linked his name with guilt and atrocity, and to such a man he must bend in subservience, so forcibly struck its anguish upon the heart of Paoli, that his senses almost sunk into delirium, at the paralyzing reflection.

That Carraccio was hostile to his interests, and that his designs were of some immeasurable extent, his mind left him little doubt of; he was become perfectly sensible that the private views of the Neapolitan threatened him with danger. The certainty of his existence being bound to circumstances of fate so closely in the keeping of Visconti, hurried him to ideas of desperation, and its resolve was the instantly annihilating of him.

"Yes, in this abyss!" he exclaimed, within his imagination, and a momentary blaze of satisfaction and triumph occupied his bosom as he continued, "he must die! Dead men can never brand their murderer. Walls, impenetrable as these, admit of no human witness; they can never be accusers; thus then will be secure, if not my entire peace, at least my future existence; it is decidedly fixed," and rushing upon the motionless and unarmed Neapolitan, he twice buried his poniard in his bosom, adding, "take this, as the reward due to the worst of traitors!"

The Signore Visconti staggered, the light of the lamp distinctly shewed the features of his assassin, and he fell, the blood flowing fast from the wound. Golfieri snatched the lamp, and hastily quitted the cell!

CHAPTER VIII.

"What dost thou mean?—thy words, thy looks, thy manner,
Seem to conceal some horrid secret."

THOMSON.

SCARCELY a quarter of a league from the bay of Palermo, and in the centre of a thick woody enclosure, stands the remains of the grotto or chapel dedicated to St. Rosalia. Skirted by the lofty heights of Monte Pelegrino, and well secured by the leafy branches of the clustering trees, it was for ages sacred to the penitence dedicated to the pious saint. Since the memorable and awful conflagration which buried a principal part of the country in its ashes, the present pilgrimage had become wholly unfrequented and deserted.* Its appearance was bleak, inhospitable, and forbidding. During many years, no human being had passed its barrier, no one dared or wished to examine the wreck of its once holy interior. Valfroni was the present occupier of its rude and isolated abode, the uninterrupted owner of its dark and dilapidated walls.

The mysterious and singular appearance of Valfroni, joined with the immense deformity of his person, rendered him an object at once dreaded and avoided. His statue was singularly formed—misshapen, embodied with an enormous hump, and altogether

* The burning of Mount Ætna is more ancient than the records of history. Its eruptions are extremely violent, and the quantity of matter it throws out is so enormous, that after digging 68 feet deep, marble pavements and other vestiges of an ancient city have been found, covered with the amazing load of earth, in the same manner as the town of Herculaneum has been buried with the matter ejected from Mount Vesuvius. New mouths, or craters, were opened in Etna in the years 1650-1669, and other times. The smoke and flames of the volcano are seen as far as Malta, a distance of 60 leagues. It sends forth a perpetual smoke; and, at particular times, it throws out, with an astonishing violence, flames, lava, large stones, and matter of every kind. An eruption of this volcano, in the year 1537, produced an earthquake over the whole island of Sicily, which lasted twelve days. It terminated by the bursting of a new mouth; the lava of which burnt up every thing, within five leagues of the mountain. It discharged ashes so abundantly, and with such force, that they reached the coast of Italy, and incommoded vessels at great distance from the island.

MACNAB's *Description of Sicily.*

so distorted and hideous, that he had sustained the general denomination of the Demon Dwarf. A large sable cloak invariably shrouded his figure; a hat, suspending a heavy plume of black feathers, partly concealed a ghastly and repulsive countenance, from which his large and ferocious eye threw a terrible glance on the dauntless beholder, who might momentarily rest to notice its terrific and supernatural character. His origin was known by no person; few had ever conversed with him; a period of two successive winters had ushered him into every entertainment Palermo boasted. There were but few circles of society in which he had not mingled; his manner and behaviour was always marked with the most profound respect; those who had met with his observations found them shrewd, and not wholly unforbidding. There was a mystic singularity about them, that his presence, although never courted, was not absolutely prohibited. No equipage, no attendants, had ever been noticed. The mode of his living and habits seemed recluse, and whether he was the only inhabitant of the ruinous retreat, no one could with truth affirm; not even had curiosity ventured, in any shape, to examine the internal appearance of the habitation, the nature of his seclusion, or the purport of his occupation.

The evening vespers in the chapel of St. Christina were nearly closing, as the sudden entrance of the Dwarf sensibly disturbed the devotion of such part of the community near to whom he meditated. The eyes which gazed on him became dim with surprise and wonder; none could recollect a former glance, none could name the spot on which he had ever before been observed. It was an evening late in the year, and every street and habitation retained its known possessor, save when the commands of religion called forth their assemblage within its sanctuary. The principal families in and adjacent to Palermo were present; there had been no departures from the town worthy of notice; there had been no arrivals; the gloomy mists of December had prohibited such change, and who the stranger could be, was a matter of astonishment and conjecture. The richness of his attire proclaimed him noble, but in what establishment he had taken his residence, none was in the knowledge of.

Valfroni fixed himself near the outer porch; he was the object of every individual's attention; each severally threw a kind of inquisitive glance, on leaving the chapel, on his dark and sullen countenance; it pourtrayed too much mystery for the silent gazer to remain long without being repelled by the terror it seemed to express. The sombre and partially lighted corridors of the chapel heightened the gloominess of the moment, and few were those who did not hastily retire, with a feeling of mingled awe and dissatisfaction. Valfroni quitted the chapel, its doors were closed, and in the same instant his figure was lost to sight. Diligent inquiry and earnest interference, each subsequent day, seemed to pervade the minds of the inhabitants. In every street all were busied in the description of the Dwarf; no one had met with him since his presence in the St. Christina aisles (a period of several days). The recollection of him had almost subsided, an intervention of several weeks ensued, and no further appearance of him had been noticed. The belief at length that the Dwarf was upon his travels, and that he had promiscuously stayed during the vespers of that evening, finally banished all further remarks on the event.

The annual solemnization of the feast of St. Rosalia is held in considerable veneration by the inhabitants of Palermo, and the anniversary is usually closed with splendid entertainments, rich pageantry, and other distinguished marks of public munificence.

The cassaro, or public promenade, was thronged with fashionables, and the beauty and elegance of the scene seemed to defy competition. The announcement of a sumptuous banquet, served up in the illuminated hall of the ducal pallazzi, called the presence of the promenaders, and, conducted by their several attendants, each party thronged to the entertainment. The sudden entrance of the Dwarf some few minutes prior to the termination of the repast, spread a disagreeable sensation in the minds of those who remembered his former appearance, and the matter being observed by the Duca, he was urged to institute that inquiry which his dignity authorised. The gaze of Valfroni was fixed upon the Comptessa Rosalviva, who, by her riches, and the great respect paid to her in public by the Duca Paoli, was an object of considerable attraction. The eyes of the guests alternately surveyed the figure of the Dwarf and the person of the Comptessa. A momentary silence prevailed, and each individual appeared astonished at the calmness and singularity of the intruder.

"Speak, stranger!" cried the Duca, in a tone rather peremptory, and who had advanced to a part of the room more secluded to which also the Dwarf had retired. "By what invitation or claim is this festival disturbed?—Your name and rank, Signore, is unknown!"

"My rank, Signore Duca, is not inferior to your own; for my name, its announcement would neither gratify nor serve you!"

"Your presence here?"

"Is it more to be questioned than another's? my rank and fortune claim the privilege."

"Then why hesitate to acknowledge its title?"

"I pray you, Signore Duca, in justice to the common feelings of mankind, forbear this idle examination; it will not profit you."

"Equivocating intruder, neither will this pretext for thy private motives, whatever they may be, avail you; learn that my will is equalled by my power; it must not be trifled with; either declare thy rank and establishment, or from this assembly my authority will dictate me to remove you."

"I will not permit such power to be exercised on the one part," tauntingly spake the Dwarf, and, throwing back a richly embroidered cloak, displayed the costliness of his attire, "nor such degradation towards the other; my sense of respect to this honourable assemblage compels me to withdraw, but, Signore Duca, many hours will not transpire when we meet, free from interruption;" and, throwing a wild and fearless eye again towards the Comptessa, he quitted the saloon. He passed by unheeded, but an inward sense of some portending circumstance crept insensibly through the bosom of most of the spectators. The Duca feared to suffer his departure thus threatened; he commanded the attendants to detain him.

Valfroni heard the summons; he paused with mysterious dignity, and, folding his arms, appeared to wait the enforcement of such command. But no crime marked his features; there was no trait that pictured guilt—no look that evinced fear; and, to the authority of the Duca, every tongue was mute, and every hand motionless. The countenance of Valfroni expressed sufficient indignation at the impetuosity of the Duca, whose ravings could scarcely be moderated on perceiving the prevailing sense of alarm, which prevented implicit obedience to his commands. At the close of some few moments, Valfroni deliberately walked through the portal, which excluded him from observance.

"The wrath of heaven follow thee to eternity!" exclaimed the Dwarf Valfroni, and a smile of bitterness shot across his dark features, as the Duca Paoli crossed the piazzi where Valfroni had seemingly loitered.

The night was dark, save the intervals in which the faint gleams of moonlight stole through the long avenues. A solemn stillness pervaded the atmosphere, and heightened the tranquillity of the scene. The Duca felt a chill when his ear caught the Dwarf's adjuration. He was ignorant of the presence of any being, considering the lateness of the hour, and the obscurity of that part of the building, and his eye surveyed the partially-lighted enclosure with a dismay that accorded with his suspicions. He drew his sword, and, in a tone somewhat peremptory, demanded the name of the speaker, and to whom that curse of vengeance was intended.

"To Paoli, Duca of Palermo!" was the reply.

"Mysterious and malignant figure, approach from where thou art, and let me behold an enemy so apparently to be dreaded."

The full gleam of the moon shone in resplendent brightness, but no particular object was visible to the sight of Paoli.

"These bombastic attacks," ejaculated the Duca, partly within himself, "are as weak as they are contemptible."

"But their hatred and resentment are not so, my Lord Duca;" exclaimed Valfroni, and he confronted Paoli.

"Madman, is it thou?" cried Golfieri, recognizing the figure of the Dwarf, and surveying with a peculiar hauteur the singular and almost pitiable appearance of Valfroni, he added, "but thou art unworthy of my chastisement, miserable abortion of human nature! pursue thy threats elsewhere, where they may be more feared; they have little effect upon me."

"There will be a time, Signore Duca, when you will shrink from them; remember the eve of San Rosalia; it is not forgotten—and there is a tongue can tell of all its horrors."

"Speak, speak! What of that night?" in breathless accents cried Paoli, and he grasped the throat of his antagonist.

"It was a night of murder; you, Signore Duca, were its chief actor!" and the Dwarf freed himself with the utmost composure.

A chilly sensation of terror crept through the veins of Paoli. The horrors of that night rung upon his ear; he had believed that every eye was closed—every form motionless that had participated in the guilt of that evening. *Who* had survived the recollection of that hour? *Who* had come forward now to brand him with the murderer's mark? It was to his mind unanswerable. He had borne the ducal sceptre of Palermo for full three years; none had dared to reproach him. He recovered from the stupor that had attacked him, and, wrought up to a kind of desperation, he challenged the Dwarf to name at once his purposes.

For some moments Valfroni was silent.

The pause gave Paoli time for contemplation; he thought it impossible, then, that a being like the Dwarf should be aware of circumstances so minute as to implicate *his* character. He endeavoured to retrace the various incidents connected with times gone by, but no recollection of the figure of Valfroni could be summoned;—not a circumstance wherein the description of such a being had been pictured to him. He smiled at the thought of fear. Might he not be the victim of idle interrogatory? The eve of St. Julian might have afforded scope for private reproach, and an innocent man might suffer from those reproaches, merely through the effect of chance. He certainly was sensibly aware as to the recollection of the event of St. Rosalia's eve, but he doubted the Dwarf's knowledge of the same, and looked upon the insinuation as arising from the accident of the moment. Feeling a momentary anger for entertaining a dread of danger, he desired the Dwarf, in a peremptory tone, instantly to withdraw from the pallazzi.

"Much requires to be performed, ere I content myself, Signore Duca, with bidding adieu to this pallazzi."

"And of what import to me? an absolute stranger, both to your person and to your affairs!"

"Not so, Signore Duca; the same spot has many an hour been sacred to our privacy."

"Thanks, Dwarf," in an agreeable tone, cried Paoli, "this last acknowledgment no longer leaves me in doubt of your having mistaken the character."

The Dwarf replied in the negative.

"But I am positive of your error."

"Indeed! The person of Paoli, Conte Golfieri, is not easily forgotten by—his friends."

"His friends are limited, and you, Signore Dwarf, he is well assured, are not of their number."

"You speak in a decided manner, Duca."

"Confident that I am so."

"Believe it; but one word,—allow me;—and perhaps, you will find, that so far as relates to matters of privacy and trust, I retain more acquaintance of such than even the most intimate of your friends. The Duca Paoli is silent, he cannot deny my promptness, but I will terminate this language. I am Valfroni, or better known as the Demon Dwarf; we are met to commune, and deviation or ceremony is unnecessary."

"To commune!" impetuously spake the Duca, "No, no;—but, fool that I am, thus to trifle with my honor and dignity, and at an hour so far beyond midnight. Hence, thou proscribed of human shape, or thy hideous form shall not protect you from my chastisement;—hence, I say!"

"The hour is far beyond midnight;—truly, Signore Duca, I defer, therefore, this matter till we meet again, and we *must* meet again."

"Never—never!"

"But who can prohibit it?"

"My own will—my own decided and unbiassed resolution."

"'Tis powerless;—thou might as well compass the wind—or impede the storm on the angry ocean.—No, Paoli, your existence is conjoined with that of mine; no earthly preventative can shield you from the assignation, I shall at any, or all times propose. Deceive not your imagination to form a contrary opinion on this point."

"This high-sounding prophetic appeal may intimidate the mind, and work upon the superstition of the weak;—in this instance, 'tis ineffective. To prove how little I heed it, I repeat my determination, and openly declare, that *should* we ever meet again, by chance only is such a meeting the result of."

"Was chance the only director, I might be deemed liar and idiot, but this is a deception, Duca, that will exist but in your mind."

"I will hazard it," hastily replied Golfieri, and drawing on more securely his cloak, was departing, when the unknown narrator detained his arm, and in an imperative tone commanded his stay.

The grasp seemed Herculean. The strength of Paoli was naturally as superior as was his mind to daring acts, but the sudden clutch of the unknown seemed to appal him. The bold grasp with which he arrested the step of Golfieri; the impression with which his voice pronounced "Stay!" awakened him to a sense of alarm; that alarm which the mind feels when combating with mystery. A kind of chilly moisture was creeping through his frame; he gazed upon the partially hidden features of the Dwarf, and resisting to the extent of his courage and strength, the familiarity of Valfroni's demand, he besought him to explain his motive for such an attack.

"This is no time for explanation;—know this much, Duca, and rest confident on its implicit obedience. In the evening of to-morrow, in defiance to that will, that 'unbiassed resolution,' we meet again;—our place of assignation shall be within the chapel adjoining the pallazzi. The hour will be in similitude with the present, hushed by the breath of night and darkness; the spot is sufficiently lighted for us to recognise each other, and there, undisturbed, we may communicate. On no pretence will you fail, Duca; nay, you must not; no power or force can prevent your punctuality. Look to it!"

"In mercy unhand me," vehemently replied Golfieri, his arm nearly benumbed with the firm pressure; "such desperate engagements I renounce; there is nought that I have to confer with you upon, nought that I wish to know."

"You have much to hear."

"Chiefly too at such an hour," continued Paoli, unmindful of the Dwarf's latter remark, or heedless of it, "when stratagem and malignity are alone on the wing for accomplishment. The characteristic importance you assume; that power and that imperious command quickly sinks into nothingness, when you name so remote a time, and so obscure a spot, for your appointments; if they be such as you would have them considered, open and honourable, unconnected, too, with the presence of a third person—be it so. I'll shrink not from the assignation; but it must be clear, and unaided by the darkness of night, or the obscurity of the cloister——"

"What, and has the mighty heart of Golfieri degenerated into fear and cowardice? Has the darkness of night, or the stillness of the cloister, so powerful an effect upon his mind, as to make him dread them. I named the hour, I selected the spot, in unison with the subject; the quietude of the night, and the lonely situation of the chapel, precluding all intrusion at such a moment."

The Duca replied not.

"But to prove that neither crime nor injury is within my intentions, to convince you that I have no need of the subtlety and the caution of the common brigand, I will be in attendance, as I now am, defenceless, and unarmed, even in your weapon's power. If this will not suffice, name your own appointment, time, or place; but it must be night. Promise me, too, the prohibition of company, and I will be in readiness, were it even the most insulated part that your excellency's memory can charge you with. So far you may see that my designs are not of the blackest dye!"

The Duca paused upon the singularity of the scene, and throwing aside further constraint or fear, "Well, Dwarf," said Paoli, "in the pallazzi chapel, at the time you signify, your punctuality shall not be exceeded by mine." Then waving his hand, the Dwarf withdrew from the piazza, and Golfieri to his chamber.

END OF VOL. II.

ROSALVIVA.

CHAPTER I.

Soft on the wave the oars at distance sound,
The night breeze sighing thro' the leafy spray,
With gentle whisper murmurs all around,
Breathless o'er the placid sea and dies away.

SOTHEBY.

THREE years had elapsed since the union of Golfieri and the amiable Francesca, a lovely boy had become the pledge of their affections, possessing all its father's features, combined with all the softer beauties of its maternal parent.

It may be in some degree imagined under what state of mind had existed the Comptessa Rosalviva; by gradual decay, she had witnessed the once heated and ardent love of Paoli degenerate into coldness, neglect, and indifference. The hatred she cherished towards the unsuspecting Francesca knew of no moderation; with Paoli she had lost every hope, and she felt sensible that the time was indeed at hand, when she would be scarcely retained in his remembrance, at least not in his esteem. In vain she had recalled to his mind his vows of early days, in vain she essayed to bring back the fondness they had reciprocally and long indulged in, and in vain were her efforts to redeem his heart, or claim even the slightest portion of it from the doting partner of his happiness; Francesca seemed his idol, and of late he had lost but trifling intervals in which he had not offered his adoration. A soul formed like Rosalviva's could probably endure every possible infliction from the being to whom all its sympathies had yielded, but that of contempt and neglect; these recollections may be traced in her earliest career, in her correspondence and intercourse with Leontini; and when the greatness of that soul was doomed to submission, in the loss of Paoli's love, its miseries, its indignance, and its pangs can be readily imagined. It is not to be supposed that a woman, with the faculties and resolutions of the Comptessa, would tamely bear with calamity; she was not moulded in that tenderness to watch the

————"canker worm of care
Creeping thro' her heart!"———

and not strive to exterminate it from thence; no, the sense of Paoli's indifference, and the reward which her enthusiasm, her sacrifices for him only, had met with, rather served to fire her brain with the madness of desperation and revenge, and under its powerful impulse she willingly submitted to it with the utmost subservience. Imagination pictured a thousand schemes for the result of her vengeance upon the perjured Paoli and his bride. Her heart shuddered at the recurrence of its early fondness, and she smothered its recollection in emotions of vindictive resentment and ferocity. The incidents of the previous evening glanced across her mind with pleasing retrospect, and the singular and peculiar menace of the unknown dwarf stranger towards the husband of her rival, seemed to bring with it a joy and a satisfaction, that she trusted might be turned to some share of profit and account. She contemplated on the mysterious and appalling figure of the Dwarf, but there was a manner and a dignity about him that failed not equally to engage her attention. He had deigned to gaze upon her with more than common interest, and the longer she reflected upon the circumstance of the evening, the more anxious her heart seemed to feel for the re-appearance of its object. Her wish of discovery, and her desire for the chance of that moment which would effect their meeting was now her most ardent pursuit; she frequented such places as might give her the opportunity of his presence. It was at no distant period wherein her efforts were rendered successful.

The soft glow of a Sicilian sky, in the middle of its most exhilarating season, had one evening invited the Comptessa to enjoy the mildness of the refreshing breezes of the almost sleeping Mediterranean for a greater length than was her customary habit. The rippling current had borne her little barque, which was conducted by one attendant, to a considerable distance along the lake (which branched from the port of Palermo through a winding track of some length,) before she observed the interval which had caused it. Her reflections were at length disturbed by the mellow tone of a lute; the sound struck upon her ear with amazement and rapture; the boat was stationary; the echo of the waters near to the cavity, from whence seemed to proceed the harmony, conveyed a gratification upon the mind of the listener of sweetest sensibility. The serenity of the evening aided the beauty and refinement of the scene, and the Comptessa indulged, for several moments, in a kind of "extatic" silence. After the melodist had repeated the strain of a soft canzonet with much taste and feeling, the voice, in notes of beautiful tone and richness, swelled into a delightful air, of which the Comptessa distinctly caught the following stanzas.

SICILIAN AIR.

Ah! how soft those rays declining,
  Scarcely resting on the wave;
Tho' late so brightly they were shining,
  Seek they now, a cloudy grave?

So droop'd love, 'mid worlds of sorrow,
  In this bosom torn by pain;
The sun will shine and smile to-morrow,
  But love to me, ne'er beams gain.

Like the leaf by night winds shaken,
  Like the flow'r by tempest blighted;
Like the sigh which sighs can waken,
  Is the heart, where hope has slighted!
Farewell hope and love for ever!
  Joy and smiles, farewell, farewell!
Like the earthquake's shock we sever,
  Love and hope, farewell, farewell!

The pleasure of the moment was too great to be parted with in silence, and quitting the boat which was fastened to the projecting shore, she essayed to seek the retreat of the minstrel. The eminence which rose before her pourtrayed a wild but pleasing sketch of nature, and as the crimson tints of the setting sun rested upon its summits, it gave appearance to some kind of building, whose basis lay buried in the deep and woody inclosure beneath. Rosalviva pursued the track that tended to give the most ready access to the half desolated retreat. The thick intervening branches of the chesnut and pine waved over the path in clusters that almost defied penetration, and it was with considerable difficulty that she proceeded further. Attaining the extent of her path through an opposite and sloping direction, the Gothic remains of an edifice which, to the opinion of Rosalviva, had originally been of a religious order, precluded further communication, and she paused, in an intermission of breathless anxiety, for the renewal of the minstrel's harmony.

There was an agreeable variety in the suspension of those moments, which served to lull the mind and ideas into a melancholy yet pleasing calmness. Rosalviva gazed upon the surrounding scenery with feelings of mingled pleasure and sublimity. The softened streaks of the declining sun were attaining their more dusky hue; its beams still hung upon the distant prospect, deepening, as they seemed to lose themselves, in the wide expanse of the Mediterranean, over whose green surface the white sail of the gondolier was seen floating, till it progressively became lost from observation. The eye of the Comptessa alternately surveyed each intervening object, and almost forgot the seclusion of the moment. The silence of the spot conveyed to Rosalviva a thrill of singular sensation, as to the result of her researches.

Pursuing the direction of a partly dilapidated colonade, she was led to the entrance of a kind of cemetry, through which a streak of light from the horizon broke through an opposite cavity, and by its aid Rosalviva more distinctly reviewed the extent of the ruin. She passed its mouldering fabric, and entering a narrow portal, was again within sight of the waters which rolled beneath her. A small grot or cavern projected itself from the acclivity, and from thence she believed had issued the notes of the minstrel; she paused,—the shadow of a human being met her eye,—it retired; her footsteps seemed to linger where she then remained, and while her ruminations were busied in conjecture, the disturbance of the trees near to her broke the reverie, and turning her eye in astonishment, the Dwarf Valfroni stood beside her.

A confusion, marked with terror, coloured the cheek of the Comptessa, and her gaze rested upon the Dwarf, under a power as it were of inability to be removed.

Valfroni noticed her agitation, and approaching, with an air of calmness and respect, urged her to forbear apprehension, and mildly questioned the purport of her presence.

Rosalviva stammered out a few awkward and ill-timed replies, and pleaded in excuse that the beauty of the scenery, and the delicious harmony she had listened to, had invited her beyond the usual track, and in an attempt to regain the shore, where her attendant remained, she had only penetrated still further into the obscurity of the abode. "You will, I trust, pardon the ignorance and curiosity of a woman," added the Comptessa, "if she has disturbed the goodly possessor of its habitation."

"This mark of distinction and honour in visiting the retreat of the Dwarf Valfroni, is too valuable not to be acknowledged, and rather demands from me, Signora, an act of courtesy, than the thought of apology or atonement."

The Comptessa smiled, and with a feeling of somewhat better confidence, she sought to meet his gaze. The features of the Dwarf were so concealed by his bushy hair, and scattered ringlets, that she was unable to trace their character. She fancied there was a pleasing expression in the shade of that countenance, and that a look of joy returned her smile.

"May it please you, Signora, I will conduct you to a path more cheerful," and leading the way, he traced back its direction towards the front part of the building, which Rosalviva had first discovered. "These lonely wilds, Signora, can offer but a poor gratification to so illustrious a visitor," remarked the Dwarf.

"They can boast a melody that might be pronounced divine, and for such a charm, they who have souls susceptible to its refinement could dwell here for ever."

"Since then, Signora, you are pleased to feel a pleasure in its wildness, may it be hoped that the hallowed spot of St. Rosalia will, as oft as leisure and inclination permit, be rendered still more sacred with thy presence."

"I could certify that promise with rapture," cried the Comptessa, and her bosom seemed to imbibe a pleasant and peculiar feeling towards the affability and manner of the Dwarf;—"indeed, my visits shall prove it."

"Thanks, thanks, I am bound for the remembrance."

The evening was growing dark, and the Dwarf requested the hand of the Comptessa, as he offered his assistance to escort her. "The evening's gloom, Signora, methinks is contributable to danger; fear you any in a spot so remote, lady?"

"Not any," was the reply.

"True; virtue and innocence are proof against fear; still, lady, your beauty may occasionally hazard it."

"You are skilled in flattery, I perceive," observed Rosalviva, not displeased with his remarks, and willing to encourage them.

Valfroni essayed to engage her hand, the effort was unavailing, and the Comptessa increased her step. The singularity of the attempt surprised her; policy, and a certain sense of prudence, withheld a favour which she still had more the inclination to grant than the power to deny; but the ignorance of the quality of the person by whom she was addressed, his rank and family, and, again, his strange retirement, severally endeavoured to dissuade her to the contrary. For several moments each maintained a total silence.

"This apparent sullenness, Signora, elsewhere would be irksome; were it observed, it would be presumed that we were almost strangers to each other, and such a mistake I should be sorry to create."

The Comptessa could not restrain a smile, as she expressed her surprise at his meaning. She interrogated him as to its definition, adding, that the claim of fellowship was not of any lengthened duration.

"Hold, Signora," interrupted Valfroni, "this is only *your* imagination."

The Comptessa paused and looked attentively in his countenance.

"Yes," resumed he, "no incident, however trivial, has lost place in my memory during ages back,—they are too securely in my keeping to be easily lost."

The inexplicable expressions of the Dwarf served to weigh unpleasantly on the mind of Rosalviva. Her courage was naturally strong, and in the present instance it abated but little of its energy; still there was an appearance of singularity in the remark, that caused her some share of uneasiness. She rested on the basis of a rugged and broken pillar, and a rapid succession of thoughts came across her remembrance; but no clue offered that could dictate by what means he pronounced with such emphasis the language which he had indulged in;—however, she treated the annunciations of Valfroni with a levity that showed her indifference, and said,—"Since, then, Signore, you have been so studious an observer of my actions and conduct, the name of my family is equally as familiar to you, doubtless."

"Equally," cried the Dwarf, without a moment's hesitation, "oh, yes; Rosalviva, heiress of Romagno, is not less frequent to my recollection than is the title myself was endowed with."

"Name that title,—name it," anxiously repeated the Comptessa, her sense awakening a series of suspicions.

"Time will reveal it—must disclose it," replied Valfroni, and, as he gazed on her features, his heart seemed to triumph.

Rosalviva almost felt sensible of an inferiority in the presence of the Dwarf, and which she in vain endeavoured to account for. Surviving the discomposure of the moment, she extended her hand, which the Dwarf, with some warmth of feeling, pressed to his lips. She urged him to speak of the events of which he hinted. Valfroni requested her silence, and motioning to withdraw, pointed to the path which led to the shore. She forcibly detained his hand, and her large beaming eye rested earnestly upon him. "Signore, wherefore this sudden haste?"

The Dwarf was silent.

"You hesitate; in mercy, name a reason, Signore."

"I have many."

"But one, Dwarf, and I am satisfied."

"Oh, no, desist in this painful inquiry; circumstances prohibit further disclosure; we must part.—Your presence here, is injurious to yourself."

"It would be more so, Dwarf, were I to leave this place thus unrequited. It can never be quitted, till I know more. Your manner, habit, and singularity, at once confound and charm me; there is a kind of inspiration in thy soul, which fires mine. You see I am candid in my expressions of feelings, and till I obtain——"

"What, Signora?" interrupted Valfroni, "be not too impetuous—obtain what?"

"That confidence you would fain withhold."

The Dwarf continued his silence, the figure of a man was observable in the distance; it struck through an opposite avenue. Rosalviva followed its resemblance as far as her sight would permit; she had not felt a sufficient dread to have implored its assistance, though the pulse beat quickly responsive to the agitation of her heart. A kind of gloom passed over her mind and spirits and she was less free in her remarks; she felt a wish to depart, yet her inclination still yearned towards the society of the Dwarf.

Valfroni sighed, almost imperceptibly, but the sound did not escape the hearing of Rosalviva, and dispersing the oppression of her bosom, she interrogated in a tone of sympathy its cause.

The Dwarf evaded the inquiry.

"And you will not dare to confide in the truth of one, who might relieve its anxiety!" replied the Comptessa.

"In whose interest, Signora, could I be thus distinguished?"

"Rosalviva proffers her own; use them, Signore, as you may think most advantageous; perhaps you may find some profit attending therein."

"Thanks, Signora, I doubt if I have capability of doing justice to so valuable an offer; in return, let me beg the poor acceptance of mine."

The Comptessa paused during a long and heavy struggle within her bosom; she thought of Golfieri's cruelty, his neglect, the happiness of Francesca, and at her hands how much she had suffered in all the miseries her soul had known, and, as they alternately fastened upon her soul, responded with the throb of vengeance; dared she repeat these thoughts, these dark wishes, to the Dwarf? Could or would he assist her in them? Might he not betray them, and might not her designs be scorned and defeated? Yet she thought him sincere; she looked back at the meeting with him and Golfieri; she remembered his menace there, and she could but be assured that the purpose of some desperate attempt had urged it. Might not he have equally suffered from the false promises, or from other causes, at the instance of the Duca, and might he not be desirous of avenging them; else wherefore wish to disturb the hilarity of such a time by his mysterious and appalling presence; his words at parting, too, with Paoli, hung upon her lips, and she repeated, with enthusiasm, their purport—"many hours will not elapse when we *must* meet again;" she mentally exclaimed, "and these were the words of the unknown Dwarf." She was too sensible of the quality of their tone to conceive the intruder in the light of a dependant; it was the language and authority of one who had much to communicate, and that in redress, doubtless, of his injuries. The idea soothed her, and she felt determined to point out to Valfroni all her sufferings; she turned her eyes upon him, he was in the attitude of reflection; there was a solemnity and a majesty in his deportment and manner that encouraged her wishes, and she assured herself that the soul of the Dwarf was not less susceptible, nor less valuable than her own; her gloominess vanished, and, in an artless and unreserved voice, she questioned his thoughts, concluding with "Who, Valfroni, has the felicity of their engagement?"

"One who has had them long, Signora Rosalviva."

"Ha! then I might presume you deign to acknowledge that you can love, Signor Dwarf?"

"I have loved almost to madness, Signora."

"Thou art not singular in that fatality, others have equally suffered, without doubt, Dwarf."

"Truly so; there are many beings in the vast range of empire whose souls have loved; years, perchance, may have recorded their passion; they may have known joy and sorrow for one selected object, and the happiness or misery of such an object was their's; but ah! mine was more; the love I cherished was not depicted in smiles, or my grief in sighs, in tears; I loved ardently, and one who could promise much, and who could teach me to believe that she felt much; she deceived me, lady, and the wound she had inflicted was permitted to rankle; but words are vain to describe that passion, the heart only wears its remembrance, and that can never disclose it." The Dwarf paused, and his eyes met those of Rosalviva.

"Oh, Valfroni," interjected the Comptessa, "thou hast a soul formed for adoration."

"Hush, Signora, such was the language of her I loved, cease to persecute my memory with its recognition,—'tis dreadful!"

"Unhappy Dwarf, thou hast my pity, my esteem."

"Ha, this is well; now, lady, I could gaze upon you till my heated eyeballs seared their sockets with watchfulness; I could chase away thy cares, I could give consolement to thy bosom, nay, might sacrifice my feeble existence were it to benefit that of your's; I will deserve thy pity and esteem, believe me." The eyes of the Dwarf seemed to convey more than usual brilliance as he smiled upon her, and while Rosalviva witnessed their expression, her soul cherished a kind of delight and animation, from which she derived unspeakable pleasure.

"Since then our wishes and ideas assimilate so closely, Signore Dwarf, their correspondence must not be at distant periods; you will give me to hope that the Castelli di Romagno shall be considered at all times open to your visits and familiar to your uses; suppose, for its first change, you favour me with its acknowledgment in the evening of to-morrow."

"With grateful pleasure," answered Valfroni, and he respectfully kissed her hand. He carefully conducted her from the acclivity to the shore, and, unmooring the boat, waved his hand in repeated adieus, as the moonlight, breaking from the heavens, lighted the Comptessa from the rocky eminence.

CHAPTER II.

Wealth now is mine, and all that wealth can give,
But oh, it gives not happiness. I've still
That fever in my brain which turns and burns
As though the spirit were flesh.

SOANE.

"Speak: what is't ye do!"

SHAKSPEARE.

AN instinctive pride impelled Golfieri from communication with the pallazzi respecting the assignation of the Dwarf, and until the elucidation of the circumstances attached should be made known, whatever might be the consequence, he felt determined to hold the most implicit silence. Francesca had perceived his repeated moments of abstraction, and, in earnest supplication, questioned its nature. He excused himself on the plea of ignorance towards its cause, assuring her that the ensuing night's repose, which it was his intention of seeking at an early hour, would doubtless alleviate its pressure.

The natural change and gloom of Golfieri's mind was the frequent observation of the palazzi's inmates. The Duchessa would repeatedly endeavour to exact from him its origin, but his silence and petulance forbade any strictness of inquiry, and when he essayed to banish it in the smiles of his offspring, the trifling reproach she fain would have advanced at his want of confidence, became instantly hushed in receiving the more pleasing feeling of his paternal fondness.

Golfieri retired considerably before his accustomed time. It was one of those cold and dreary nights which shut out intercourse beyond the small circle of familiar associates. He looked from the window of the pallazzi in intent awe; the faint and intervening gleam of moonlight pictured to his sight the shadow of the Dwarf as it glided beneath the portico of the adjoining chapel, true to the time appointed. Golfieri withdrew himself from the casement, fearful that his presence might be noticed. The Dwarf closed the door of the chapel, and the next instant the scene appeared wrapt in obscurity. A presentiment of some evil would have intruded itself upon the mind of Golfieri, but that he considered his opponent was unarmed and unattended, and even within the walls of his own pallazzi. He reminded himself, too, that the assignation was the choice of the Dwarf, and if it were for crime, or for any sinister purpose, certainly some other spot would have been selected, rather than the one which he had chosen, and where the domestics of the Duca, had he thought proper, might have been placed in security, and unperceived by any eye save his own. He reproved his apprehensions and weakness, and dispersing every fantastic suggestion which his brain had coined, he looked to the meeting only as a matter of communication, when probably matter of national or more private import, might have induced the Dwarf to impart them to his ear only.

He quitted his apartment, and by the light of a small lamp, partly concealed, (which he carried,) entered the chapel. The feeble glare of the light burning within at the sacristy of the chapel, threw its dim and shadowy reflection along the aisles through which Golfieri hurried with agitated step. The small portal by which he had entered, from a private communication formed through a secluded avenue of the pallazzi, was closed with a cautious quietude, and holding forth the lamp, he surveyed the cold and dismal edifice with feelings of a strange and dubious nature. The footstep of the Dwarf precluded further sensations, which the blank appearance of the scene, and its singular formation was about to give rise to; and the Duca awaited him with as much energy and confidence as the incident could permit. Looking earnestly to the Dwarf, and in a voice rendered audibly impressive, he cried, "Now, Dwarf, nor time nor place yields encouragement in such a night as this to unnecessary parley; speak to the full purport of thy wishes."

"Your precision," replied Valfroni, "is worthy of commendation; it shall not be trifled with; the hoarse night winds rush heavily and bleakly through these aisles; yonder dormitory is less open to its chilly blasts—follow me, Golfieri."

The Dwarf pointed to the folding doors at the extremity of the aisle, and motioned Golfieri to proceed. He obeyed the entreaty in silent submission. The imperative and familiar command of the Dwarf awed him into an unconscious subservience, and with almost a superstitious dread, yet retaining an indignation at the thought of harm, he entered the more gloomy part of the building—"I should hail thee, Dwarf, as a friend, or why this ceremonious observance; say thy name."

"Valfroni; did I not at our first interview announce it?"

"True; and thy country?"

"Your's, my Lord—Sicily; forbear further inquiry; my family, my friends, cease to exist; and for my origin, it will not avail in the present moment."

"These replies, Dwarf, are enigmatical;—your purposes?"

"Aye, now we speak on points of interest; answer me, then, Duca, has life and dignity sufficient charm to bind thee to its influence, or darest thou meet the gaunt despoiler of all earthly care with resignation and fortitude?"

"To what end do these inquiries result? and wherefore art thou, unknown Dwarf, their interrogator?"

"In pursuance to an allegiance I have long sworn to effect the accomplishment of. Trace back the few latter periods of thy life, and tell me, Duca,—nay, this curled lip and disdainful smile colours not thy feelings, I know them too well,—therefore, speak if thou canst, whether the recollection of such times is unspotted by infamy—its verdict exempt from retribution?"

"Presumptuous and insolent enthusiast! Is it for reproof like this thou hast dared to break in upon my privacy, and vauntingly to claim my attention? Maniac! (for so I must deem thee,) fly from this spot, or the excess of my rage will dare me to deeds which even the sacredness of this roof will not prohibit; go, or be the arbitrator of your own immediate doom."

The contempt and vindictive passions of Golfieri had been harrowed up to the extreme of desperation; it amounted almost to madness, and, under its control, he seized the Dwarf amidst a burst of excruciating feeling, and but for the equal strength and resistance of Valfroni, it would have terminated decidedly fatal.

"Now, thou recreant Dwarf, since thou hast created my vengeance, take the punishment it merits; thy life is in my hands. Either confess thy dark and subtle motives, or consider thyself its just victim—this moment shall be thy last."

The eyes of the Duca threw a malignant glance upon the struggling Valfroni. He disengaged himself from the hands of Paoli, and replied,

"Thy threats are as weak as thy vaunted power, Duca. Dost thou believe I venture here unguarded, though unarmed? No!—Carry thy vengeance into execution,—but remember, for every particle of blood thy madness might shed, the daggers of a countless band of partisans will invoke its penalty. Thinkst thou, too, that I should thrust myself on the point of this poniard," (for the Duca had unsheathed a small sword, which he usually carried,) "had I not known that there was an ample strength in reserve, to close up my wound. Misguided Paoli,—look to thine own life, nor resign it with such seeming exultation."

The Duca smiled, but it was under the influence of feelings which he almost shrunk from acknowledging. He could not but own their tendency, and as the changed and wild expression of his eye viewed the singular form of Valfroni, a gloomy presage of guilt and dismay passed over his soul, and which seemed to him to be charged with convulsions of mingled horror. There was, in despite of his utmost resolutions, a tremor crowding within him, which as he attempted to address Valfroni, the faltering accent too clearly betrayed. He felt his heart throb in painful suspense, and he implored of Valfroni to terminate so unpleasant a meeting. "Tell me," he cried, "what is it you desire, and I will endeavour to see it realised; dost thou seek power? has ambition a flame within your heart, that you would fain cherish?"

"It has, it has," interrupted the Dwarf, "and I seek it, Paoli, at your hands."

"Thy abstruse and singular mode of conduct were not the best testimonials of thy right to its favors," spake Paoli.

"Do not mistake my meaning, though, Duca," calmly rejoined Valfroni, "'tis not power, command, or a desire of precedence, either in rank or riches, beyond those of my fellow creation; it is the desire of rewarding those by whom Valfroni has suffered injury. Can the Duca Paoli subscribe to this?"

"He would have you to point out those aggressors, and probably *some* advice or assistance might be offered by him."

Valfroni paused for some few moments. A severe and derisive

smile was upon his lip, a threatening expression seemed fixed upon his brow, and the power of some dark and immoveable purpose appeared to hold a dominion over his thoughts. "Answer me then, Duca; what advice canst thou offer, in behalf of the man who could first betray the confidence of a friend, and who could, in cold blood, complete his treachery by the assassin's knife? who could——"

"Hush, hush!" interrupted Paoli, for the words of the Dwarf seemed to appal him; the portrait held up to him was too close in resemblance with his own, to view it without embarrassment; yet still persevering in a kind of temporary assurance, he replied, "such a man, Dwarf, ought to suffer by the laws of his country."

"And their decree would pronounce his death, Duca; judge I correctly?"

"It would; and for whom does this language appeal?" questioned Paoli, and he assumed a more composed and dignified demeanour.

The interrogatory agitated the bosom of the Dwarf; there was a confusion of strange and perverse ideas flashed throughout his imagination, and amidst their engrossment, the name of Paoli Golfieri involuntarily passed from his lips.

"Paoli Golfieri!" echoed the voice of the Duca, and the intrepidity and firmness of the speaker seemed the more forcibly to alarm him, as he looked upon his unmoved and strange countenance. "In what instance canst thou couple the name of Paoli with such an act?"

"Had he ever the title of a friend among his acquaintance?" resumed the Dwarf; "can he remember whether there ever was the man to whom he professed the most ardent friendship, the most sincere esteem? Does he remember whether he ever forfeited his sentiments of honour and regard, and does he not remember to have made such a friend his victim!"

"There was one who deserved all this," shouted Paoli, in an expression of madness, which harrowed up his senses at the Dwarf's recital. "And he met with his fate," he added, still wreathing with a violence of rage, that told the unsubdued and reeking torment of his soul.

There was a trifling space of time which marked their mutual silence. Valfroni perceived the tumult that existed in the brain of Paoli, and enjoyed it with a satisfactory triumph.

"I knew him," cried the Dwarf, "I knew this victim; I heard his last gasp escape him, and I saw the hand that caused it; therefore prevarication, Duca, is needless. Shall I tell you that your victim was my kindred,—Leontini di Vivaldi;—one to whom I owe every gratitude, and for whom I would contend with every danger. I appear here, Signore Duca, in the character of his avenger,—nor can I relinquish it while existence——"

"His avenger?" repeated Paoli.

"Yes, Signore Duca, the law of his country demands it, and the right of his kindred will enforce it; and even though the ducal coronet binds thy brow, it is not the more exempt from the punishment due to such a crime. I come, Signore Duca, to the presence of the tribunal, which governs Sicily's rights, to pronounce my claim; nor all their honors, nor all thy riches, can buy them from the fulfilment of their duty. In the face of Heaven I make my charge, to the hearts of my country my appeal."

"And its decision," murmured Paoli, within himself, "is but too certain, can be but fatal." He reflected for some moments and he felt with it

"All the horrors of a guilty mind."

"And is the incident which ended Leontini's existence never to be blotted from memory? Will not the hand of sovereignty, extended to his hapless kindred, be in some degree an alleviation for his loss; perchance it might be, Dwarf, that thou hast enemies;—some who may have scorned your hopes, blighted your endeavours; speak of them, and to such beings shalt thou deal out destruction; name the word, and I have hearts bold enough to rid them from your recollection."

"Doubtless," replied the Dwarf, and his countenance and gaze had resigned part of its apparent venom and malignity.

"Hast thou," resumed Paoli, "from ties of consanguinity, friends thou wouldst fain reward? Knowest thou the man, who in the black hour of adversity, (if such a moment you ever felt,) administered to thy wants and gave thee even a hovel's protection?

Speak of him, and his repayment shall be riches and dignity; nay, speak of what you will, so much does my poor heart and soul relent for the untimely death of the Signore Leontini, that I would commemorate it only with acts of mercy. Now, Dwarf, thou hast my power and inclinations at thy command; use them as befits thy most special, and thy most desired wishes."

That this confession would have been the resource of Paoli, may be expected, seeing how deeply his guilt was unfettered, and how incapable his strength of resolution was of drawing Valfroni either from his calmness or decision of purpose. Threat or taunt was of feeble avail; it was an instance of policy to change its tone; could he by signification of his remorse, and a well formed narrative of penitence, purchase over the commiseration and respect of the Dwarf, whatever might be the price of such an instance, his determination was to hazard it. He knew that the person of the Dwarf once within his grasp, and his secrecy and silence within his keeping, the dread of danger vanished, and he bore still an unimpeached and spotless soul. He perceived that his harangue carried some encouragement; Valfroni mused upon its feeling, and an occasional smile played upon his lips as the rapid succession of ideas passed through his brain.

It was a satisfactory moment felt by Valfroni; the terms upon which Paoli seemed willing to secure the silence and friendship of the Dwarf, were flattering and auspicious ones; the result of his contemplation taught him to engage with them, and he intimated that so much was he desirous to render the penitence of Paoli more lasting, and to witness his acts of goodness, rather than be their prohibitor, that to his liberality of mind and to his exemplary principles he yielded his appeal, and added,—"So long, Signore Duca, as I retain your confidence and your generosity, the Dwarf Valfroni is silent as the grave."

"Thanks, thanks! My pallazzi, my wealth, my kingdom, are all in your care; make of them as thine observations and thy friendship warrants."

"I shall not be unmindful, Duca, of the extent and greatness of my trust."

Paoli seized the hand of the Dwarf, and pressing it with exulting warmth, he said,—"This pledge is sacred."

Valfroni bowed, and exchanged a pleasing smile.

"Come then, Dwarf Valfroni, the night has already far advanced; no other roof must form thy shelter but the one which covers Palermo's Duca; to-morrow, when we meet, to the Duchessa you will permit me the introduction of the Marchese Valfroni."

Valfroni acquiesced. The Duca refreshed the lamp he had brought with him, and requesting Valfroni to proceed, he led the way towards the state apartments of the pallazzi. The Dwarf was conducted to one almost unparalleled for richness and embellishment, and the Duca bidding an adieu, he was left to future reflection.

Thus far was secured the silence and subservience of the Dwarf Valfroni, and happy in its attainment, the Duca Paoli once again resumed the air of composure. Valfroni, locked in the solitude of the chamber, gave vent to the various ideas that floated across his mind; the circumstances of Leontini di Vivaldi were their principal import.

It is remembered that in gratitude for the restoration of a life doomed by Paoli to destruction, the Signore Leontini had undertaken his journey to Reggio, where the mission entrusted to him by the Neapolitan Visconti was with willing pleasure entered upon.

The subsequent morning witnessed his departure; the Neapolitan received him to his embrace, and hoping his safe return, they parted,—it was an eternal separation!

The brightness of a soft Sicilian sky animated the prospect of Leontini, and as his sight seemed to measure the immense space that pictured itself before him, his heart felt a genial throb, in viewing the sublimity of the Creator. A chain of mountainous passes, beneath whose narrow and winding declivities the path was just distinguished, mingled with the clusters of numerous pine and cork trees, that scattered themselves upon the rising borders of the scene, encouraged a pleasing and romantic train of contemplation, and Leontini freely indulged them, while the slow but certain step of his mule tracked the course of the steep and rugged road, from the shelving and rocky summit of the last wild and variegated eminence that linked itself with Palermo's boundary. The small but beautiful town of Monte Real extended itself to the right of the port; and along its gently sloping ascent, Leontini pursued his route. Its aspect was of the most enchanting and picturesque kind; from the rude passes he had just left, the scene was mellowed into a delightful landscape. The light appearance of the villas dispersed throughout,—the lines of olive and other trees thronging upon its heights,—the half-tenanted remains of the abbey, just rearing its turret through the intervening vista,—the serpentine road, refreshed with cooling streams that spread themselves from the overflowing cascades and surrounding *jet d'eau*, which are numerously discovered upon its environs; the extensive sheet of Mediterranean reaching to the isles of Lipari, studded with the barques of the Sicilian trades, and other frequenters of the coast, afforded at once a most delicious and brilliant prospect.

Leontini occupied some few minutes in reflection; then, turning from the scene, he emerged into the almost entangled path, and made for the nearest town. The romantic and even terrific appearance of the mountains which he passed, their perilous heights rendering approach impracticable; its acclivities impregnated with rugged piles of rock, and other masses of immense structure, scattered as it were by the bold hand of Nature, above numerous tracks and descents, which, excluding from the craggy and canopied steep the light of day, seemed to pourtray

"Dells of gloomy horror."

The mist of evening was enshrouding the brow of the lofty heights; Leontini had travelled several leagues, and felt the effects of its fatigue. Gazing from a projecting ascent through the distance which lay before him, a small but wretched building appeared the only habitation within sight, and to its inhabitants he directed his course. It was a rude although cleanly hovel, shelved in the hollow of one of the mountains. The wild thyme and heath briars grew upon its path, and the vast range of cedar and pine trees served to partially shade it from observation. From its eminence, the main road was seen winding through an uncultivated waste, till the black and impenetrable appearance of the forests terminated the track, through which, at intervals, a faint speck of the Mediterranean was just distinguished.

The door was opened by a hardy and cheerful-looking

mountaineer, who, surveying the appearance of Leontini with some apparent good humour and caution, he made a formal obedience. He inquired the distance from the next town, and, finding that it was several leagues, he purposed sheltering at the hovel for the night. The mountaineer repeated a hearty welcome, and throwing some fresh fuel upon the hearth, the red flame reflected brightly on the walls of the hovel. Its interior afforded but little, either for observation or entertainment. A flask of choice Greek wine was offered to the Signore Leontini, and, partaking of some dried fruits, with a large oaten cake, which was presented, he felt somewhat refreshed.

The close of the following day brought him to Capo Cefalu, and, engaging with a small galliot trading to Messina for an exchange of some rich merchandise, he was speedily within sight of the ancient and opulent port. Making a temporary abode at Porto Real, he sought some gratification in its rich and varied prospects. From a rocky ascent adjoining Fort St. Katharine, a scene of the most peculiar grandeur presented itself.*

The heat of a Sicilian sun had decreased, and only its beams lingered on the calm surface of the Faro, (or straits,) leading from the entrance of the port, amply defended by majestic ridges of moun-

* "It has often been remarked, both by the ancients and moderns, that in the heat of summer, after the sea and air have been much agitated by the winds, and a perfect calm succeeds, there appears, about the time of dawn, in that part of the heavens over the Straits, a great variety of singular forms, some at rest, and some moving with great velocity. These forms, in proportion as the light encreases, seem to become more aerial; till, at last, some time before sunrise, they entirely disappear. The Sicilians represent this as the most beautiful sight in nature. Leanti, one of their latest and best writers, came here on purpose to see it. He says, the heavens appeared crowded with a variety of objects; he mentions palaces, woods, gardens, &c. besides the figures of men, and other animals, that appear in motion amongst them. No doubt, the imagination must be greatly aiding, in forming this aerial creation, but as so many of their authors, both ancient and modern, agree in the fact, and give an account of it from their own observation, there certainly must be some foundation for the story. Giardini, a Jesuit, has lately written a Treatise on this phenomenon. The celebrated Messinese, Gallo, has likewise published something on this singular subject. The common people, according to custom, give the whole merit to the devil, and this is much the shortest and easiest way of accounting for it."

Brydone's Tour through Sicily and Malta.

tains, upon which art had completed what was originally the rude and sublime outlines of nature. The town of Reggio, stretching its towers to the "blue horizon," met the eye of Leontini, and musing for a moment upon the purport of the mission which caused his presence there, a sigh escaped him for the unfortunate bride of the Neapolitan Carraccio.

CHAPTER III.

I burn, I throb, my pulses beat
I feel thy rankling arrows now;
They tremble in my bleeding brow,
And pierce Reflection in his filmy seat.
In heights of pain my heart is tost,
And all the meaner sorrows lost.

DERMODY.

THE Dwarf was punctual to his promised meeting. The Comptessa enjoyed a peculiar kind of delight in his visit, and it was expressed in a reception of the most cheering welcome. "I would rather, Comptessa, meet with the fare of a guest less valued, than be the participator of entertainments like these; they do but form obstacles, probably, to our meeting, and tempt us, by artificial means, to resolutions which alone ought to be the work of calm and reflection. But permit me to speak of what may be of greater import. Since my presence here, the Duca Paoli has made me inheritor of his sole confidence; through the entire range of Palermo's dominion, the Dwarf, hitherto spurned and avoided, has free scope, power, command. He will shew it. *The wealth, kingdom, pallazzi*, all in Paoli's claim, are *in the Dwarf's care*—mark you that, Signora—and he is desired *to use them as his observations and friendship warrants*."

"Oh no, impossible, impossible," shouted the Comptessa, with a peculiar force and insanity of expression, that failed not to pourtray how gladly she received such an instance of information; she clasped the hands of the Dwarf,—"To what, Valfroni, does an event like that originate? Oh, do not falter, tell me all, and I will reveal to thee every feeling and every wish my heart possesses—ah! it would be happiness indeed, dared I to think that Valfroni's wrongs, and he must remember such intimation was given to Rosalviva, had received atonement from the hands of the Duca Paoli."

"They have, Signora, in some degree; but *wealth and kingdoms* cannot hush sufferings that I have known; they may, for a temporary period, but the storm is still gathering, though hidden, and must, at a future interval, burst forth."

"This is comfort to my soul," remarked the Comptessa; "other clouds, equally blackened, and fraught with impending danger, shall hover in conjunction with those thy imagination forms, and in one destructive crush shall the proud Duca Paoli perish. 'Tis sweet, Valfroni, to have a partner in an act of great and vindictive revenge;—thou wilt be mine?"

"Nay, Signora, ere I could possibly subscribe myself to this, I would know the extent of that cause by which it is derived."

"Scorned, insulted, and blighted love," unhesitatingly pronounced the Comptessa, and her eyes fully revealed the rage and indignation of her soul; "can there be causes, Dwarf Valfroni, more calculated for severe punishment than these?"

"None, none," answered the Dwarf, and a more than usual fire of countenance beamed from him at the moment of exclamation. "I have one day yet to come, when I must make out a similar penalty."

"Forget it not, Valfroni, but inflict it to its full extent; curses upon the viprous being who forgets the vow of love."

"The curse of every torture fall upon such an one as you have pictured, Comptessa! May the blood of every nerve within them scorch, and wither them up, as fire breathed from the maddened hydra! May agonies most acute fasten upon their heart, and in the hour of death may their hopes and their prayers be as loathsome and as abhorred as their pangs! May the great Creator, bounteously as his mercy is extended to fallen sinners, curse them! Let their grave be in the depths of hell—their souls for ever in its fires!"

"Yes, yes," impassionately rejoined the Comptessa, and she viewed, with eyes of gladness, the ardour of Valfroni's thirst of vengeance, "thou hast fondly loved, and thou hast suffered?"

"I have, Signora."

"And yet thy mistress was fair, lovely, and spoke with such

seeming truth, that you could have staked, probably, every power on earth in compact with her faith and affection," resumed the Comptessa, and, in tracing out the description of Valfroni's lover, she gave the resemblance too of Paoli's.

"I could have done all that human strength and human art could accomplish, to have perfected the happiness of this creature. What a thrill of strange and peculiar passion its recollection brings on my soul; that time when I used to gaze on her, through hours of gloom and sadness. We met, Signora, often, but not always happily; there was a kind of adversity that crowded upon our hopes, and chased our affection; her tears would heighten the melancholy of the scene; but when Valfroni spoke of love and happiness—when, in the soft embrace of innocence and sincerity, his bosom pillowed her form, and his heart throbbed with intelligence that recited schemes of future felicity—Oh, then, her look, her voice, and her smile, was indeed a Heaven. She would press her lips upon my brow, that ached with terror and oppression, and her kisses would alleviate its pain; she would tenderly clasp me, and, in the full glow of her affection, she exultingly then would exclaim, 'we shall yet be happy!' With this, who could have but loved as I did?—Madness as it were, I cherished it, and rather than have forfeited it, would have encountered torture, destruction and death."

The Comptessa was silent, an apathy seemed to reign over her senses, and though she gazed full upon the flushed countenance of the Dwarf, its sense was void.

"And think, Signora, when, at the moment my bliss was most perfect—when there was a cup offered to my lips beaming with such richness and such sweets—she—she alone dashed it from me—with her own willing hand she snatched from me the last hope, and the last throb of joy that ever warmed my bosom. You may imagine, in some degree, that state of misery which the distressed mariner suffers when his little bark, containing all that is valued by him on earth, is overwhelmed in one immense gulph, and, wrecked and desolate, he views the scene that has brought with it his horrors and his ruin. I stood—the motionless statue of grief and despair; there was no arm offered to lead me from my wretchedness—to sooth my suffering; she had fled from me, and with her, human happiness."

"And this deceit was practised to obtain another more deserving?" replied the Comptessa, somewhat interested in the narrative.

"Not more deserving, Signora;—he could but love her. More than I would have done for her, to shew my sense of felicity and to secure that of her's, could not have been the attainment of man; but there was some charm that diffused itself in her bosom, inspired by her new lover, that existed not but in the sun, of whose beams it was constantly reposing; and for this charm she bartered her promises; all those ties which serve to bind human nature in one formation of comfort and joy, were burst asunder; she took his heart to the unison of her own, and mine was flung from her unheeded and unpitied."

"But she relented?" cried Rosalviva.

"Never, Signora; she rioted for an age in the excesses of her love, and the guilty passion of her paramour."

"She lives yet in it?"

"Time, Signora, has brought on a satiety in the mind of her lover, and he has turned from the object of his once magnified idolatry; in the arms of one more endearing he loses the wanton smiles of his late mistress; it is ever the case attendant upon affections engendered like these. You, Signora, seem to know some little feeling, with regard to the correctness of my observation—has the Signore Duca Paoli deserted charms beauteous as thine? impossible!"

"He has;—but he shall yet learn the vengeance due to insulted affection. Thou hast deigned, Dwarf, to tell me of thy sufferings; they are but parallel with mine—nay, do not start—I once had a lover, kind and faithful as yourself; he seemed to bestow upon me every care and every hope, but the high blood within my bosom rushed impetuously, and my heart was swept away in its torrent. Oh, to the ear and senses of woman, what penetrates so quickly as the sweet balm of adulation. Paoli was then my admirer, he lavished it upon me with unceasing hand, and, blinded by its infatuation, I became lost to shame, truth, and honour. I quitted the presence of one who would have made me blest, and fled with him who now has rendered me wretched."

"And the lover survived his ruin?"

"Thanks to Heaven he fell; my disgrace, my end, he can never know; he died, Signore Dwarf. I will not assume vanity sufficient to mark the event, as derived from the result of blighted joy;—but he ceased to breathe more than during a trifling elapse after my union with Paoli."

"Better thus," observed Valfroni, "than to cross thy path with the bitter taunt of violated vows and perjured principles."

"Rather should this hand shed the blood that warms its heart, than Rosalviva suffer the momentary horror and torment his presence would create—oh, it would sink me into the earth!"

"And thou, too, art really wretched?" ejaculated Valfroni, fixing a look of earnest inquiry on the commanding outline of Rosalviva's countenance.

"'Tis a wretchedness, Dwarf, I scarcely know how to delineate; 'tis not the abject sorrow, the bitter grief, that dries up the current of every young and branching hope; it is indignation, scorn, and resentment combined; and its unities burst upon my soul with the fever of agony and revenge. For Francesca has he relinquished the Comptessa of Romagno—tell me, Dwarf, if an adder, whose sting has penetrated the most sensible part of thy nature, crosses thy step and lingers there,—what should follow?"

"Its destruction," replied Valfroni.

"It should, it should," eagerly echoed the voice of Rosalviva, gladdened in the coincidence of Valfroni's ideas with her own. "But a woman's courage is not ever at command; much as the reptile may have wounded, she might recoil at the moment its venom is seen."

"There are instruments invented by the art of mankind, to deal destruction out in every possible shape, and there are hands to wield them, Signora;—the viper, whose dreadful touch you have felt, should lose its sting; and in losing that, you enjoy the satisfaction required."

"With your aid, Dwarf Valfroni, methinks the spirit and resolution burning within my bosom could blaze forth in all its strength; thy temperance would enable me to deeds, I had not confidence otherwise to think upon.—You, too, feel an equal pang, and for its affliction no one could yield a better reward. Shall I claim thy services?"

The Dwarf mused.

"You see I am prompt, Valfroni; but I need not point out to one so capable of judging by experience the enthusiasm which is carried with it; my first glance directed to Valfroni told me that there was a sympathy and a suffering in his bosom akin with that of Rosalviva's. She has not drawn an incorrect portrait. Valfroni is sensible that the Duca Paoli has wronged him; he has also Rosalviva. What further remains, but, in unison, to seek atonement, and by one act reinstate the composure and peace of mind he so indignantly lacerated."

"Yes, this might be effected, Signora, justifiably and safely," rejoined the Dwarf, in a tone of the most calm and decisive kind.

"And *must* be effected," repeated the Comptessa, and her hand pressed more fervently that of Valfroni.

"Dost thou know, Signora, or rather dost thou remember, that the unhappy period which terminated thy parent's, the Conte Reo Cardoni's life, was singled out by the assassin's art."

"It was," replied the Comptessa, and a gloom momentarily overwhelmed the brightness of her features.

"Thou also wert sworn to avenge it, the oath was bound in compact with thy soul's destruction, dared you to fail."

"It was; but how know you this?"

"It was too publicly known and recorded, to have escaped me, or aught beside were their sensibility awakened to its interests. How hast thou performed thy covenant?" interrogated the Dwarf, after a space of time, in which there had been a complete silence. "Nay, do not descend to offer a frown, Signora," for he perceived that there was an alteration of visage and a cast of expression that augured her displeasure with the familiarity of the Dwarf's inquiry, "unless I do but hear the most minute description, how can I possibly administer aid?"

"True," murmured the Comptessa, and a sigh of agony seemed to escape her.

"You falter, Signora Rosalviva, is the assassin known to you?"

"Would he were; my broken promises and my neglected duty to my parent's destruction should meet atonement, in my immediate consignment of the recreant to the scaffold. 'Tis true, that the affairs of the heart have been more the care of Rosalviva than those which ought to have marked the duteous zeal due to her father's remains; but God will forgive it!—It has slept, but it now shall be my first thought, my first accomplishment."

"And thou wilt forget, then, thy injuries from Paoli;" remarked the Dwarf, as he beheld the kind of fiery ardour which vented itself in the wish of persecuting the assassin of Cardoni; "one must actuate the other, and both may be decreed, finally and irrevocably."

"Thou canst give me comfort, Valfroni," placidly cried the Comptessa.

"Willingly, and to prove further my sense of such, promise not to shrink, and I will point out thy father's murderer!"

"My father's murderer!" shouted Rosalviva, and a temporary wildness took possession of her faculties.

"Aye, Comptessa; I will not deceive you; the hand which guided the weapon to the heart of the Conte, in the piazzi of St. Marc, on the eve of St. Rosalia, was one thou hast often pressed."

The eyes of the Comptessa grew dim; there was a singular and mystic manner about the energy of the Dwarf that alarmed her, and she began almost to doubt his natural agency. She looked with an involuntary dread upon his cheerless countenance, and a sensitive shrill of terror seized her.

"Speak," she pronounced deliriously, "in candour, do not keep from me his name; my lips can blast it; speak, Valfroni."

"And thou canst positively, were it the dearest friend on earth, resign thy bond, in obedience to thy father's last command, and thy oath of allegiance."

"Assuredly; no tie on earth could make me relinquish the promise sworn to at the dying pillow of my parent."

"Signora, thou hast treble vengeance and treble claim; the assassin was——"

The Dwarf paused, and looking cautiously to the portal in the distance, from which his fancy formed approaching footsteps, he drew more closely to the Comptessa, whose agitation and impatience were manifested in the convulsed sob, and the breathless vibration of her bosom.

"Quick, quick, Dwarf! his name?"

"Paoli Golfieri!"

A violent and horrid shriek witnessed the Dwarf's harangue,

and she sunk for some moments, in a state of stupor, into the arms of Valfroni.

"Oh, God! oh, God!" she replied, on recovering her self-command, "this is dreadful indeed!"

The state of her feelings may be imagined to be those of the most afflicting and the most harrowing kind; she looked back at the wide career of sin she had run through, hand in hand with Paoli, with her father's assassin; the man she was bound by oath the strongest to hurl to punishment and death. Her senses seemed to reel within her; she shuddered to sketch the retrospect, she trembled to think of the future. For a short time her fine form and features were enshrouded in the most dejected and most abject appearance, nor could all the consolements of Valfroni dispel from her mind the intense pain and pressure of calamity that bowed it; a wildness and an utter abstraction alternately succeeded each other, and to the various remarks of the Dwarf Valfroni, she scarcely was heard to acknowledge reply. A goblet of sparkling lachrymae stood beside the couch of Rosalviva, and flying to its delusive and exhilarating relief, her mind and ideas obtained a fresh colouring.

Valfroni had detailed to her so minutely the incidents connected with the fatal catastrophe relative to Cardoni, and the frequent occurences that arose in her recollection since that period, relative to the conduct and manner of Paoli, served to render doubt at once fruitless. She recalled the singular ardour with which he sued for the character of the assassin, when the Padre Vivaldi had presented her with its outline, and urged her pursuit of it; and the more attentively she had recurrence to the past, so much was she the more convinced of its unfortunate reality. The night was already far advanced, the dim reflection of the lights in the apartment threw an unusual tint of darkness around it. The figure of the Dwarf, as he sat beside the Comptessa, scarcely moved, and there was a stillness solemn as it was unpleasant.

"If the Dwarf Valfroni," ejaculated the Comptessa, "wears a heart like mine, what will it not accomplish."

"He has a heart, Signora, bold and revengeful—can you but prove firm?"

"I will prove a giant's strength, a giant's soul," triumphantly replied Rosalviva, her eyes expressing the excess of passion that rested in her heart, and, at the same time, she drank deeply of the intoxicating beverage before her.

"Well then, Comptessa, it is for yourself to determine, whether the disgrace and destruction of the Duca Paoli be immediate or not—dost thou still love him?"

"Oh, shame and horror, I do, I do!"

"Wouldst thou have him survive it?—wouldst thou yet enjoy more of——"

"I would but see my rival, Francesca, tortured—say death—and then learn how far the feelings of his soul will reveal themselves towards her loss—this done, the proud Paoli can form no excuse for the denial of my fondest boast, Palermo's Duchessa—but this I doubt—his heart seems woven with her's, and she has acquired an ascendancy over it that holds free and entire dominion."

"And forgotten thee?" implied the Dwarf.

"Oh! yes, cold and frigid is the resemblance of that passion which once he inherited, and which oft he would pourtray."

"And if Paoli, sensible of thy value, and unmindful of the decease of Francesca, welcomes to his heart thy hopes and thy happiness, what follows?"

The Comptessa was unable to reply; she felt the agony of such a moment; she felt her fancy rise to scenes of splendour and bliss, in the acceptance of Paoli's hand and dukedom—but again her mind was appalled on its reflection that such an union was with the assassin of her parent. She uttered these suggestions to the Dwarf, but his persuasive and unerring tone diminished their poignancy.

"You may still preserve thy oath, Signora, and still enjoy the highest happiness!"

"Ha!" violently cried the Comptessa, and her enthusiasm seemed lighted up with more than usual brilliance; she seized the hand of Valfroni and pressed it to her heart—"and the terms that could secure to me this invaluable enjoyment?"

"Francesca no more, you claim at once the fiat of your wishes."

"Granted," replied the Comptessa, and her mind was rivetted to the remark of Valfroni.

"What is the sequel?" resumed he; "his refusal gives him to the scaffold—his acquiescence, the summit of your expectations—this done, there only remains for you to demand the wealth and possessions of his dukedom to your own consignment—think then what will be your power, your rank, and your grandeur—warn him that Palermo holds one being who can prove his atrocious guilt in the assassination of Reo Cardoni—ask of him if you shall point out to the tribunal of his country that charge, which will compel this being to disclose all his heart is in possession of—will he not shrink from the idea with horror? This much accomplished, you only can pronounce whether he lives the husband of Rosalviva, or falls the doomed assassin of thy parent."

"But didst thou not say, I could enjoy both these attainments?"

"Yes, Signora, but not for ever—at least if thy father's loss and his value be considered worth recollection. I said thou mightst still *preserve* thy oath; but why wouldst thou seek the mutual existence of these attainments? Tell me what possible feeling you can have towards the man who wantonly deserted thee—who, while he was presuming to cherish a flame for one, he was destroying the peace of another—has this man the soul left of former days?—no, it has gone. Makes he you the partner of his splendour on voluntary terms? Does he not purchase it by your silence? and can such an one retain a power of thought or commiseration in the bosom of Rosalviva? Surely not. The wealth of Palermo absolutely in her sole possession—can she then not find cause to proclaim to the world the assassin of her parent? Can she not tear off the mask he has long concealed himself with? Her country will applaud the deed, and she may reign, as it were, amidst the warmest of honour, and exultations, at the act of magnanimity."

"And Paoli perishes," she pronounced at the termination of Valfroni's detail.

"As traitors should perish," cried the Dwarf. "Do you forget your wrongs? or do you shrink from the task? Indeed I thought the Comptessa Rosalviva had a more lofty soul, or I should not have deigned to presume upon its guidance."

"No, no, this is irrelevant," impressively spake the Comptessa, "I can do all that becomes me—I can fulfil my oath—but how, mighty Valfroni, can the existence of Francesca be parted with? Might not the deed at once destroy our projects? Might it not lead to detection? Who can be *her* executioner?"

"This is with facility accomplished; my introduction to her excellenza will favour me with sufficient opportunity for every purpose, and so ably (pardon me, Signore, if I over-rate my own poor ability)"—the Comptessa smiled, but she snatched his hand to her lips, and its pressure testified the sense and rapture she felt for his zeal and superior knowledge; "I repeat, so ably could it be effected, that no sign or evidence of destruction can be adduced; suspicion shall not have the smallest crevice for its purposes; no individual being should know, or can possibly discover, the symptoms or cause of her death, so secretly could I stop and undermine the heart's pulsation of this idol, Francesca, that she shall sink into the icy embrace of dissolution, ignorant even herself that its approach is so near, and at once so decisive."

"Oh, most powerful and astonishing Valfroni, what have I not gained in having thee?"

"Peace, Signora, I will detail the conclusion. Francesca's indisposition will be so slight, but so certain in its result, that it must be supposed the natural ordainment and interference of Providence only is the cause of her departure to an early grave."

"This is power, this is sublimity most wonderful!" cried Rosalviva, and her bursts of rapture were vented in continual plaudits and testimonials of the sense of Valfroni's value. "And to what agency does Valfroni owe all this grand and masterly acquirement?"

"Poison," audibly answered the Dwarf.

The Comptessa momentarily startled—the calm and expressive manner of the Dwarf, and the singularity of his observations and disclosures charmed and fired her soul with more than grateful ardour. "Poison!" she repeated, and her tone almost seemed to fear the safety of its effect.

"Yes, Signora, and of so pure and subtle a nature, that not the slightest trace or distortion of feature can mark the victim's fate; its efforts are slow, imperceptible, but will never fail; languor and weakness will be its attendants; yet no reason can be construed more than the mere relaxation and apathy of mind, which at the best of times, and in the strongest of constitutions, will have free egress. This compound, Comptessa, will be given in her beverage, she was pleased to accept from my hand, (by the way) this day at her husband's banquet—a draught of choice wine which I selected and recommended!—it can be repeated to-morrow, and with it can be infused the compound I speak of. Some hours will elapse ere it proceeds to work upon the mind and spirits of the partaker, but its effect and its success will arrive."

"And thy hand, Valfroni, will administer this?" exclaimed the Comptessa, almost overpowered at the sensations of her delight.

The Dwarf paused.

"Oh, do not keep me in suspense; you have raised my hopes to an enviable height; do not, even with your silence and hesitation, blast them."

"I have, doubtless, signified, Comptessa, the plan which would produce your happiness; but of what right or authority has my interference? The Duchessa Francesca never wronged me; indeed, to speak impartially, I should conceive her too amiable; and why am I to be the destroyer of her days?—Why should my soul be charged with her murder?"

A shriek of discordant and painful moment escaped Rosalviva, and she looked with pitiable inferiority at the unexpected and galling remark.

"Oh! Valfroni, how have you tortured me? This state of my wretchedness surpasses in every degree that which I have ever yet known; it is cruel—it is unkind, indeed."

Tears followed the expression of Rosalviva in rapid succession, and her sobs were violent. The Dwarf gazed on her with the most cordial tranquillity, and in his breast there appeared to exist a world of new and indescribable sensations. He extended his hand to the Comptessa; she received it, but her grief really manifested the absorbed and harrowed state of her inward suffering. They were the first tears nearly she had through any means acknowledged—they were bitter ones. The Dwarf had fixed his eyes intentively upon her; he ventured to kiss her lips; he repeated this familiarity, and the warm blood again was renovating her exhausted nature. She turned her swollen eyes, still wet with their tears, towards him, and scarcely beyond a whisper, cried, "Is there no price that can be offered, Valfroni, for this signal act of service?"

The Dwarf was silent; but her pressure of his hand to her bosom, which heaved with excessive emotion; her flushed countenance, and her convulsive respiration, separately told that feelings of a warm description were animating her heart.

"To which do you allude?" asked Valfroni, "the compound can be procured at no great price; but if you mean the service of Valfroni, he must reply, that no sum on earth can purchase it."

"Oh, miserable and degraded woman that I am, to unburden my heart, and to unite it with one I thought deserving in a mutual cause, and thus to be renounced.—Valfroni, I did think thou hadst more sympathy and more fondness."

"Thou wert not deceived;—listen, when I state, that no price, however great, can purchase this act that leads to your eternal welfare; I do not deny but that it is otherwise to be obtained."

"Tell me,—tell me the means, and I will hope to deserve it."

"I have much of your confidence, Comptessa, truly; I might, for the arrangement of this design, hope more," insinuated the Dwarf, and he surveyed the tremulous beating of her bosom, which had become somewhat calmed, yet still fluttering beneath its anxieties.

"Thou shalt have the utmost of thy hopes, Valfroni, in completing so great a task as that you have commenced."

A pause again ensued, and for some trifling elapse, a mingled sense of embarrassment was felt by each other. The Dwarf drew her more closely to his arms, and, looking mildly upon her partially smiling features, he implied, "The young heart which first ventures upon the world, Signora, sets out girted and bound with honour and virtue; tempt but to possess it, and it renounces riches, threats, and all that might be imagined to realise it; it passes further through the throng of admiration, and in an unsuspecting moment, escapes from its chain, and, to the voice and supplication of the urchin-boy, denominated Love, yields that which kingdoms, treasures, and ages, could not have won."

The Comptessa smiled with peculiar pleasure at his figurative sketch, and she suffered him to press her lips, which she returned with a seeming fondness.

"Shall I illustrate still more, Signora? Even thus may be applied the services of Valfroni. No price could engage them; but, in the smiles and pleasures of Rosalviva's arms, they are irrevocably sealed."

"Dwarf Valfroni, thou hast art and power to win the sternest heart. Oh! who could resist the fascination of thy voice?—Live in Rosalviva's smiles,—her arms are opened to thy bliss."

"Enough,—enough, divine Comptessa!—We both are happy."

CHAPTER IV.

————————At this hour,
This solemn hour, when silence rules the world,
And wearied Nature makes a general pause,
Wrapt in night's sable robe; these cloisters drear,
And charnels pale, shooting across my path,
With silent glance, I seek the shadowy vale
Of Death.

PORTEUS.

ON the lofty summit of a steep rock, commanding an entire view of the villa Monte Real, stood the Castle San Viedo; remarkable only for its beauty of situation and the tranquillity of its solitude. It had been the occasional retirement of the Duca Reggio, and during his existence every care was taken to render the loneliness of the spot and the wildness of its appearance more desirable and more attractively picturesque. Paoli had renewed at intervals an attention to the improvements, and as the mild season of the year approached, or its more serene period, there was usually every requisite adopted, to invite the visitor to an autumnal sojournment at its rocky seclusion. A banquet, given in honour of an annual festival, was signified at the ducal pallazzi, the subsequent day of Valfroni's meeting with Rosalviva; and in the height of enthusiasm, he had with his most earnest punctuality infused a sufficient portion of the compound into a glass of wine called for by Francesca, and which the wary Dwarf took especial care to procure for her.

The ensuing morning brought with it the result, Valfroni knew would be experienced; a slight drowsiness, and a mental stupor visited her, but as the cause was supposed to arise from the fatigue of the previous evening, scarcely any notice was taken of her languid depression.

The day advanced, but instead of the accustomed hilarity of Francesca, there was the stupor, with all its general effects, and which the certain properties and government of the potion could not, as the Dwarf implied, fail to operate.

A slight intermission of fever was at times observable, and seeking only the aid of some cooling beverage, she confined herself to the quietude of her chamber. The evening found her much in the same situation, and Paoli considered that change of air, and the more invigorating breezes of San Viedo, might be beneficial towards her recovery. The distance from Palermo being only a league, he gave the necessary orders for her conveyance; and while the last departing rays of a bright sun rested on the suburbs of Monte-Real, they reached the Castelli.

At intervals the spirits of Francesca enlivened, and indulging a few moments in an ordinary glow of animation, she receded again into a kind of dejection, and seemingly negligent of conversation, or the efforts made to amuse her, she would recline absorbed in the arms of Paoli. The time that would witness its final effect upon Francesca was come: and on her retiring for the night, she apparently entered on her eternal slumbers. Early in the morning, the Dwarf Valfroni visited the Castelli San Viedo; his presence diverted in some measure the time of Paoli until noon, ere he thought of disturbing Francesca.

Language is somewhat deficient to do justice to the feelings and astonishment of the Duca, on beholding the form of Francesca wrapt in death. He summoned assistance; but every art was unavailing to restore her.

Paoli gazed upon her with emotions of tenderness and sorrow; he pressed her lips, but they were cold, the damp chill of death had fastened upon them. He was led from the corse, amidst the struggle of some few finer feelings, and secluding himself within his apartment, looked back at the visionary existence of the past.

Anguish filled the bosoms of all who were familiar with the perfections and the kindness of Francesca. Violent cold, supposed to have been received in her too suddenly retiring from the intense heat of the banquet, she having been observed to hasten to the terrace, where the powerful effect of the night air, must doubtlessly have seized on her delicate frame. Those who knew her less, imagined it an event ordained by the immediate dispensation of heaven, and while they heaved a momentary sigh for her loss, exclaimed, "the will of Providence must be abided by."

The Dwarf consoled the gloom of Paoli's mind, and at the period of her interment, he undertook the attention due to the ceremony. By the counsels of Valfroni, the "pomp of state," and the unmeaning grandeur attendant upon the bier of departed rank, were avoided, and he was persuaded to suffer the burial to be performed with the utmost privacy and solemnity.

"Who can bear," added he, "the multitude, with gaping mouth and gazing eye, in assemblage, to usher forth their useless exclamations, and the mourner's ear to be wrung with lamentation? Even, Signore Duca, the presence of relatives are but oppressive; we are sensible that the decrees of God are just, and cannot be reproved. Great as we feel the loss of those most dear to us, still, at his righteous and manifest decrees, it is not in the power of man to avert them, or should he repine. Life, at best, Signore Duca, is but a perilous and stormy ocean; they who hasten the fleetest along its current to repose in the haven of a better world, ought to excite sensations of happiness, rather than those of grief, in the bosoms of us who are doomed to be parted from them."

"These are just remarks," answered Paoli, his mind rather more cheered, than in the early state of the occurrence; and looking upon Valfroni with an earnest eye, he added,—"But we cannot help the common weakness of our nature. He who had known a Francesca, and had felt the short, but too happy period of an union like that I thought to experience, cannot refrain indulging in a sympathy and regret at its untimely closure."

The arrangements for the interment of Francesca were deputed to Valfroni, and the serene hour of midnight witnessed the removal of the corse to the cemetry of the ducal chapel in the Abbey of Monte Real.

The night was dark;—the black clouds that chased each other through the arch of heaven, gave but trifling intervals from the display of the bright features of the soft and "moonlit world." The winds were so gentle, and the face of Nature so solemn, that the hour and the occupation seemed enveloped as it were in a complete and almost mystic tranquillity.

The interior of the Abbey was hung with sable habiliments, and escutcheons of state, rendered visible by the many tapers burning around the catafalque and the altar. The mourners, and the few attendants that witnessed the ceremony, knelt with pious resignation during its performance, and as the deep tone of the organ swelled with its requiem, their love and veneration for the object showed a reality in tears, that spoke more than an abundance of language. The termination of the same week brought Paoli again to the ducal pallazzi and the condolence of Palermo.

Rosalviva had witnessed in secret the progress of her wishes, and through each degree of Valfroni's assiduity she rewarded him with the riches of sensual and enthusiastic love.

"And thou hast done the last duty to Palermo's Duchessa!" cried Rosalviva, the evening after the funeral; "Valfroni, when can I enough repay these disinterested but zealous services?"

"Rosalviva," spake the Dwarf, (their intercourse had made the pronunciation of her name now at all times familiar,) "there is yet greater enjoyment for thy vindictive passion. Francesca is not buried."

"Not buried?" and the looks of the Comptessa evinced a wild and singular feeling.

"My wish to afford gratification to you still more exulting, led me to delude the pious devotees of the church, and instead of consigning to the peaceful seclusion of the tomb, the corse of Francesca, I chose to have it immersed within the grating of a ruined vault of the castelli, and in its stead, solder up the coffins, which were sufficiently weighty to avoid suspicion."

"And the body of Francesca?" rapturously inquired the Comptessa.

"Is where I named; when the night's deepest gloom comes on, if Rosalviva has courage, she shall view it, amid all its baleful and deadly solitude."

"She will; and the sight of its livid resemblance shall afford bliss to her soul, in mockery of the fair form, and the bewitching features that captivated her doting husband, and caused the wretchedness of Rosalviva.

"And to what purpose can it be further consigned?" asked the Comptessa, at the close of a short but triumphant interval.

"Only to that of our pastime! It will yield comfort to Rosalviva, to be enabled, as her fancy desires, to muse upon the wasted and decomposing form of the once lovely and engaging Francesca,—will it not?"

"Beyond measure, Dwarf Valfroni; this act magnifies thy worth, and binds me to thy interests for ever."

"I doubt not my reward," replied Valfroni, and his lips wandered with repeated warmth over her charms.

The intense obscurity of the atmosphere served their purposes, and as the Pallazzi di Romagno was hushed in repose, the Dwarf, accompanied by Rosalviva, for whom he had provided mules, journeyed towards Monte Real. Their path lay through the most remote and unfrequented part of the forest, verging from Palermo; the rapid flashes of blue lightning from the sultry heat of the night, flitting through the branches of the dark cypress, the poplar, and the lofty pine, with the intermitting roar of distant thunder, which at times vibrated in dismal echoes o'er the craggy precipices, then rushing through the winding avenues of the traveller's route, and terminating in dreary response down the immense steep, whose measureless abyss seemed to lead to other worlds, produced an electric effect. It was not heeded by the Comptessa, but occasionally halting for a moment, she would gaze upon the wild and fearful scene around them. The rhapsody that floated across her mind, at Francesca's death, and the opportunity of viewing her pallid corse, in commemoration of her visionary existence, dispersed at once the dread of danger, and afforded her mind and spirits an unusual thrill of delight and animation. The spiral tower of San Viedo was before them, and they alighted at a narrow entrance in the southern angle of its steep ascent. The solitude of the spot precluded observation, and they made fast the animals to an adjoining column.

"This, then, leads to the grave of my victim?" said Rosalviva, "oh, its dark and impenetrable mazes convey a sensation of more sublimity than all the gilded porticos Palermo can command. Welcome, silent and mysterious solitudes! I hail ye with rapturous emotions; thy roofed and unexplored recesses shelter the bones of Francesca! Quick, Valfroni! to the tombless corner of earth that contains the Duchessa."

The Dwarf had provided himself with a lamp, and turning its reflector, they proceeded along the partly dilapidated building.

A total silence witnessed their progress; their separate thoughts seemed wholly to ingross their minds, during the pause of some minutes, till at length they reached the vault where was deposited the Signora Francesca. It was narrow but lofty, and its impregnable walls doubled its security. The Dwarf closed the grating, and they surveyed its interior.

Upon a bench of red granite was resting the body of Francesca, enshrouded in a thick and richly furred robe of sable cloth. Her head-tire was of snowy whiteness, fashioned like that of the nuns of Saint Viedo, but over it was partially drawn a cowl of velvet, lined with ermine. On her breast rested a crucifix, richly studded with brilliants, which was affixed to the girdle that confined her robe, by a massive chain of pure gold. In her hand was a rosary, elaborately carved, and by her side was placed an illuminated missal, nor were the usual appendages of death forgotten. The crossed bones and the fleshless skull were laid on a small table, before a calvary, which had once been the ornament of Francesca's private oratory, before which stood a small taper, that shed a dim and solemn light through the dull and darksome cell. A chilling sensation of terror rushed across the bosom of Rosalviva at the gloomy abode, and she caught the arm of the Dwarf with an apparent dread of some horrid catastrophe.

"Does the heart of Rosalviva sink?" questioned the Dwarf, while the reflection of the lamp threw a shade over his dark features, that rendered their expression unintelligible.

The Comptessa made an effort to resume her prior courage and firmness, and, in a tone harsh yet faltering, she exclaimed, "Shew me the corse."

The Dwarf disengaged part of the cowl that concealed the countenance of Francesca, and, with the light of the lamp, the Comptessa gazed upon its placid and still smiling expression. There was not the slightest change in its appearance, since when the "festive hour" marked her presence, save that the rosy hue of the lips had faded, and had left a pallid colouring. The gratification of Rosalviva was alternately succeeded by that of guilt, as she viewed the body of the Duchessa.

"And is it here, Valfroni, that thou wouldst keep the corse?"

"Here, that thy sight can be, at frequent periods, gratified; when the silent and death-like stillness of the night can guide us to the dungeon; she needs not to be more secure."

"But the Castelli San Viedo!" replied the Comptessa, seemingly dubious of its secrecy; "would not the hollow and horrible vaults beneath St. Rosalia be a safer mansion?"

The Dwarf mused.

"*That* is a spot sacred only to our own footsteps; it may perchance that in our visits *here*, the eye of busy curiosity might pursue us—alarm would be given—the cell, remote as is its situation, cannot be unknown to the inmates of San Viedo; and then think, Valfroni, what would be the result of such a search!—discovery of the body!"

"She shall be borne, then, to the deepest vault of St. Rosalia," pronounced the Dwarf, assured of the more infinite practicability of the suggestion, "the eye of Heaven alone can be witness there to our meetings!"

"Hush, Valfroni, that expression makes my heart shudder and hang within my bosom, swelled in horrid emotion; speak not of observation of deeds like these, much less that of Heaven's!" She trembled, and an inward throb fastening upon her soul, it acknowledged its subservience and weight of guilt.

The Dwarf laughed; it was in a bitter and derisive tone, and the sepulchral silence of the cell gave to it an almost unearthly vibration. "I cannot resist this levity, Rosalviva," he cried, "when I hear you speak thus *morally* and *piously*—mind we are not doing penance to St. Christina's shrine, nor are we——"

"But hold, hold," interrupted the Comptessa, "this is not a time for the indulgence of idle moments; the corse," and she pointed to Francesca, "must be removed."

"The increasing approach of light, ere we can attain Palermo, will not give us opportunity for the present; it must remain until the evening of to-morrow, and with proper arrangement she shall be conveyed to the retreat of Valfroni."

"And yet the incumbrance, and the mountainous path, will preclude, and I fear defy our attempts."

"We will not thus hazard them, Rosalviva; from the terrace

balustrade of di Romagno you can descend, a small boat shall bear us to the skirts of this building—there, in waiting, you will look for my return with Francesca. The obscurity of the place, and the darkness, will not afford the least chance for detection; even were it observed that the barque was in waiting, suspicion could not be attached—our persons are unknown, and the immense covering which enshrouds Francesca cannot betray it; this done, the black foam of the waters carries its burden to the landing shore of Monte Pelegrino."

"Delightful!" rapturously shouted Rosalviva and her manner pourtrayed her returning sensations of triumph.

The Dwarf extended his hand, which she clasped with an avidity, and kissed with repeated ardor.

"Thy directions and thy judgment are boundless, Valfroni; who could oppose them? or who could defy their purposes? Oh! thou art truly devoted to the scarce deserving Rosalviva!"

"Dismiss these panegyrics," briefly replied Valfroni, "you fully repay their deserts, believe me."

Rosalviva again leaned over the corse, and gazed, with exulting pleasure, upon its senseless appearance. Even amid the pressure of these extacies, she could but admire the divine features, and the beaming looks of sweetness and purity that once gave animation and lustre to the form of Francesca.

The hour of the following midnight brought the Dwarf, agreeably to his intention, to the cell where was placed the body of Francesca. Rosalviva had with difficulty been dissuaded from accompanying him during the occupation of the event. The night was tremendous, and the face of nature so convulsed, that it required almost superhuman strength and courage not to be appalled at its horrors. The vast space of horizon was thronged with dark and rushing clouds; the wind swept, in hollow and stunning echoes, through the forest, and the rain fell in torrents, united with the intense and vivid flash of incessant lightning, followed by such strong peals of thunder, that the confidence of Rosalviva was defeated, and she shrunk from the dreadful contention and rage of the "fury-fraught element." She urged Valfroni to delay their intended mission, but he would not be biassed from his purposes, and closely shielding his person from the storm, he was speedily within the walls of the Castelli San Viedo.

The stream of light that guided him along the subterranean passage, leading to the dungeon, was with difficulty preserved. The building appeared shaken to its foundations, and the deep moan of the winds, passing through the avenues, conveyed an universal sense of horror. The Dwarf pursued the track undismayed, and, closing the grating of the cell after him, he again gazed upon the Duchessa. He grasped the sylph-like form of Francesca within his arms, and traversing, with the utmost speed, through the isolated and broken arches of the Castelli vaults, he rested it upon the fragment of a pedestal, and, beckoning to a figure who was musing in the distance of an adjoining colonade, they together conveyed it to the boat. The tempest had abated, and the stars reappeared with a more than usual brilliance. The surface of the waters was still in agitating motion, and the current hurried the little vessel with an uncommon rapidity, towards the projecting shore of Monte Pelegrino.

The stillness of the hour, and the night's tranquillity, seemed to render the scene in capacitude with the incident, and the Dwarf led the way, still supporting the body of Francesca. A companion, called Julian, habited as a page, and who had been discovered at the retreat of St. Rosalia, in earnest attention upon the Dwarf since his confidence with the Duca Paoli, preceded him; and while in one hand he retained a small lamp, he assisted in conveying the habiliments of Francesca. Reaching a secure vault, whose entrance was through a rocky division in its walls, he took the light from the attendant, and cautioning him to remain silent, his figure was momentarily lost in the thick gloom that spread itself before the eye. The Dwarf was not absent but few minutes, when he returned, and they traversed the passages leading to the habitable part of Valfroni's abode.

CHAPTER V.

Amid the vast horizon's stretch,
In restless gaze the eye of wonder darts
O'er the expanse.

SOTHEBY.

So contraries on Etna's top conspire,
Here hoary frosts, and by them breaks out fire.

COWLEY.

THE blue streak of morning lighted Leontini to the port or landing of Reggio. The long track of the Mediterranean rolled smoothly beneath the vessel, and as the soft ray of dawn broke upon the surface of the waters, its appearance seemed to unite in the blue horizon, that of the "ocean world." There was a delightful silence,—it gave rise to a sublimity of thought, and a sweetness of melancholy, that were mutually interesting.

At the extremity of the town was situate the Strada di Zelto, the habitation of the Senor del Capucio. The humble and retired appearance of the spot denoted its denial to wealth or splendour; but there was a respectful quietness, and a degree of neatness about it, that spoke the industry and care of its inhabitants.

An aged Neapolitan, on whose brow was scattered the wintry hairs of time, welcomed the appearance of Leontini; but, to his inquiry of the Signora Carraccio, he heaved a struggling sigh, and in mellow tones replied, "Wearied, Signore, with care and the weight of mental suffering, she left this dwelling but few days since. Palermo was the extent of her journey,—her husband—but no matter; he has deserted her, and the poor creature's heart hangs upon its last thread.—Never do I expect, Signore, to see her more: there was an expression in her countenance, and a peculiarity in her manner, when she grasped the hand of Capucio, that told him it would be their last earthly meeting."

The sympathy of Leontini was sensibly awakened to the remarks of the Signore Capucio, and which but too fatally accorded with the outline of the portrait sketched by Carraccio.

Leontini signified the purport of his visit, yet was at conjecture upon what condition to render final its completion. The arguments of the relative of Visconti were, that she had quitted Reggio for ever! However, he resolved to entrust the packet to the care of Capucio; and, upon his return to Palermo, if the Signora had not departed, she would be in possession of his arrangement.

He begged the attention of Capucio to his mission; and if any other directions were formed contrary to that he now had fulfilled, he purposed by written communication to forward them.

An involuntary sigh of sensibility stole from Leontini, as he mused upon the ill-fated happiness and destiny of the bride of Carraccio. His anxiety to return to Palermo by the most secluded route, and to inform the Neapolitan of the nature of his tour, induced him to quit Reggio immediately, and without difficulty or delay, he retraced his track again to Messina.

Not a star lent its aid throughout the vast vault of heaven, to illumine its "wide world," as, faint and bewildered almost, the Signore Leontini, from one of the heights of Messina, stood absorbed in a reverie of meditation. The whole scene appeared wrapt in obscurity, save the intervening flashes of quick lightning that traced its serpentine track along the skies. The moody silence of Leontini was disturbed, as his eye, diverted from its "nothingness," gazed upon the awful and grand appearance of Etna. Far above the most towering eminences, just descending, in appearance, from the veiled heavens, the red volumes of smoky flame displayed their illuminating and majestic power. The tranquillity of the spot where Leontini stood,—the vast space around which the streaming light from Etna seemed to render visible, and the tremendous chain of mountains just distinguished by the occasional appearance of the yellow moon, united a prospect at once magnificent, horrible, and gloomy.

The mind of Leontini was disposed to realise a gratification hitherto unthought of; and, engaging a guide, with mules, he pursued his way, making Etna his most direct and principal route.

The road extending from Messina is romantic, lofty, and furnishes the traveller with views his eye can scarcely hope to survey; so varied, so wild, so picturesque, and so extensive, are its objects. It were impossible, likewise, to conceive the luxuriance and the aspect of the immense ridge of mountains, leaving just path sufficient for the footsteps of the mule, along distances of many leagues. Here, too, are seen mingled with the wildness of nature, fruits, shrubs, and flowers, the most delightful and in abundance. The cinnamon, pine, and jessamine, which also enclose them, and which are profusely scattered, interspersed with branches of the Indian fig, and other singular but beautiful productions, diffuse a fragrance at the same time, that when refreshed by the light dews and the gentle breezes, emit a delicious odour.

Passing Giardini to the left on the sea coast, there is little change, either in the scene or its journey; the same bold romantic imagery presents itself. On arriving at the small town of Taorminia, a change of conveyance is offered, and in addition to the guides, there are sbirri or guards, who are hired for their protection along the island, and according to the weight of the employer's purse, so are their services and vigilance extended. Yet, strange as it may appear, these men, whose character and crime have been, during a long career, marked with the most dire and hardened colouring, and who have with difficulty escaped the wheel or the scaffold, are in their new capacity treated with the utmost cordiality, protected and even revered. Their courage is generally strong, and the most perfect confidence and fidelity is reposed in their care and attention. They have also the power to chastise any acts of dishonor, knavery, or impositions; and frequently punish with instant death, such as endeavour to injure or deceive their employers. They usually precede the travelling equipage, well-mounted upon their mules, their carbines ready for action; also pistols, which they carry out of number, as well as sidearms; although in some instances, in passing through the most desolate and unfrequented places, reserves of Sicilian banditti have been known to loiter, and these guides, for a share of the plunder, turn chief actors in the scene of slaughter. Indeed the robberies and attacks of this kind, and at this part of Sicily, are enormous.

There is a small tract of land, which Leontini was near approaching, that bears a most appalling character. From this spot, (Val Demoni,) numerous brigands nightly wander, and the utmost perseverance of the Sicilian government have found a failure in attempting to extirpate them. Nature has formed a barrier sufficient to preclude the strongest force or the most spirited attack, as the immense caverns and subterranean passages beneath mountains, where access is deemed impossible, and which form such peculiar shelter, that no one beside those acquainted with the tract can ever discover them. Still it may not be amiss to point out, that, according to an adage of "honor among thieves," the banditti of Val Demoni reverence this particular to its full extent. At times, when the profits of their *profession* are less at command, they raise frequent loans from the adjacent districts and inhabitants, who mostly from fear, and partly aware of the strict sense of *honor* and *honesty* that is manifested in the kind of transaction, make no scruple of thus serving them; and so precise and correct to the time and promise of repaying them are the banditti of Val Demoni, that their exploits are desperate, and their perseverance in the obtainment of booty, in order to fulfil their payment, that they willingly bear the stain of murder, rather than that of dishonor.

Guiseppe Fazzelo was the leader of a small brigand, occupying the chief range of the Val Demoni mountains. The traits of this man's character were peculiarly great; to the most intrepid and daring courage, which amounted even to ferocity, was added an invincible firmness, a strength of mind, and an intrepidity scarcely equalled; a man whose public deeds in the Neapolitan territory had shed more human blood, and had been the propagation of more vile enormities, than almost any malefactor registered in the lists of those who had terminated their existence on the *gibbet*, or toiled at the galleys; yet was there a mildness and serenity of countenance and manners, a sense of honor, and even virtue, and a conduct and principles altogether allied, that amidst the rugged and unwholesome covering that formed his exterior, there was a heart within, destined for a better sphere.

Some few leagues from the retreat of the horde commanded by Guiseppe was a monk's cell; it was a little spot raised by the hand of Nature; its enclosures gave him food, and its springs and rivulets a beverage. The bounty of the few bettermost inhabitants, an occasional donation, and the liberality of the stranger, who wandered by his sanctuary, and to whom the monk would trace out the hundred tales, connected with one rill or mountain, he would bend in gratitude for the few pistoles bestowed upon his narration.

Time, and little need of further wants beyond the lap which Providence had opened to him, had amassed a small sum, and which he held in "goodly store;" bequeathed it in acts of charity, and relieving the poor wretch who strayed, friendless and homeless, to his rustic and holy shed. The humble stock had at times given aid to the momentary necessities of Guiseppe Fazzelo, and it had again been remitted with reverential esteem and gratitude. It was from instances of this kind, that a brother of Fazzelo, and one of the band, endeavoured to serve his own purposes. He hastened, during the calm of one unsuccessful night, to the cell of the Monk, and in the name of Guiseppe he urged the immediate loan of a few ducats.

The Monk received him with all due esteem and veneration, and, in a tone of truth and suavity, he replied, "Ah! Signor Otto Guiseppe, thou know'st well my zeal in compliance with the claims of thy good brother, Fazzelo; but, in the present instance, my wishes are thwarted, inasmuch as I have blest an unfortunate but pious family of the nearer mountain, beyond the valley here, with my utmost value. The late storm had swept away the stock and herd, he was possessed of, and rather than the tears of his wife and the hunger of his children should appeal in vain, I offered, with cheer, to reinstate his little stock. Oh! the grateful humiliation and enthusiasm paid me by this relieved circle, and the warm appeal to heaven in thanks for His bounty, administered through His servant, would have repaid me, had it been twenty times the amount, and never again to be returned." The old monk murmured a prayer and looked to heaven.

"Psha!—this preaching, Monk, is ribaldry; so, you were fool enough to suffer the whining crew to get thy money?—Tush! my mind misgives me; I don't heed it; the toil of so many years would not have been parted with in a moment.—Come, Monk, the money."

"Indeed, and I am pennyless;—you mistake me. Return hence in a few days, and the amount shall be at thy brother's service,—for in such a period has the borrower of my simple store undertaken its repayment."

The robber paused, and surveying the snow-clad features of the Monk, he cried: "But I know not how to return, thus empty handed;—this idle tale may appease me, but it will not serve Guiseppe; you know, Monk, the irascibility of his temper. St. Matteo only knows what might be the result. Come, look to thy secret hoard."

The Monk shook his head, and again repeated his inability of compliance, adding, "Indeed, as the Holy Creator is witness, so am I destitute, beyond the staff and scrip of his goodness."

"Well," replied the Brigand, "I would advise your reverence to seclude thyself closely till the money be forthcoming; venture not abroad, nor even see Fazzelo, should he appear here to be satisfied of the denial. I must appease him, or the consequences are great. Keep secluded, I say; I will return some few days hence."

The robber departed, and the Monk repeated an Ave Maria. The evil star of the poor Monk seemed to hover over him, for in crossing a narrow brake, to administer a supply of herbs and balsams to the disorder of a dying muleteer, whose hovel skirted the mountain, and who had entreated the comfort and assistance of the priest, the bandit Guiseppe crossed his path: with trembling and palsied distress he saw his approach, and in agony of despair, he sunk upon his knees, and implored the mercy of the robber.

"And why this solemn appeal?" questioned Guiseppe, surprised at the Monk's agitation and dismay.

"Alas," he replied, "I have not the money yet! spare me! do but send thy brother Otto in the evening of to-morrow, and it shall be thine."

"This sort of language, priest," observed the leader Guiseppe, and his demeanour was that of hauteur and astonishment, "is to me an enigma; speak fully its meaning."

"Indeed," repeated the Monk, still in tremor, "I have not the money."

"What money, priest?" questioned the robber, and he looked at the Monk sternly.

"That which thy brother Otto, Signore Guiseppe, came yesterday to demand for thy use."

"My use! my brother Otto!" severally exclaimed the leader, equally surprised and in ignorance of its meaning,—"mistaken priest, I have not needed thy money, nor have I commissioned Otto to seek it; thou art mistaken."

The Monk assured Guiseppe of his brother's visit, and further added the reason why he was prevented fulfilling the demand.

"Well," answered Guiseppe, "thou shalt see, holy priest, who had the necessity of borrowing the money.—So, then—follow me, and the matter shall soon be decided."

They proceeded in silence for some miles, till the entrance of the cavern brought them to a salute with a robber on guard at the pass. Guiseppe desired the presence of his brother, who, not aware of the discovery, instantly obeyed the summons; his eye met those of the Monk, and an instantaneous glow of shame and confusion reddened his brown and swarthy countenance. He awaited not the charge, but commenced a series of defence and apology, that had led him to the endeavour of imposing upon the Monk's liberality and confidence.

"Fool and knave," retorted the leader Guiseppe, "these excuses will avail not; an act of duplicity like this, Otto, cannot be palliated; to the purpose,—didst thou ask the Monk for this sum in the name of Guiseppe Fazzelo?"

"I did!" after a momentary hesitation, answered the sullen Otto, and he darted a scowling look at his brother's seeming superiority.

"Then thus he rewards thee," exclaimed the leader, and, raising his carbine, he shot him through the heart. The robber fell lifeless, without a single groan; and, in the utmost composure, Guiseppe turned to the Monk, whose tremor and alarm were raised to the highest pitch, "Senor Monk, you are satisfied that I needed not your money, nor will countenance a dishonest act."

The Monk raised his eyes to Heaven, and, uttering "Jesu Maria," shook his head, unable to speak further.*

Leontini's confidence in his guards felt somewhat lessened, as he listened to the narrative of his guide, on their approach towards Val Demoni; and he looked for a meeting with its inhabitants under apprehensions of no very favorable kind. The equipage of Leontini, however, passed onwards in safety, and he reached the

* The outline of this narrative is authentic, and passed in the month of May, 17—. I have heard it detailed by natives, and I am further informed of it in "Brydone's Tour through Sicily." See Letter 4th, Vol 1.

ancient town of Catania in defiance of banditti and their terrors. The ruins of the once populous town of Catania presented an appalling picture of its early grandeur and greatness.*

From the scene which surrounded Leontini was discovered a sublime wreck (if it may be thus termed) of nature—innumerable masses of lava covered the ground over a space of several miles, and rendered a passage nearly impracticable, yet those thick clusters of cork and chesnut trees, absolutely rising from the lava, gives it a verdant and luxuriant colouring; leaving these fields, rich vineyards meet the eye, and numerous habitations, half desolated and choked in nitrous ruins, appear in "rugged piles."†

As the dim and misty vapour of night increased, a prospect of astonishing description displayed itself. From the summit of the Monte was seen pouring forth, in torrents surpassing description, the liquid flames of deep crimson fire; showers of enormous

---

* It was entirely ruined during the earthquake which happened in January, 1693. Many remains of antiquity are seen in this unhappy place: such as an amphitheatre, and several heathen temples. The cathedral (converted now into a Christian place of worship,) was one of those temples. Luberius, who was a Roman Consul, (and perhaps Proconsul, or Governor of Sicily,) built this magnificent edifice for a bath to himself; which bath, in succeeding ages, was converted into a cathedral church. But the terrible earthquake, already mentioned, began upon the 9th of January, 1693, and became so furious, that upon the 11th day of the said month, it tumbled down in a heap of ruin the whole town. The earth suddenly opened in several places, and quickly swallowed up those whom the fallen materials of the houses had spared. Eleven thousand persons, who had fled into the cathedral, imploring the Divine assistance with fearful cries and moans, were in an instant absorbed into a sudden rent of the earth, and buried under the ruins of the church, which fell down upon them. The catastrophe happened at the time when the priest was giving the benediction, and only the minister of the altar, and about an hundred people who were before it, escaped. Nothing remained of the cathedral church, except the chief altar, and two small chapels on each side of it; the rest of it became a heap of rubbish, with eleven thousand souls buried in a moment under it. *Macnab's Description of Sicily.*

† The city of Jaci, or Aci, and indeed all the towns on this coast, are founded on immense rocks of lava, heaped one above another, in some places to an amazing height; for it appears that these flaming torrents, as soon as they arrived at the sea, were hardened into rock, which not yielding any longer to the pressure of the liquid fire behind; the melted matter continuing to accumulate, formed a dam of fire, which, in a short time, run over the solid front, pouring a second torrent into the ocean. This was immediately consolidated, and succeeded by a third, and so on. *Brydone's Tour through Sicily.*

stones, mixed with lava, rushed likewise, in devastating horror, along the sides of the mountain—while others were thrown, by the violence of the crater, to an immense distance—and the noises which the perpetual eruptions occasion is such, that the sense of hearing at length becomes void, and the mind and ideas stunned! Ascending further towards the height of the mountain, the ground is absorbed in a thick and pure covering of snow; to the incredulous this may appear as bordering upon the fabulous; it might be imagined, in support of the opposition to the existence and appearance of such, that, from the intense heat of the lava, any possible congealment of snow would not be likely; but it is positively so far the fact, that indeed the revenues and income of the bishopric of Catania, "arise principally from the sale of snow on Monte Etna! one small portion of which, lying on the north of the mountain, is said to bring him upwards of a thousand pounds per annum;" a singular but certain proof of its value and estimation.*

Massa, a writer of eminence, states, "that in some eruptions of Etna, the lava has poured down with such a sudden impetuosity, that, in the course of a few hours, churches, palaces, and villages, have been entirely melted down, and the whole run off, without leaving the least mark of their former existence." It is in instances of this kind, therefore, the inhabitants calculate on "snow famine."

Another writer of great credit, in speaking of its eruptions, gives the following anecdote, and which is submitted verbatim. "A vineyard, belonging to a convent of Jesuits, lay directly on its way. This vineyard was formed on an ancient lava, probably a thin one, with a number of caverns and crevices under it. The liquid lava entering into these caverns, soon filled them up, and by degrees bore up the vineyard; and the Jesuits, who every moment expected to see it buried, beheld with amazement the whole field begin to

---

* Ætna furnishes snow and ice not only to the whole island of Sicily, but likewise to Malta, and a great part of Italy, and makes a very considerable branch of commerce: for even the peasants in these hot countries regale themselves with ices during the summer heats; and there is no entertainment given by the nobility, of which these do not always make a principal part; a famine of snow, they themselves say, would be more grievous, than a famine either of corn or wine. It is a common observation amongst them, that without the snows of Mount Ætna, their island could not be inhabited; so essential has this article of luxury become to them.—*Brydone's Tour through Sicily.*

move off. It was carried on the surface of the lava to a considerable distance; and though the greatest part was destroyed, yet some of it remains to this day."

The guides of Leontini, fearing that the dangerous passes, on the part of the mountain to which they had approached, would convey a terror, they motioned to return. The ideas and astonishment of the Signor were, however, incomplete, and, as he proposed quitting the region of Etna early the subsequent day, he felt determined to continue in the source of further gratification. The impenetrable dusk of night obliged the travellers to halt for some trifling period, and for a few hours they met with no very uncomfortable shelter. It was a large cavern, La Spelonca del Capriole. The sun-rise from this ascent was the richest view Leontini had ever beheld—he doubted if it ever could be equalled. The immeasurable distance of ruins, divided by forests, interspersed with rivulets, shrouded partially with delightful foliage, and the extreme height he appeared to stand above the "habitable world," gave it a wonderful and supernatural appearance. It would require the pencil of a bold hand to sketch out the prospect of such an expanse; perhaps at no point of the world is there combined the awful, and yet magnificent formation of that scene, which is spread to the eye from the summit of the mountain called Il torre del Filofoso. There cannot be greater justice done, in the tracing of this outline, than to conclude our present chapter with the drawing from the pencil of a late traveller.

"The immense elevation from the surface of the earth, drawn as it were to a single point, without any neighbouring mountain for the senses and imagination to rest upon, and recover from their astonishment in their way down to the world. This point or pinnacle, raised on the brink of a bottomless gulph, as old as the world, often discharging rivers of fire, and throwing out burning rocks, with a noise that shakes the whole island. Add to this, the unbounded extent of the prospect, comprehending the greatest diversity and the most beautiful scenery in nature; with the rising sun, advancing in the east, to illuminate the wondrous scene.

"The whole atmosphere by degrees kindled up, and shewed dimly and faintly the boundless prospect around. Both sea and land looked dark and confused, as if only emerging from their original chaos; and light and darkness seemed still undivided; till the morning by degrees advancing, completed the separation. The stars are extinguished, and the shades disappear. The forests, which but now seemed black and bottomless gulphs, from whence no ray was reflected to shew their form or colours, appear a new creation rising to the sight; catching life and beauty from every increasing beam. The scene still enlarges, and the horizon seems to widen and expand itself on all sides; till the sun, like the great Creator, appears in the east, and with his plastic ray completes the mighty scene. All appears enchantment; and it is with difficulty we can believe we are still on earth. The senses, unaccustomed to the sublimity of such a scene, are bewildered and confounded; and it is not till after some time, that they are capable of separating and judging of the objects that compose it. The body of the sun is seen rising from the ocean, immense tracks both of sea and land intervening; the islands of Lipari, Panari, Alicudi, Strombolo, and Volcano, with their smoking summits, appear under your feet; and you look down on the whole of Sicily as on a map; and can trace every river through all its windings, from its source to its mouth. The view is absolutely boundless on every side; nor is there any one object, within the circle of vision, to interrupt it; so that the sight is every where lost in the immensity."

CHAPTER VI.

All that wild despair,
And jealousy and madness can inspire,
Raged in her bosom with consuming fire,
And roused her to a desperate deed.

She would pierce
His senseless heart, and wring his very soul.

Miss M. G. Lewis.

DURING an interval of several days, the gloom of Palermo was deeply manifest in the sudden decease of the amiable and respected Francesca. The ducal pallazzi had been closed to the interruption or interference of public matters, and within its seclusion Paoli appeared to indulge in a sorrow that was far from being feigned or alloyed.

Visits of inquiry and condolence were at length daily followed up, earnest and enthusiastic as their respective interests were most apparent. Joy lighted up in the young hearts of many devotees to the Duca Paoli's magnificence, and a new flame of admiration; nor were less zealous in their desires to bend before sovereignty the paternal part of Palermo's nobility. Already, in the perspective of their imagination, was sketched the outline of alliances, honors, and anticipated preferences, in behalf of a second union with the young Duca.

The Cassaro, upon the first public festival subsequent to the "cessation of sorrow," presented an unusual brilliancy; one glance from the Duca Paoli gave to youthful ardour a hope of further "glory;" and even in the withered form of age and debility, it removed from its painted and artificial beauty, a *wrinkle*, and a *few years*, at least.

Rosalviva beheld all these appearances with exultation; she knew their aim, but she felt satisfied in their fallacy; sensible that only to *her* power and charms, would Paoli be subjugated. As calmly as her bosom would permit, she had to the present period suffered to remain dormant the mingled feelings of affection and sensibility, at Paoli's seeming chilliness towards her.

At length she conceived further delay was unnecessary, as regarded her interests, and her unity with Paoli; and considering every object that had hitherto stood between her, and her hopes, to be banished, she essayed, with her utmost power of skill and blandishment, again to engage the still melancholy Duca. She sought him in the most unfrequented paths; she met him—but oh! how great the change of a few weeks. Sorrow was visible in every line of his features, and his manner cold,—repulsive.

She ran to embrace him;—she caught his hand, and her kisses were lavished there with enthusiasm,—"Paoli," she cried, "this has been an age of torture, since we last met. We will not part so easily now!—bless thee!—bless thee!"

Her passions had seemingly attained their heated ardour, and she fell on the bosom of her lover with rapturous feeling. But the warmth, the genial glow of his heart had fled, and to her fervent and affected endearments he returned a look,—a reply, so distant, so unforgiving, that its very tone pierced her to the soul; it seemed to leave with it a pang that she dreaded to examine.

Francesca had engaged such of his heart as was worthy of retainment, and her loss afflicted him severely. In vain were the endeavours of Rosalviva applied to divert his mind from her memory; all the softness, the modest and almost celestial habit, that was her constant covering, was before his eye, in every glance around him; and other objects afforded but a sorry atonement for the vacuity her absence created. The charms, and bold, but still beautiful countenance of Rosalviva, were a kind of horror to him; his sight shrunk from their dignity and expression, with a sensibility that told sufficiently its distaste, and its no longer gratification in the possession of what was once his idolatry.

It was not imagination only that whispered to the Comptessa the failure of Paoli's affection, and that she no longer retained a power she could never suppose to have decreased—it was unhappily reality. She recurred to his whole correspondence and conduct, it was then with difficulty she could be persuaded that such a man had ceased to regard her; it might be merely the effect of languor and inattention; but she felt too sanguine of her claims upon his heart, to wholly give up the idea that she would still live the successor of Francesca's dignity and rank. Her restless spirit in the controul of a great action, caused her too much torture and compunction to remain long under suffering, and she determined to come at once to the conclusion of her hopes.

"Now, Paoli, Providence has ordained the arrival of that hour which gives me to thy arms—that proclaims me thy wife."

The Duca was absorbed in a silence.

"Speak, and tell the joyed Rosalviva that her happiness and her raptures are mutual.—Oh, what a lingering period has it appeared."

"Hush," in a monotonous and chilling tone, interrupted the Duca; and, as he passed his hand across his forehead, he seemed to feel an inward agony and horror. "Name not," he added, "the past,—speak not of happiness with me,—I know it not; the world is darkness and delusion to me,—thou need'st not strive to share it."

The Duca slowly traversed the apartment, still fixed in the intense and silent reverie of his mind, while the Comptessa, awakened to a feeling of surprise and alarm, surveyed his altered figure during moments of singular emotion. Assuming the levity usually attached her, she cried, her voice attaining a sarcastic, though not an unpleasant tone, "And is the heart of Paoli left upon the tomb of Francesca?—Is this the enthusiasm—is this the kind of conduct due to Rosalviva? Never can I think that the senseless heart, and the sterile soul of her you were pleased to honour with the rank of Duchessa, can outweigh the sacrifices mine have made, to shew its estimation of the value due to the Duca Paoli!—certainly not; beside, what are the contents of thine epistles, which were combined with the announcement of such an incident?—'Remember,' saidst thou, 'to you alone am I bound by every tie that can constitute happiness,—by every pledge, human or divine! These bonds can never be broken.' And is this but fiction?—Am I to believe that you have become insensible to the affections deserving of the woman who has done that which I have?"

The tear seemed rushing from its concealment, and Rosalviva wept, but they were not honest tears,—they were not those pure and genuine offerings of sincerity, that originated with the sympathy of pure and refined affection. She was prepared for a scene like this, and they were, in some measure, resources to which she looked with safe dependence.

Paoli beheld her grief with calmness; indeed, there appeared to exist within his bosom, a series of painful and excessive feelings, such as denied union with any other.

It was obvious to Rosalviva, that respect to the memory of Francesca occasioned all the gloom and sadness of Paoli's mind: he had acknowledged it, even to her, and, by that confession, her soul was stung with the most poignant anguish. Pride, mortification, resentment, and the most baneful of human passions, crowded eagerly within her bosom, and her eyes turned with hatred and indignation upon the being who could have so willingly forgotten the charm due to her merits.

"These are moments, Rosalviva," cried Paoli, somewhat sternly, "which, for the sake of our united feelings, should be spared. I am indisposed, and must retire; you will excuse my inability of remaining longer in thy presence."

The agitation of the Comptessa seemed unrestrained, and in its excess, she threw herself at the feet of the Duca.

"Unfeeling Paoli! to wound the heart devoted to thee as Rosalviva's is; it is not meet that I should deserve coldness and severity at thy hands; look at me, humbled, and prostrate to your mercy—to your affection; thou canst not spurn me."

Her tone of voice was that of supplication, and she detained the hand of the Duca, whose apathy was still apparent. "Oh, let me call to mind all those hours of former bliss; let me retrace, Paoli, those moments, when the heart knew no joy but in the exchange of each other's passion. Think what pleasure they both have derived; think what thou hast taught me to believe, to hope; and answer, thyself, if treatment like the present should be its inheritance. Paoli thou art only mine, nor can I even exist, unless in thy acknowledgment. We will not part!"

"Wretched woman! oh, God! oh, God!"

The ebullition of Paoli's grief and feeling was a painful spectacle, and the more he gazed upon the features of Rosalviva, there was a coldness and a disgust clinging round upon his heart, that poisoned his imagination in the recollection of the past. The short period of singular but real felicity he had known with Francesca, had so changed him, the purity of *her* smiles and affection had wrought such penitence within his bosom, and had charmed him with so endearing a passion towards her, that to contrast the extravagance and excess of Rosalviva's hitherto voluptuous and sensual passions, only roused him, on viewing the retrospective, to shudder and recoil, and while he looked upon the object by which it originated, a convulsive pang of horror and remorse shot across his anguished brain. When he recurred, too, to the unhappy destruction of the victims of his then impeding joys; when he thought of the motives that ridded Leontini of the world, the fate of Vivaldi, the progressive list of enormities that had followed these, the death of the refugees, the assassination of Carraccio, his soul expired nearly within him, and he felt himself too much abandoned, to kneel to the throne of mercy, to deign to look to heaven for pardon.

"Leave me, leave me," he uttered, in the ardour of his thoughts, "nor sun, nor light of heaven, should shine upon beings estranged from our God, as we have been. Oh, how great is the enormity of our sin! Go, go, Rosalviva, in the bosom of St. Rosalia's confidence and sanctity, do thou seek the peace and comfort which only can prepare thy mind and soul for the dreadful coming of futurity. Mine revolts even from the hope, from the thought of this after world, this future existence. Oh, the struggles that rest here,—here, in my bosom, are agonizing, indeed! The world is madness to me. Begone! begone! I am nearly upon its brink; stand aside; the precipice once gained, I pass into death and oblivion with safety; away, nor check my progress!"

The sanity of Paoli's mind seemed deserting him; the infuriated look, the terrific awe that revealed itself in his glaring eye, the convulsion of his limbs, and the burning heat of his brain, severally told the internal suffering and weight of torture.

Rosalviva was paralyzed nearly with rage and astonishment; its excitement, however, manifested sentiments within her, that vented themselves in bitter menace and irony at the weakness and imbecility of Paoli. "Insulting fool and madman!" she retorted, "this bigotry of enthusiasm will not serve thy apostate purposes. Thou hast sworn to Rosalviva too firmly; thou hast proffered thy love, protection and fidelity in terms too binding, too securely registered in deeds of blood, to escape from her thus. What! and has Palermo another Francesca to pamper to thy sickly appetite? Disgraced and perjured insensate, who has taught thee thus to whine and simper out these *pious* tenets? What has this *devout lesson* cost thee? Ha! ha!" here the wild and hoarse laugh of the Comptessa echoed in avengeful fury, "and thou thinkst by its recital to mock the state of Rosalviva's wretchedness, to colour thine own apparent principles of sorrow and atonement? Poor misguided wretch! thou wilt live yet to know ages, worlds of torture and ignominy. Aye, thou! Paoli, Duca of Palermo! pious and doting mourner of Francesca! The apostate, the murderer Golfieri! hear me, hear me! Thou hast brought down upon thy head, thine own sentence, thine own horrible end. Yes, thou art upon the brink of thy destruction, truly. I will lead thee to it, aye, and safely. Bid me not *stand aside*, for it is *I alone* that can usher thee into that *oblivion*, and pass upon thee the murderer's curse!"

Paoli stood horrified; the colour and the appearance of health were blighted upon his cheek; his appearance was more spectral than human, and he at length reeled insensibly upon the floor. The feelings which had been most predominant in the bosom of Rosalviva had crushed those of minor description, and were incapable of being repressed. She had not wished to have been thus indignant; she had hoped to soften his mind into compassion and returning fondness, without extraordinary art; but failing in this, and distressed at the replies of Paoli, her violence knew no bounds, and in its turbulence, she openly disclosed her desperate intentions.

The heart which has felt the most enthusiastic love, is as likely to know the most extreme of hatred; to this the ingenious Rochefoucault adds,—"It is impossible to love a second time, the person we have entirely ceased to love;" and such had seemed the power and feeling of Paoli to the Comptessa Rosalviva. Coldness and contempt to her were the worst of punishments; she could have endured his reproach, his anger and his resentment; she could have borne all the infliction his haughty spirit could have created, but the thought that there had lived within his breast a sentiment of feeling towards another woman, in precedence to that for her; the thought that he could pass her in scorn and contumely;—that he could forget her in willingness, and in sacrifice to the respect for a Francesca, produced feelings of the direst rage, and worked her brain to a delirium almost beyond madness. Again she wept most violently, but it alleviated not the wild and hysterical throbbings of her brain. She glanced at the still prostrate figure of Paoli; rather than being glorified with its seeming weakness and inferiority, she conceived it to be merely a wariness to give a pretext to his silence; and in the indignation arising from the idea, she vented forth her utmost anger.

"Look up, wretched Paoli," she added, "awake to all the horrors and the miseries of thy ducal inheritance,—the scaffold!—the scaffold can only repay the insult and scorn heaped upon the neglected and deceived Rosalviva," a loud shout of maddening laughter followed the expression, and her features attained a satanic triumph.

Paoli was indeed awakened. The taunt of Rosalviva pierced his soul, he turned towards her, but no longer did there exist in his bosom a feeling like that which earlier days had kindled. Contrasted, at limited intervals, were the ideas and resolutions of Paoli; during one moment his frenzy rolled back in equal torrent with that of the Comptessa,—at another his mind and spirits appeared chained to some deadly and unconquerable spell, and under the power of its anguish, he was lost to sense or animation.

In one of those moods, opposed to her violence, he retorted,—"Thoughtless and ungovernable creature, of what avail is it to thee that I suffer? Will not the same blow that terminates my career—end also that of thine?"

"Never!" pronounced she, "where is the eye that has ever seen,—the hand that can point the heiress di Romagno——"

"Mine!—mine!" interrupted the Duca, endeavouring to restrain the cause of her vindictive harangue.

"Thine, madman!—will the accusation of a murderer be accredited?—Never; thou diest, abhorred and cursed."

"In guilt, thou art the superior; to thy charge is dated all the unhappy and fatal deeds of Paoli Golfieri: when he reposes quietly in the grave, thy bosom will be——"

"The soul of thine can never *repose quietly*;" cried Rosalviva; preventing the continuation of the Duca's remark,—"seek not to appropriate the atrocities of thy dark career to *my* contriving—I deny it. Listen for one moment: we will imagine the recollection of the past, and the several events that have registered themselves in the minds of our communion to be made void; let there be not one instance for us to pause upon, or that need be expatiated—all shall be destroyed; but reflect, *illustrious* and *worthy* Duca, on the period of time prior to our interview. Call to mind that event, which, on the eve of San Rosalia, enlisted thee in the lists of assassination, and fixed upon thee the murderer's mark; it can never be erased—an oath was taken before the pious ministers of heaven to avenge the fallen Cardoni."

The Duca shuddered, as the recollection of that affray struck upon his mind, and his clasped hands pressed against his forehead with disordered emotion. The Comptessa had paused to witness the effect of her language upon the feelings of Paoli; she resumed.

"That oath was mine; it will now be accomplished. Spirit of my parent! look down upon thy repentant offspring, she will fulfil thy latest decree; yes, recreant! thou hast saved me from perdition, and brought it justly upon thyself. For thee, so blindly were my passions and my endeavours guided, I could have welcomed the fate due to souls laden with the blackest of crimes, whose existence, fraught with love like mine, taught me to despise every feeling, to defy every danger that threatened its felicity. Mark, how oft I despised and banished every curse that memory heaped upon me, and for thee! For thee, I could have gone down to the dark and horrid tomb,—the apostate's tomb; my oath should have been buried with me. So long as happiness and Paoli's love had blest me in this world, Rosalviva would have smiled at the dread of punishment in that hereafter: she would have done this, and blest thee; think, then, how she must have loved,—and such a love thou hast savagely—wantonly annihilated. A word more, and we part——"

"Maniac!" reiterated the Duca, the agony of his mind having worked him up to a degree of rage and defiance of horror, "Quit the pallazzi with safety; or there are dungeons beneath it that will never resign thee."

"And thou darest—thou commandest *me* to fly? Poor reptile! My voice alone destroys thee. Palermo's tribunal, ere the night of to-morrow, shall pass sentence on its culprit—on its Duca! Death is its sequel; nor can the power of mortal interdict the decree."

The piercing glance of the Comptessa, was directed to the ashy features of the Duca. She perceived the prominent convulsions that passed within him, and, in a tone of stern and powerful confidence, she said, "Thou art satisfied of this, my power, and my resolution to bring about thy deeds of infamy, and to seal their punishment!"

The Duca uttered not a syllable.

"Didst thou not hear? Thy reply."

"The light of heaven will surely shine upon thy corse before I leave thee, if thou retirest not from the pallazzi; my feelings are desperate. I have nought to lose; earth is a hell sufficient, and life is its torture. Francesca's dead,—away! thou canst not doom me to more existing purgatory. Look, thou serpent, I have a dagger!"

"And I dare thee to its use! I came not unprepared; and thus

I inflict, at least, some portion of my revenge; the scaffold shall complete it."

She drew from her bosom a poniard, and in the uncontrouled frenzy of the moment, she directed it to the breast of Paoli.

The stroke, which was aimed thus desperately, was averted, and to her singular astonishment, by the momentary resistance and interference of the Dwarf.

A silence prevailed some few moments; the sensations of the Comptessa and those of Paoli may be equally imagined. Valfroni still detained her uplifted arm, and in an attitude of mutual defence, he still between them.

"Signora," he cried, "this is madness indeed!"

"Foiled! Ha, ha, ha!"

A hoarse and boisterous shout of laughter followed the act, and she swooned in the arms of Valfroni.

"Retire, Duca," in an under and impressive tone spoke the Dwarf, "seek thy chamber; for the restoration of the Comptessa I will be answerable."

"Thou wilt give me thy presence speedily, Valfroni," cried Paoli, "I would devote some few hours to thee in private."

"It shall be so."

The Duca withdrew.

The revival of Rosalviva was marked with a strange and sullen perturbation; her eyes were fixed on the Dwarf, and their expression sufficiently pourtrayed the displeasure she felt at his sudden and abrupt conduct. "And is this the amity of Valfroni? Has the Signore Duca at length purchased his kindness and care? Lives Valfroni the dependant of such a being?" severally and hastily interrogated the Comptessa. "Fallacious, indeed, is the promise of man!"

"Signora," rather sternly replied Valfroni, "such an insinuation I have not merited; be not too harsh in thy suppositions; the removal of Francesca, is some proof, that my will and inclination to thy service, is far from being deemed trivial; thou art unkind and unjust."

"True, I have confided in thee, Dwarf Valfroni; forgive my apprehensions."

"I do; I have not been an idle spectator of this scene, believe me. I witnessed it narrowly, and knew that an act as *was* attempted would inevitably terminate it, if not by yourself, Rosalviva, it would have been the Duca's, and I was not willing thou shouldst have fallen such a victim, either to thy own passion or that of his. Am I deserving reproach?"

"No, no, thou art praiseworthy indeed; how can I deign to consider Valfroni capable of acting injudiciously? But say," and she looked earnestly round the apartment, "the Duca?"

"He withdrew; and claimed my attention to him in private, as he quitted the room."

"Better so," observed the Comptessa, "but we lose time, and we are in Paoli's power. I need not repeat to you the tenor of our interview, since you acknowledge to have been its participator; say then, the conduct to be pursued; point out the immediate destruction of the Duca, and the abandoned Rosalviva with rapture subscribes herself obedient to its performance."

"To-morrow, Signora, this decision shall be made final!"

"And why such delay?"

"It were policy, Rosalviva, to effect as much caution as possible, and first I will learn the nature of the Duca's communication; we then shall more fully determine. And that can be within this hour," continued the Dwarf, observing the impatience of the Comptessa.

"And we will meet again at the Castelli di Romagno."

"In one hour, Signora, depend upon my punctuality," replied the Dwarf, and conducting her through the most secluded avenues of the pallazzi, she hurried back to her residence.

CHAPTER VII.

I owe thee thanks, and in good hour
Will I repay thee, for that thou thought'st me, too,
A serviceable villain.

ZAPOLYA.

"DWARF VALFRONI," exclaimed the Duca, after a conversation of much length, during which his mind and ideas were thronged with furor and despair, "add to the ill-fated list of Paoli's deeds this new one, and thou art the arbiter of his fate,—his destiny; do with me as thou wilt. Oh, the weight of sin and blood presses so heavily upon my heart, it were annihilation by piecemeal, an inhuman death to suffer under its torture; I cannot endure it, my brain will burst. Oh! agony,—agony!"

The Duca covered his features; the feverous throbbing of his bosom, and the pitiable state he appeared in, excited a feeling near to commiseration, and the Dwarf Valfroni gazed on him sensible to such.

"This penitence, Duca Paoli, removes, in some degree, the weight of that sin which thou endurest," calmly observed Valfroni, and the tone of his voice conveyed a kind of tenderness, in consideration of the anguish of Paoli. "She did threaten thy life, 'tis true;—still it decrees not, that thou should'st—"

"Do not moralize, Dwarf Valfroni," interrupted the Duca, "to ears like mine, its sound is horrible. Speak of blood, of death, and I'll listen—I'll obey.

"I cannot plunge deeper in the gulf of infamy," in a frantic gesture cried Paoli, at the close of some few moments' silence. "Hell has chained my soul so fast to its limits, I cannot,—cannot escape. Rosalviva, thou hast been its curse, thou hast prefixed its doom, and thou must also suffer; yes, Dwarf Valfroni, she shall die;—my own hand shall ask her blood, myself alone shall be her destroyer. I repent me, thou shalt not be stained with this crime,—but thou must not betray me!" The voice of the Duca at this moment faltered, its tone was so imploring, his manliness so humbled, and his appeal so pathetic, that it was painful to see the wreck of such once illustrious and commanding dignity. He again repeated,—"Thou *wilt* not betray me?"

Valfroni was still silent.

"I require but this, Dwarf;—the deed finished, I am thine—thy power alone can govern me; speak, to the agitation and alarm of a soul like mine, silence, or delay, only the more tampers with its scorching flame."

"I will be silent, then," replied the Dwarf, "I will aid thee; I am not unused to the sight of human blood, and fear not to witness thine effort.—Thou art resolved?"

"On Rosalviva's death, Valfroni?"

"Aye, Duca."

"Firmly! Heaven nor——"

"Hush—'tis enough!"

"There are vaults, Duca, beneath the fabric of St. Rosalia, unknown to the most scrutinizing search; long habit and perseverance during my abode there, effected, perhaps, in the first instance, by the most singular accident, served to make me alone master of its deathly and subterranean recesses. Thither, in the solitude of this night, the Comptessa shall be invited. I need not bid Paoli to mark the sequel."

"Thy endeavour be accomplished to the contrivance of Rosalviva's presence *there*, and the design is complete!"

"To that, Duca, I bind myself. On the repose of the pallazzi, meet me at the basis of Monte Pelegrino, an avenue, canopied by the dark cypress and the wild fir, branches to the water's margin. There I will await ye; in the mean time I hasten to secure the Comptessa."

"My deity!—my deity!" shouted Paoli, and he embraced with ardour the Dwarf Valfroni,—"Thou art Palermo's best treasure!"

"Thou wilt be mindful," coolly observed Valfroni, and he quitted the apartment.

Fatigue, and the harrowing state of Rosalviva's mind, had overpowered her, and she sunk exhausted upon a couch on reaching her chamber. She laid for a time insensible to her grief and resentments, save that the recurrence of the past, and the swelling emotions of her soul, still occupied place in her mind, under the most nervous and fevered state of her slumber.

The faint streak of day was departing, and the evening's partial light acknowledged that she had slept some hours. The sultry heat of the season had assisted to lull her faculties and senses beneath its languid allurement, and since that she had endured of late the loss of so much of her natural rest, the few hours' sleep, (alloyed as they doubtless were,) still benefited her by its refreshing aid. She arose, and amidst the light just discernible, stood the Dwarf Valfroni, in musing quietude.

"I would not disturb thee, Rosalviva," he cried, taking her hand, "and have been thy guardian here, through a continued interval;—thy dreams were busied," said the Dwarf.

"They were partly, nay, chiefly, of yourself, Valfroni!"

"Thou would'st strive to flatter," he pleasantly remarked, "but I can excuse it, Signora;—it is hoped that I have some claim to thy private, and even thy sleeping moments."

"Thou hast; but, forsooth, I did not admire the tenor of these intrusive phantoms."

"And what could render them thus unpleasant?"

"I dreamed, Valfroni, that, in the storm of a dreadful night, thou appearedst in a cloud of streaming fire, and hurrying me from my pillow, ascended, in the most astonishing manner, to the height of an immense cliff; beneath the frightful precipice was open to my sight an abyss, where the bodies of numerous beings seemed reposing. There were others, too, in apparent torment. I saw, too, the corse of Francesca, and it was as perfect—as beautiful, as though she had slept only! I saw, too, Paoli; he seemed to endure the tortures of the damned! My heart shouted as I gazed, and I was wont to turn me, to offer thanks to thee—a cloud burst over us, and thou changedst—oh! Valfroni, how terrible didst thou appear to human eye."

The Dwarf facetiously smiled, and, taking the hand of Rosalviva, cried,—"ha! Signora, thou art pleased to sport with the feelings of the poor Dwarf—this is not worthy of *thee*."

"No, I would not for worlds do that, Valfroni, but I can never forget the spectacle of such a moment—thy tremendous stature—thy demoniac visage—and thy fiendish smiles were appalling; I shuddered, and exclaimed 'Valfroni!' 'Here!' thou replied, and a burst of laughter escaped thee that petrified my soul, and rang again in horrid echo around us, 'not Valfroni, but thy destroyer;' and in this instant, I felt thy grasp at my throat; thou wert about to hurl me down the dreadful steep; I shrieked, and in that alarm my slumbers left me—oh! it was truly horrible." The Comptessa evinced all the internal horrors of her mind; and, as the Dwarf essayed to press his lips with her's, she recoiled from it in strange and fearful dismay.

"Thou wouldst indulge in the belief of this vision it seems, Rosalviva, or why this coldness?"

Rosalviva had, indeed, conceived a more than common interest, and a more than usual alarm, at the recollection of her dream, and she felt some degree of reluctance, in suffering herself further in the power of the strange and singular person of Valfroni. She thought upon the probability of his deceiving her. Might he not delude her into the imaginary success of her schemes, and might he not betray her to the Duca? Might he not have become his creature, and might she not be his victim? These suppositions severally took possession of her mind, and the more strongly she recurred to the incidents connected with Valfroni,—his sudden conciliation, too, with the Duca, and, subsequently, his attaining so much of his confidence and power,—the less she felt disposed to trust herself within the guidance of the Dwarf. She feared, however, to disclose her suspicions, but endeavoured by artifice to discover more particulars, that might present an outline of his origin and character. Her features brightened, and she caught his hand with a kind of pressure that testified her returning warmth and ardour. "I will cease to think of what might cause displeasure, for even a moment, with the Dwarf Valfroni. I have to apologize; forgetting, likewise, that I prevented the communication of your result with the Duca."

"True, Rosalviva. In few words, our victory is decisive; the night's coming gloom brings the Duca to the chapel vaults beneath St. Rosalia; there I have promised to commune with him!"

"But wherefore in so singular and remote an auditory as the chapel vaults of St. Rosalia?"

"The better to gratify my vengeance. The body of Francesca shall be the first object shewn to him, and the vault which contains it shall also be his eternal grave."

"Then we dispatch him there?" eagerly questioned the Comptessa.

"Without you would prefer that his *excellenza* should linger."

"Oh yes, oh yes," earnestly interrupted Rosalviva, "this will be greater revenge, and, in daily tortures, he will awake beside the corse of his bride, in witness of her fast and putrifying dissolution."

The Dwarf was silent.

"Will this mode of vengeance not gladden the heart, too, of Valfroni? oh, it must, it will!"

"In the distance you can accompany us, and be the spectator of all that ensues," replied Valfroni, unmoved at the vehement and rhapsodic display of her feelings.

"In St. Rosalia's vaults?"

"The same, Rosalviva; I have promised to reveal to him sights that will gratify him."

"And he was amused in the probability of this promise?"

"He was, and awaits anxiously for the moment," answered the Dwarf.

"That moment which may be termed his final one with life?"

"Even so, Rosalviva, and that moment past, the recompense of the Dwarf Valfroni is——"

"Gained in his revenge," remarked the Comptessa, as if in anticipation of his conclusion.

"Greater than that, sweet Signora; its recompense is with *thee!*"

"You would over-rate my thanks and my gratitude, Valfroni," facetiously implied the Comptessa; "but I will not forget these services, and even when worlds—distant worlds divide us, I will with joy look back to the hour that gave me the friendship of the Dwarf Valfroni."

"And dost thou anticipate a separation, Rosalviva?"

"From whom?" eagerly asked the Comptessa, and her agitation and surprise was somewhat excited at the strange interrogatory of Valfroni.

"From the Dwarf," replied he, and the energy of his tone seemed to convey an unusual asperity and strength; "no, Rosalviva, thou canst never leave."

"Singular being," replied the Comptessa, and she felt disposed to indulge in the train of observations which came from, and which seemed to amuse the Dwarf. "Nay," she added, "tell me by what solemn and mysterious compact I am chained to thy will? Will not even my sacred meditations, my repose, my solitude, be exempt from thy interference?"

"Does, then, the thought of Valfroni's society seem to afflict the Comptessa?"

"Oh, no; but how is it to be imagined, that, shut from the world, as will be her determination, the Dwarf Valfroni can seek or hope for society with her? This act, which invites Paoli to the spirit of his wife, gives thee thy revenge, as well as mine. We have nought more, Valfroni, to communicate; and the link which now binds us, must *then* be broken."

"It will only be in death so," gloomily answered the Dwarf, and his voice appeared to sink into that sepulchral tone, which the darkness of night, and the loneliness of the mind, appears to create.

"Do we never part?"

"Never, Rosalviva—never! Immure thyself within the darkest recess of the earth; frequent that isolated spot, where the pure light of heaven never yet beamed, nor the voice of mortal ever cheered;—select that path in existence the most appalling—the most dreaded; thy shadow keeps to thee still—so will mine; aye, never to forsake thee! Death only can part us; and, even then, my soul, unappeased, would welcome dissolution, to join with thee in the other regions."

Rosalviva shuddered. The half fabulous, and the half solemn meaning of the Dwarf, caused her no trifling sensations of terror; there was a presentiment seemingly clinging to her soul, that produced disagreeable reflections, and she felt the icy chill of its alarm; her heart swelled within her, and the attempt at utterance was, for some minutes, resistless; she leaned upon a couch, and her respiration was heavy and convulsed.

The Dwarf viewed the contention of her faculties unmoved, save that there was a kind of derisive contortion of feature, mixed with a calmness, and a still apparent good nature, that was difficult to be accurately defined.

"This is misery of strange apprehension;" murmured Rosalviva, as the faint glow of animation warmed her feelings.

"Misery!" repeated the Dwarf, "thou art wont to bestow harsh terms really upon sensations wrought up by the sole guidance of yourself."

"Alas! I am ignorant of this mysterious harangue, nor do I wish to pause upon its purport. The Duca Paoli—the Duca!" impressively urged the Comptessa, anxious to banish the thought that opened contemplation on the future.

"The Duca will be in waiting at the skirting of Monte Pelegrino in due time, be assured. In order to avoid observation, we will repair thither prior to his arrival; in one of the most secure avenues of St. Rosalia, thou shalt be a witness of the deed that consigns him to eternity."

"And we mutually decree, then, Dwarf Valfroni, that, in the vault which contains the corse of Francesca, the Duca is to be immured."

"Decidedly thus: a lamp, which I have provided, will, in giving a constant flame, light him to his diurnal horrors; its glare, though feeble, is sufficient to shew the decomposing remains of Francesca. How long a time his soul can banquet upon this prospect, is not for ourselves to determine; it is enough to know, that a fate wretched as this, mankind need not invent more agonising, to avenge the injuries received from his most deadly foe; *thou* wouldst not wish beyond, Rosalviva?"

"Nothing beyond; and, for the safety of the vault?" asked she.

"There is no human being," replied the Dwarf, "possesses the slightest clue to its situation, or could even approach it; beside, ere the bars of that dungeon could be removed,—secure as I can make them,—the body of Paoli will be long returned to its native dust, and the earth can tell no tales."

"The night grows late," observed Rosalviva, "we had better depart."

"Willingly;" cried the Dwarf, and, through the most silent parts of Palermo, leading towards Monte Pelegrino, they cautiously proceeded. The occasional gleam of moonlight afforded them a direction along their path, and at the close of an hour, they attained the dark and desolate building, once sacred to St. Rosalia.

The passages were not new to the eye of Rosalviva, and she looked around them with a familiarity and satisfaction. The more deeply she emerged within the subterranean avenues, notwithstanding the mildew and dampness that hung about their walls, and the thick chilling gloom, (that the light, which they carried, scarcely seemed to penetrate,) the greater was the predominance of that vindictive passion, that kept alive all her feelings and faculties, with perfect submission and gladness. Paoli would be speedily within her grasp; it was a triumph, indeed, to reflect upon, that the man who had doomed her parent to a premature grave, and who had broken her heart, would terminate a life horrible as would be his. Her acquiescence of leaving him to his own wretched and lingering death appeared to be moved. She considered that further torment might yet be given him.

"What," she whispered to the Dwarf, "if we were to leave the Duca to his own contemplation? one night, Valfroni, of such horrors as must be his, fettered beside the mouldering corse of his wife, would be worlds of death and pain; and then to awaken him from these, to finish them upon the scaffold, would be an excess of joy to *me*, that not all thou couldst ask should purchase it from me. Say, Dwarf, shall it be done?"

"It might," coldly replied Valfroni, at the same time replenishing the feeble light of the lamp; "We are near the vault of Francesca," added he, "thou must remain in this recess, Comptessa, until my return with the Duca. On thy silence depends the security of Paoli; move not, I beseech thee, from this spot. Were it known that thou art here, be assured the Duca would suspect treachery; even a sight of thee, until we attain the interior of the dungeon, would inevitably destroy our purposes; therefore, on no pretence, or anxiety, leave this cavity. The light placed in yonder broken arch will not be observed, and from within its dusky enclosure you will easily perceive our approach; enveloped closely in your cloak, you can follow,—anticipate the remainder. It must be full midnight; so I'll to Paoli."

Distracted and torn by feelings of alternate horror, crime, and repentance, the perilous Duca awaited for the meeting with Valfroni. His mind and senses had become so distracted by continual torment, that he dreaded to pause; he would gladly embrace whatever destiny might befal him, in preference to the ignominious one that had been threatened to him by Rosalviva; to perish thus, he would never yield; with his own weapon would he have destroyed his excruciating existence, rather than suffer the fate due to his enormity of crime. "It is my last remaining hope," he apostrophised, in the midst of his ruminations, "it is the last decree that seals the doom of Paoli. Ministers of darkness and vengeance, oh, I dare not look to my God! I dare——"

"Hush, hush, Signore Duca," cried the Dwarf, who had appeared during the appeal of Paoli, "thy God can bestow mercy, where there is penitence."

"The anguish which rages here in my bosom, the fire upon my brain. Oh! Valfroni, it is past utterance; when shall I know peace?"

The Duca raised his eyes to heaven, they were uplifted several moments, a tear stood tremulously within them, it seemed to give relief to his burdened heart, and in a voice almost inaudible he sobbed,—"Cardoni, thou art there; my crime were expatiated in the miseries I now endure! Leontini, my murdered friend, oh! if thou couldst witness the compunctious throbs that tear my soul, thou wouldst bid me die and end them.

"What did I not forfeit in losing thee! To what extent of crime did I not plunge in, when I became thy betrayer! tears of blood rush from me, but they will not suffice; oh, I am agonized indeed; remorse, remorse, thou hast fixed thy sting here! 'tis dreadful."

The Dwarf felt pity, and he supported the nearly exhausted frame of Paoli, during a period of severe struggle and anguish. "Come, come, be alive, Rosalviva is fixed to the spot devoted to thy purpose. Thy weapon gives releases to all thy terrors."

"More blood!" groaned the Duca, and the pale and livid marks of death seemed almost to triumph over his countenance. "My soul shrinks from the sound, my arm will fall nerveless, ere I can strike the blow that marks me deeper with the stain of murder."

"Nay, but think, unhappy Duca, upon the alternative. What oughtest thou not encounter in avoiding a scaffold; think of such a fate, reflect on such a death!"

The Dwarf grasped the arm of the Duca, who, unable to subdue the kind of stupor that came over him, yielded to the impulse of Valfroni's power, and in hurried step they entered the chapel of St. Rosalia.

CHAPTER VIII.

——————When I see
These frantic transports of despair, I joy
To have preserved thee. Live. To see thy anguish,
Will more complete my vengeance. Thou shalt live.
SINNETT'S *Atreus and Thyestes.*

I stand immoveable, like senseless marble,
Horror has frozen my suspended tongue.
YOUNG.

THE retiring footsteps of the Dwarf were listened to by the Comptessa, as he quitted the range of vaults, with an elated throb of ardour, and in the silent meditations of her mind she traversed the dreary space of the cell, during several impatient and troublesome moments. The silence of the sepulchre, and all its gloom, exceeded not the loneliness of the recess wherein she awaited the return of the Dwarf. She had not courage to meet the reproach of the past, she feared to judge of the future, and the better to avoid the anguish of thought, she endeavoured to discover the grating that opened to Francesca's vault. At such a time, in such a spot, and with all the horrors that may be supposed to have fastened on a heart like Rosalviva's, guilt and fear would have at once decidedly prohibited the attempt, but such a dread was not prevalent in her bosom; her courage failed at the idea of retrospection, but her personal temerity, in wishing to obtain access to a sight of the Duchessa, was not in the slightest degree perceptible, and she snatched the lamp with a determined boldness, once again, and alone, to gaze upon the livid corse of her victim.

A narrow archway branched from the vault, leading towards the grating which closed its extremity, and having carefully observed the manner by which the Dwarf had previously gained admittance, she adopted the same process. The walls of the cell, and the few pillars that supported its lofty roof, were covered with a sable cloth, which the gleam of a lamp that was affixed to one of the columns just distinguished; at the end of the vault was laid, upon a small erected throne, a coffin, over which the deep pall was spread and the other insignia of the "charnel house," equally discoverable, met the sight of Rosalviva. A canopy, bearing the arms, and the partly dishevelled banners, of some illustrious family, waved above the bier, and various lineaments of ancestry were scattered about the cemetery. Rosalviva startled, and pausing during a moment's consideration, she found that she had entered a different vault to that which contained the corse of Francesca. She was proceeding to retire, when the appearance of a black curtain, in an adjoining circular recess, caught her attention, and as she viewed its dismal folds, a sudden emotion from behind the drapery riveted her to the spot, and she felt the blood chilling throughout her veins, in supernatural horror.

The folds of the curtain were again distinctly seen to move, in a kind of cautious disturbance; in vain she essayed to recede, her steps seemed clogged with some dreadful and heavy burden, and she remained in a state of insensibility, and yet as if awaiting the appearance of some dreadful mysterious disclosure.

The alarm of Rosalviva ceased in proportion as she felt convinced that it was ideal, and slowly recovering her usual spirits, she tottered to one of the columns for temporary support.

"Madness and horror seem to oppress me," she faintly articulated, and a cold shuddering at repeated intervals came over her. "Oh! these dark and chilling vaults, my every step seems to echo as though with guilty tread! these walls even have curses for me, and in the awful pauses and moaning of the hollow wind, there rises a voice that appals me! Hark, nay 'tis hell to be thus absorbed! Why should sense and feeling be so strongly fettered? idle phantasies! shrink, shrink not my soul; think on what I am! think on what I have suffered, and thy scorned superiority shall nobly triumph. Paoli Golfieri, thou diest!"

A wild and coarse shout of laughter followed the exclamations of the Comptessa, and horrid were its echoes along the distant passages.

The whisper of the Dwarf Valfroni in an adjoining archway, roused the attention of Rosalviva, and she rushed through the avenue to meet him. The grating closed violently after her, as a sudden grasp of her hand moved it from its stationary position. The electric dissolution of worlds could not have been imagined in more awful shock, as did the tremendous peal reverberate throughout the entire space of St. Rosalia. Her agitation was heightened in the extreme, and she sunk almost breathless against a projecting crag, in the recess where Valfroni had commanded her to remain. The visage of the Dwarf caught her eye; and the harsh meaning it conveyed, the terrible and appalling glance directed to her, and the loud and angry tone with which he pronounced, "Rosalviva, thou hast trifled with my interdiction," harrowed up her entire senses. "Disdainful woman, what might not have been its consequences? this curiosity of thine is wrong: didst thou know its dangers, thy life would have been forfeited, rather than thou wouldst have endeavoured to have learned them; speak, what hast thou seen?

"Answer," again stormed the Dwarf, after a pause, wherein the silence of Rosalviva was maintained, with a kind of obdurate and indignant feeling, rather than otherwise; "The grating of yonder cemetery has been unhinged, and thou didst venture to explore its deathly and horrible interior! Speak, rash and ungovernable woman, what hast thou seen?"

"The resting place of the dead;" replied the Comptessa, and her mind and tremor had given way to a courage, and an unconscious degree of defence, that caused her to assume a more than expected intrepidity of reply; "hast thou such forbidden mysteries, that I—Yet all this is evasion.—Is the Duca within reach?

"The Duca is but few paces distant."

"It is resolved," urged the Comptessa, "that we, during some few lonely hours, confine him in the vault with Francesca."

"It is!"

"Hasten then, Valfroni, this much; for already the dampness of these subterranean habitations has given me a chill, and I feel anxious again to see the light of heaven—to feel the air of humid nature."

"But then thou wilt not leave me?" questioned the Dwarf, and he glanced a look at her, which seemed intended to penetrate the interior of her soul; "what are the terms of the compact? I have forgotten."

"Indeed this is, in the present moment, wholly irrelevant;" replied Rosalviva, "my mind is too much engrossed in the accomplishment of our design, to consider of matters more trivial. Have I not offered thee, Dwarf, all that riches may command?"

"And all of which I utterly disdain;" spake the Dwarf.

"Oh, cruel and tormenting Valfroni; thou hast a dagger—sheath it here!" and at the same instant she bared her bosom, grasping, too, the hilt of his poniard, which the Dwarf imperiously and with facility extricated from her hand: "Yes;" she cried, "sheath it here; and let my fears terminate. Thou knowest not, that suspense and delay to the feelings of womankind, are at once cruelty and death. Be kind, then, and if thy power is not equal to thy inclination—if Paoli has bribed thee to renounce the sacrifice of a life, so justly doomed to suffer—if thy nature, pitiable and relenting, withholds itself from the deed, in mercy—in mercy, tell me, and seek not by an invention of purposes, to impede or crush my wishes. I discharge thee cheerfully from thy pledge—will still revere thee, and think, too, that thou endeavouredst to serve me; but vengeance must not be parted with; for to the scaffold will I with gladness summon this recreant and perfidious Paoli. This much, at least, thou canst assist me in, Dwarf Valfroni; come, then, since I have brought forward for thee, this confession, reverence it, and we will part."

"I would not deign to interrupt the volubility of thy eloquence, Signora," sternly remarked the Dwarf, "now thou hast spoken, I will hasten to remove this suspense thou talkest of: further delay shall be also unnecessary—listen, thou art deceived."

"Deceived!" echoed the voice of the Comptessa, and a variety of strange and perplexed ideas instantly rushed across her mind.

"Yes; the time is at hand, when the award of a rapid career of crime like thine must be measured out, and the fate it merits will have its course; follow me, and this scene of fiction shall be dissolved—your own eyes shall behold—"

"Ha, then my fears are real!" shrieked the Comptessa, as with frantic gesture she interrupted the strain of Valfroni's command, "I am betrayed; and thou art, indeed, the monster—the demon, whose shape, in my dreams, I have witnessed; but thou shalt be foiled:—Dare to pollute me with thine abhorred touch, and this dagger, which I have secreted for its due purpose, shall terminate a deed of treachery like that of the base and abortive Valfroni! What are thy purposes?—Speak, let me know their worst and most darkened colouring, that I may be the more enabled to resist them."

"Follow me to the cemetery yonder," cried the Dwarf, "and thou needst not further inquiry."

"Is it thus you would allure, then, your victim?—Has the Duca Paoli obeyed thy wishes; and does he loiter to laugh at the subdued Rosalviva? Oh, yes, I see it all; I see all thy damning accursed duplicity, thy sin, and thy horrid treachery; yet, strive to effect thy designs, if thou darest!" Here she snatched from beneath her cloak, the poniard concealed there, and, frowning in the most severe contempt and rage upon the Dwarf, she cried, "Now, Dwarf Valfroni, I will pass; oppose my egress from these assassin haunts, the consequences shall be fatal; and, for this, thy joint plot, the light of the forthcoming day shall avenge it; and then, Paoli Golfieri," looking earnestly round the archway, in suspicion, that among the dim shadows before her, she should recognise the figure of the Duca, "Murderer! Heretic! Coward! Take my curses,—bitterest curse; it shall ring upon thine ear while the grasp of death is upon thee; it shall hiss around thee till thy latest breath, and then invoke the wrath of God to thy everlasting torments. Now, Dwarf, I will pass."

"Thou shalt not pass," reiterated the Dwarf, and with his hand he forcibly detained her; "thy suspicions, and thy charges are equally wrong; it is thine own act and deed that hath brought thee to this state. Valfroni is no monster—is no demon."

"The world has nominated thee such, and thy black and dark actions proclaim thee one;" shrieked the Comptessa, her eyes darting the most fiery and avengeful glances.

"Thou liest; Valfroni can defy that world to prove one act that unites him to guilt."

"Is not thy appellation universal throughout Palermo?"

"What appellation?"

"The Demon Dwarf! And what but crime and atrocity can give it such authority?"

"The credulity of fools might have it so; but the appellation was my own, in every place, in every cause, society, and all engagements during my habitation here, I pronounced it thus—the Demon Dwarf! There was mystery in its sound, and I endeavoured to profit by it. The huge and hideous frame of *body* only, could sanction the title; the mind, the mind, Rosalviva, was of a different order."

The voice of Valfroni, during the conclusion of his replies, lowered itself, and there was a kind of calmness, a retentive recollection of something that seemed more than in a common degree to engross his manner and his meditations. The Comptessa was inclined to feel a terror creeping throughout her. The changed and altered tone of the Dwarf had filled her imagination with fresh mystery, and under its power, she felt less capable of resistance, than had it arisen to that imperative and authoritative repulse, which she conceived must have followed.

"And what canst thou mean?" urged Rosalviva, in fearful and comfortless feeling, "this singularity and horror breaks upon my mind with strange impulse; how couldst thou hope to profit by thy assumed mystery? And how hast thou profited? Didst thou originally, in the hour of misfortune, with thy wealth and thy hopes, become a wrecked and abandoned man?"

"I told thee that there had been a time when I ventured to nourish the fairest flower, that ever Nature produced; I told thee, that it lived in my bosom, and grew there rooted with it; I told thee, that from its fragrance and its dewy blossoms, I enjoyed all my pleasing comforts; to constantly gaze upon its richness and lustre, I said, was my daily pride, and my care to add freshness to its bloom; oh, I cherished this flower into so divine, and into so enchanting a treasure, it was my deity! And I told thee, too, that, in such a moment, there appeared a sting, a barb from beneath this flower; and, in an unthinking moment, it struck into my heart, and perished there; the flower withered in its cold and desolate bed, and bloomed no more. There was once a voice, too, the only one in the world that could have recalled my dreaming soul from its blighted and tortured sleep; for you must know, Comptessa, that until the sound of that voice awakened it, ages had bound it beneath its slumbers: but thou hast heard my history, and it were tedious repetition to speak of it here; follow me to the cemetery, thou shalt know the utmost."

"And what have I there to behold?"

"Paoli Golfieri, fettered to the embrace of Francesca."

"Oh, God! No, no; thou dost but mock me," in agonising frenzy, cried Rosalviva.

"Away! and be satisfied; away—away."

The Comptessa instantly yielded to the impulse, and rushing through the avenue gained the iron grating. Valfroni removed it, and she emerged into the vault.

The Dwarf closed the grating upon her; she awaited his approach, but the silence, and the darkness, (for he had taken the lamp from Rosalviva,) convinced her, that he had departed, and the fatal truth seemed to disclose itself, that she was now, alas! wholly in his power! Her situation rendered her dreadfully violent. The small lamp beside the bier gave the most feeble light imaginable; she revived its dimness, and guiding its reflection round the vault, cried, amid the fervour of her intense sufferings, "Paoli Golfieri! I call thee to answer this treachery. Spirit of Francesca! I charge thee, too, with its origin! I charge thee with the destiny that befals me!"

The concealed recess at the extremity of the vault again caught her attention, and she rushed towards it. Throwing aside, in the violence of her agitation, the dark drapery, to her horrid surprise, the figure of Francesca stood before her! Pale, and in the habiliments of death, the form of the Duchessa, as she appeared in the dream of Rosalviva, gazed stedfastly upon her. The glare of a brilliant lamp, suspended above the statue appearance of Francesca, correctly pourtrayed the unaltered countenance. She could not look upon it; an icy and poignant thrill of horror coiled upon her heart, and, with a convulsed shriek, she sunk upon the earth. The drapery closed itself immediately.

The Dwarf Valfroni, through a further cavity entered the vault; in a voice of terrible power he recalled her to animation, and, snatching her from her sunken and exhausted position, he cried, "Look up, Rosalviva! thy time is near. The fiends of despair and darkness await you!"

"Valfroni! my *preserver?* my betrayer?" faintly exclaimed the Comptessa, the wild glance from her eye bespeaking the kind of dread and horror her soul entertained.

"Thy preserver *once*,—thy avenger *now!*—Look at me, and

peruse these dark and stern lineaments of an injured, a desperate being!"

"Oh God! I see them. I see the fierce lightnings of thine eyes, and they seem to scorch me; but why should they blast *me!* Thou, Dwarf Valfroni, and this—this *living* spectre. Oh! mystery! mystery! what is it? what art *thou*? art human! or fiend? speak, and crush my miseries!"

"Wonder not if I had become fiend, indeed, wretched and hardened woman; my heart is still human. The wound thou caused, stamped me with desolation. I did not die and curse thee. I lived for this hour, to triumph over thy falsehood, to repay thee, in the terms due to thy evil and dreadful career. To sting thee with the adder's most loathsome venom. Once thou wert sunshine to me, and my every happiness was in thy beam; it was snatched from me, and thy dark and inhuman soul meditated my destruction. It failed,—I became free, and lived to rend thy heart by a meeting like this. Look at me."

"Valfroni! Valfroni," fearfully and sobbingly cried Rosalviva, and her courage scarcely allowed her to look towards him.

"No, thou mayst avert thy gaze, but it cannot shut out from you the horror of my presence. Darkness, nor all the powers attendant, can exclude from you, him that thou hast wronged, Leontini di Vivaldi! Look at him! He stands to wring thy heart. Look at me, the tomb restored me; my sight must palsy thee; if thou hast one chord within thy breast, now will I break it. Abandoned, and apostate woman! And see, see thy intended victim triumphs upon thy fallen and disappointed hopes. Francesca lives! repentant too, Paoli is joined with her, and thus they behold their intended destroyer!"

The Dwarf, aided by some contrived and hidden power, immediately withdrew the drapery in the recess. Paoli and the Duchessa stood enfolded in each other's embrace, and in the same moment, the members of the Jesuit tribunal entered the vault, and surrounded the appalled and astonished Rosalviva.

The person of the discarded and injured Leontini appeared from beneath the artificial character of the Dwarf Valfroni, and assuming the dignity of manner his feelings best encouraged, he regarded the Comptessa, with a stern and reproachful glance.

A terrible and awful scream escaped her, at the wonderful

events before her; she uttered several daring and incoherent imprecations, but the interference of the judicial authorities silenced them. In the dreadful and convulsed state of her sufferings, she snatched from her cloak the poniard, and fearlessly plunged it through her heart! "Here has been my enemy," she exclaimed, "thus I reward—Oh! God! mercy! mercy!"

The blood flowed impetuously; it was a blow decidedly fatal. She swooned upon the earth—the last struggle was upon her—she expired!

CONCLUSION.

> Bliss is a shadow, shrinking from the view,
> Lost in the distance in obscurest gloom;
> The aerial phantom we thro' life pursue,
> From reason's dawning till we reach the tomb.
>
> PARGA, *a Poem*.

THE lines here quoted pourtray but too fatal a sketch of happiness; and, for this imaginary treasure, what will human power not encounter with? What will it not sacrifice? A soul, formed like that of Rosalviva's, is not a common one; such an one does exist certainly, but it is a dreadful possession. The violence of passion is like a whirlwind, bearing all the finer sentiments of the heart before it!—Like an eruption of a volcano, it desolates the spot where virtue would have flourished! It is progressive in its inroads, till, at length, it amalgamates itself so closely with our existence, that it perishes the mind, and, subsequently, dooms its victim to a wretched and certain fate.

Leontini and Rosalviva, though very different characters, were each actuated by the same motive—the desire of revenge. But Leontini had a reverence for the laws of Omnipotence, and was of too high and noble a mind to imbrue his hands in blood. Injured as he had been by Paoli, he could not resist the pleadings of mercy within his bosom; he was moved to pity by his sincere penitence, and left him time to make his peace with his Creator. In his disguise of the Dwarf, he had fathomed most accurately the heart of Rosalviva. He certainly urged her to those deeds, which he knew he could, in a moment, prevent being accomplished. The arm of the Comptessa was raised against herself; Leontini had neither opportunity nor power to prevent the desperate deed, and he was guiltless of her death.

During his residence at the ducal pallazzi, the unfortunate wife of Carraccio had pleaded to him for a knowledge of her husband's fate. Leontini beheld, in the humbled, and, to those of the Ducal establishment, unknown, mourner, his first love Viola di Morini. The Neapolitan was no more. Leontini imparted the melancholy tidings, and shortly took Viola to his arms—a fond, a devoted bride.

www.ingramcontent.com/pod-product-compliance
Lightning Source LLC
Chambersburg PA
CBHW011352010726
47494CB00008B/2285

* 9 7 8 0 9 7 9 2 3 3 2 6 5 *